the sun's attendant

A DIPTYCH

Charles Haldeman

SIMON AND SCHUSTER · NEW YORK · 1964

To Renate

First Printing

Library of Congress Catalog Card Number: 64-10796
Design by Betty Crumley
Manufactured in the United States of America
By The Book Press, Brattleboro, Vt.

Contents

LEFT PANEL

A *cage went in search of a bird.*—Kafka

To my young friend Stefan Brückmann—this
notebook as a cage to find you out.

—IMMANUEL DE BRIS

Paris, June 1955

SUMMER SOLSTICE

All right, Immanuel, have your way. But don't forget to bring your map and calendar—the plot will have to be *your* hack work. And if you don't like the game, go away; it could be I enjoy it even less than you.

I know what I'm saying; all the figures in my memory-at-large wear the same swollen mask, stake the same greedy claims on me. They've been crowding me for so long they all look alike. I prefer them that way; I can pretend they're perfect strangers. (Question: "Stefan Brückmann, will you identify this body?" Answer: "Not if I can help it.")

But it seems I've agreed (weak, deferential child!) to call the roll for you (*more* hours in the snow). Well, bear with me; it will hurt to make their faces out again, and I don't want to be the hero of pain—mine *or* theirs.

Still, behind my acceptance of your challenge to go "cage seeking" (gravedigging would be more like it) I detect a diffident flicker of hope—that somewhere, in all the muck I'll have to plow through, a diamond (or a dime) may be patiently lurking as my reward.

In any case, the dead will be on time.

A nice *traditional* beginning: I was born on February 1, 1929, at a Gypsy horse auction being held near Nauen, a town west of Berlin. My father, Janos Brückmann, was a pseudoromungrish *Waldbobui* who claimed descent from Michael the Voyvode's minstrel sergeant and the granddaughter of Count Athanasios Kalman—to whom, as you may not know, Baron Walther von Säule zum Pfosten, emissary of the Emperor Sigismund, granted pilgrim's credentials and a letter of safe conduct in 1425 or thereabouts. (No questions, please.) My mother was a *chali* (which means to a Gypsy about the same thing that *Schickse* does to a Jew), the daughter of a middle-class Berliner named Schnee. She was nineteen when she took to the road with my father, and she never saw her family again.

My godparents, who had come over from the winter camp at Weissensee for the fair, were Karel Szeklecz (known as Tito), a *Lallery* fiddler whose parents had come from Bohemia to Germany in 1901, and his wife, Maria, a *Volksdeutsch* Hungarian girl who in her youth had been an aerialist with Mundt's traveling circus. (But she had fallen in Prague, injuring her back, and never had the nerve again to undertake anything more daring than a foxtrot.)

Tito used to tease me (this was when I was ten or so, in Budapest), saying I'd been so tiny that my mother hadn't known she was carrying me, and had dropped me without noticing in the snow outside the covered wagon. If my father, coming home with a newly acquired mare, hadn't almost stepped on me, they'd never have known I'd been born, he said, and from lying all day in the snow my fingers and eyes were frozen solid. Could be—I have my father's complexion but my mother's (Schnee-blue?) eyes, and of all the candidates for the violin who ever lived I had the stiffest fingers. Anyway, everyone was so upset by my mother's unsuspecting *balitshtido* (she was exiled immediately to another wagon while ours was scrubbed from top to bottom) that nobody remembered to give me a bath in cold water. Or maybe it didn't seem necessary.

My Gypsy passage: bow, scrape, edge on by. A ballet of formal greetings. Face to face and backward out of range. Laughter from the sidewalks.

Tito and my father emerged triumphantly from an all-night prebaptismal drinking bout with a Gypsy name for me: *Murshkar*. Their announcement of it sent Maria into hysterics; she immediately insisted on seeing for herself. During the inspection it suddenly dawned on my mother what the name meant; she flew at my father and threatened to cut his eyes out if he was seriously thinking of hanging such an epithet on me. "Say what you really mean!" he shouted, and a brawl ensued. My mother prevailed in the end, and they named me Stefan—a proper name for a child born at a horse fair. But for Maria I was always Murshkar. (Don't think I'm going to tell you what it means, either!)

June 13th

Memoirs write themselves, you say. So much the worse for them, then. I've decided to introduce Edith, your hero's present peril, into the scheme, just to keep things going during the frequent intermissions.

Here she comes: a smile, aloft, an Indian brave in a doeskin coat, waving her pocketbook like a tomahawk. If I could just forget her for five minutes, I'd fall in love with her on first sight all over again.

When and where did we meet? At a Left Bank bookstall on an early summer afternoon. She was looking at etchings and I was searching for the *Illuminations*. The sky had no color at all, but the eye-level city was yellow-green and red with posters, already photographed, demobilized by wind. I had been almost five months in Paris then, half in a trance, wandering around, sitting hours by myself in cafés and cinemas.

The wind had disheveled her hair; she seemed vaguely distrait. On an impulse I spoke to her; she laid aside a boudoir print and looked me over. "*Vous n'êtes pas français?*" "*Non,*" I said. "*Ni moi,*" she said.

She let me buy her a coffee and *fine* just down the street. (The awning flapped, our napkins blew away.) Her name was Sonya, she said; she spoke five languages and made her living doing translations. "*Et vous, vous êtes poète.*" "*Non, pas encore.*" "*Mais oui, vous êtes poète,*" she insisted, "*j'en suis sûre.*"

We walked up to Montparnasse, where we ran into some friends of hers. "*Bon soir, Edith!*" they cried. I must have looked rather confused; "Sonya" laughed uproariously and said she had wanted to know how it would feel to have a Russian name for a few hours. We all went down to her place on the Quai. She put on some jazz and then some Debussy, and we drank a couple of bottles of *rouge*. When the others left we made love. Afterward she began to talk. It had been months, she said; or didn't I believe her; it was true. I was an exception to the rule, small people are usually too quick, she said; was I perhaps a homosexual? Poets often are, she said; they can't help it; she didn't mind. She was sure I was a Jew, I looked like a Jew, was I a Jew? She chattered on and on like that; it became more and more zany. She was happy, that's all. Finally, just as dawn broke, we laughed ourselves to sleep.

He grew accustomed to his face, once he had accepted the fact that it was turned inside out. Until then he had always avoided mirrors and walked by windows obliquely, to keep from encountering himself. That's me.

Don't get restive—I'm still warming up.

The first six years of my life were spent mostly in the family *vardo*—that is, horse-drawn wagon—on long meanderings throughout Central Europe. My mother bore two more sons during this period. Junker and Lodo. But my first sure memories are of Budapest, during the winter of 1934–35. Tito (who was playing the cafés) and Maria lived behind the Hotel Passy. We all stayed together in a huge dense room with a wood stove. I had a toy zeppelin. Tito was forever practicing; my father was restless to be on the move, and he and my mother fought incessantly.

Memorial photograph of my mother: her hair lies back and forth upon her head despairingly; two slack, heavy braids lean on her shoulders like futile, pale forearms. . . .

I moved in with Edith; for a while we did nothing but make love. She set the conditions for it, ingenious and hungry. But circumstances had to be just so; if they weren't, then she adjusted them, and I played along—or else. I was wildly in love with her, but she ran the show. I was her monkey, her puppet: a toy xylophone on which she pounded out whole concerts. I was astounded by the range, the wild notes she got out of me; this jealousy was *mine*, this delicacy, this fever. Under her emotional pommeling a brand-new erotic "I" took shape.

Eventually, of course, we reached the limits of our particular collusion: she ran out of octaves and I lost my patience. I began to want her to be more solid, more consistent, without so much pretense, no matter how brilliant her devices might be. That was when things started to go wrong with us. Edith loves love, but she doesn't really love. Only her timing is good.

June 17th

Persistent acid burn in the top of my stomach. Slightly bilious. Anything to avoid almost everything. My well-known malady.

Every morning I ran out for fresh croissants and butter, while Edith made coffee in a huge filter apparatus that produced a good dozen cups. I had begun to work on the poems, however hesitantly, and she was (ostensibly) doing some kind of translating work for an Egyptian "director" named Rugby Wagbat (that's what it sounded like to me!). He seldom paid her, but she couldn't resist his mustache (she said), and so she kept on working for him. She usually came in around five or six in the evening, laden with *baguettes*, cheese, fruit, paté, and a bottle of cider or wine. I'd break off then and we'd have a little picnic on the bed. When we finished she'd go over to the desk and take a look at my day's production.

She wasn't a generous critic (happily); she didn't give me a chance to form bad habits (or any habits at all). She knew I wasn't writing for her; that made her all the more demanding. But if her intuition told her that something I'd written was artificial, or lazy, or off the top of my head, it usually was. I wasn't always happy to admit it; often I got horribly irritated at the way she scolded me—but the next day, when I sat back down to what I'd been so proud of, I had to admit she'd been right. Many times I sat all day and just scribbled aimlessly, drinking coffee after coffee until I got the shakes, knowing that any minute she was going to come bounding in and demolish me. I had just so much time to myself and no more—time enough for a kind of frantic descent, like an athlete scrambling down a rope into a pit, a mad rush to gather as much memory-trash as I could hold on to and still haul myself out and get things sorted before the whistle blew. It was fatiguing, but it built up my self-critical muscles. Even after twenty offspring, my stomach didn't sag.

Full of milk, the baby hangs in her embrace, looking as confused and estranged as Joan of Arc at the stake.

June 18th

Edith angry is like Snow White with a lump of apple stuck in her throat. We fight all the time. None of her accusations are quite true, but there's no use in my trying to refute them; very shortly now they *will* be.

Charity bizarre: love's end vicious ...

In the winter of 1935–36 my father, at the head of a string of wagons, insisted on trying to cross the Vistula, which had only recently frozen over, rather than pass through Cracow; and halfway across, the ice gave way. Ah! but the back door flew open as the wagon went down, and the chest in which I was sleeping simply floated out. I didn't even get wet. But the rest were drowned. That's how easy it is, I want you to remember.

Vautrin is discovered in the latrine, anxiously scrubbing his hands with Bab-O.

June 20th

We're sleeping with a sword between us now . . .

I was carted back to Budapest and left with my *kirvo* and *kirve*, who in the meantime had moved to Janko Picza Street, in an almost entirely Gypsy neighborhood. Maria, who had no children of her own (perhaps because of her fall), had grown very fat—to make room for me on her lap, as she said; I came to love her as I had never loved my mother. Good perspiring Tito of course thrust a violin into my hands immediately, and for two years I scraped away bravely, long after it had become painfully obvious how hopeless it was. By the time a boy is seven, you can tell. I did my best, though; I could see what it meant to him. Maria on the other hand (undoubtedly influenced by all the noise I made) wasn't the least bit sentimental about the matter. Anyone could tell I wasn't meant to play the violin, she said; the cafés were already filled to overflowing with little old urchin-virtuosos; why didn't he just let me be? Tito was too proud and too determined to give in, but his enthusiasm for my (nonexistent) progress slowly lost fire, until finally, one day when I was murdering his favorite *friss*, it fizzled out altogether. He wrenched the fiddle from my hands and shouted, "Your fingers are too weak!" Having thus condemned me to an unmusical life, he stamped out furiously to get drunk. He had every right to feel crushed: the violin was his life, his soul, and the one child who'd been granted him had proved incapable of sharing it.

(I could tell she resented my presence next to her: she kept breathing the other way.)

June 22nd

Motif: the Summer King. Drunkenness, derangement, dismemberment . . .

I have a large purple birthmark in the small of my back. Maria said that all children born during the first three days of February are marked, inside and out, and she used to shed a lot of fruitless tears lamenting my misfortune.

June 26th

Well, it's come to this: we spent the entire evening together without speaking. We ate at a so-called Greek restaurant, sat like stones through half of *The Diary of a Chambermaid*, walked slowly back to the Quai, climbed the stairs in stages, got undressed, fell into bed with the light on and made love like two wild animals. All that without a word.

PATIENT (*belligerently*): I'm as good as anybody else.
PSYCHIATRIST (*scornfully*): Hah! With only one leg?
PATIENT (*pleadingly*): But what difference does that make?
PSYCHIATRIST: How the hell should I know? I'm not in your shoe.

June 29th

Moon died four years ago today.

Disastrous wound, expanding in the dark, fingering the minutiae of wreckage . . .

Sixty-odd crucifixions and not a Jesus yet.

Angels in smocks, prescribing feathers in illegible handwriting. I can't find my smelling salts. *Tant pis!*

Summers we went out in a rented wagon to the villages of the *Puszta*, and Tito played at peasant festivals. Once we traveled as far as Brno in Czechoslovakia, and Tito won a bull in a fiddling competition. We tied it by a rope to the back of the wagon and dragged it back to Budapest (it was the thinnest bull in all creation by the time we arrived), where we sold it (I swear!) to a kosher butcher.

July 8th

Edith is on her way to Barcelona. Cool farewell at the Gare d'Austerlitz. She'll meet her father there—hasn't seen him since she was ten years old. Her parents separated in 1941 in Vichy. Her father went to Spain and then on to Argentina, where he made a fortune in beef. Mme. Garcilaso (a White Russian) returned to Paris with the child, and they've been here ever since. The mother is a dotty old duck, smokes cigarillos despite a bad heart, was a ballerina in her youth. Good time to go and see her—Edith is always shutting her up at the best moments.

Provisional epitaph. He loved her through one filthy winter, sunk in a funnel of bedclothes and lingerie, in a room overlooking an alley. Empty stove and one convulsive window. Regrettably, it wasn't that way at all. Grievers are not inclined to fantasy.

July 22nd

Two weeks now: eat and sleep, sleep and eat. My stomach has stopped acting up. Edith's vacation is doing *me* good—haven't you noticed?

Back to the grind.

We didn't go far in the summer of 1939. Just far enough. During the first week of September (yes) we started across the border into Austria on the way to Körmend, where a harvest festival was going to be held. The Hungarians let us through, but the Austrians told us the border was closed. Tito started shouting and so they searched the wagon and made us show our papers. That did it. Mine had my parents' names and places of birth on them: unmistakably German. A telephone call was made; in an hour a car arrived with three policemen and a fat civilian in it. They asked a thousand questions; Maria became hysterical and Tito was trembling with rage, but there was nothing he could do. I was held and Maria and Tito were turned back, forcibly. I began to scream, and I could hear Maria crying my name long after their wagon had disappeared from view.

It took the police a week to sort things out; in the meantime I was kept under lock and key, and the wife of one of the customs men brought me meals and made sympathetic noises. Finally, I was carted off to Vienna and after a few more days was shipped to Berlin like a jungle specimen (with a lady trapper from the Viennese police as escort).

A committee of three was on hand to greet me at the station: my mother's brother (hard to say uncle) Willi, his fiancée Ada (a muscular blonde) and my grandmother (Herr Schnee had died in 1935). They tagged along to the police headquarters and, after the signing of numerous papers, were allowed to take custody of me. None of them looked too happy about the acquisition, especially Willi, who was sporting a party badge and wore black boots that came up to my waist.

July 24th

This snow on my shoulders is really the doings of pigeons. One of those statues that cities are full of.

After old Schnee's death Willi had shown no interest in the family business (health foods), so the running of the shop had been left to two employees, though Frau (*Witwe*) Schnee herself audited accounts and spent much of the day on the premises. When Willi joined the party in 1937, they sold their house and rented a small apartment in Moabit. I slept on an old couch in the kitchen—it was the best bed I'd ever had.

July 25th

Coffee and cognac at four with Edith's mother (dwindling tangerine, gilded ear lobes, high-heeled birdfeet, still crouched for flight thirty years after the full stop in her right knee). She was overjoyed to see me without her daughter for a change. I'd forgotten how deaf she is; for two hours we sat and shouted at each other (contralto and tenor at three paces). Her love for the ballet endures; every night she perches in the wings, on a cloud of nostalgic regret; onstage the beloved mechanical sweat still pours, the fairy thighs and pistons pound the boards: scorched gauze, tired crepe, tinfoil. On the toes of her weak-ankled memory, she is lost in identical bobbins, the fifth spun swan in the second rank. The mind unwinds, a late finale: "*L'Ostende, naturellement . . . Oui là! Gitanes, ils . . . Qui?*" (Entr'acte, the hands aflutter, clock with a twenty-four-hour face) . . . "*L'Espagnole . . . Ma petite Edith, elle . . . Mais la guerre . . . A dix-huit ans . . . Autrefois! . . . Son premier amour!*" (She explodes with laughter and bounds from her chair.) "*Comme moi!*" she cries, "*O la la!*" She attempts a pirouette and loses her balance, the brandy topples, I catch her (not it) just in time. I hear her heart out loud, she reaches for a cigarillo, her temples are pounding, she smiles weakly. "*Merci!*" I flee.

The earth so seldom firm enough to grasp or grapple with. It's my face against the invisible faces all the way.

Much of the furtiveness with which I was shuffled around from office to office seemed pretty unnecessary to me. My tameness was extraordinary. Willi was taking precautions—the whole affair must have been quite embarrassing to him. By the first of October I had been duly inscribed at the *Zigeunerdezernat*, had been issued an identification card with "Gypsy, Mixed Breed, Second Category" and my right index fingerprint on it—and through some magical instinct of self-preservation on Willi's part, had even been smuggled into a proper school.

I was two or three years older than every child in my class and made almost no friends at all. The teacher, whose name was Brun (I think), regarded me with extreme wariness, but only occasionally showed any real impatience. I don't believe I gave her as much trouble as she'd been told to expect. The first big surprise to everyone concerned was that I didn't put up the least resistance (not that it would have done me much good), and after a few months I began to do rather well. (Suddenly, right now, I recall very clearly Brun's face and the smell of the wood paneling and steel in the train carriage coming up from Vienna. I wonder why . . .)

I did have one short-lived friendship that first year with a boy named Iro Hulse. He was not quite eight, but he was as tall as I, and very slender and pale. We walked about the halls together, sat next to each other in class and spent our recesses talking very quietly in a corner of the yard. We exchanged magazines, and he gave me a tiny lapel pin (a Stuka). Every day his mother was waiting for him on the steps when school came out; she was a small, fattish woman with black hair and a fur-collared cloth coat. Iro would wave to me, let his mother take his hand, and together they would walk off. Suddenly he stopped coming to school, and I was never able to find out why.

July 31st

The moon between sessions of rain . . .

Twelve hours of sleep, with the same silly dream question piping up in my head over and over: "Is it *chemically* possible?" I woke up around five, soaking wet, my covers on the floor, got up, drank some water, then went back to bed and fell asleep again, soundly this time, and slept until eleven, when I awoke with the tail end of a good dream:

A room in a pine shack (American). A man and woman with

heavy bodies are lying naked on an unmade bed, on their sides
and facing each other. I stand in the door and regard them.
They know I'm there but don't seem to care. They are caressing
each other gently, and perspiring. I can almost make out who
they are. The man is hairy and pinkish, the woman smooth-
skinned and dark, with large molelike nipples. They are not
attempting to excite each other; perhaps they have already
made love. I feel only a mild curiosity. Their flesh seems to
glow; it possesses an intense quality of life. A warm sensation
of response wells up in me; suddenly I know that they *belong*
to me.

Frau Schnee began to find me moderately tolerable after a
while. And to give her her due, in the two-and-a-half years she
"had" me she never once laid a hand on me, and seldom spoke
harshly. For some reason I frightened her a little. Sometimes
she came close to showing tenderness, but always with a strange
reserve, in the way that women attracted to a dog will touch it:
compulsively, with a quick, delicate, daring movement, never
stroking or truly caressing. Once she said, tilting my chin up
with two fingers, "You have *her* eyes"—meaning my mother's—
disguising her ambivalence with a sort of reproach.

A man murdered his wife with a sledge hammer, so they sentenced him to life imprisonment with hard labor, and set him
to work in a quarry crushing stone with the exact-same weapon.

August 2nd

We got hungry, said the ex-legionnaire, I can't tell you how
hungry we got. Our hunger became so substantial we tried to
eat it. We washed it down with air, but when it hit bottom it
broke into a million pieces and each piece grew into a hunger
as big as the first. After a while there was no way we could eat
it all. Even a feast of hunger will stump a starving man.

Running over the top of the urinals in the *pissoir* is a kind of trough into which water has leaked from above. The water is greenish-gray with slime and tobacco. A runty, bewhiskered old man wearing a porter's hat has been standing next to me, casting furtive glances in my direction. Suddenly he coughs, *Aha!*, spits a tiny fish into the trough, then turns and leaves.

Rationalized: Theresa Neumann, Jean Genet, Tom and Jerry, the First World War, the thin skin of this planet. I never allow anyone to peel an orange for me.

M. Fantin-Plustard, vest unbuttoned, forgotten napkin in his collar, whizzes by the Opéra on roller skates, shaking his tiny fist and shouting '*Con!*' at passing motorists. In front of the American Express he collides with a Vespa and throws up his lunch: snails, sole, partridge and rice, wax beans, endives, Gervais, pears and last year's *blanc-de-blanc*.

A young man is painting his own skeleton in the Rue Jacob.

August 4th

Well! A card from Edith: Gaudi's "Sagrada Familia." Thank God she doesn't miss me.

The Schnees had a day maid who had been with them for years, a gaunt woman of about forty known only as Feldt, and unmarried. She prepared meals, did simple housekeeping and laundry and later (when Willi left) tucked the old lady in at night. Feldt and I got on beautifully; she even remembered my mother (vaguely, I must say) and told me what a beautiful girl she had been (which was all I wanted to hear).

Feldt and I had a daily ritual: I would sit in the kitchen and write out my lessons, and she would slipper about her work quietly. Once in a while I'd ask her a question, and she'd slip on her glasses, take up my copybook and hold it close to her nose (pretending to read), then put it back down softly, take off her glasses and declare in a hoarse whisper, "I'm afraid I can't help you, dear." Often I asked her things I already knew, in the hope that she might just once have the pleasure of knowing an answer. But she never did. Anyway, when I'd finished my schoolwork she sat down beside me at the table (after having prepared hot *mukafuk* for us both) and took up the apparently endless story of her life wherever she had left it off the day before. She was better than any soap opera, and I was an ideal listener, it seems. Whenever (every day) she read just the right look of sympathy on my face, she would burst into tears, and weep (also in a whisper) great rivers of tears into her *mukafuk*. I'd start to laugh then, upon which Feldt would shut off the waterfall abruptly and begin to glower at me. Then I'd try to stop laughing (you can't imagine how severe she could look when she wanted to) and start to hiccup, and suddenly she would explode with laughter too, and sipping her *mukafuk*, say, "That salt was just what it needed, *Spatz.*"

But Willi—Willi took great pleasure in mauling me—pinching me, twisting my arm and so on. He used to come in at eight or so in the evening, usually with Ada, and if I wasn't in bed he would bellow, "Ah-oh! Time for a bath, *Dreckskerl!*" and drag me into the bathroom (with Ada close behind, giggling maliciously), strip me, turn on the cold water in the tub, dump me in it and begin to scrub me with a dog brush. The more I screamed, the harder he brushed and the more hysterical Ada became. When he had tired of the diversion Willi would lift me up to the mirror and say, "Just as dirty as before, it seems to me. *Gut*, we'll try again tomorrow."

I was deathly afraid of him. The thought of running away may have entered my mind on occasion, but the far more horrible vision of Willi in pursuit always chased it right back out again.

Trying to remember the names of some of the children's magazines that Willi occasionally brought home with him: *Onkel Anton's, Die Goldene Stunde, Deutsche Jugend, Flieger und Matrosen.* He never handed them to me directly, but just left them lying around under *Der Stürmer* and *Der Völkische Beobachter.* One day Feldt handed me an old, battered copy of an Indian book by Karl May; I had struggled through half of it before Willi pounced on it and burned it as decadent literature. He was all set to give Feldt hell, too, but she cut him short in a fierce whisper: "Don't be silly," she said; "It was yours in the first place."

August 13th

Another card from Edith (peasant drinking wine from a goatskin). Postmarked Seville.

The old man sitting beside me in the waiting room leaned over, opened his battered suitcase and took out a tiny New Testament. I caught sight of an ivory crucifix and something that looked like a mummified foot. I had thought he was chewing gum, but suddenly, absorbed in reading, he spat, and a toenail landed on my shoe. Hurriedly he knelt beside me and retrieved it, then looked up at me (penitently) and asked, "Can you still put your foot in your mouth?"

"No," I replied. "I'm sorry to say my guru has forbidden it."

Mock air raids. Willi's voice in the streets . . .

His child knew the dog he had given her was breakable, so she smashed it like a china dish. Weeping, he swept up the pieces and laid them carefully away in a drawer, to reproach her when she grew up.

August 15th

During the summer of 1940 I ventured alone into the slums around the Alexanderplatz, where many Gypsies were living (and by this time much of the remaining Jewish population).

There I became acquainted with a settled family of Romanichals named Doehr. They had no regular income, but all of them (there were eight children—three boys and five girls—mother and father, grandmother and I don't know how many aunts and uncles in the *immediate* family)—all of them were musicians of one kind or another, and they got along. Because they weren't a traveling family they hadn't been bothered much by the police. (For a great many other Gypsies it was quite different, though—restriction of movement and employment reduced them rapidly to a life on the criminal fringe, where they didn't last long.)

Up till the year before, all the younger children in the Doehr family had even been attending a school for Gypsies, and the oldest boy, Christoforo, had been called up for military service in the early days of the war. (But after two months on the Russian front he was suddenly recalled; for a while he worked in a chemical plant in Friedenau, but eventually he suffered the same fate as the rest of his family. Time enough for that.)

August 16th

Edith again, this time Toledo. Her father has a touring car. Distance has changed her clothes; my cloistered world (insofar as she is still in it) is lined with picture postcards.

ME: I used to be able to talk to myself profitably.
YOU: And now?
ME: Everything I say seems to be to you, no matter what.
YOU: Yes, but I'm all ears.
ME: Mm.

August 17th

All my life I've been seeing other people off. My own travels have been inconspicuous, to say the least. Anyway, three weeks respite from the sword (flaming?).

Rolf, who was the next-to-the-youngest Doehr and just my age, sang and played the guitar in a café called Zum Siegerkranz. He and I became the closest of friends. By the end of the summer I was going to meet him almost every day; as long as I was back by six-thirty, Frau Schnee never pressed me for explanations. But one day I was careless: we went together to the café and I didn't get away until a little after seven. By the time I got home Willi had come; he was waiting for me at the door. He beat me mercilessly, but I absolutely refused to tell him where I'd been. Finally Ada became frightened and made him stop; I was bleeding from the mouth and nose. After that I was confined to the house until school began again, and my grandmother (who was just as afraid of him as I was) had to make him a full report on all my movements. It was almost six months before I saw the Doehrs again.

No one wants to inherit a garden.

A puppet show (or a film in color—but where?), Frau Holle. Pillows being shaken and the down, as it fell, turning to snow. Upturned faces—the orange-brown of cedar or glazed clay, dolls' faces ...

Just before Easter in 1941, Willi was called up. Ada left a few weeks later to work as a switchboard operator in Metz. Frau Schnee fell into a state of dutiful, premonitory mourning, and I decided it was as good a time as any to run away. I went straight from school to the Doehrs' one evening and proudly announced my decision. The seven of them who happened to be on hand at the moment promptly sat me down and gave me a good long lecture on what that would entail, and the upshot was that I was back in Moabit within three hours of my departure-for-good.

Life in a tin trough with steep sides ...

August 22nd

I'm beginning to envy myself the emptiness of this summer.
With you and Edith gone I can pretend I am alone. I never
knew before that I could *play* at it. If this is what is generally
known as irresponsibility, then even that has unexplored resources.

Feldt took me to a film once. If she'd been caught doing it, it
would have meant as much trouble for her as for me. It was the
first film in my life, and I didn't see another until some time in
1947, in Coburg. I don't remember much about it except that
the star was Emil Jannings and that it was a comedy. Recently
I saw a revival of *Der Zerbrochene Krug*, with Jannings in the
role of Richter Adam, and it seemed to me that this was the
film I had seen then, but perhaps it wasn't. That day I was
hypnotized by the experience itself, by the pure sensation of
movement in light; it was almost overwhelming. Jannings reminded me for some reason of Tito; I watched him openmouthed all through the showing and didn't hear a word of
the dialogue. I've never known a deeper sense of loss than the
one I felt when the puny house lights came on at the end. No
cry, no severance, no tragedy before my eyes has ever transported me further or affected me more deeply than that first
contact with the *sattispil* (Rolf's word for *Schattenspiel*): it
washed me out with light.

I fell in love with Jannings; his face mingled with Tito's,
and the heavy *fact* of his body, overlarge and brilliant, his tragic
clownlike tenderness, bred a memory of touch so real and in-
delible I carried it with me for years.

It wasn't until a little less than a year ago, here in Paris, that
I saw another of his films—almost thirteen years after the one
in Berlin. It was *Tartuffe*, with Werner Krauss. I enjoyed it
tremendously, but somehow it was *only* a film; I couldn't find
the magical Jannings I remembered; as for Tito, he had fled

forever. In the months that followed I set out to see every old film of his that came along—twelve or fifteen at least—hoping against hope to redeem that image. Needless to say, I couldn't; perhaps my eyes have hardened (or my heart), but it was only rarely that I felt myself brushing the edges of recollected illumination, of a day when Emil Jannings, huge and fumbling shadow wreathed in light, laid his gentle fingers on my uninitiated heart.

Sleep in a damp place, a rancid moldering quilt on my naked body, small animal and human sounds from behind thin walls. Outside more rain.

Doehrs every weekend again. The war was young; Berlin was like a fairground. Then in October the word came that Willi had been killed in Egypt. Frau Schnee enjoyed a nervous collapse; when she grew tired of it she began to emerge from her room for the evening meal.

A tired-looking, heavier Ada showed up for a few days over Christmas. She had married a corporal (in Nancy) and was already pregnant. She and my grandmother sat together for hours, tearfully turning the pages of old albums. And when she left she kissed me.

August 24th

Telegram from old Parris this morning: Moon's Aunt Libya died a week ago. Who else would have bothered to let me know? Does it matter?—all the lines are down.

I remember a funeral in Budapest, around 1938. A wealthy *hadnagy* had died, and half the Gypsies of Hungary had lined the streets to wail him to his grave. I sat perched on Tito's shoulders and watched and howled as loudly as the rest (without an idea why). Beside the hearse (open coffin, top-hatted corpse, his pipe and purse, guitar and watch fob) walked a

Catholic priest hired for the occasion. Just behind came a
string band of Gypsies (strengthened with *gorgio winds*), and
then dozens of hansoms and carriages smothered in bouquets
and wreaths and half-naked children.

What I want to recall is this: at the moment the hearse was
passing directly before us a young man (probably a close relative) suddenly sprang from the crowd, and before anyone had
realized what was happening or could stop him, deliberately
set his foot in the path of the wheel. The hearse was tremendous, the wheel was faced with iron, and his foot was crushed.
But that was what he wanted: the terrible pain loosed his
anguish and grief, and he screamed until it seemed his head
would burst. A great responsive moan rose from the throng; it
surged forward toward him; and clutching his head in both
hands the young man fell into it.

What I want to ask is this: From what absolute level of
suffering arises such euphoric certainty?

One day in the summer of 1942 a little man dropped in and
informed Frau Schnee that my presence in school the next year
would not be "desirable." For a moment she seemed to wake up
and remember me. She became flustered and began to look
dangerously white, and the man (only a civil servant, after all)
apologized, mumbled the usual words about orders and duty,
left some papers behind and departed.

For a few hours my grandmother regarded me sadly, her
head tilting oddly with regret, but by nightfall she had lapsed
back into her own private world of adequate forgetfulness.

Disillusionment. The fingers of your only trusted friend tighten
on your throat, and his familiar smile begins to fade. You
realize (as your tongue swells and slowly fills your mouth)
that he has come to believe you love life more than *him*. But
which do you regret more: his mistake or the loss of your
life?

August 26th

It is (still) raining. I'm the last customer in the bar. The cashier has dozed off, the waiter is reading *Jean Christophe*. People come and go outside, under the awning. I've had at least half a dozen coffees in the past two hours, and now I react with a jump to every little noise. Poem with a ballpoint on several napkins, tearing the (scar) tissue easily . . . just these two fragments:

If the ashes of the trees
are washed by winter
then my hands will be the torches
that ignite the birds.
Their hunger will assume all dead men's eyes
and be consumed by fire when summer dies.

No bone can bend a syllable,
no scar carve names on its infliction,
no word be found to bind the wound
that only other wounds can heal.

Fräulein Feldt, after a whirlwind romance with a widower Huguenot butcher, became Frau Michelin. Her place in the household was taken over (*erobert*) by a lumpy Hausfrau named Mecker, who invaded bodily, eyeing me like a stain that had to be wiped from the rug.

This time I ran away for good, or rather, I simply began to spend so much time at the Doehrs' that at last I was living there. No one cared any more, now that nobody was apt to come looking for me. In the end I was dropping in on my grandmother like a visitor. (Quaint picture of an afternoon: old lady with watery eyes and vagrant mind, small dark accidental boy, ersatz coffee, papery cookies, all wrapped in blackout. Where was the war?)

At Christmas I came with a small gift, a piece of embroidery done by *Oma* Doehr. Some of my grandfather's relatives were there, come up from Leipzig for the holidays. They had no idea who I was, and made much of my "friendship" with the old lady.

That was the last time I ever saw her; after that I didn't really have a chance.

Noah knew but he didn't have much time. Days piled up like garbage (Laurel and Hardy), skies dripped, pairs poured in and leaned back in deck chairs, shedding their camouflage, laughing rudely at his Jewish premonitions. Think of it: all of them, furry, horny, feathered, seasick, bouncing about somewhere out there on the waves, confident and uncomfortable in the nosy *Beagle*. Two apes, one dove ...

The survival of defeatists.

August 28th

Just for one last light note I'll tell you about the final Gypsy wake held at the café Zum Siegerkranz. It was like this. Things were beginning to warm up nicely, Herr Schorsch the proprietor had just broken into the third keg of home-brewed schnapps, and the dead man was well on the way to being joyfully forgotten, when one of the magician's three eggs (which had been planted in the pianist's pockets and were expected to bring forth pigeons) turned out to be real and rotten. As soon as the news reached the nose of the third violin, he made an ugly (if appropriate) comment on his instrument, startling the sword swallower so badly he almost swallowed his sword. Now quite by chance the organ-grinder's monkey (or somebody's monkey) chose precisely the same moment to sink his teeth into Madame Fatima's thigh (on a generous spot not quite covered by her tights). The offended woman let out an earsplitting scream that froze everyone in his tracks, kicked the beast halfway across the *Stube* and proceeded to direct a violent stream of abuse at its owner—a vocal performance so vile and so brilliant that the magician, the violinist, the pianist and the sword swallower, up to then unresolved, immediately began to emulate it at the top of their lungs. The mourners, not wanting to be left out, picked up the threnody in their own way, and in no time flat the air was thick with bottles, chairs, bodies and whatever else lay at hand.

Well, the police came (of course) and unfeelingly put an end to the lamentations. The whole thing was illegal in the first place, they said. *Streng verboten!* They carted everybody off but me and Rolf, who had had the foresight to squeeze ourselves and most of his guitar into the dumb-waiter. We were too scared to move until early morning when Schorsch returned, weeping and bearing in his hand a placard that said: CLOSED BY POLICE ORDER. His was the real bereavement of the day.

The success of exhibitionism depends on the illusion of spontaneity. Or?

August 30th

For "Sonya"—a story.

For weeks at a time you were almost totally unrecognizable. When I finally worked up the courage to look you in the eyes, I landed harshly on something real but very much apart from everyone but you. And since I had no name for anything outside myself, I could only watch it but not name it. In your eyes I followed the flight of an identifiable but unnamable bird. It headed directly for the sun and hovered for a single blinding second in the smoke of its own silhouette. And then I always lost it. But there it was, and again, there! No mistake.

Of course you never dreamed that I'd seen it. Despite your vast dissimulation, the logic of your movements, the plans that trembled on your lips as you were waking and died of ague before the day was out—no, you never dreamed.

I began to pursue you, dear heart, a silent urging lover; I dogged your eyes as they scattered from wall to wall and out of the windows over the city and its rotten winter landscape. For months our bodies did not exist except as ambulant caverns full of echoes and audible blood, short days the racks on which they broke. We lived as eyes alone: two double doors never exactly opposite each other, maneuvering and fretting, snatching points of rest on vacant objects, moving on.

At last the spring convened; it found us exhausted at opposite ends of a room, wide-eyed and blind. With it came the panic of inertia, a barrel of flies, and the heaving first deep intake of breath.

You spoke first (as always). The sun coming in the window roused gooseflesh on your arms. "Strange," you said; "suddenly I'm cold enough to die."

I shuddered and said nothing.

"Maybe I *am* dead." A kind of afterthought.

The sun nudged my foot and I kicked it away. All of a sudden you looked at me; in your eyes the sun darkened, the bird was poised there calmly. It spread its wings.

"You didn't even care enough to bury me," you said. "That's the least you might have done. You made me the goat. There aren't any prohibitions . . . bury me, too."

The bird lifted itself slowly, hovered for an instant, took a firm grip on the air and sailed away. You averted your eyes; I sat down unhappily.

"Am I really responsible?" you asked. But I didn't trust you enough just then to reply.

In the night you came to me. Your body was warm, and in the dark you seemed to have put on weight miraculously; your flesh was unstippled and immediate. I was still suspicious; I took you grudgingly and without satisfaction. You said nothing afterward, but I know you did not sleep.

Next morning I rose and went into the living room. The doors were open onto the little balcony. It was early and damp but growing warm. The sun was smeared obliquely and stickily across the floor. You were up and hard at work, moving about nervously, lean as before, wearing shorts and a sleeveless blouse, attempting a dozen things at once. You seemed to take

no notice of me, just went on watering flowers, shoving furniture about, emptying ash trays, wiping surfaces—hopping from
one thing to another inefficiently, the slack dejected flesh of
your upper arms and thighs wagging like loose bowstrings. And
as you worked you talked to yourself (it could not have been
for me)—an absent, distracted running commentary on your
movements, nothing more.

I felt a spurt of fear; the word *insane* occurred to me. Perhaps
I was threatened with the recognition of my own madness. But
if I had been, I would have attributed it to you. I would have
put on the mask of remorse, or even guilt. Yes, I might have
felt that too, at least some emotion deeper than the real shame
that made me fear to witness your despair. But I made a mistake: I let my shame move me to pity you—that was vicious
enough.

You felt my pity on your back like a cold hand (or did I
really touch you then?) and you shivered and ran away. I was
left with nothing to do. I began trying to restore the room to
its earlier order, but my memory of it was imperfect. When I
moved the table I discovered a dead, unidentifiable, namable
bird. I picked it up and let it burn my hands with stolen
sunlight.

That was the last day of our life together. That.

September 1st

Moved today. Rue de l'Ancienne Comédie (appropriate as I
could make it; houses infested with retinal roaches, one ruin on
the run-down heels of the next). Today two small boys passed
by me arm in arm. One of them had a stain on his shirt front,
and I felt suddenly mortified.

In February 1943 the walls of the last non-Aryan pocket of
Berlin came crashing in, and the furies swept through: Berlin
police, S.S., Gestapo checkers. They turned the houses inside
out in the Alexanderplatz. The few remaining Jews had held
their breath so long already, the blow came like a *coup de grâce*

—but surprise would be no word to describe the effect on the Gypsies.

I went down with the Doehrs like a last-minute suitcase. No one had asked for me; I was just bundled along.

We waited in the streets for hours before they moved us off. Long gulfs of silence, the coughs of an impatient audience, shuffling feet, hands rubbed or clapped for warmth, like hesitant applause; and then, slowly gaining in volume, a swell of voices and sighs and cries in an impossible orchestration: notes of disbelief and query, long bars of argument, brief phrases of despair; drowned single instruments in polyphonic chaos, lost arrangements conducted by fear out of silence. To this day I can't listen to certain works (of Bartók, Schönberg, even Richard Strauss) without starting to suffocate. Can it be that music belongs entirely to remembered states of being?

Too much distance—not so much the distance of time though as indifference, *real* indifference.

After three days in a detention camp (cage), we came up for selection. I was wedged in between Rolf and Ulla, the youngest Doehrs. The examiner looked rather disconcerted to find a boy whose name was nowhere on his list. He demanded my name impatiently and I started to cry. "Doehr's not your name!" he cried, and I was sure they would send me away. But a fat man came over, an inspector, wearing a big smile. "My name is Kluge," he said. "What's yours?"

I told him and he asked me very gently if I had a card, and I nodded and gave it to him. He whispered something to a guard and in a minute or two he was holding my file in his hand.

"Second category," he said. "Where are your parents?"

"Dead." I replied.

He glanced at the file. "Your mother's relatives?"

"Dead."

Still with the same smile he asked, "Your grandmother too?"

"Yes," I said, and it was the truth, in a way.

"Do you live with these people?" he asked.

"Yes." (With leaping heart!)

"Mmm," he said, and carried the papers over to a desk, where he scribbled something on them and stamped them. He came back, "*Also gut*," he said. "Go with them, then."

So we passed on together, out into the yard where the trucks were waiting. We were carried to Stettin freight depot (by which Rolf and I had walked so many times) and transferred to railroad boxcars, twenty or more to each one. Around midnight the train pulled away.

An old story by now, but no less mine.

Palette from here on out: scorched earth, Prussian blue, vitriol, cyanide and blood lake, horn green, canary yellow, all possible flesh tones, rose madder and madder, white lead, and a black so black it lets your eyes through and then punches holes in them.

Off at the zoo, muzzling peanuts through armor and wire. Short-necked children, vitamin deficiencies. Wives and mothers gobble bark and leaves, rub and jostle one another with shopping bags, crush the pets and gardens under foot.

I haven't learned the language of the hunt yet, but here I am, just the same.

September 4th

Dream. A dispensary. Riveted gray-white walls of a ship interior. Three-decker bunks along the bulkheads (echoes of the scatological latrine-bath of other dreams). A slow washing-in of red, rust and yellow. Many young men, all displaying injuries of some kind (not battle wounds), are lounging about. A few are lying on their bunks, others congregate in the center of the compartment, not far from a round hatch. A naked boy appears (or has been standing there without my having seen him). Virtually his entire body is covered with the scar membrane of a horrible burn, like a caul. At first glance his genitals seem to have been destroyed, but then I realize that they have been melted to-gether and are now *protected* by a semitransparent covering which is an extension of the caul. It is evident that the boy has been "healed" and that he is prepared to leave any time now. Looking at me, he complains that he should have been left to die; no one else pays the least attention to him. He walks about, mumbling. I sympathize, *from outside*, with his sense of impo-tence, with his futility, which I somehow share.

Through the hatch (the round one) comes a nurse (odd mixed resemblance to Edith and someone-no-one else); she immediately launches an attack on the naked boy. She claims (for the benefit of the others, who now stop talking and listen respectfully) that this young man himself was solely respon-sible for his injury, that he had done what he had been told time and time again not to do (something about a boiler). And when he says he would rather have died, she shouts that that is only an additional proof of his ingratitude, and a lie to boot. "Would you like to die right now?" she asks; and he shakes his head.

Throughout the tirade he has listened with head bowed. His lack of protest is also related to our "shared impotence," I feel, and I blush at his humiliation, wanting and yet not wanting to have been a witness to it. In spite of the logic of the nurse's remarks, even the *justice* of them, I am furious with her for having appeared, for having intruded like a self-appointed chorus into the *intimacy* of my dream to deliver a vindictive catalogue of the circumstances of his misery, now, at the time of his release.

Analyze it yourself.

September 5th

I knew it. Edith is back.

APHELION

No wardrobe inventory of trials and tribulations.

I suppose there are plenty of reasons why others want to look back—to delineate, to accuse, to remind, or simply to record—but I can't find my way back into that world. I am sure that it existed, but now I can only invent metaphors and relate certain incidental memories. Two (hundred) years.

It is impossible for a man to live in the presence of death, in the immanent, continuous presence of it—impossible, at least, for him to accept it as a natural condition. But it isn't the same for a child. I know; I lived in death itself, not merely in its vicinity. I went through puberty without really noticing. My body seemed to commence with death; it had no other definitions, and so I grew by accident.

It was the same for most of us children, those of us who survived. We developed an odd kind of patience, unthinkable to adults—a restraint of impatience, you might say. We lost weight, our bodies became covered with sores, and everything we reached to touch was already dead. Yet we breathed energy, real energy in all that deathly space, and managed to live without hope—*prior* to hope. Our compound was the world, the only one we knew or expected; as long as we lived we floated in death, buoyant in it with the air of an impossible optimism.

I'm distorting. I felt tempted to say that we were handled like grown men, but didn't react as they did. But although that might be a way to talk around some unthinkable things, it would still be a falsification. We were children, though we didn't know it; we were immune, oblivious, to any *crime* being perpetrated against us. What crime? the opportunity to be a child in a world that recognized none? We were barely conscious of ever having been children. It's easy to take away a *man*'s liberty—it's so often an illusion to begin with; as for a *man*'s freedom, in the abstract, what is it? But a child's freedom is another matter: self-evident, fragile, exercised and not internally perceived. Only when the knowledge of death—I mean, the consciousness that life is not infinite after all, or that, on another level, life is something *questionable*—is imposed on the free wheel of a child like a brake, and a cruel one, he stops in his tracks, and forthwith offers up the simulacrum of a man. An odd sense of autonomy, of *license*, persists for a time, but even this atrophies gradually, and grows worthless and encumbrous —more worthless even than the loss of liberty for a man, who after all has lost only his illusion, and to whom real freedom may for the first and last time be revealed as a proud affirmation in the circumstances of his personal, selfless death.

For us though, death remained impersonal and ubiquitous, and the threat of it meant next to nothing. Inflicted pain was the outer boundary of our fear for our *selves*. The door to life had been shut in the instant we were about to pass through it. And when it opened, when it seemed to open, when you told us it had opened again—one fine day that smelled like all others and was not—we were left standing on its threshold unable to move: bodies of children casting shadows of men, forward, out through the door, out into life. But unable to move.

As for me, I am still standing there, and I would give anything not to be. I see a multitude of men outside. Their feet, their shadows, their bony shoulders brush my shadow, the shadow of the man pretended, man portended. They stop and stare at me, with curious eyes, with wounded eyes, with eyes I cannot fathom, with eyes expressing loss, confusion, despair— even scorn, if I don't imagine it. And each one (this is the terrible thing!), as he crosses my shadow and moves on, drops a word, a single word and always the same one, like a great vindictive secret or accusation.

Time! he says. Time!

What do they mean? What is it that I do not understand, even now?

(Bunions, blisters, callouses and leper's wounds to kiss and point at!)

We came to the outer walls of a monastery. It was raining. We had come a long way and there were too many of us; only a few could be taken in. The rest were turned away, condemned.

Above the gates stood an inscription: IN LABORE LIBERTAS. A sound retreat, a model of the universe (its concave heaven, convex hell), inhabited by monks who wore the cloth of a most exclusive order and were bound to their Lord by an infrangible oath.

As novices, we had to swear away all claims to nationality, all earthly goods. Our heads were shorn, our bodies cleansed. We were given new, blue names, and we donned odd filthy habits. We fell asleep in huge outrooms, in straw-filled boxes, embracing each other's heads with bare feet. We spent profane, unproven days in quarantine, wolfed dusty bread, choked down the phlegm of our prescribed humiliation. One last chance to meditate in silence, castigate the flesh, prepare the soul for vows.

Not a monk in a carload of us, though.

September 10th

An anonymous guitar . . .

Where O road do you end?
Not at home, never home.
Where O love do you lie?
On the hill, all alone.
Where O road do you bend?
Where I will, when I will.
Where O love do you bleed?
From my heart, on the hill.
Where O road do you lead?
To a hill, far from home.
Where O love do you die?
On that hill, with my rom.

One remembered, a hundred forgotten. Smoke.

Z for *Zweifel, not Zigeuner.*

After a couple of weeks, all but me and Rolf were taken away and gassed. We would have gone with them too, except for a scout from the "Construction School" who came through the block and pulled us out as likely builder-candidates. There were stronger boys on hand—we just happened to be standing closest to the door.

Rolf didn't last long; he wasn't cut out to be a carpenter or mason. He got through the training period all right. And afterward we were assigned to the same work squad. But it was for an outdoor construction job—a new cluster of barracks being built at breakneck speed—and it rained all the time. Ice water. Rolf started to wet the bed and to wake up screaming in the middle of the night; he was certain to be transported at the next selection. But one evening, after a grueling six-hour roll call, he collapsed in a fit of coughing and tore his lungs out during the night. The next morning he was dead—just like that—and except that another boy had to be chosen to fill the quota three days later, I'd say it was better that way. It *was* better for *him.*

Aus dem Totenhaus ...

> So many years have passed
> and suns have risen
> since you and I lay down
> in separate places—
> I fell asleep, you made
> the grave your bed.
>
> Now even from the house
> of death, your prison,
> I hear your voice resound.
> How near your face is!
> But when I weep, I drown
> among the dead.

Most of the other Gypsies at the "school" were from Eastern
Europe and spoke little German. They huddled together in a
tremulous knot of tribal superstitions. Even though Rolf could
speak Romany very well (much better than I), they regarded us
both with suspicion. After Rolf died I had little more to do
with them, and in a few weeks I was switched by the *Blokovi* to
a *Kommando* with a group of German Jewish boys, most of
whom were from Berlin.

September 18th

Strange, since your return I've started sleeping again. Loud,
crazy, disturbing dreams every night, but at least I fall asleep
without much difficulty—for a week or so I suffered a real
kicking insomnia.

Leftovers.

The sects complain the bowler's ruined propriety, the fallow
helmet, loss of yeast and vest, the golem fleeced, the sabbath
zwieback.

Rabbis are spending champagne on soap and glue; Vienna is
prating pansies to brag their bones.

Merchants are no longer sure of Canada: its puppet strings
were snipped by Vichy scissors. Spectacles, hats and rings went
down with boots.

Only the blank uncounted Sunday flies fill their ears like inedi-
ble puddings.

Swollen prunes and spilt milk mingle with the natal flow and
the honey of Canaan.

The reason, deterred from untouchable candy, is weeping:
Theresa and Saxon, one joke, risk of beechwood and birch, rose
and bell, roof and sweathouse.

Mennonite witches boil frosting in canebrakes: moored to the towering pamphlets of organ-grinders, sacked under laundries for chocolate stains.

Obdurate witnesses, martyrs to cornets and kitchens, children ditched by birds: hands up, regretful.

The black knight, his knees on the lilies, is prone to watch Solomon's daughters, made septic with swords, wash down in single file.

The rosebuds have nowhere to hide from X-ray eyes.

Down a single white corridor, an intern's diapered grin stabs their groins like a hypodermic.

Outside, eclectic bows are scratching backs and fogs on barbs, raising smoke from caesuras, pomp and fire from circumstances: shepherds of the cross and dove, our Spanish acquisitions. The orchestra swells and goes by like a Swiss delegation, blinder than ever to hotbeds of orchids and hoed corteges. A wake of thistles, the lost eyes of godawful cartoffal soup, a barrel of resin, a handful of lime twigs inter my heart, scraping an ultimate jam tone from an urchin's intestinal cell-o.

After ten years in various monasteries, the master of our guild escaped in his own way.

Then: my body like a model range of bones, strapped to a board on display. A male nurse from Prague explores its craters without anesthetic, down to bedrock. Eruptions are provoked.

Three days in 21A (the lions' den) while a crust forms, then up and away to a new block.

September 21st

Morning in autumn
a bath of air from blue bottles
white walls and underwater grass.

Can you distinguish figures, hear
her voice in absence, offered
to the god, his fractioned body?

Golden was from Garwolin, in Poland, and he was a kind of
supernal supernumerary to the *Blokovi* in the new compound
to which I was assigned. All sorts of unverifiable stories had
been circulating about him since the day he arived in early '43.
The first one I heard was that he had gone off with Polish
partisans in 1939 and had been caught three years later wearing
a German cavalry officer's breeches, Russian bearcoat and the
Légion d'Honneur and smoking American cigarettes. But the
very next story, told with equal conviction, claimed he had
been a hermit, had eaten leaves and lived in a cave. To the
Jews in the block (most of whom were German or Czecho-
slovakian) he was a legend in the flesh; but his invariable
answer to a question regarding the truth of a particular story
was: "Believe what you please, my friend. If it pleases you, yes,
why not believe it?"

He was a gigantic man, almost six foot six, with a huge head
and hollow eye-sockets and bulging eyeballs, and a broad frame
which his terrible emaciation flattened and emphasized. His age
was unreadable: he might have been anywhere between forty
and sixty.

Everyone called him *"Rebbe,"* but whether he was a rabbi in
any strict sense of the word or not, he *was* a holy man, and a
magnet that drew the block, Jew and non-Jew alike, into a
unity by its presence.

Though I'm quite aware how unqualified I am, I want to try to
reproduce a few of Golden's words here. I was young and I
knew nothing, I was not a Jew, I have only an imperfect
memory to rely on, confused with distance and echoes of later
things. Still, I want to try, being as faithful as I can to him and
to the circumstances. I had forgotten him, and now, suddenly,
here he is.

Every night he performed the same ritual. He would speak a few words, only a few, in the silence after lights were out, then pause and say, "Let us remember our names," and after a second, "Isaac Golden, Garwolin." Then every person in the room was expected to speak up with his name and place of origin. And whoever had died, or had been transported, or who no longer responded, would have his name spoken for him by someone else—by the person in the next bunk, or by the one who had taken his place, or by Golden himself if anyone faltered. On his last night in the block, when there was little more left of him than a voice and a pair of eyes, he alone supplied over *two hundred* names.

Do not laugh when the moon is in waning! But worse still to frown. The Tempter himself laughs and darkness falls into the heart. If you doubt, doubt greatly! Feel potent despair! Fountains of strength spring from our exile, in spite of ourselves! Let us remember our names . . . Golden, Garwolin . . .

When is true progress possible? When all our sins have been forgiven. Progress is the path the World-to-Come takes already. Fear neither stillness nor change. Though *this* world is our doing, we *will be forgiven*. Yidden! Strength! Let us remember our names . . .

Every freedom but the last, true freedom must be sacrificed; only when you have accomplished this may *your* freedom be realized, and not even the most jealous of gods will require it of you. But a man who claims more than one true freedom has no sacrifice to offer, and even the least jealous of gods will require his life of him . . .

In my youth I was given to hours of black melancholy and terrible loneliness. Aged twenty-two I went to Warsaw and walked in the streets. I felt no one around me and threw myself under a streetcar. But the Lord embraced me as I lay between the rails, and the wheels passed me by on both sides. Then

I knew that I had to go on, that I was not alone. To go on! That is to be a Jew. To go on, and on, and on. Toward Him, Blessed be His Name. Let us remember *our* names . . . Golden, Garwolin . . .

The Holy One, Blessed be His Name, is *at* your side, not *on* it.

Do not cringe! Do not forget your names! What great power they have! The heavens hang from them, and the angels in those heavens hang from them. Your very bodies are systems of worlds depending on your names. Be strong, collect your selves, for the tiniest worlds and the most infinitely enormous are founded upon your single existence, and your name. Let us remember our names . . . Golden, Garwolin . . .

A *musselman* has lost *only* his name, but with it every access to the World-to-Come. Stand at the gates and look in; never turn around!

I ask you: Could I ever have imagined these eyes I have now? When I close them I still see them suspended like great white bulbs above me. They are horribly mine now, but *mine* still, and though for a moment I quaver each time I see them hovering there, they close when I order them to, go out like lights and go blind on my sleep. I have shut them off from hunger, blinded them to death, forbidden them to dream; I have forgotten all but the voices and names of the dead. And I shall not relinquish myself to my terrible eyes, not surrender my name. Let us remember our names . . .

Never fear! In time everything will be elucidated!

The following aphorisms are about as many as I can recall (with any certainty) of the many thousands that sprang from a game which Golden invented one evening. He called it "The World-to-Come." The only rules (if you can call them that) were that the World-to-Come had to be spoken of always in the present

tense, and as one word, a unity real and recognizable—*given*.
No one was permitted to use his aphorism as a wish-vehicle;
imaginative reflections were not allowed. There are no inven-
tions in the World-to-Come, said Golden, and for a long time
he supplied all the phrases himself, until others began to catch
on. Pretty soon whole work squads were mulling over aphorisms,
disputing like scholars around the stove or in the latrine, trying
to fix their conceptions of the World-to-Come in words that
would show they really had caught a glimmering of that world.
For Golden remained the sole and final authority.

Now, thinking back, I realize that I was witness to an
astounding phenomenon: with his little game, Golden succeeded in rekindling a genuine religious fervor in those around
him; he inspired even the simplest, most untutored little Jew
in the block to an attempt to articulate himself, the validity of
his common human longing, and lent him insight into an enduring, good, *created* world anchored in the tangible world and
yet transcending it, transcending the horror of his surroundings,
transcending even the memory of past suffering. He helped each
man redeem in himself the forgotten truths, the dissipated
substance of his childhood, of the faith which is the birthright
first of all of children, their *domain*. They *know*, they are not
crippled by their eyes; their faith is not founded on appearances
or intimidations. When a child acts, he acts in accordance with
a truth that may not be seen or held, but which is present to
him as a vision is present. And his act is then an expression of
his being, not the mandate of a need to become anything other
than what he is already.

Each time anyone believed he had an acceptable contribution,
he rushed to Golden directly after rollcall and presented it for
his approval. If Golden thought the phrase needed polishing he
would say why in an encouraging way, but he wouldn't allow
the submission of a revised version on the same evening. The
instant Golden nodded approbation, however, the aphorism
was published with great enthusiasm and became an object of

avid discussion. Often it happened that the same phrase would be presented a number of times, with only minor alterations; but this was quite acceptable: only in the World-to-Come can two people say exactly the same thing, Golden said.

The World-to-Come is not beyond; it is already indestructible.

God, the People, World: these are the three cornerstones of the World-to-Come.

Nature is not a word in the World-to-Come.

The World-to-Come is not bounded by Nothingness.

Murder is always later than the World-to-Come, loneliness always prior; neither is in it.

True speech is heard only in the World-to-Come.

The hand commands the eye in the World-to-Come.

Whatsoever the hand touches or the eye sees becomes a prayer in the World-to-Come.

In the World-to-Come there are no indifferent realities or neutral truths.

Force is forceless in the World-to-Come.

Eden is the ground on which the World-to-Come is founded, but the two are not apart in space or time.

Longing is the knowledge of exile from the World-to-Come.

No one is ever born dead in the World-to-Come.

Machines grow like vegetables in the World-to-Come.

Guns exist in the World-to-Come, but there are no targets.

Waiting is forgotten in the World-to-Come; attendance is rewarded by response.

No two things or beings may be compared in the World-to-Come.

The World-to-Come presents no surfaces.

Hell is present in the World-to-Come as an empty receptacle, like a vase without flowers.

All bodies bear fruit in the World-to-Come.

In the World-to-Come angels are redundant.

The mathematics of the World-to-Come is one of plenitude and not of multiplication.

In the World-to-Come, men fly without wings.

Art is the only crime in the World-to-Come, but it is never committed.

Sins are harmless in the World-to-Come: bees without stingers.

All men are Jews in the World-to-Come.

September 27th

Dreamed of myself and Hannes Däumler. We were wearing white overalls and were planting juniper. No guard in sight; I kissed him and awoke.

Polish aristocrats, Latvian sailors, Ukrainian muscles . . .
    We owned our nudity, wore it like fish through disinfection chambers, carried it licketysplit by the hawk eyes of surgeons, four hundred rickety, slippery mimes of health.

On the eve of my fifteenth birthday, the monk-corporal who was calling the roll crooked his white-gloved finger at me and ordered me to report to the monk barracks. I doubt that he knew why, but from the pleasure he took in telling me my presence was desired there, I'm sure he thought he did.

When I arrived, floating with terror, I was greeted jovially by a high-ranking monk. Congratulations were in order, he said: the Reich was making me a birthday present. Someone in Berlin had made a regrettable mistake, it seemed: I was not a dirty little Gypsy-second-category after all, but an up-to-now camouflaged Aryan.

First of all (of course) I had to be moved from all danger of (further) contamination. This was accomplished immediately: I was delivered into the hands of a *capo* from Limburg, who saw to it I received a (hot) shower, a new headshave, a thorough delousing, a quick lancing and dressing of all more prominent boils and abscesses, several hasty embraces, a clean track suit with matching soccer shoes, a piece of (real) cheese (also from Limburg), more caresses, two bowls of soup (from the bottom! of the vat), a parting kiss, a re-tattooing (*E* for Education), and a bright red badge with *D* on it.

After this I was shifted to a special camp for Germans and stuck in a block among newly arrived Aryans (imaginary cross section of Berlin during the late Weimar Republic): pimps and malingerers, clergymen, habitual (but petty) criminals, street-walkers, flagrant homosexuals, minor politicals and families of politicals, and people denounced for hoarding, illegal radio reception, loose remarks or any of a hundred other offenses.

The gates are busy, you can't imagine! People are lined up for miles to get in or get out or get *back* in, all of them weighed down with bundles and infants and trunks. I try to look as official as I can, and oddly enough they get more angry with each other than with me. Maybe they respect my youth, or my uniform, or recognize some deep imperative, or feel an unaccustomed shame. *I* do.

For a while nobody seemed to know what to do with me. I was too young to be offered the "opportunity" to join the army, and I wasn't exactly a person (loudmouthed child) who could safely be planted back in Germany among unwitting civilians. My new status was confirmed in one way though: I was handed a metal disc entitling me to visit the bordel in Block 24. I exchanged it for a sweater.

September 30th

How would you like me to be? Quiet persuasiveness is a gift I don't have—and I'm not a steamroller either. Maybe I expect too much of you (of everyone?). There's a good sharp point on my emotional pencil, but the eraser's all used up. Understand? It's pretty damned inhibiting.

Finally I was transferred to a small farm in the monastic complex and assigned to a greenhouse of wood and glass (even the nails had been largely replaced by pegs). The larger area (Raisko) was worked mostly by women, but in the greenhouse Czech and German male prisoners were engaged in the germination of seeds provided by a botanical supply house in Münster (health foods before the war).

Hannes Däumler was almost twenty when I met him. He was an odd-looking boy, half a foot taller than I was. His legs had grown out of all proportion to the rest of his body; his pelvis stood out like an ox yoke; above the waist he was still an undernourished adolescent. He was horribly sensitive about his height. Often when we were walking together he would suddenly jackknife his legs, bringing his eyes down to the level of mine, and then shuffle along in a ridiculous crouch, "just to see how the world looks from down here." He had straw-colored hair, so that his shaven head seemed to be topped with a white velvet skull-cap. He had narrow green eyes, a laughably tiny nose and fleshless lips and the most *capable* hands imaginable —broad and hard, beautifully balanced, but not at all delicate. He handled the plants on the farm with great tenderness; every seedling he set thrived. He was in love with the feel of the earth, with the fragile, minute touch of green life between his fingers.

He took me under his wing and taught me what I had to
know. I learned fast. When spring came, all rain, we moved
from the greenhouse into the open and planted our pharma-
ceutical seedlings in neat, numbered rows. On our knees by the
boots of visiting monks (fairly seldom) we tended and plucked
and reset all through the summer, gradually browning in the
sun, lean as planks but gorged with pilfered vitamins.

Hannes's father had died of a "heart attack" in 1937, in
Sachsenhausen, two years after his arrest for "party-inimical
journalistic activities." Hannes and his mother (who was of
aristocratic birth) had moved to Düsseldorf; he had been studying sculpting at the School of Fine Arts when, in 1941, someone had decided that he and his mother were also enemies of
the state. They had been sent to Buchenwald, and his mother,
if she was still alive, was there now. Hannes had no idea why
he had suddenly been transferred to Raisko to become a
gardener, but it was "far better" than what (whatever it was) he
had been doing at Buchenwald.

Footnote. There was no shortage of ash and bone meal, but
sacks of real compost from Germany and northern Poland had
to be used for the fertilization of edible herbs consumed by the
monks or packaged for the army. But when shipments were
delayed we were obliged to make do with the local product.
Now, even if the monks had known how impure (racially
speaking) their parsley and their peppermint occasionally were,
I doubt that they'd have cared very much; no, another more
distant, recondite ethic was being satisfied in the use of German
dung. But we were careful about which herbs we nibbled on.
We *knew*.

Our greenhouse (and four others) were under the general
supervision of a man named Gustav Lokowandt. He was a
political prisoner, though anything but an ordinary one; often
he was away for weeks at a time, and it was rumored that he
had known Hoess in the days of the *Artomanen*. Hannes had
seen him at Buchenwald, too, where he had seemed to perform

some sort of peculiar function as liaison between prisoners and monks, and where it was obvious that someone outside was keeping a protective eye on him. Hannes knew of many people whom Lokowandt had helped, and he often wondered about the strange coincidence that had brought them together on the farm within a few weeks of one another, but even though he was in Lokowandt's good graces (then), he was unable ever to find out anything about the unusual state of "privileged disgrace" into which Lokowandt had fallen.

The first sight I had of him was about a week after my arrival. Hannes and I were watering shoots of basil on the incubation table when Lokowandt came through with Dr. Caesar and a couple of monks. They stopped and watched what we were doing for a few moments and then moved on. Lokowandt whispered something to Caesar, who glanced back at me and laughed, saying: "Well, it's not the first bastard weed Berlin has sent us." I must admit, next to Hannes I looked about as Aryan as an eggplant.

Physically, Lokowandt was a strange mixture of both primitive and refined characteristics. His oversized peasant head was poised on a slender neck, and he had a narrow chest that branched off into short, fleshy arms with incongruously tiny hands. He was exactly my height at the time—around five foot six, I'd say—yet, just to give you an idea how large his head was, his eyes were a full inch below the level of mine.

Yet only the most superficial memory of his face remains. His *real* face (which I later saw, and which I shall never forget) was not the face from the farm; in fact it seems to me now that there he was another *plasma* as well.

A barn beyond Finsterwalde...

How many times in all the years between have I awakened in the middle of the night with pounding heart and a mossy taste in my mouth, unable to make out the walls and windows among

which I had fallen asleep, lost still in the landscape of the
dream, a landscape from which all color had been drained, as if
by snow or by a brutal white humidity.

I see a black medieval carriage drawn by two white chargers;
it comes close by; curtains part; and suddenly his face (a
glimpsed palimpsest) is present for an instant (tiny eyes, low
forehead, cropped red hair already graying, yellow teeth); he
smiles and asks in a throaty, taunting voice, "Ach, where is
your Hannes now?"

Hannes and I played a game: the game of consolation. Analogy
for toy swords, dry friction and toothache, if you want to know.

What ever happened to Wilhelm Busch?

Keep away from the kitchen!
I had known a few *piepels*. Some of them had had no choice:
their eyes, their hands, their little rumps had given them away.
But others played the whore. As for the rest (of us), when the
wolf showed his purple head, when that ugly knout popped out
from behind the tree—we ran, we hid, we promised and
avoided.

I'm the victim of certain self-inflicted prohibitions. I have
one great doubt in my heart, one that will never be resolved in
the World-as-Is. I remember in snatches where and how, the
hide-and-seek, the awful letdown. The flight goes on. All these
years I have harbored dangerous resolutions for the sake of a
private totem-to-end-all-totems, rejecting the slightest reminder
of desire. But all I can be sure of is that there are no fabulous
restorations (like those of fairy tales or animated films); the
shattered mirror cannot be repaired, but every fragment is still
a mirror. The fence is electrified and the first touch is glue.

Still, Hannes and I did play the game of consolation, and it
was what it was.

Lokowandt knew without a word. He read it all over us.

Hannes tired of the game long before I did. Then Lokowandt stepped in. Hannes began to fill out in his shoulders and brought me extra rations. We went on playing, from time to time, but the peculiar, separate, unspoken confidence of our game had been destroyed. Hannes (at twenty) lost his innocence; I didn't understand what that meant just yet.

The subtleties of memory are all superimposed; I'm afraid I've made myself out to be something other than I was. Hannes, wiser and older, out of another world but obliged to adapt to the same monastic rigors as I, reacted with instincts I did not possess, recognized things that were invisible to me. He was able to manipulate circumstances (for a while and to a certain degree) with a feminine, acquiescent caution that was his by age-old, race-old heritage. I had no *instinct* for survival—I floated. For Hannes to survive, he required the faculties of a man, and he did not fully possess them; I lived because it never entered my mind that I might not—if this was reprehensible, then I am still open to the same reproach.

October 10th

Last night I bought a little prostitute some drinks and took her out to eat. Afterward we went to my hotel. She undressed immediately and sat very erect on the bed. She had a beautiful back and a long neck, and a wild face with unsteady eyes. She was ashamed of her breasts: she had had two abortions in close succession and they were still swollen. I decided suddenly I didn't want to sleep with her. I offered her money; at first she refused and then said, "If you can afford it,"—not ironically, but in an almost apologetic way. She was barely twenty. I walked a way with her, she told me the usual tale of woe, but only because I asked her to. Then she said she wanted to be alone. It was still fairly early. I almost asked her to come back with me, but didn't. I fall in love too easily, you know, and not just with little whores, either. But I fall out of it just as

quickly. Casual sex tempts me, and then means nothing afterward. Perhaps I'm simply incapable of fidelity, of loving anyone
for long, or deeply . . . any more?

On some Sunday afternoons in late summer, Hannes and I
took long walks out into the garden complex. Peculiar inter-
ludes of grass and breezes, a prickly sky, flat stretches of black
and green merging imperceptibly into a steaming horizon,
docile animals and far-off peasants haying. An illusory bucolic
world, perfect and unbounded for an hour.

As autumn came on, a sea of yellow rose around us, ma-
rooned us, turned us in upon ourselves. Hannes grew uneasy, an
odd discontent preoccupied his face; at certain moments on
our Sunday promenades, when we simply stood gazing off into
an untellable distance, or sat side by side (I touching him), I
felt a dim premonitory melancholy, heard the faint overtures
of a knowledge I was not ready to receive, but which Hannes
possessed already. I pressed him to talk then, about anything:
his parents, the other camp, his studies, childhood. But he
knew my curiosity had other roots, and he grew taciturn,
blushing like a shy criminal when he looked me in the eyes.

Winter came; it rained every day. We stood together in the
greenhouse handling plants automatically (letting them pass
through us), seldom speaking, owners of fingers rather than
tongues, brushing one another occasionally, as if by accident,
and apologetic (for the first time) for the consciousness of
touch.

One day he said to me suddenly, "I can't any more"; and he
went to another bed to work. I ran after him. "Leave me alone,"
he said, and thrust his hands like spades deep into the soft
earth on the planting table. He glanced at me with eyes like
a frightened animal's, then turned away, and I was called back
to my work.

December. Lokowandt was away. I hounded Hannes in

our free hours; he ignored me as much as he could. Do you know what I'm talking about?

He turned on me. "Why don't you leave me alone?" he said, trembling. "But why?" I asked, ready to cry. "There's no why," he said; "you'd be making things easier for us both, that's all." "But what have I done?" I cried. "It's not what you've done," he said; "it's what I *am*. You wouldn't understand. Now just leave me alone."

One night in early January, long after lights were out, he came and wakened me. His face was glowing oddly in the dark. He pressed something into my hand—half an orange! I hadn't even thought of one for years. "Eat it now," he said. "I took half, the rest is for you."

Lokowandt was back; he had been to Germany. He had told Hannes that within a few weeks we would all be moving to the west. Where exactly he didn't know, but the Russians were drawing near. I fell asleep again with the taste of orange in my mouth and dreamed of Hannes's strangely luminous face.

Until the day we departed I hardly spoke to him again; his brief visit in the night was swallowed by the dream that had followed it. He spent almost every evening with Lokowandt. A tall monk moved into the greenhouse and supervised the boxing of plants that were to be shipped away before we left. Nightly, great bonfires lit up the sky over the monastery. Fog and snow the same sickly yellow-brown.

Finally, one evening toward the end of the month, we were instructed at roll call to be ready the next morning to leave. Before dawn we were lined up outside the block, shivering and stamping our feet. And then just waited. Around eleven o'clock a contingent of monks showed up, far more irritable than usual. Lokowandt appeared for a brief moment, held a hurried conversation with Hannes, smiled right through me, and then went away in the company of several monks, all of them carrying filing cases under their arms.

Around midafternoon we were marched off to the monastery itself. Just inside the gates, between the two outer rings, thousands of prisoners were milling about. We filed by carts from which we were handed two loaves of bread and a tin of "stew" apiece. A little Czech named Calek, who was between me and Hannes, took custody of the pound of margarine meant for the three of us. We were warned that these were a week's provisions, but many prisoners were already gorging themselves (to the great amusement of the monks). It was long after dark when we passed out through the gates again, for the last time, between rows of guardian monks with submachine guns (to bar our re-entry, no doubt).

As we moved away over the crusted fields, our lines flowed as tributaries into a greater stream already on the move. Only the sound of our feet on the frozen ground: the brittle, shuffling tread of a gigantic human millipede. The night air turned white with breath and body heat; the shouts of guards congealed like tiny icicles in our ears. I couldn't see over the shoulders of anyone around me, and I looked up. The full moon appeared overhead for an indistinct moment; it was far away, but no farther than anything else. I welded myself to Hannes; our hands froze together.

At daybreak we were allowed to lie down for a couple of hours in the snow. Many never rose again; there was a scramble for their uneaten rations. Others were dragged along by their companions. We spread out gradually into a loose herd. It was more difficult to walk by day; at night we had been drawn along by contact, by the anonymous magnetism of darkness, but now the vision of distance and a sense of helpless separateness made our feet heavy, let us stumble easily. Sometimes, when the monks weren't looking, we stole brief moments on the runners of the sleds loaded with their baggage.

Hannes and I were strong in comparison to most; we possessed the relatively privileged bodies of those who had had "enough" to eat. All the same, Hannes soon began to show signs of weakening, and had finished his rations long before me. Calek

and our shares of the margarine vanished in the first few hours. Around us hundreds were dropping—and how many had already died, with or without the help of the monks (who could stand no signs of weakness)! We had been among the last to leave the monastery, and the fields over which we passed were studded with corpses (some already black and half-covered with snow) like stumps of trees or single tortured branches.

On and on we moved, and steadily the number of marchers dwindled. Hannes began to talk to himself; for long stretches he forgot me entirely, and I (at his heels like a dog) watched him stagger along; his head seemed to float detached just a little ahead of his body.

We crossed the Oder near Cosel, then marched north along its banks, through village after village, through fields with abandoned and starving animals. We stopped in hamlets, in the squares, huddled around the frozen fountains, while Polish women crossed themselves and sometimes brought us turnips, or handed us bits of bread. We drifted like grounded birds, past mines and quarries, burned-out camps, half-empty settlements. We crossed the paths of other marchers who had left before us, and sometimes walked parallel to them across great frozen stretches, before losing them again. At night the wind carried to us the sound of artillery fire, of Stalin organs, or single spurts of gunfire, coded messages from the woods; then the monks fired tracer bullets low above our heads (to keep the wolves away, they said).

And every time we struck a larger town we learned that we had come an hour or a day too late for the last transport. Ten days went by this way.

On my sixteenth birthday (give or take a day) we reached Breslau. It was still smoking from an air raid a few hours before. Not more than a fifth of those who had begun the march had finished it. We assembled in the freight yards and after a great deal of counting and recounting were finally loaded into boxcars. I caught a brief glimpse of one of the Jewish boys from the "school," but had no chance to speak with him. Hannes began to wonder if we were on our way to Buchenwald, and if he would find his mother there alive.

A transport of troops from the Eastern Front stood on a siding; they stared at us with haggard eyes until their train pulled away. There was no way for them to communicate with us, but they couldn't take their eyes off us. None of the blindness of civilians or railroad men.

Faces in windows, eyes (boys with hairpins in their forelocks, blondes with home-set pin-curls, capped bald men with mustaches): who wondered?

Our destination turned out to be Gross Rosen. After a week in a shaky wooden firetrap of a block (three to a bunk) we were issued new, slimmer "travel provisions" and piled into boxcars again. In two hours we were back in Breslau (which had suffered an even heavier bombardment in the interim); from there we moved northwest, stopped in Cottburg for six hours or so (to take on more prisoners; no room even to sit down then), and on to Libben. We spent the rest of the night there and moved at dawn. Hannes was absolutely certain this time we were headed for Buchenwald.

Others have described these things more graphically than I. Looking back on that journey is like staring into a pool that reflects my face as it is now, and mirrors a seemingly bottomless dark world in reverse behind it. The cold gives way; hunger is pluperfect; the pace is the same impeded crawl; the landscape that rubs by loses all relative shape, accelerates to a blue blur, and then disintegrates. Nothing remains but the colorless perpetuation of a movement completely internalized.

All ends are indescribable and inexplicable to me. Only in rare moments of transition am I made aware of the passage of time. No thrill of accomplishment: another severance is announced, another threshold has been crossed. But sometimes, for an instant, in the very act of crossing, the future or a clear intimation of it appears clearly before my eyes, outside of time, as a signification of new movement.

This time the transition began when we left the monastery; the journey itself was a fitful series of false terminations; it did not end until it had carried me beyond my powers of conscious endurance. I can't help but be erratic in my recollections of it; the past ran me down in the present, and left the future to pick me up in its own good time. Whatever exists of me or that journey now is in the nature of inherited characteristics—genes of my succession of myself. And what isn't in me I have to invent—for myself, *of* myself.

Where? Half an hour out of Libben. The train suddenly sped up. We pressed to the apertures to see. Nothing; gray daylight like smoke through the cracks. The sound of an airplane, thin, the whistling of air, the train rollicking from side to side. We leaned against each other, jostling like cattle. Then: a whining sound from somewhere, from both sides; short clatters of gunfire. An explosion; we tilted backward, to one side, in a carnival wheel. Cries, crossed blades of light, the titter of machine guns. Another explosion, as if under us, a sudden metallic scream: we begin to slide and pile up, the car is leaning, leaning. A violent stop, the car is thrown on its side, a great outcry. I strike my head.

There is a light, a square cloud, directly above me; it begins to expand. My feet are up in the air. Moans, voices. There is a sharp pain in the back of my head; I strain to right myself in a mass of bodies. Groans. Hannes, where is Hannes? I cry out his name. Ah! he is beside me, half under me, he is bleeding from the forehead.

We struggle to our feet. Everyone is heaving and shoving; the dead and the injured are a carpet. The car has a wall it didn't have before; the light above us is an open door!

Hannes didn't want to go. He kept saying insanely, "We've got to get to Buchenwald!" Some had already managed to scramble out. Shouts from outside, single shots. A prisoner, struck by a bullet, toppled back into the car. More and more were pulling themselves up through the opening. I made Hannes go, I screamed at him frantically until he fought his way up and reached back down for me.

The air above was bitterly damp-cold, shrill with voices, the frantic cries of those still imprisoned in other cars. The train lay on a long curve of track, at least thirty cars, with us near the end. The locomotive had rolled over and lay smoking, well off the tracks, like a ruptured can. Some cars had remained upright, others teetered on their sides, held up only by their couplings. From the middle of the train to the back the cars had piled up in a zigzag line back and forth across the tracks.

The only monks to be seen were far away, up near the front of the train: they had guns, but they were cautious about getting out into the open with them. The plane was still up there. Except for one other freight car much farther up, ours seemed to be the only one that had sprung. But we were in luck: both turreted cars had been put out of commission. The one behind us had suffered a direct hit; the other (behind the engine) had been thrown on its side. On the inner curve, behind the wrecked locomotive, the monks had set up a gun from which they could control the field on that side; the snow was dotted with the bodies of a few prisoners who had tried to cross it. On the outer curve, however, the monks were moving back slowly, obviously watchful of the plane. Occasionally one of them would mount a boxcar for a moment and fire a few bursts into its locked interior.

The plane came down again, strafing across the locomotive, then banked around and swept low along the outer side; the monks dived for cover. Hannes and I sprang down on the same side and set out as fast as our legs would carry us. At first we ran a long way back, beside the tracks, keeping as many cars as possible between us and the monks. We ran without looking back, stumbling across the plowed, frozen earth, lurching through patches of snow. We gulped the icy air with open mouths; it was like having all your teeth pulled out at once. The plane came down again directly at us, dipped its wings, and began to fire over our heads; we didn't dare look back. After what seemed like hours, the cries and the sound of guns grew fainter. I glanced over my shoulder: there was no one behind us. We had put a good two kilometers between us and the train. I shouted to Hannes, who was at least thirty yards ahead of me. He looked back and wilted to the ground. I caught up with him and sank down beside him. The sole of one of his shoes had come completely off; the top hung around his ankle like a funnel, his foot was blue and bleeding. For a while we sat heaving like bellows; the air we breathed out was no warmer than what we took in.

We had escaped, it seemed.

The rest has no periphery, no frame, no form; it is a nightmare without entry or exit. I don't even know exactly how long it lasted—five weeks or six, at least—but it might have been as many years, or only one long winter night that overslept the spring.

Neither in it nor out of it now.

There are only two principal actors in this winter charade (I can hardly call it a drama): a pair of youthful vagabonds or ragamuffins (one tall and blond, one short and dark). Toward the end (when there is almost no time left for him to make his appearance) a man with red hair comes on. Additional players in the piece have little to do but cross the stage, singly or in groups, pushing carts, riding old bicycles, loaded down with baggage and animals and all sorts of household paraphernalia. They are of all ages and sexes and shapes, and are dressed as warmly as possible. There must be enough of them to sustain the background movement throughout; no single person may appear twice in exactly the same guise.

The time is near the end of the Thirty Years' War (1914–45), somewhere in Germany between the Neisse and the Elbe. The stage is bare except for a backdrop of trees and covered haystacks. There are no acts or curtains; the lights are dimmed from the very beginning and remain that way (except for occasional brilliant flashes from both wings) until just before the "end." The piece is essentially an improvisation and requires no audience for its performance. The mere presence of the persons on stage is enough to keep things moving.

The two young vagabonds, both of whom are dressed in a grotesque hodgepodge of worn and outsized garments, wander round and round in devious circles; occasionally they may backtrack, but they never take a direct route across the stage. In the beginning, the taller boy (who walks with a limp) is seen wearing only one shoe; his other foot is bound in rags, and he leans on his younger companion. Frequently he sits down and starts to sing in a heart-rending voice unlike his own. The melodies are recognizable, but he seems to have forgotten the lyrics; only such terms as *Mutti, Kind, Heimat, Herz* are intelligible. As the two boys stumble along, this taller one does most of the talking. Though there is a suggestion of hysteria in his voice, he is still fairly coherent; but as time wears on, his speech becomes more and more of a disconnected monologue, until finally it makes no sense at all.

The following incident occurs in the early part of the play. A hussar (or renegade monk) begins to track the two boys and finally waylays them. They turn on him however, knock him down and beat him senseless. Then they strip him of most of his garments (the taller boy takes the shoes) and leave him to lie half-naked in the center of the stage, where he withers away (or is dragged off secretly).

From time to time certain members of the supporting cast (peasants, deserters, refugees, factory workers, knights without horses or armor) stop and stare at the two vagabonds. A few even try to strike up conversations; but the taller boy either bounds away like a frightened deer or springs wildly at the stranger and scares him off. Only the younger boy ever approaches any of the passing figures, and then while his companion sleeps; he dances or does pantomimes for food, most of which he saves for his companion (who always wakes up ravenous and ill-tempered). Food is not easy to procure: it is a time of dire want; he has to display increasing ingenuity and showmanship to coax even a shriveled tuber or a drop of milk from the peasants.

The play goes on like this for weeks.

Then, suddenly, the bursts of light from offstage left become more frequent. Much of the dialogue is drowned by great peals of thunder; this makes no difference, however. The boys begin to discard some of their clothing and to walk rapidly in smaller and smaller circles. Finally they come to a full stop and lie down. The background movement ceases; the lights come up a little and another backdrop comes down: the outline of a barn and in the distance, on the left, the faint intimation of a river. Horses whinny and stamp. At this point the red-haired man, bearded and in tatters, enters the barn. He makes his way unsurely across the stage, then stops a few steps short of the sleeping boys and stares at them. Suddenly he lets out a hoarse roar; the boys sit up, startled and afraid. The red-haired man points a finger at the taller boy; both boys cry out in recognition, as if this were an old friend. The taller one springs to his feet and waltzes away with the red-haired man to the opposite side of the stage, where they sit down and start to converse in exaggerated whispers, madly gesticulating. The younger boy, who seems too tired to rise, crawls to the center of the stage and tries to hear what they are saying, but he can only make out single, isolated words from both of them, words such as *Vater, Verbrecher, Verleumdung, Verrat,* and he cannot understand why these words should be used. After a short while he is overcome by fatigue (though he does not want to be), and laying his head on his arms he falls asleep. Horses are heard again, exaggerated whispers. The lights go out and the play goes on in darkness.

No scream will ever be loud enough.

All that night I wandered in and out of an inconclusive, disjointed dream, cooking up endless dream plots to avoid the need to urinate (what else?). But some great truth seemed reachable through my dreaming, a truth quite apart from my body and its stupid interference, and so I pursued it. But whatever it was avoided my grasp, and finally my body became a solid obstruction and would not let me fix my promised vision. I grew resigned in my sleep then, and punished my body. I dreamed I was dead, and dreamed of waking in a cold light. But my body became disgusted with all my evasions and brought on real daylight, to fade the false light of my sleep-death and open my eyes.

"The horses are the first to notice" (old German proverb). Who else has used the horse as a sacrificial animal, letting its blood like a bull's, feeding it sanctified oats?

The *rom* call the horse *Grai*, which means "God's gift." It is a great crime to slaughter a horse or a dog, or to partake of their flesh; anyone who does so is called *kushpulo*, and among the German Gypsies this is the most damning word of insult.

Lokowandt may have spared the horses and me, but he is still *kushpulo*.

The horses (a dray and two mares) were trembling and shuffling about in the rear. I stood up and went to them, thinking to warm myself on their bodies. But they backed away when I tried to touch them, staring at me with huge distrustful eyes, jostling each other nervously, breathing steam. I turned away and for the first time saw Hannes lying on his back in the straw. I smiled and took a step toward him, imagining he was still asleep. I spoke his name aloud, then saw his open eyes, his dark protruding tongue, and I knew he wasn't sleeping. He was green, Hannes was all green. I shuddered involuntarily and knelt down to touch him. Through the open door, sunlight came pouring in across his face: he began to glow with an icy-green light. Two blackish marks stood out on his throat; his eyes had no irises, they were completely green too. I tried to shut the lids and couldn't. I tried to force his tongue back into his mouth, and couldn't. I was very deliberate about it, but I couldn't. I got irritated and stood up, thinking, How stupid he looks! I was ashamed of him for looking so stupid. I returned to the horses; they shied away still, showing their teeth threateningly. I grabbed up an armful of oats from their bin, ignoring them. They knocked against me. I went back over and dumped the straw on Hannes, covering his face, hiding his green mouth and eyes.

For a moment I stood there staring down at him, and then I was seized with violent tremors that yanked me out into the yard. I was conscious of everything that was happening to me, but felt as if I were standing a short distance outside my body. The mist was lifting, the air was tinted with a thin, bilious yellow. I heard the sound of artillery fire, clear separate bursts on all sides. Almost casually, the thought of Lokowandt entered my mind, and instantly a sharp pain shot through my bladder. I shrank. A great liquid spasm of fear and nausea swept over me, opening every pore. My knees gave way wetly and I sank to the ground.

It was almost noon when I came to. I was soaked in my own filth. I felt as if I had been turned inside out. I got to my feet slowly, with no sensation of weight whatsoever, and began to run. To fly. I reached the river; it hadn't been far away after all. I found a battered rowboat, without oars and half full of water, pushed it off, fell into it and passed out again.

Seven weeks later I came round; I was in an American field hospital near Halle. It was there I learned I had survived the war.

AUTUMN EQUINOX

The celebrated historian Ebn Athir relates that when he was at Moussoul on the Tigris, in the year 600 of the Hejira, there was in that country an epidemic disease of the throat; and it was said that a woman of the race of the Jinns had lost her son, and all those who did not condole with her on account of his death were attacked with the disease; so that to be cured of it men and women assembled, and with all their strength cried out: O mother of Ankood, forgive us! Ankood is dead and we did not mind it!

—THOMAS KEIGHTLEY, *The Fairy Mythology*

November 2nd

For almost a week now I've been avoiding this book assiduously, but I can't afford to leave it any longer if I'm ever going to get through with it. (I don't say *finish it*, because in spite of all the climaxes, there is no denouement.)

If I were to pretend that "I" is one consistent being (outlived the war, outgrew his childhood), then the years from the end of the war until I arrived in Paris would have to show the slow peeling away of an innocence that was only a veneer—in a flaying process that actually began in 1945, but whose effective pain had been (mysteriously) deferred until now. It wasn't that way, though: pain never came late; it was always directly proportionate to my naïveté, my unsuspectingness. What I *have* learned is that pain I can anticipate is not unbearable; but such already-learned lessons jump the gun, and are apt to estrange frail sympathies, *mon vieux*. Or do you already know who I am?

I woke to summer. For three weeks it had been touch and go; I'd been out, really out, absolutely still except for a violent heartbeat, as if I'd been sprinting in my sleep. I don't remember a thing, but I wouldn't be at all surprised if that was exactly what I was doing—running for my life.

Then I suddenly started to talk, in spurts—for hours, for days at a time, and my temperature returned to normal (*up* to normal: I'd been brought in frozen and I'd stayed that way). They began to think I might live after all. The doctor (whose name was Walowitz) said that by some miracle there wasn't a sign of tuberculosis. He asked me questions about things I'd said when I was delirious. I'd been arguing, he said, with invisible people, impersonating them all; much of what I'd said had been quite coherent; once I'd delivered a long apology for not opening my eyes, or not being able to, and had then turned around and wept, and in a different voice had accused myself of pretending to sleep. What had happened to me? Where had I been? But I couldn't remember then, or I didn't want to. Not yet.

For two or three weeks I still went on sleeping for twenty hours a day. I had to learn how to eat all over again. Solid food of any kind hurt my mouth; my stomach was in terrible shape— it looked for a while as if I might develop an ulcer. But gradually I developed a real craving for milk, and that made everybody happy.

Illnesses are pets. We fondle them for a while and then grow tired of them, only to discover that they can't be thrust off easily. They are our habits and we are theirs, but they know us better than we know them; they feed on our unspoken needs, rely on our delayed impatience. The trouble is, they never know when to stop; as soon as they become too demanding, we have no choice but to get rid of them. Yet the loss is one we can't really afford: not only does it strip and empty us, it leaves us helplessly open to the backlash of our overextended dependency as well. We've loved them after all, it seems; we simply couldn't bear their love for us.

Walowitz took a great liking to me. He was born in Berlin and had gone to America in 1934, straight after medical school. He was married and had three children, lived on Eastern Parkway (the "Rue de la Païs," as he called it), in Brooklyn, and had been a consultant in a big general hospital, with a private practice as well.

He was by no means a very religious Jew, but he was a rabid advocate of circumcision. He used to say that the worst punishment that could be imposed on the Germans would be to forbid them potatoes and then circumcise all the men. Anyway, when he discovered (in the course of things) that I had a phimosis, he could hardly wait until I was well enough for him to get at it. I didn't like the idea at all. He told me, Think, if you ever get to New York you can go swimming with me at the Brooklyn Hebrew Center, and nobody'll ever know the difference. That wasn't much comfort, but he got his way in the end. (I took him up on his swimming invitation, too, in 1953—but that's another story.)

November 5th

High up over my head, the great span of a bridge rears and arches out of sight. Somewhere the visible downcurve must begin, but as I walk I am still stepping into my shadow. I'd like to know how much further it is to noon; but so far I haven't met a soul coming from the opposite direction.

In early July of 1945 I was transferred to the DP camp near Halle, a barbed-wire enclosure of individual barracks in a former German army post. The camp was divided into tight little national compounds by the refugees themselves; for a time even the latrines were segregated. I found myself squeezed in between "Little Germany" and "Little Hungary." No one paid much attention to me; only once in a while some chauvinist from the German clique would ask me if I was sure I was where I belonged. That question helped restore my sense of humor.

In Halle I met Moon.

Jesse Byrnes was his real name, but Moon was what everyone called him ("from the time I was knee-high to a grasshopper"). And it fit: he had a full round face with a halo of crinkly auburn hair and was disguised (only disguised) as an American infantryman. In reality (I was the only one who knew), he was the King of Summer, spoke an indecipherable tree language and visited the camp incognito one day in every three.

He was a powerful man, tall as a tree trunk (his beer-paunch, which was meant to complete his army disguise, only made him more regal-looking). He was the quickest and yet most relaxed, strongest and yet gentlest man I've ever known. He was a zoologist by profession, had been trapping and stuffing animals from the time he was fifteen, had been bitten three times by rattlesnakes and once by a black-widow spider (cut and suck!), had shot mountain lions in Montana and painted backdrops for the Museum of Natural History in New York, was all set to head for Africa on an expedition when war broke out, spent two years in Seattle, Washington, giving judo instruction, then requested combat duty and got it, was wounded in the hand and won the Silver Star, and now had nothing in his head but to get back to South Carolina and settle down.

Of course, all these details came later, when he began to write to me (and I had become able to read what he wrote). During the brief period in Germany he was a demigod pure and simple to me; and this impression colored everything I learned later. Right to the end. And still.

He was married to a girl named Aphra. She was from the same small town (Parnassus) and the same age as he (twenty-nine in 1945). He showed me photographs of her: a tall, haughty-looking young woman in white dresses and extravagant hats, posed on porches and lawns and always a little out of focus (or perhaps my memory is).

Now. Why should Moon have taken a liking to me, out of all the thousands who passed through Halle? I'll tell you later on why *he* believed he had. I knew better, *know* better. I know I responded to him with a whole heart from the first moment I set eyes on him; no one can ever say that the love he inspired was the result of any calculation on his part. I'm not really interested in "deeper motivations" either; no matter what he saw in me, or was searching for, no matter what I came to realize of his tragic incompleteness, an element of innocent predestination (redemptive word!) was present in our first meeting—and no later analysis, no later rationalization, no confession of eventual failure can ever erase it.

I say this for myself no less than you, Immanuel.

Moon could draw beautifully, and he was a natural mime: when he wanted to tell me something or ask a question he would either draw me a picture or act it out, and I began to communi-

cate with him in the same way. By the time (in August) that I
was transferred to the refugee camp in Coburg, we were "con-
versing" fluently in an improbable salad of words, gesticulations,
signs and pictures. I had begun to study English, too; but Moon
remained totally inept with German.

He came down to Coburg as often as he could, and for hours
we carried on like a pair of grunting, face-pulling, epileptic deaf
mutes. It may very well be that what he "told" me and what
I understood (and vice versa) were seldom exactly the same
thing; but we were relying on sympathy, on resonance, not on
the results of any rational, self-explaining exchange. We experienced a kind of freedom in our intercourse that became revela-
tory of self.

We never had any privacy; there were always dozens of volunteer translators, interpreters, curious scoffers and onlookers. But
we shooed them away; we weren't going to be stifled or inhibited by their interference. What did we need of exegesis? Moon
was a phenomenon; I grew relaxed, *wildly* relaxed and released
in his presence. There was no danger of misunderstanding; each
of us manifested himself in acts of pure spontaneity, the other
was always an ideal foil.

One Sunday in early October I suddenly realized that what
Moon was trying to tell me was that he was leaving, that he was
finally going back to his summer kingdom, that the war was
over for him too now. I was struck senseless; everything broke
down in the instant I understood. The tears began to stream
down my cheeks; for an instant I *saw* myself weeping, and then
I saw nothing at all. Moon got down on his knees and pulled
me close to him. He tried to speak, tried to say things with his
hands, but his voice, his gift of gesture had fled him; he began
to cry too, softly. It embarrassed him, he took a deep breath,
released me suddenly and stood up. Shaking his head he backed
away. And then he was gone. I couldn't move. For a week, for
weeks, whenever I opened my mouth to speak in ordinary,
known language, an overwhelming urge to scream welled up

in me and, frustrated, turned to tears. So I had lost him too.

But it wasn't to be that way. Just before Christmas I was told that Mr. Jesse Byrnes of Parnassus, South Carolina, had taken steps to adopt me.

The next three years have a strange complexion. Moon was a distant legend, dreamed, uncertain. In Coburg the view from every window, every face, was the same perturbed or disappointed ruin of itself. Seasons came and went repetitiously, the visible world played the same succession of scenes interminably, round and round like a snake with its tail in its mouth.

I lost contact with every sense of causality, with every derivative state of things. My eyes were fixed on a single unimaginable hope that nonetheless was an act of my imagination. Daily necessities, contiguous things were nothing more than a practical test of resistance, of staying power . . .

That first year after Moon's departure was the loneliest and yet, in a way (small comfort!), the most reflectively formative year of my life. For the first time, the burden of a separation that was not necessarily final lay on my shoulders. Suddenly I had invested love and confidence in another human being, of my own accord—it was a new and dizzying sensation. Up to that moment everything in my life had been decided for me, out of my hands. Now, unexpectedly, I had to accept the fact that the built-in impossibility of guilt incurrence had been removed, and that my child's innocence of what had happened to me could never be used as a prop or apology.

November 11th

(Last night.) There's just one thing I'd like to know from you, Immanuel: What drives you to pursue my bursts of ridicule, to *cultivate* them, in exactly the same way a *clochard* pounces on castaway cigarettes? If you go around following smokers, you must know the butts you snatch up so proudly weren't thrown away for *you*. And the fact that you can still glean a puff or two doesn't make you any less a scavenger.

Moon began to write; he had decided not to go back to New York and had taken a job teaching high-school biology. His letters were full of incomprehensible (to me) passages, but packed with sketches and photos. Even when I could read English moderately well, the world of which he spoke was so unlike any I had ever known that I invested it with the same intentions, approached it through the same internal postures and receptive gestures with which I had listened and replied when he was present. My eventual adoption had no other meaning to me at that time (but what better sense could it have had?) than the promise of a restoration of touch, the resumption of our peculiar duologue—on a more subtle plane perhaps, but still, essentially, an acted resolution of two incongruous worlds.

In the summer of 1947, at Coburg, I had a brief affair (say) with a Polish girl whom I'll call Alma Shem. She was four years older than I, and she had been through hell. All the members of her family had been killed; she had been brought to Germany as a slave laborer. Between 1942 and 1945 she had worked in half a dozen factories and was even a gravedigger for a time. When the Russians closed in on Stettin in the last days, she and some other women had run away from the farm where they were working and set out for the west. After a grueling trek during which she became separated from the others (she told me then), she finally reached the Allied lines. She was determined not to return to Poland, and had stood her ground successfully against all the various repatriation committees. She hoped eventually to get to Canada; she had an uncle there somewhere, if he hadn't died in the meantime.

Alma wasn't beautiful, although you could see she'd been born to be. Her face had become a kind of leathery mask for suffering, a face tanned and scarred by wear. Yet the bones were strong and clean, and sometimes, when just the right light fell on them, her original face was suddenly restored, and it glowed with a freshness and purity that took my breath away.

Shortly after her arrival from Wildflecken she came to work beside me in the camp kitchen. I don't recall which of us spoke to the other first, but she was the only person up to then with whom I'd exchanged more than a few words, in the whole camp.

We began to make love right there in the kitchen, on a make-shift bed of benches and blankets; she was the first woman in my life. Yet I find my memory of those evenings weak: I remember only that she was always very quiet and strangely self-involved in her lovemaking, almost passionless, even though the sexual invitation, the initial one, had been hers. She seldom made a sound, just lay there wrestling with herself. She was afraid of losing herself, of letting go, but I didn't know why. As for me, my attempts to make love to her were self-directed, exploratory; and I was too grateful (yes!) to make demands she couldn't fulfill. It must have been a little grotesque.

After several weeks she was transferred to the storerooms, and our nightly sessions came to an abrupt stop. We went on seeing each other in the evenings, but only once did we ever make love again.

It was a sweltering night in September; we had taken a long walk in town, down to the river. The kitchen had been our accomplice; neither of us had sex on his mind, really, but it was a hot night, and dark, and it happened more or less of itself.

Everything had changed, for both of us; we realized it almost instantly, but we couldn't stop that easily. Things had built up inside me to a crude erotic impatience; Alma too was suddenly almost viciously passionate. I lost control of myself; I tried to hurt her. She began to gasp and make odd little noises and to tear at my back. My nerves gathered into an excruciating knot, and I pounded my body against hers, trying to make them untie. But suddenly I drew back, I don't know why, and looked at her; she had her teeth clenched and bared and her eyes were wide open, wild. I groaned and pulled completely away, exploding. She fell back; for a moment she couldn't catch her breath.

After a long silence we started to talk, hesitantly, hiding our faces from one another. And she told me that she and the other women with whom she had been fleeing at the end of the war had been overtaken by a patrol (does it matter whose soldiers? she asked) and had been raped she didn't know how many times; after the second she hadn't resisted; she hadn't even fainted. What did it mean? They had killed the others, but they hadn't killed her; at least a dozen men had possessed her and then let her lie . . .

What could I say? that I didn't know what she was asking? that it meant nothing? that I was sorry for having forced myself on her, for having aroused her, for having made love to her at all?

Nothing. Neither questions nor answers existed.

We never spoke again. Perhaps she went to Canada.

Thousands came and went like breaths of air, undifferentiated and unremembered, adjuncts to life on the lowest physical level. I dwelt in almost perfect anonymity among a hundred thousand refugees—alike, unalike, dead, alive, suffering, beyond suffering —thrown up like driftwood by all the rivers of Europe into the great lost-and-found of Germany: a vast terminal with endless platforms on which we stood, unticketed, watching witlessly as an endless train went by without stopping, treading on glass while the girders above us rained down their final splinters, whenever our milling feet caused the earth to tremble.

How many times was I interviewed? A paper facsimile of myself accumulated—eleven feet long, a rectangular effigy of words and photographs and fingerprints weighing over two hundred pounds. A conditional coffin for the useless descriptive data, the dead ends of memory and ruined history that for some reason still insisted on calling itself Stefan Brückmann.

In early 1948 I was transferred to the DP camp in Mannheim. Until then all efforts to verify my declared origins had been in vain. The trouble was, nothing whatever could be found concerning my father, there was no record of my birth in Nauen, and the files of the *Zigeunerdezernat* had been destroyed by fire. It *was* learned that Frau Schnee had died in 1944 (of natural causes), Willi's war and party records were uncovered, and my mother's birth inscription in Mariendorf. Nobody could say I had invented them, but nothing connected them with me. The attempts to locate Tito and Maria Szeklecz drew a complete blank, and the Doehrs, to all intents and purposes, had never even existed.

No one seemed to doubt that I was some kind of German (what kind was another matter), but a great many legal questions had to be settled, I was told, before I could be declared one. So far not a single person had turned up (or *been* turned up) who could attest to having known me. The I.R.O. workers were more than patient under the chaotic circumstances in trying to run down possible clues. It took time, that's all.

That's all.

At first I worked in the kitchen (as in Coburg), but in the late summer, with the help of Mrs. Irene Morton (a social worker from Chicago who not only had been in Germany since the end of 1945 but also had spent almost two years in Berlin under the Dawes Plan in the late Twenties)—with her help I got a job on the outside (a thing not normally allowed without loss of all DP privileges). In the beginning I was on a rubble-clearance squad, but later, after the currency reform, she found me a job on a construction gang. It paid almost nothing, but I needed almost nothing to stay alive (although by this time I had had to assume responsibility for my own food), and I was proud of my self-sufficiency. The money that Moon sent from time to time I spent on lessons in English; there were plenty of people eager to give them at a few marks a week, and I used half the American soldiers in Mannheim as conversational guinea pigs. I read (or attempted to) almost every book in the ragged compound library (mostly dog-eared servicemen's pocket editions) —everything from *Bring 'em Back Alive* to *You Can't do Busi-*

ness with Hitler and *How to Win Friends and Influence People.*

My German co-workers were generally bitter and apathetic; most of them were married veterans, and they complained about everything—the miserable wages, the *Amis* and their cars and cabarets, having to eat white beans and powdered potatoes and salted butter ("wasn't even *this* bad at the front"), the hiring of Poles and Czechs from the camp—everything. Somehow the word got around that I had been in a *KZ-Lager*; I wasn't going to try and tell them the stories were true, was I? They wanted to know, but they wanted a negative answer. So I kept to myself as best I could, and let them worry about it.

Moon wrote that he'd been elected game warden of Parnassus County. I didn't have a very clear picture of what that meant; I envisioned him wearing a green uniform, carrying some kind of blunderbuss and a staghandle knife and walking through lofty, tame green forests, his step dampened by a soft rotting bed of needles and loam. All the animals talked—why not?

Whenever he mentioned his wife Aphra (with whom he was having difficulties), I relegated her to the more sinister side of the mythical world that was gradually taking shape in my imagination; she was the most treacherous and at the same time the most beautiful goddess in my Olympian Carolina. But there were other names that came to populate it: Ora, Parris, Libya, Vesta—vague outlines in a hard purple landscape where the sun shed light like chalk.

When I met them in the flesh, they were anything but gods and goddesses. But I suppose that most of the heroes of escape literature (Moon's letters, for example) are based on pretty disappointing prototypes.

One day that spring Mrs. Morton returned from a trip to Berlin and sent for me. She opened a door in her office and a fat, tired-looking fortyish blond woman entered, terribly excited

and flustered, and fixed her eyes on me, let out an awful wail
and tearfully threw her arms around me, scaring me half out of
my wits. She began to stammer my name (my name!) over and
over again; I stared pleadingly over her shoulder at Mrs. Morton, who smiled and nodded encouragingly, apparently quite
moved by the scene. I didn't have the vaguest notion who the
woman was; I would have sworn I'd never seen her before in
my life. Then Mrs. Morton said, "This is Frau Ada Würgel,
Stefan." The woman pulled back slightly and peered into my
eyes, tears streaming down her face. "Stefan, Stefan, *Liebling*,"
she said. "Don't you remember me? It's Ada, *Ada*." She bit her
lip and begged me to remember.

Ada? *Willi's* Ada? It dawned on me. This was Ada?

"Ada?" I asked, incredulously. She nodded solemnly. I was
speechless and suddenly embarrassed. Ada turned to Mrs.
Morton. "Yes, yes, this is little Stefan," she said, and began to
weep hysterically, and had to sit down.

It was Ada, all right, much the worse for wear. But Mrs.
Morton had found her, God bless her!—a living, breathing
anchor in the past, *my* past.

The next thing I remember she was talking a mile a minute:
her husband, Roman Würgel, the soldier she had married in
Nancy, was an engineer; they would adopt me, I would come to
Berlin to live with them, they had three children and a big
apartment and Herr Würgel made good money, he wanted me
to come, she wanted me to come, the children wanted me to
come, and oh! (more tears) it was all so *unglaublich*, she was so
moved, *wie ein Wunder* it was, and now it was going to be so
hübsch in Berlin for me.

Mrs. Morton said I should make up my own mind, that the
important thing was for me to be "re-nationalized," but that I
shouldn't say no out of hand, it could still be a year before
I knew about America, despite the Refugee Bill. Of course I
waited; as grateful as I was to Ada, I had to wait for Moon.
Anyway, within two months I was (again) a German national,
and somewhere the right wheels finally began to turn.

Except for a letter I'd received from Moon in April, announcing his imminent arrival (which seemed, after two months went by without a sign, to have been just one more false alarm), I had no warning of his coming. If Mrs. Morton herself knew, she didn't let on—and since she wasn't very good at hiding her feelings, I rather doubt that she did.

In any case, I was called to her office one fine day in June; she met me at the door, tearful and twitching, and ushered me through the anteroom with all the trembling solemnity of a guide through a minefield. Not a word; I broke out in a cold sweat. At the door to her inner sanctum she stopped, turned to me, raised her hand in a cautioning impresario's gesture, smiled mysteriously (archly, terrifyingly) and opened the door.

There he stood!

I'll spare you most of the details of the next half hour, only informing you that Mrs. Morton, who enjoyed a sentimental blood-bath as much as the next man, stood by and gurgled with anticipation while Moon and I eyed each other like a couple of shy gladiators. When the combat began she retreated to a neutral corner and shrieked delightedly while Moon yanked me off my (twenty-year-old) feet and proceeded to pound me black and blue with joy. Not a single coherent syllable was uttered; we just howled and groaned and grunted and bounded about while Mrs. Morton cheered.

Moon didn't look a day older; his temples had advanced steadily toward the back of his head and joined ranks around the last outpost of hair, but he had grown leathery thin and his occupation paunch was gone. As for me, I'd grown taller and filled out considerably (comparatively speaking, that is). Moon swore up and down that I'd changed completely, but if I had, I hadn't felt it.

I've never had a very good idea of what I looked like at any given moment of my life. The *me* I see in these memoirs is always the latest mirror version of myself, no matter what kind of descriptive inconsistencies and monstrosities that makes me guilty of. Usually (and it's probably a good thing) I don't see anybody at all.

Moon hadn't come until he was absolutely certain he could have me, and then he landed on the scene with all the weighty self-assured impact of a messenger from the gods (or a last-minute stay of execution). For all the speed and urgency shown in dispatching me from the camp then, you'd have thought I was a rotten leg up for emergency amputation—another minute and it might have been too late. Between the moment Moon arrived and the moment we got out of the plane in New York, exactly six days elapsed.

The first suitcase I'd ever owned in my life was a going-away present from Mrs. Morton; everything I owned in the world went into it, with room to spare. (P.S. Three years later it was stolen in the Trailways bus station in Albuquerque, New Mexico.)

The four years or so that are still to be described are the most recent to memory, but I am going to skip over them in large part, and move almost immediately to the crucial incidents of my sojourn in America. The jump may seem radical, but I'm not writing a novel; I don't have to plan or balance things out for the sake of dramatic effect. Oh, I know you'll be full of doubts (Where did you learn this or that? What about . . . ?), but most of what has happened to me is equally unbelievable to me; even my writing this, the fact that I am sitting here in this miserable little sunless room, in this most touchy, most facile of all cities, trying to call up memories of other planets, other rooms, is just about more than I can grasp.

For the first few months in America I felt I'd been set adrift in space, without relative bearings of any kind by which to read my size or position. I didn't know if I was a pinpoint or a map; I clung blindly to Moon, like a barnacle on a space ship.

Can you believe it? I had come to depend on my late and (I had thought) hated environment; it had become a next-to-natural habitat. For seven years the air I'd breathed had been twice breathed already, the food a thousand times digested. I had been an anesthetized cell in a cumbersome, wasteful body that possessed one great ravenous stomach, a greedy pair of outsized lungs and a tiny superfluous brain. Yet it hurt to be excised from that body—and when I realized that I hadn't been removed simply in order to be transplanted into another similar one, I had my first unmistakable taste of the *fear* of death.

Now, looking back, and with the knowledge of all that came after, I can see that the whole matter had very quickly gone beyond the simple (or not so simple, in its own right) question of my adoption. I was always *there*, of course, as the concrete object of Moon's efforts. But when he had returned to America and faced the first obstacles, and found that it wasn't going to be easy to have me just like that, the perspectives of the situation began to embrace a much larger personal problem than the question of his relationship with me-in-particular. *Who* I was began to be of secondary importance; that someone was *there* mattered more.

And as time dragged on, and so little headway was made, it came to seem to Moon that something else was at stake; his ingrained resistance to time, to procedure, to law itself ultimately, was being thwarted; and this provoked him to a furious activity which, at the same time as it called forth his best qualities, caused him to pass dangerously beyond the redeemable circumference of our *personal* relationship. I became his crusade—or someone with my name did. Though it would have hurt him terribly had he been conscious of it, the cost of his success in obtaining me had been greater than his love for me; it depleted his inner fund of self-assurance and weakened the walls of his independence. In some mysterious way I was expected to shore them up then, to *restore* them; I was to be the return on his investment. In a sense then (and I must bring myself to say it) he *bought* me. Not for what I, singly, offered him (nor even for what he needed of me directly, humanly, nor for the sake of what he had responded to back in 1945), but to underwrite his very existence.

What I am saying here is awfully schematic, I know, and it may seem that I am exaggerating or distorting the matter into an absurd complexity. But I don't know how else to say what I am trying to. I am speaking *now*, after almost four years in America, and four years after his death, of a man I came to regard then, there, as a specimen of a vanishing race, a race with *no ethnic complexion*. What I am telling is not meant to discredit him, but rather to clarify (for myself) both his failure and mine. If it were in my power I would portray him as a tragic figure—gifted, generous, willfully mistaken, fighting a losing battle from the outset and fighting it heroically, quixotically. But I cannot embellish; he was struggling for a boy's freedom in a boy's world which he desperately clung to until it was too late for him to relinquish it. He resisted and despised the so-called man's world around him with a kind of frenzy—not because he was not a *man* (he was), but because his masculinity too was based upon a boy's glamour-concept of maleness: courageous, absolute, infallible, and in the last resort *sexless*. His innocence (and he *was* innocent) was obstinately based on a refusal to grow up, or rather to grow into a world that disclaimed such innocence. And so he and the world rejected each other, and watched each other jealously, distrustfully out of the corners of their eyes.

November 22nd

Old Parris's third taxi (the first a legacy from Moon's father, who died in 1937). The trip down from New York, just the three of us, the first time (except for a couple of jeeps) that I ever rode in an automobile.

Ivy, Lee, Guy, Amy, Ruby, Furman, Rosa, Tabitha, Emory.
. . . Black-widow spiders, outhouse and woodpile, wasps' nests
in the rafters.

God's chewing gum stuck like a wart under Aunt Libya
Mauldin's right eye. Rimless glasses. A high-ceilinged house
that smelled of mildew, leather and gentian.

Molasses, mustard greens, slices of congealed grits fried in
sausage fat. Buttermilk biscuits.

Butter-churning, ice-cream cranking, rock salt and pickled
peaches.

A Sunday drive to Walhalla—thin air.
Lightning scars in the pasture, natural blue clay, pure on the
banks of the branch.

Fresh peppermint, iced tea. "Dope," alias Coca-Cola.

A plaster life-mask of Moon aged twenty-four. Stuffed, shedding animals: a fox, an owl, an eagle, weasel and possum—
Moon's first taxidermy.

Old radios in every room, like model wooden churches, the
heavy yellow parchment dial-doors.

Doodle-bugs, June bugs, lightning bugs, chafers. A rain of
froglets.

Hannah Savannah, breasts like watermelons—"Lawd, Masta
Steve, how you do favoh yoselfl"

Miss Lemon, boarding-school teacher, at the piano. The
Gospel Songbook, brittle sheet music: *I'm Tying the Leaves
so They Won't Come Down*, *It Ain't Gonna Rain No Mo'*,
Whispering, *America I Love You* (You're like a sweetheart of
mine!) . . .

Whitewash.

Moon's mother (Ida May Byrnes) wringing a rooster's neck in the backyard.

St. John's bread, knots of sycamore.

The remote heartbreak of night trains, klaxon dirges. To feel a continent . . .

Aphra, in a Roman dressing gown, lets down her auburn hair (to the small of her back) before a three-faced mirror.

After a year and a half of tutors (including Miss Lemon, whose forte was history) I was packed off to an insignificant, imperceptible prep-school–college about forty miles away. It was Baptist and Bible-ridden and musty, and full of shell-shocked, chalk-fingered old recluses, effeminate seminarians and smooth-cheeked crewcut religious fanatics with Scotch-Irish names. My only friends were a handful of ex-GI's—non-Baptist Italian-American pre-med students from New Jersey (Cliffside Park, South Orange, Hoboken), with names like Lauricello, Venza, Corsi and de Bari. They augmented their allotments with basketball and refused to be fazed by the division of the campus into male and female restricted areas.

In March of 1951 Aphra ran off with a lawyer named Oakley Prescott from Columbia (Aunt Libya wrote me); Moon sold his partridge and quail pens, his frog tubs and baby alligators and took off for the mountains, and Ida May (D.A.R., Red Cross, Tamassee, Sewing Circle, Methodist Mothers, Calhoun Society, and Eastern Star) reappropriated the old house.

When I returned at the end of the spring semester, badly dented by my first bout with "formal education" (three chapels a week and a run-down roommate named Rob Roy Mac-Dervish, who spent half an hour on his knees every night, praying out loud, before hopping into bed to masturbate till dawn), I went to stay with Aunt Libya, who with Moon away was the only one of his relatives who'd have me. Aphra had been more or less tolerant, but his mother was completely allergic to me. The first time I met her she turned as white as only a well-girdled Southern gentlewoman can, almost threw up, gasped something about "octoroon" and flew off to bed for a month. After that she simply pretended that neither I nor her obviously demented son existed.

It was her doing, in a way, that Moon never resumed his work at the museum in New York after the war, and I'm sure she pushed Aphra into leaving him as well. She was one of those people who are always doing what is "best for others"— i.e. one hundred per cent God-fearing, righteous, overbearing, intolerant, self-centered and murderous.

For weeks there'd been no sign of Moon, and no one knew where he was exactly, just "somewhere up in the mountains." It was a listless, distracted interlude in my life; during the first year and a half I'd hardly stuck my head out of the door unless Moon was with me. Now it was as if I had come to a different town, as I began to explore Parnassus without him. I walked through shaggy streets whose frame houses were lost in trees and vines and shadows, alien to their history, their ancestral secrets, the old women rocking on porches. I stood stranded on naked Main Street, among barkers and medicine men and orators, stung by the strong smell of dung, the nostalgia of rain in the air, dusty sidewalks. I was a stranger to drugstore interiors, to the perfumed aisles of five-and-tens, the musk of woolens; quiet witness of barbers and overalls, and bare feet dyed red by years of clay. I remember Hoot Gibson, Bob Steele, Ken Maynard, the Three Mesquiteers—endless Republic and Monogram productions, serials, popcorn and neckers, the incontinent felt of the dark. I wandered far down by the mill, the baseball field, into vast grassy meadows on days so wet you couldn't make the sun out. I went into a two-ring circus near the Negro gospel hall (with its windows all gone), heard colored voices awakening second-rate animals, moving the flea-bitten freaks to tears, and paid seventy-five cents to see a real hermaphrodite unveil. Beef stew was still a dime at Lewis's

Café; the pool hall was black inside, a cave of vagrant sounds. Last year's senior class came home on leave (before Korea); Jessica Bivens and Rosamund her sister rode by with flying hair, back from immortal finishing schools. I lived the still green requiem of Sunday mornings: empty streets, straw fans and Fords, white-shirted on the courthouse lawn, my eyes wide open, an untouched untouchable astray in the swelter of Parnassus and its never-glory, locked in by *kudzu* and pickers and red-clay no-man's land. And I was deceived by its surface, its accessible peace. But what untold violence lies just beneath the skin of such a place!

I had not stopped subscribing to people, to appearances and manipulations; but my passive adventure was almost over. Moon is my last creation: the stepfather of my fictional infancy. Now I have only to live out the last episode of an obsolete existence and I'll have come full circle. Watch me help him die.

He showed up one evening at suppertime and sat out front honking his horn and shouting my name. I ran out ahead of the others. The car was a dirty wreck, and he was too. When he saw me coming he grinned broadly and cried, "Steve!" But he didn't get out of the car.

I went up close to the window on his side. He stretched out his hand; he was shaking. His eyes were bloodshot and he was wearing a month-old beard. He grabbed my arm and pulled me close; his breath stank.

"How are you, Stevie-boy?" he asked.

"Fine," I said.

"Well good for you," he said. "You can see I'm not." And laughed.

"Get in," he said, in an oddly confidential tone. "We're going to take us a little trip." Old Parris was limping around from the back of the house. Aunt Libya was crossing the porch; she waved and started down the steps. Moon glanced uneasily in her direction. "Get in," he said, more urgently.

"All right, Moon," I said; "just let me get a few things."

"No, now!" he whispered, harshly, and gave me a shove toward the front of the car. So I ran round and got in on the other side. Without a word to either Aunt Libya or Parris, we shot out of the driveway.

In a few minutes we were on the Brevard road, moving into the foothills. Moon wasn't talking, and I was glad; he was a good driver, but he wasn't in any condition to talk *and* drive. He had a bottle of white lightning on the seat beside him; every time he took a swig he offered me the bottle, and when I shook my head he simply shrugged. We had all the windows open; the air blowing in was like hot water.

We began to hit the hairpin turns; Moon's driving was becoming more erratic by the minute. If there had been a car coming toward us any of half a dozen times, we'd have collided head-on or gone over the edge.

We passed the turn-off to Rocky Bottom and the entrance to the old CCC camp, doing seventy miles an hour. Just this side of the state line we suddenly veered off to the left onto a little dirt road. Moon slowed down; it was getting dark fast. Then he began to talk, without looking at me. "Steve," he said, "there're a couple of things I'm going to tell you. I want you to listen and not say a thing unless I ask you to. Okay?"

I nodded, and felt my stomach draw up ominously.

"I'd've told you a long time ago, but I didn't know exactly how, or maybe I didn't have the nerve. Not that I really do now, but I've decided to tell you. I wish you'd take a drink. For me."

So I did, and threw a coughing fit. He laughed. "That's my boy!" he said. "Well. This all happened a long time ago; I guess by now most everybody except me who had anything to do with it 's either forgotten or 's died. It was when I was eighteen years old—in 1934.

"I never told you I had a twin brother, did I? Well, I did. His name was Edmund. He's a long time dead now, died of polio the next year after this happened, up in Virginia at school.

This was what it was: it all has to do with a lynching, and one I'd almost forgot about too, until just a few years ago. That's the reason I'm telling you this now—I mean, you have to do with my remembering it.

"There was a white girl named Louise something from the mill village who said she'd been molested by a colored boy, and a bunch of fellows down at the pool hall got all drunked up and talked themselves into doing something about it. It was common knowledge that she'd been fooling around with about everybody, but they said that didn't give no black bastard any privileges. Anyway, Edmund and me were with 'em, though they were his friends, and they teased me into coming along. They were just going to rough the boy up a little and give him a scare, they said, that was all. So I went, feeling scared and shaky but kind of important all the same. I hadn't been drinking, but Edmund and the others had. Well, we drove out to an old ramshackle farm not far from Six Mile and took that boy from his family and drove off with him to a place near the Keowee River.

"The minute I laid eyes on that colored boy I began to lose my big stuff—he couldn't 've been more'n sixteen, and maybe because I looked younger than Edmund, even though we were twins, he kept looking at me, not saying a word but with big scared eyes like he was asking for me to help him . . ."

He paused for a few seconds and cleared his throat; he was trembling. He glanced at me uneasily.

"There's no point in telling you what kind of things they did to that boy, my brother included. I didn't, I couldn't, I got sick. They'd meant to kill him all the time. I couldn't move, I watched, and they killed him all right, I mean they tore him to pieces.

"When they were through they pitched him in the river, and we all piled back in the car, nobody talking, and drove back into town. About a week later I broke out in boils and never stopped having them until the time I went to New York four years later. I didn't have a notion there was any connection with the lynching, but now I'm sure there was. Neither Edmund nor me ever mentioned it either, to anybody or even to ourselves, and like I say, he died the next year.

"This isn't just a confession; there's a reason for telling you, but it isn't easy to make it clear. I saw some things in Germany I never thought to see if I lived a hundred years. I'd seen my buddies die before my eyes, sure, that was one thing, but those places, those camps we rode into, that was something I wasn't ready for—that nobody was, I guess. I started to have dreams where I saw the lynching all over again, every night, but with a difference: it wasn't Edmund who was helping—he wasn't even there—but me. And the boils came back . . .

"When I walked into that compound at Halle a few weeks later I was in a state, I wasn't sleeping hardly at all. And when I saw you standing there, just you, one day, I felt all of a sudden like hell had opened up right under my feet. It wasn't that you looked like that boy, not exactly, not your color or anything like that, though I guess you were about the same size—no, it was the look in your eyes that was the same, like you were asking me, begging me to help you. All over again."

He took a deep breath and looked me in the eyes. An uncertain smile flickered across his lips. "Do you know what I'm getting at? I want to ask you a question now, if it's not 'way too late, like you was the man and I was the boy. And it's this: Do you think that maybe the things we've done, or let be done, things we're guilty of no matter how, keep on being done by us—you know—are what we *are* and always were, and there's no way we can ever change them or make up for them?"

I shook my head. "No," I said.

He seemed to consider my answer; for a long moment he was silent. Then, suddenly: "You wouldn't lie to me, would you? It's no good if you're just saying that because you think it's what I want to hear. I've got to know if I did the right thing by you, by taking you, by bringing you here—if I made up even a little for the other—and for Edmund."

He stopped the car; we'd been just creeping along.

"No, you've made it up," I said. "If it's up to me to answer."

We sat without speaking. After what seemed like hours he said, "I guess you know that Aphra's left me." The dashboard lights made his face look puffy; he rubbed his eyes with his fingers. "Maybe you can tell me why . . . because I don't know."

I shook my head helplessly.

"Yes, you know," he said, almost accusingly, I thought.

And I asked the most selfish, stupid question of my life: "Because of me?" I swear, I thought it was the reply he wanted from me, but he opened his eyes as though I'd struck him, and dropping his head on his arms on the steering wheel began to cry like a baby. I put my hand on his shoulder; he shuddered; for a long time he couldn't stop. Finally he drew up.

"Where's that bottle?" he asked. "I've got to have a little drink."

"Don't," I said. "Please, I'm sorry."

He laughed. "What are you sorry for? Just give me the bottle if you know where it is." Just then he found it himself on the seat behind him, took a long pull and handed it to me. "Have some more," he said. "Puts lead in your pencil."

He started up the car; we drove on silently. I don't know how to describe the feeling I had watching him: physically it was a swelling, hurting pressure in my chest and throat, but emotionally it was something else entirely; I could literally *feel* something inside him trying to work its way to the surface. I didn't imagine it, it *was* an instance of real empathy with an inchoate, buried substance—as though another self were trying to articulate itself for me. He was afraid of it though, unreasoningly, stubbornly afraid; and he held it down and defeated it.

We rounded a bend in the road; lights up ahead. The moon swam up over Mount Eaton, revealing a small lake. I heard the rush of a waterfall; it was suddenly cool.

Moon blew the horn; two or three men appeared; one of them had a shotgun in his hand. Moon stuck his head out of the window and shouted, "Put away your firearms, boys!" And they shouted back in greeting.

We pulled into a tiny tent camp not far from the shore of the lake. Two or three jalopies and a pickup truck were parked near by. We got out and Moon introduced me to his cronies: eleven of them, tall and scraggly brush-apes, mountain boys, with names like Clyde, Oliver, Lloyd. They were running a gigantic still. Moon went over to it, silhouetted by the red glowing boilers.

"How's it getting on?" he asked.

"Third run today," said Clyde. "Number two showed a seam 'bout an hour ago, but it'll hold."

"Hope you know what you're talking about," said Moon.

For a long time we sat around the fire and talked, passing the bottle. Every once in a while somebody got up and went over to the still (more like a baby locomotive) to stoke the fires or let steam or check the output. Quiet, careful talk—these were men of few words. The bottle went round.

Moon stood up. "I'm going to take me a little swim," he said. "Who'll join me?"

Guffaws. "It ain't Saturday night," somebody said.

"I will," I said and got up.

We went down to the lake and stripped and waded in. The water was stinging cold. I'm not a good swimmer—I'd only begun to learn that same year, in a pool, and I've always been afraid of the water. But that night I walked out to my neck in icy black water, losing my body to it by inches, and wasn't afraid. Moon swam off with strong strokes, out of sight. By the time he came back I was already on the shore, hopping up and down to get warm.

We went straight off to bed then. Moon and I had a small tent to ourselves not far from the waterfall, higher up than the other tents, among tall pines. We wrapped ourselves in rough blankets and lay down; Moon began to snore immediately. I lay awake for a long time, trying to fathom him, myself, the events of this particular day.

It was still dark when I came awake. Moon was tossing about and mumbling in his sleep; I couldn't hear any other sound, not even the waterfall. It was as though the world had shrunk to the narrow dimensions of the tent itself. Moon was making strange little sounds; I couldn't see more than the outline of his body, but from its movement I realized he was crying in his sleep. I edged over to his side and propped myself up on my elbow. I laid my hand on his forehead; it was wet. He turned his head and groaned and opened his eyes.

My hand was still on his brow; for ages he stared up into my face, and then, with a sudden, spastic movement, he flung his arms around me and pulled me down on his chest, with my face to his, and held me there tightly. I could feel his heart pounding close to mine; his breath was thick against my face. He began to shudder and squeezed me even tighter. I could hardly breathe. With one hand he began to stroke my head, heavily, flatly, the way a child learns to caress. He was still making those strange, snuffling sounds. He stroked my back, breathing more and more heavily.

I was permissive; I wanted to let him know I loved him. But something else was happening inside him: he was having his way, and he was losing control.

Suddenly his mouth was open on my face, and I panicked. I couldn't help it. I strained to pull out of his bearlike hug, but he only held me more tightly. His hand on my back was heavy and hot as an iron. His mouth was groping for mine. "Please, please," he said; I twisted my head back and forth frantically, and tried to push his face away.

Abruptly he relaxed and released me. He half rose; I could make out only the glistening whites of his eyes. His head brushed the ceiling of the tiny tent; a shower of condensed droplets fell. The waterfall had become audible again. He hung over me like a great bear, his arms dangling loosely, swinging his head from side to side agonizedly. Suddenly he threw back his head and howled, as though a knife were being twisted in his heart. He hauled himself to his feet, a naked giant, uprooting the tent, restoring the night. With a vicious heave of both arms he freed himself of the useless canvas and stumbled off down the hill.

The moon was gone. I sat on the rubber tent floor, bobbing with cold, with abject fear. I couldn't see or hear him. No footsteps, nothing. Then, below, a car door slammed. The sound of ignition, a motor turning over, the clash of gears without clutch. Scattered voices: the others awakening. I stood up (I hadn't thought I could) and didn't dare to move. There was a brief, terrifying silence. Then I heard a thin, whining sound and the bumping rattle of a car in motion. Five seconds, ten, then suddenly a crash: metal against metal, one clean sound. Instantly a brilliant flash of light, a split second later the roar of an explosion; another flash, a second explosion, and a tremendous column of flame shot up from the still. Both boilers had blown.

How we got him out alive I don't know; his entire body was on fire. We rolled him in blankets and laid him smoking in the back of the pickup among chunks of cord oak. I climbed in the back beside him, wrapped in a blanket. No one spoke to me. He was alternately screaming and passing out, screaming and passing out, all the way down the mountain, all the way into town.

To admit the existence of pain (how not to?) and to be ready for it, ready to *take it*, is one thing; to pursue it or welcome it or submit to it for the sake of knowledge, or experience, as an act of ostentation or even as a despairing declaration of its inevitability is altogether another. I don't pretend to know the meaning of suffering; sometimes it appears to be necessary, but that is not its meaning. What I do know is that if it is inevitable (as I'm so often told) only those standing outside it are in a position to condemn it, and it doesn't do the sufferer himself much good either to dispute its justice or to have others do it for him. And there's not much point in debating, *while we are suffering,* the question of whether we have invited our pain or it has invited itself; it can be confronted and (possibly) defeated only when it is *present.* The expectation of it (*Angst?*) is most likely its incipient presence.

And no matter what our suffering (present, past, or presumed inevitable) may seem to reveal to us about the nature of the "world" or "the human condition," pain is not made more desirable. I admit, pain does come to mean a great many things to those who have passed through long sieges of it. *Afterward.* But not even death itself proves the *need* to suffer. In fact, the very *occurrence* of death may be a sign that we are not *necessarily* bound to be eternal victims of a world we ourselves have corrupted, and that what we call suffering is only the penalty for that corruption.

November 29th

There is one story that Moon told me while we were passing through Virginia on the way down from New York, in which he must have been referring to his twin brother Edmund. If so, it was the only time he ever spoke to me of him, even indirectly, before that night up on the mountain.

It seems that on his way home from the war Moon stopped off in Roanoke (I think it was), Virginia. It was where his "brother" had died, he said, and he'd bought some flowers and gone up to the cemetery to lay them on his grave. He didn't recall where his brother was buried, and the caretaker couldn't find a record of the interment either, so he set out to find the plot by himself. At first he passed systematically from marker to marker, reading the inscriptions, but when an hour or so had passed and he still hadn't come across his brother's grave, his movements became more erratic; he began to wander from one side of the graveyard to the other, hoping (rather superstitiously) to chance upon the stone. (He told me this with his eyes fixed on me, in an offhand manner, and smiling; but I remember wondering why his lips kept jutting out in a kind of resentful pout as he talked.) Often that afternoon he'd sat down on a low headstone, taken off his (new) straw hat, mopped his brow and tried to call up some recollection of the funeral or a later visit to the grave, but he couldn't even remember his brother's face (or his own?), much less where he was buried. (He laughed and said, "I thought, here somebody's gone and pulled a good one on me—maybe this isn't even the right *cemetery!*") Evening came. This frustration of his good intentions angered him; it was obvious he would never find the grave before nightfall. In desperation he began to look around for a stone, *any* stone with his brother's death year on it—and when at last he came upon one (a stillborn infant's grave), he threw his flowers down disgustedly and fled.

He was still smiling, still pouting, and still staring at me—so hard that his eyes grew shiny and filled. "Funny," he said, "that same night, on the train going home, I made up my mind there wasn't anything or anybody was going to stop me from getting you over here . . ."

For as long as Moon lived I was to be *his* orphan.

But as he lay dying (one whole week), with lidless eyes and unable to speak (or beyond speech), I think perhaps he understood (don't ask me how!) that he himself had been the only true orphan, and that his life had been no more than an obstinate and sometimes tortured refusal to accept his essential aloneness.

In that week, when his body had already taken leave of him and hung preoccupied with its own private plaything of pain, I like to imagine now that he was able to abandon all pretense. I want his death to have been a negative victory, at least—to have canceled its own absurdity and set him free—of me, of the responsibility for the waste of his life, of his investment in me.

Moon's real life was lived in the process of dying: the huge blister his body had become sealed him off from time, and in granting the respite of absolute freedom, let him know how near and yet how far he had always been from its human equivalent.

Aphra came up from Columbia, without her lawyer but with his Buick, just to satisfy herself that Moon was really going to die. She rushed into the clinic in a dark-blue dress (like a wind-driven thunderhead), surveyed the bed and its contents with a look of shocked distaste, ignored the smattering of family (all suddenly evil-eyed), glanced sharply at me, registering something between fear and disdain, and then fled.

As for the others: they sat, they closed their eyes, they talked in torrents, one gushing into the other. Obsessive talk, and mostly of incongruous things: words no good unanswered. In their own way they were begging his forgiveness, but to no avail. One by one they lapsed into silence, then awoke a few seconds later and stood up looking around frantically, as though a voice from nowhere were calling them away. And they came back, day after day, for more. What did they hope for? God only knows. As long as Moon just lay there, two eyes projecting themselves into space out of a heap of bandages, with no sign of life except a faint respiratory shudder, they seemed bent on humiliating themselves in installments, laying themselves bare for his invisible judgment. But there was nothing forthcoming; another day or two and they'd have torn the bandages off to get at him.

I sat, and watched, and heard the vague undertones of life, still humming, still *in him,* and I felt the reproach of having to attend the death of another man; for it was this approach to death that was unbearable. When he finally sank and didn't come up again, I felt an incredible relief: *that* was familiar. There is something mild, something beyond sorrow, in the pure facticity of the human form in death, like a portrait of sleep that can be looked upon without concern for the sleeper. (Or monastery furniture; natives of the monastery landscape; even more impersonal, the frayed, unraveled cloth of flesh. The dead are all alive in dreams.) When we mourn, we don't mourn corpses.

His relatives fell into a magical hysteria to raise him up again. Good Christians all. To see him there, removed from future recriminations, an effigy convulsed with laughter, infected them with rage. They turned and looked into each other's eyes, verified their fury, and fell to wailing not in grief but in communal frustration.

But his mother was the prize mourner. She, who had virtually disowned him, indulged herself splendidly. What was left of him lay in a sealed coffin in the tiny room where he had been born. The wisteria on the porch stank. The adjoining parlor, where the mourners were gathered, was thick with flies. Huge wicker baskets of lilies and flags stood everywhere. The ceiling fans revolved slowly, like gigantic dragonflies. Celluloid collars were melting. There was a low wash of voices. I sat with Aunt Libya Mauldin and held her hand. Suddenly, at the top of the stairs, his mother appeared—gaunt, unveiled, white-faced, on the arm of her brother. It was a moment of great drama; even the flies stopped humming as she wilted on the top step, regained herself, and then, half-reliant, half-dragging on her brother's arm, allowed herself to be rung down on the performance like a final black velvet curtain.

The only gift Moon ever expected of me was acquiescence, pliability, obedience. I was not expected to love him, and certainly not to understand him. He was content if I did his bidding. His love for me couldn't help but be inconsistent; he could make it justifiable to himself only through a successful remolding of his acquisition, and that was more than he could manage; everything about me got in his way—my age (which he had *never* been), my foreignness (which frightened him), my use of his language (which hadn't been a problem at first), my unfathomable background (which irritated him in spite of himself), my color (in spite of my blue eyes, that too), his own unconscious internal concerns (which governed his *ethics*, so to speak). If only (yes, if only!) he could have *accepted* the established, unbridgeable distance between us (and seen that when you love, this distance has no meaning)—then perhaps, only perhaps, the crisis that led to his death would never have been provoked.

And yet, soon or late, his death was *appropriate*. Only the sacrifice of his confounded adolescent vanity could have made him a whole man. Ever. As it was, what I have just said about myself applied to Aphra as well (*mutatis mutandis*): he could not bear to be loved by anyone he hadn't first adapted into a kind of slave-accomplice—and he made both Aphra and me become gradually hateful and unrecognizable to ourselves.

Aphra was a vital, passionate, opinionated woman; Moon tried to desensualize her and the role of statue did not become her, so she ran. As for me, he was ready to give me everything (the woods!) in exchange for total approbation; he wanted me to be his son (unengendered), his apprentice, his blood brother —call it what you like—one or another of the facets of his childish idyl: a world of muscles and harmless smut and guiltless decisions, beautiful but impossible.

Nothing was so deeply fundamental to his character as his antagonism toward restrictions of any kind, whether physical or artificially imposed. All his life he struggled to work himself through the fine mesh of public and social ties that lies over the essential formlessness of American life. Even his love for "Nature," for wild things and wild places, was the inverse side of his distrust of their independence, their separateness. In ordering, in taming them, he was playing an elaborate, ambivalent game of fatality, deliberately provoking otherwise inert forces (or at least basically amenable ones) to resist him and be put down. City and forest, sophistication and crudity were stamped heads and tails on him; the alloy of his character lay in between, hardened in an auto-erotic dream of immolation.

Dark-skinned Abel (red or black) is murdered and therefore eulogized. Cowboy Cain has a price on his head and an unrelenting, growing posse on his trail. One day they close in and mow him down; from then on the ballad of conscience is his only epitaph and his only reality.

After a great deal of wrangling (and pressure by Aunt Libya's lawyer), the family came to the legally unavoidable conclusion that I had the right to a son's share of Moon's estate. If claiming the money had been up to me (which it wasn't, for good or ill) I'd have let them choke on it; I couldn't have cared less about it. Aunt Libya encouraged me to go back to school. I tried, but it was no use; after a month I left. The illusion of what I was to become, who I *was*, had been destroyed. There was no recognizable center which I could regard as myself, or as a point of departure for a self to be. I was a something that had come from nowhere and was going nowhere—a vector visible to others but in itself unaccountable.

December 3rd

All aimed arrows strike the bull's-eye by accident, although it is possible not to believe in accidents.

I began to wander, from town to town, always farther inland. I reached the Rockies and, repelled by them, turned southward and back. Two years I drifted, sometimes working, mostly not. I avoided trains and seldom hitchhiked; usually I took buses, with endless accordion tickets, got off in unlikely places, stayed an hour or a day and got back on, in and out of a kind of sleep-read-sleep-talk-stop-start-sleep, on and on through the slow transitions, the wastes, the geographical paradoxes, the dry primitivity, through the inexplicable familiarity, freak electricity and sudden clarity, the named placelessness of the American continent, transported by an absurd, fluid, heart-breaking dream of distance.

I moved on and on, through infinite depots and aisles, down platforms and main streets and highways, through the only new, the only real cities there are, over the only earth that seems unowned, that maybe isn't owned and never will be, in and out of prehuman settings, through a Nature that takes no account of men, whose men do not believe in her, whose wind and dust and forests, whose grain fields and whose summer conflagrations repudiate their own roots, their imposed edges; whose inner meaning, once defined, defies the tongue that tries to tell it, puts out any eye that hesitates for long.

And everywhere I went I talked to people and more people. I talked insanely, brokenly, inspiredly, incessantly, moved by my lostness and the readiness of those to whom I talked to identify themselves with it, by their deep desire to share. I talked to the oldest people in this world, to its real refugees—all of them struggling to throw off their skins, convinced against all reason that there must be a way, *still*, and willing to reveal to a stranger in immediate, striking phrases their fragile, naïve longing—but so promptly, so urgently, so pleadingly, that any doubt about its honesty was swallowed in the first great urge of recognition and response. I have never known such a frantic, effusive, *convincing* demonstration of the buried truth in anonymous human beings—of the insistent, naked presence of it beneath the obvious weakness and confusion of their outer lives.

And I rediscovered the Moon I had lost in 1945, a thousand times over.

I'll always remember this about America: not its chaotic, often brutal face, which is like a razor blade held up by surface tension, but the unique fluid of its inhabitants, who despite the fact that they are still homeless manage to preserve and some-

times dignify in their displacement a crude but human predica-
tion of hope for a new life.

December 4th

All my thinking is done out loud or with my hand; I can't treat
the past (or memory) as though it existed in a space on which
I could reflect. Only if I open up, out loud or with my hand,
do I discover that it is *all there.*

A great many random moods and whims have contributed
to the unevenness of what I've written, and I've contradicted
myself on every other page, I know; but these vagaries originate
in the changeability and instability of *Now,* not in the content
of the past. I sit and write and watch words appear with a kind
of wonder; my fingers itch with a peculiar agitation. A child, a
young man, has taken shape, a self I cannot, with the best will,
believe was ever me—a child locked for years in a prison of
wordlessness, one who doubted nothing he was told and nothing
he heard, remembered everything and only recently found out
that words belong to him as well.

To be sure, the dead were never kind to me; they preyed on
my credulity, and for a long time I had no choice but to do
what they wanted. Was I alive then? yet? A useless, impene-
trable question, existing prior to the voice that can put it,
prior even to any doubt that could betray a genuine belief. My
hand asks it now though, tasting its own reticence and mine in
words complaining the passage of everyone else's time in a
funereal era.

No, I was never really that child, and the ties that connect
us are devious and circumstantial. *My* life is only now beginning
(as they say), my *proper* life, I mean; no birthday, no more
history, no past impounded, nothing out of reach of hand or
eye, no dead men walking in my shoes or on them.

A visible hand can tilt the moon for a change!

A legend has to go on being what it is, and not rack anybody's brain or break his heart. There must be answers to questions and ends to roads, and promises must be kept.

Who knows? Perhaps one day the absent faces will all be restored.

Our origins are never what we think they are. Mine estranged themselves from *me*—not the other way round—in a succession of shocks (all monotonously the same) to which I feel a really callous indifference. Perhaps this is a dangerous admission, but if I've learned nothing else, it's that the easiest thing in the world is to become an orphan. The almost impossible task is to go on *being* one, even under the best [*sic!*] of conditions. Home is not where *I* started from. I am sure of this, even though my body is forever disputing the fact; whatever I remember it insists on relegating to its own order, and whatever I succeed in forgetting it recalls for me in obnoxious detail. I am your presence, it says (a little shrilly); there is no death before me or without me, and without death you need expect no day of miracles, no resurrection.

In its own rather limited way my body is right, I suppose, but I owe it no tribute; as the tomb of the past, it is surely the vehicle of birth and rebirth, but it doesn't generate new life, not of itself.

December 6th

"*Denk' ich an Deutschland . . .*"
Do you know what you're doing?

Last night, for the first time in several months, I sat down and reread my poems. None of them mean much to me any more, I find (not too surprisingly)—a few lines from the Berlin poem ("Children in the furnace of his own reflected eye/Balance on the tightrope of the sun . . . Who is the bright musician/Who strums my eyes?"), some parts of "Monastery Rain," and

"Nachtverzehrer" (the most successfully dishonest of them all). Other than that, nothing.

After Moon's death I began to have a recurrent dream—of a huge, somehow familiar house, always the same inside but with an alternating exterior (sometimes like the white Colonial house in which Moon was born, sometimes like a Central European brick apartment house at twilight).

I was given to know that some unspeakable crime had been committed in the interior—what crime I didn't know, but over and over again I scoured the rooms, from cellar to attic, always with the same feeling of anxious exhilaration, until I knew it (or dreamed I did) more intimately than my own self. But I couldn't uncover a single clue to the crime.

The dream persisted even after I returned to Europe; the white exterior gave way almost entirely to the brick one—that was the only difference. It began to irritate me, and so I devised a scheme to exorcise it: I would write a series of poems, draw a kind of waking blueprint as I dismantled the house; all to uncover the crime.

During those first months with Edith I raged through my dream house like a demon-detective, tearing down walls, ripping out staircases and partitions, until (even in the dream) I had gutted the place and hauled its innards into the daylight of words.

Left completely alone at the time (and obviously I didn't want to be), I'd have plotted and dreamed and gnawed myself down to the bone (witness the artist as skeletal monster!) Yet the poems (for me, at least) were not the real issue of our relationship. Edith came (like a bony nurse with a kit full of homeopathic incentives) in time to aid but too late to effect a cure. There was nothing we could exchange: moody willfulness was her bad habit, tight-lipped introversion mine; we walked on different floors, breathed different air, invented holidays for our compulsive gifts and forgot real anniversaries. I used her selfishly at times, out of a kind of desperation; and she gratified herself with outrage. But no solvent could melt us both at once.

Anyway, the poems got done: the proofs of demolition—metaphors for floor plans, epitaphs for rooms, postulates for a geometry of memory. But now I find that nothing is alive in them, nothing really coherent; not one of them is able to extend by an inch or an instant its own immutable space. And even though the house is empty, its shell remains intact around a space that still contains a crime.

When we cease to believe in distance we begin to hate the nearest thing at hand.

December 8th

It is raining in Strasbourg; the Rhine smells of snow and carborundum.

December 9th

Here we are.

Afternoon itinerary: Hebelstrasse, Zwingerstrasse, Kettengasse, Wolfshöhlenweg, Fauler Pelz, Endemannstrasse, Gaswerkstrasse, Schlachthausstrasse, Grabengasse.

There was a tiny, perfect, hidden pocket in his uniform. The day he discovered it he transferred his loose change to it; by the next day the coins had worn a hole, he lost them, and now this ruined secrecy is a known and bothersome defect, although it is still hidden.

Barbara Speer ...

Three days after his successful *coup d'état* the general committed suicide out of nostalgia for the voice of a murdered radio announcer.

Even the warning that this would be a fiction was fictional. Fodder for the machines of the third person.

All those who have "been through" something are taken hostage by those who haven't.

Poetry and firing squads; your childish, expedient, heroic, phony, eighteenth-century holy-war philosophy.

December 13th

Dear Immanuel: Every failure is not of the same order. If you attempt to dismiss this "book" because of its irregularity or its lack of art, or if you are prepared to be "disappointed" in me because of it, I feel sorry for you: you miss the point entirely as to why I let myself be talked into keeping it. And if you discount it because you've been *planning to* (which wouldn't surprise me in the least), just to ratify certain wavering emotional defenses in your (not-so) secret self, then you will have to pay, eventually, for your presumption and hypocrisy. Even if I should supply you with something you expected (masochistically?), you would still have to disregard the substance of what I have tried to tell, to touch, before attempting to tear the book apart intellectually—for *whatever* personal reasons. The imposition you *intended* in handing me this notebook was not an incidental or momentary thing, and you *know* it. That is why I say these things now, just before returning it to you. I feel no sympathy for you at all; I wanted, in a kind of vacuum, to try to shed my past, and in freeing myself of it (if I could) to make you a gift of it, as a reproach, or rather, *admonition*. I should have realized from the very beginning how compromising that would be, but I was naïve enough to convince myself it was some sort of *exchange*, or dialectic, you wanted. Now I know that it is *me* you want—I can see it, hear it, feel it in the ill-contained anticipation of triumph that you have become: an anticipation that has gradually perverted and obstructed every honest intention I had. And I am left with little more than frustrated pity for you. (I even pity you now for having to deal with these words, and for having to discount them as well. It will seem easy at first—but later?) Each time I see you now I am overwhelmed by a sensation of abject pessimism which I have never experienced in my life before, about the ultimate possibility of any genuinely human intercourse. I don't know why I generalize on it, but it is real, and I can't bear it. Precisely in those moments when I am ready to speak from a full heart, with real passion, real love, in those moments when it is not the past I am ranting about, or *time*, but my own present self—this instantaneous flesh and blood—I am suddenly, brutally stung by the awareness that you are only *posing* as my listener, that you are hearing someone else, preparing words for someone else, that your eyes glued on my face are seeing not me but another; and then all I want to do is hurt you (as now), to lash out and strike you (as now), reach you and make you receive, painfully (as now), the only gift I have to give to you or

[*Here the entry breaks off and is not resumed.*—EDITOR'S NOTE.]

December 14th

I have been unjust and unfaithful to a great many people in my life and in this notebook. Selfishly, in the last resort. But every recorded moment is a forgery; we have to give it a particular shape it never had, if only to certify our distance from it, and from our past selves and involvements.

On another deeper level of myself, where things are not recalled in fitful fragments, but lie out of conscious reach in a slow residual sediment, I have been stirred more and more during the writing of this book by the affective *presence* of those whom I was describing as dead. In themselves they were none the less dead, but I began to realize that despite my reluctance to touch them, to *handle* them, my attempts to hold them at a safe, semifictitious distance were actually the surface expressions of an effort on that deeper level to make them speak, to call them forth in my heart as apprentices to my voice.

Golden's is the only voice that holds its own apart from mine, the only face that hasn't faded. From the moment he announced himself, unawaited, in these pages, I have not been quite the same. His rediscovery (although I didn't realize it then) was the instant when all this became unnecessary, and the burden of purely personal history was lifted.

Let us remember our names, he said; and I say Yes, let us remember our names—the names of the living for their sake, and the names of the dead not for their sake but for our own and that of the World-to-Come.

Where else is the World-to-Come, if not in this *mimesis?* Not *there* certainly, not in the there of the dead who want to pull us down to them (though we are their only salvation), nor in the there of our meaningless beginnings, which would have us all be orphans till kingdom come; not in the wasting *facticity* of a death which is the senseless habit of our mechanical lives, nor in the trivial sufferings (yes trivial!) that make us the prisoners of our own isolation—no, not there, but *here* in the very thrust of life on which we feed and which, fed back by us, lets the future, the only future, take place from us; and where our names, remembered, spoken, are all names, now, before, to come and always.

I've played this game long enough now. Whatever comes from here on will have to put itself in my way—it's not going to overtake me from behind.

HINGES

STEFAN BRÜCKMANN

NACHTVERZEHRER
(NIGHT-DEVOURER)

All night I lay
awake, I swear I did not sleep;
uneasy horses kept and ticked
irregular fleshclocks, and licked
my face till day
broke. Yet I awoke.

In dreams of mud
I froze; out of paralysis
I rose (such fallacies!), grew cold
and sank again. A tale was told
(deep in my blood)
of murder, and I heard.

I woke asleep,
or slept awake; it's all the same.
But once he cried my name, or seemed
to, clearly. Tell me, if I dreamed
it, why I keep
on dreaming that one dream.

—*Déjà-vu*, Vol. I, No. 2 (January 1955)

Look at death as a body, your body, and your life as a wound upon it. That body does not know you, it knows only that the wound is causing it pain. When you say that your life suffers pain, what you mean is that your body has felt the wound of your life. Be careful then—your body death will try to heal its wound. Fight for the wound which is life; you will learn to distinguish between the pains it suffers in its own defense, and the pains of death, which are only the pains felt by the body wounded with life.

For the body would not know of life except for pain, and without the defensive convulsions of death, life would not suffer pain. Life makes death feel its bodiliness, allows it to *have* a body. Otherwise death would not possess a body, and it does not want to.

Even if we were to regard the original wound as an accident, we could not call its self-consciousness a chance occurrence. Evolution is a word dictated to us by the body; it is not a continuous process, nor even a process—it is the already-present end of the first act of creation. That which evolves is pre-eminent, every happening is an indirect attempt to realize what has already been spoken. Nothing is presupposed, or caused; everything is already *there*, for *us*, just as "The People" was already inherent, in and from the moment the body of death was spoken out of chaos.

But life is not yet irreversible. Everywhere but in the World-to-Come, life is still dependent upon death, even though it is only through this contingency that death has been granted a body. As I have said, death does not want its body, and as it struggles to heal its wound and sink back into oblivion, it feels more intense pain, and its discomfort increases. Take care! There is great danger: the wound can still be healed. And should it be, the body would dissipate. Our only warning is the pain of life itself, a pain present instinctively even before the consciousness that life is a wound. This instinct is the first safeguard of the act of creation; in fact, without it there would be no creation. The moment in which an awareness of the nature of the wound is born is also the moment of the first genuine challenge to life: this is the hinge on which creation turns, the moment from which the very impulse and perpetuation of life as a wound is made to *seem* sinful. It is the moment of the Fall. But just as life, as a wound, depends on death, as a body, for its sustenance, for its realization, Man himself could not begin to realize himself until his fall had wounded Eden. Man will return *at once* to his original home, which has never ceased to exist, in the very moment that his wound becomes irreversible—that is, when life is no longer healable by death.

Then the body will no longer decay; it will be given over entirely to life, and *there will be no death*. This does not mean there will be no body; life without a body is a blasphemy in the eyes of the Holy One, Blessed be His Name, equal to the affront of death without a wound.

This victory of life over death is not a personal victory. Only when we, I mean The People, are irrevocably established, when life is all there is, only then will we realize that the victory of the wound over death has been the defeat of *Nothingness*. With the death of death, there is no *after*, and nothing will *occur*; pain will cease to be pain and will display its true nature, which is joy. Death for us now is an ostensible state of the decayable body of each of us, of the body that bears the wound of life. The victory of the wound alters this state, abolishes it, transforms it, renders the body transparent, continuous, perfect. This is the only, the *promised* immortality, and the birthright of creation.

Auschwitz, January 1944

JESSE BYRNES

November 20, 1948

Dear Steve,

I guess you must have been wondering what's happened to me, it's been so long I haven't written, but it's not that I've forgotten you or anything, I've just been running around like a chicken with his head cut off and I didn't even have a minute to sit down. I'll try to tell you what's been going on.

Like I told you last time I decided to run for the office of Game Warden. Well I did, knowing I was a whole lot better suited for the job than Roy Childress who'd been sitting on his tail for twenty years doing nothing while all the fish were being blown out of the water and birds being shot out of the sky, sparrows and all, and young timber being cut. I thought it would be an easy thing to convince people that this man was no better than worthless in his elected capacity. Well it wasn't, I can tell you. It was my first attempt at politics except for talking about it. I didn't know what I was in for until the campaign started and then I learned fast. It seems it isn't so much what you do as what you claim you're *going* to do that brings the voters around, and there's no lie big enough it can't be repeated until you've got everybody believing it. The only thing I could really harp on was what old Childress said he *had* done and what I knew he hadn't and never had a mind to. That was his big soft spot, he'd had plenty of time to take care of whatever he meant to and not just promise every time an election came up, so I went right to work on that. I told people that Roy hadn't been further into the mountains than Rocky Bottom for over fifteen years and that was true. On up beyond you could get away with just about anything you had a mind to, and there wasn't anybody to say no. I said if they elected me I would appoint all kinds of deputies who would roam around those woods and make sure the law was enforced. I said I would pick these men from men I know up there who have lived there all their lives and are not just town people who couldn't wade across a creek if their life depended on it, and that I planned to spend most of the time up there myself seeing to it that the taxpayers' money was being put to good use in restocking lakes and streams and prosecuting anybody who thought he could wander around toting a shotgun any old time he felt like it. I covered the country from one end to the other and everywhere I went more people were turning out to hear me. I'm not a very good talker, never was, but I know these people, I speak the same kind of language they do, and when it comes to woods and wildlife there isn't a person for a country mile who has made that his life the way I did, and so they listened to me. Well when the word got around to Roy about the kind of crowds I was drawing he got scared I guess, because he started running around all over the countryside like a chicken with his head cut off spreading lies about me, and when people didn't pay the heed he expected them to he had no other choice but to start claiming he was going to do all the same things I was. That was a big mistake on his part because people started to laugh and yell questions at him that he couldn't answer, like hadn't he had enough time to do them already. Finally you know what he did? He came to my house and told me if I would withdraw from the race he would make me *his* deputy. I was going to lose anyway, and that way I would still be able to do most of what I wanted to. Well I told him we'd see who was going to win and in the meantime he'd better be a little more careful about the kind of things he was saying about me personally because if he wasn't I might even be obliged to haul him into court. Well he got red as a watermelon and stomped out of the house fit to be tied. That was three weeks ago, since then we have had the election and I won hands down. About the only votes Roy got came from his pool-hall buddies and now I don't think any one man ever hated me so much in my whole life. But I reckon that's the way politics is and there's nothing I can do to change it. . . .

January 25th, 1949

. . . I hope you have got the package, these things always take a long time around the holidays, but we mailed it before the tenth of December and there's no reason why it shouldn't have arrived by now. The wool socks were knitted by my aunt Libya Mauldin herself, who keeps asking all the time when you are going to get here. I can only tell her just as soon as I get an answer from about *five hundred* letters. Sometimes I get so riled up with all the delays and *investigations* I could just sit down and cry, there is no way to push the whole thing out of my mind and let the red tape wear itself out, I keep thinking there is something more I should be doing. There is just no *reason* why it should have taken almost *four years*, it's not like I was trying to take you from your *family* or something like that. But what am I doing making you listen to my complaints, it's as much of a burden for you as me. I guess all we can do is just sit and keep on going about our work as best we know how and try not to think about it until they make up their minds to let you go.

I didn't know what else to send you for your birthday except this check. I know you are working and earning your own money now but I know they don't pay you very much and I want you to have the things you need until I get there. Not get sick or run down or not have enough to eat. How are you, boy? It's hard for me to think of you being already twenty years old, you must have grown real big by now, though I couldn't tell from the photo you sent what you look like underneath, with all those winter clothes you had on. But take good care of yourself, and whenever you need some more money don't be ashamed to ask for it. I'm real proud of the way you write now, your English is a damsite better than mine already, that's for certain. Aunt Libya Mauldin said you sounded like a fine young gentleman with good upbringing, and I told her yes that's what you are. . . .

GUSTAV LOKOWANDT

Excerpts from three rather peculiar articles in the East German-Soviet propaganda weekly Morgenrot, *under the pseudonym "Georg Brand"*:

... No self-respecting Hun ever wants to be on the *side* of the gods; if he can't *be* one himself he gets nasty. But Siegfried, the dear boy, is dead when so-called German history begins....

The millennium in the interim, the passionate devotion to traditional, practical and bourgeois values—these are all post-mortem sophistries to cover up a raving Hagen complex. What German wants to be purged this side of the vale? Not even Goethe. Only with the *Götterdämmerung* and the subsequent destruction of the world can the death of *Junker* Siegfried be absolved.

The *Nibelungenlied* is a guilt-history in which the German's hatred of the encumbrance of spirit [*Geist*] by matter (leaves and mistletoe twigs and bric-a-brac) is given pious vent. The *Edda* can claim with some right to be a real mythology, but our *national* version of it is an obsessive saga that perpetuates an act of present, not prehistoric murder. Through its schizophrenic (Christian-dualist-barbaric) generalizations the question of guilt is mystically deferred, until someone (not Hitler, after all) resurrects both Hagen and Siegfried in one body; the only outlet till that glorious holocaust is in a theatrical world-immolation à la Oberammergau: Wagnerian auto-da-fé.

(27.II.46)

... I looked forward through all those years of *protective* arrest to the hour in which I should once more *function* as a free man. If I paid for that hour with concessions and repetitions, it was in the certainty that one day I'd cease to pay and all the others who continued to cling to their spurious freedom at my cost would have to reckon for it.

When I say "others" I don't mean my jailers; they were committed fools, when they died they had the looks of cows or dogs on their faces. No, I mean all those silent countrymen of mine who refused then to valorize, but who believed and still believe there is a way to the *future* in adamant faith and hopeful words. To me their rejuvenated idealism is anathema, their democracy an ant heap, their handless God an empty threat to bolster up their lie of a new life founded on the old. . . .

(29.III.46)

. . . but what a joke [the attempts on Hitler's life]! None of the conspirators was ready to die in the act, it seems, but they were all overjoyed to be put to death along with thousands of others (many of whom they had rejected) on gallows and hooks in Gestapo catacombs, crying, *"Es lebe das heilige Deutschland!"* just as soon as the Führer's immortality had once and for all been proved to their superstitious satisfaction. . . .

Fat mayors, late intellectuals, Iron-Crossed priests, uneasy officers, the discontented, the slighted, the overrefined: they sat down in secret seminars to hatch their plots, wet with perspiration, atremble at their daring. And like schoolboys they immediately forgot what they had come to discuss; it was more fun to talk if they imagined their project to be a *fait accompli*. Enthusiastically they fell all over one another with suggestions for games on the bridge once the troll was slain. So they schemed and deliberated, not on how to kill him, but on their activities *afterward*, when they would bask in the beautiful adulatory sunshine of world delight and their own glory, which they for some reason called "Germany." They lost themselves in such fairy realms of post factum that the factum was doomed from the start—not merely to failure but to abject impossibility. Their feeble attempts at assassination were so unreal, so amateur, so cinematographic, that if Hitler *had* died it would have been because of some quirk which neither they nor he had taken into account.

The complicated attempts to excuse or rationalize the mess they made of things are inane. They simply never put first things first. (There is no need for me to point out that this is a time-honored national trait; the mere thought of what might have been, *otherwise*, induces historical vertigo.) Any one of a dozen persons could have killed the man, at the cost of his own life, more than once; but that would have brought the dream down to earth, and required the assumption of truly individual responsibility. As for the volunteers from outside the ranks of the exclusive, they were shuffled about like playing cards until they wore out, or until the "right moment" had passed and they had to "get back to the front." Besides, who could be sure of a volunteer's personal motives? Schoolboy masturbation societies are always reluctant to admit new members. . . .

(30.IV.46)

POLICE PRAESIDIUM, CITY OF V——

Bureau of Missing Persons   V——,January 5, 1952
Ref: 45/827/L: 6/050152   Nifelheimerstr. 46–50

To:
Frau Hilde Lokowandt, nee Laufey; widow
St. Veit
Waldstrasse 3.   Registered!

Re: File 45/827/L; Gustav Lokowandt; Missing Person

Honored Madam!

Your letter of inquiry dated December 16, 1951, is herewith respectfully acknowledged. To our great regret we must inform you that there have been no new developments in the case of your son Gustav Lokowandt (alias Eichel Brand), born on

May 11, 1897, in St. Veit, and that, under existing statutes, and barring receipt of information that would point to his still being alive, the search for him will be discontinued on the 31st of the current month, at which time he will be declared dead, and our files on him will be closed. Notification of legal procedure pursuant to such a declaration will of course be sent you by the authorities having jurisdiction.

Considering the fact of his earlier disappearance (*vide*: our letters 2/180647 and 3/090847), we realize and agree that he *could* still be alive under another name, but inasmuch as not even you, his mother, have received any communication from him whatsoever since early 1942, and since we have been unable to uncover a single trace of him since 1945, there is little or nothing more that we can do. You must understand that his own concealment of his identity after 1927, and his possession of false papers during the period 1931–41 in Berlin, greatly impeded the efforts, both here and abroad, to track down persons who might have known him before the war, and with whom he might have re-established contact afterward. The last editor of *Die Mühle*, Herr Heinrich Deckeler, who did have business relations with your son during the time he bore the assumed name "Eichel Brand," was able to supply us with many details of his prewar life, but attests that he has not seen or heard of him since 1941. If you remember, it was only due to the chance discovery of his name during the processing of lists of persons sentenced to Buchenwald for political offenses that it was possible to trace him there in 1942, and then to Raisko/Auschwitz in 1943 (*vide*: our correspondence 4/231148). Both the protocol of his trial and his political dossier must be regarded as lost or destroyed; even if they should turn up at some later date, they would be of dubious value in the matter with which we are concerned: too much time has passed.

To summarize: the last traces of your son of which we may be certain are: (1) that he left Raisko/Auschwitz in a political transport sometime in late January 1945, and (2) that his name exists on a roster of German prisoners departing for Cottburg on the sixth of February 1945 and destined for Weimar/Buchenwald. This same train was bombed and strafed by American aircraft just outside Luchau on the same day, and in view of his subsequent unlocatability, we are obliged to conclude that he was a victim of that attack.

Should you have further inquiries, or should any new information that could lead to our establishing his whereabouts fall into your hands before the 31st of this month, please do not hesitate to contact this office.

[Seal]   [Signed] F. NEBEL
Certified: (Facsimile)   Commissioner
B. I. FENWAY, Major, U.S. Army.

IMMANUEL DE BRIS

. . . but in a war, every city is in some way an open city, at least insofar as its men are opened and laid bare to themselves. Only those cities which were *declared* open endured in a physical sense, of course—that is, their buildings remained standing and usually not so many inhabitants died.

But on a deeper level, these cities died as surely as the bombed and devastated ones—died by default and not by murder—and we, their already naked men, died with them, embalmed in our few remaining pretensions: our precarious pride, our commitment to a city *ethic* which was to have been our salvation when the smoke had cleared. . . .

Just think: we were abandoned suddenly, anticlimactically, left with institutions and posters intact, surrounded by familiar alleys, corners, promenades, hotels, *bistros*, shops, clubs, fountains, monuments, landmarks—and not one of their bland faces was scarred or troubled by any of the physical or spiritual torments that had ravaged us men so terribly. The occupation turned out to have been a *preoccupation*. Here was our playground handed back unable to be mourned, calling for the same allegiance, dirty with the same indifference, demanding

the same hours, hounding us with the same old history-plus-four.
In the midst of this, in the first moment of genuine stillness
and reflection, on the first Sunday of our "new lives," we knew
ourselves to be horribly and irrevocably burdened—with an internal destruction having no external counterpart on which to
build, from which we might derive one word of comfort, one
mute ruined sign of gratitude.

                              —*Arrières-pensées* (*Paris*, 1946)

*"I'm only now beginning to understand some things about
you," said Edith de Bris.*

"Good for you," said Immanuel.

"For one thing, I know why you married me."

"Oh? That's interesting. Tell me, why did I?"

"You were jealous."

Immanuel laughed. "Of Stefan?" he asked.

"No, quite the contrary. Of me."

I first met Stefan Brückmann in the spring of 1955. An ephem-
eral periodical called *Déjà-vu* had somehow landed on my
desk and contrary to habit I did not relegate it to the trash
but sat down and began to look it over. It was devoted entirely
to a series of poems by "Stefan Brückmann"—tight, delicate,
personal little poems in English—and three or four of them
made such an impression on me that the same afternoon I
wandered over to the Quai d'Anjou, hoping to learn the whereabouts of the author from the "publisher" of the review.

As it turned out, *Editions Edgar* (a fourth-floor two-room
flat from whose windows one could just make out the pointed
cupolas of the Hôtel de Sens) was the home not only of Mlle.
Edith Garcilaso, translator and editor, but of my young quarry
as well. He himself greeted me at the door: Mlle. Garcilaso
was out but would be back shortly; could he help me? I said
I was not personally acquainted with the mademoiselle, I had
come with an inquiry. So he asked me to come in, offered me
his hand and announced his name.

He was extremely slender, of medium height, black-haired and dark-skinned, and had the most volatile blue eyes I've ever seen—like strongly tinted alcohol. His movements were nervous but at the same time oddly precise; somehow they evoked a sense of inner duplicity, as if he were mimicking his intentions by executing them. His French, though quite fluent, was pronounced with a curious deliberation and spacing of phrases. When I remarked how little his accent resembled that of all the other English-speaking people I knew, he laughed and said that wasn't so surprising, he'd spoken three languages before he ever learned a word of English. Oh, and what were they? I asked—but at that moment Edith Garcilaso came in, loaded down with groceries, and took over. She was a striking young woman, fine-featured and angular, and two or three years older than her lover (who turned out to be twenty-six years old, though except for his eyes he didn't look a day over twenty). He retired to a corner and sat listening with a bemused smile as Edith began to answer all questions addressed to him: he was a German, she said; he had arrived in Paris about a year before after some years in America; she made no mention of his Romany background. We came quickly to the reason for my coming; about the poems as well she spoke with managerial self-confidence, and he did not interrupt or open his mouth. I felt a little stupid. It was obvious that my homage meant next to nothing to these people. Stefan's amused indifference irked me no end; but at the same time a number of things about him aroused my curiosity. When I left I asked him to come and see me in the next few days.

He showed up alone, and seemed to be quite willing to talk about everything but himself. Each time he felt I was asking him to make a personal revelation he retreated quickly to the same strangely abstracted distance. He was immensely alert; nothing escaped his attention. But once a remark disappeared behind those eyes of his it seemed to become a part of him, as much as if he had digested it. Never an immediate reaction or response.

And his laughter: it was indescribable; it parodied everything, and it always came at the most unlikely moments. At first I thought it betrayed a purely infantile desire to demean things; only much later did I understand that this boy-man was trying to reach beyond his pain, and in the meantime was using his laughter as an anesthetic. The agitation I felt in his presence grew, as I began to see him more and more frequently. Without knowing exactly what I expected of him, I developed a real *need* to talk with him, to *be* with him.

The information (when it came) that he was part Gypsy intrigued me. Superficially he was every inch the dark-skinned, high-strung, unpredictable romantic image, but his eyes, which betrayed such great suffering, and his words, which *denied* it in a manner that can only be described as oracular—these two warring characters produced a phenomenal tension of being which I could never fathom or grasp, and which went far beyond any possible preconceptions I might have had of the purest nomad. I have never known a person to speak reflectively with such dissociation as Stefan did when he spoke of himself. It took ages for him to *condescend* to answer the more direct questions I put to him about his past; and when he did, the answers he gave seemed to me so discontinuous as to be almost entirely worthless or unbelievable. I accused him of lying (preconception!); I accused him of willfully disregarding the inner consistency of events, saying that occurrences which are not set in any sort of intelligible order are apt to appear unnecessarily cryptic. To which he replied, "You asked me about my past; the things you call cryptic are all that's left of it." I resisted the impulse to say I felt he was striking a pose, but remarked rather peevishly that even the present would be empty for someone for whom the past was meaningless. "I didn't say it was meaningless," he replied; "but whatever meaning it *still* has is both cryptic *and* present. The past is dead and digested, and as far as *I'm* concerned, all chronologies are fictional. I couldn't care less for *my* past—we all own everybody's, with our im*pa*tience—that is, if we're really alive."

A few days later I handed him a blank notebook, and rather jokingly said I wanted to see just what a "fictional chronology" would look like. No hurry, I said, and then spent a tremendous amount of effort, both intellectual and emotional, pushing and coaxing him into beginning. I was sure that once he did, he wouldn't be able to stop, and that as he went on, the natural laws of literary expression would take over automatically.

You must judge for yourself whether I was right or wrong. I can only caution you to be prepared for an unorthodox work which, though it contains elements of journal and memoir and poetry, is not consistently any of these. Stefan's notebook is essentially formless, reflective as much of its author's changing moods and inner states as of a determined attempt to produce a consecutive account of the events of his life. Despite moments of great introspection, it is not an effort at self-analysis; Stefan succeeded in preserving (whether intentionally or not I do not know) in his writing an atmosphere of the same passionate distance, the same disavowing, erratic sense of *presence and nothing else* with which he confronted me personally. And yet, no matter how many irregularities in tone, how many uncertainties in style, how many contradictions exist, a knotty thread of truth and time does bind his fragments and render them accessible.

In July Edith Garcilaso left for Spain. Though she and Stefan had not parted on the best of terms, he stayed on for a time in the flat on the Quai d'Anjou. I myself traveled to Normandy for the August holidays and remained there for a conference in early September. By the time I returned to Paris Edith was back; she and Stefan had parted, and he had moved to a little hotel in the Rue de l'Ancienne Comédie.

(At this point, as a matter of what may seem to be irrelevant information—as far as the notebook itself is concerned—I shall inform you that in February of the following year Edith Garcilaso and I were married. Whatever general conclusions the reader may draw are his own affair; his knowledge of the fact of our marriage is indispensable to his understanding of certain things which I shall say about the role Stefan ultimately played in my life, beyond the journal.)

For a month or so after my return I hardly saw Stefan. Edith and I began to keep company. The trip to Spain and the break with Stefan had changed her, had tempered her eager aggressiveness and made her seem more feminine somehow. She had known when she left that time was running out in their relationship, but I think she expected to be the one to terminate the affair, and his defection before her return came as a shock to her ego, and even scandalized her just a little. But neither harbored the other any lasting ill will. Stefan knew I was seeing her, but he never mentioned it—nor, to be perfectly fair to him, do I think it had any bearing on his outbursts against me in the notebook.

After his separation from Edith, the tempo of his writing changed (I recognized this only when I had the notebook in my hands, of course; as long as he was working on it I avoided making too many inquiries, and he was never the one to volunteer information); he began almost immediately to sound greater depths in himself, in his past. A genuine urgency heightened his language and powers of concentration, and the facile distractions of the first section (my division) fell away abruptly and almost entirely. In a way, his radical dissociation of himself from Edith was a legitimate and even inevitable result of the struggle that began with the writing of the poems and was renewed in the notebook *as an act*. The same is true of his sudden break with me a few months later, in Germany. But it was a long time before I could show the same equanimity in regard to his desertion of *me* that Edith did toward his abandonment of her. For almost two years I kept the notebook locked away; when I finally let her read it she said, "I always knew he understood me, better than I wanted him to, in fact—but he had *you* nailed down."

It was Edith's idea to translate it. I told her she would only be wasting her time, that it was hopeless to expect it to take on a shape it did not already possess; what meaning could it have for anyone else? But she persisted, and I gave in. When, after almost a year, she handed me the manuscript, and I reread the notebook in my own language, I received a severe shock: I realized that I hadn't really *read* it at all before. For the first time it was brought home to me to what an extent Stefan had penetrated my life, had *wounded* me. Not by what he had written —no, by his *presence*, the conscience I could never grasp and had only half sensed. These were reimpressed on me through the reading of the notebook in French. Reimpressed, did I say? They struck me in the face.

Such a delayed reaction is never easy to explain—to one's own satisfaction, at any rate. And I have stubbornly hesitated to attribute to Stefan the power of a catalyst, right to the present moment. But this is being blind to the *significance* of the notebook; what it declares, unmistakably, is that Stefan's entire life had been a series of encounters in which every attempt to hold him, or enslave him, or make him anything other than what he was, ended (inevitably, it seemed to him) in the catalytic destruction of the other. If he is to be believed, this effect he had on others was not intentional—quite the contrary—and any attempt to explain what took place, how the effect was brought about, is as idle as to try to deny its occurrence. To all intents and purposes, what happened simply *happened*, with a seeming inevitability that terrified him. When he began to feel the pattern repeating itself in his relationship with me, he ran from what he regarded as an imminent disaster that I myself was inviting, and of which he, *once again*, would be the un-willing agent.

In the past two years I have sat down more than a dozen times to write an introduction to the notebook, but with each new attempt I found most of what I had written the previous time to be immaterial or inadequate, and often downright em-barrassing. This time, too, I am aware of my inability to say what I want to. But I have found the courage to confess my own inadequacy, and to admit in writing, if only to myself, that what I have been trying to do for so long now is to nullify, or at least obscure, the damage Stefan did me, the *necessary* damage, and to prepare a biased Baedeker to the notebook that would serve as an airtight alibi for me as well.

All my false starts (some running to thirty and forty pages!) are adequate evidence of its (his) intense impression on me. Looking over them now, I am dismayed at the vicious ingenuity, the intellectual vehemence with which I have "defended" myself. There is nothing objective about them; they are pages written in dead earnest—ferocious, jealous, resentful, written by a man with no one looking over his shoulder, least of all himself.

At this point I expect someone to jump up and shout, "Charlatan!" After all, the notebook is only what it is and nothing more, and I never played more of a role in it than that of a backboard and offstage ear; if I was deaf it was my own fault. Be that as it may; Edith has left me, the notebook has become the masochistic consolation Stefan predicted it would, and now these recollections are providing me with a breathing spell; while I apply my weary wits a little more, you will have time to whet your knives.

In early November of that year I received an invitation from a student literary association at Heidelberg, through its acting secretary, Frau Barbara Speer, to pay a visit to that university just before the Christmas holidays and deliver a few informal lectures on *résistance* poetry. I had become acquainted with Frau Speer and her husband Paul in the summer of 1952, when they were camping in Provence, at the manor house of a mutual friend, a well-known expatriate German surrealist. I had liked them both; they were enthusiastic and intelligent young people, and Paul had already established himself as one of the most brilliant young poets of postwar Germany. That was the only opportunity I had to talk with them, however; it came as a severe jolt to read in July of 1954 that Paul Speer had killed himself in Frankfurt, at the age of twenty-seven. If the invitation had come from anyone else I should probably not have accepted, but wishing very much to see Frau Speer again, and finding myself free from more pressing commitments just then, I wrote to her and said I would be happy to come.

The idea to ask Stefan to accompany me on the trip was rather a last-minute impulse, in which I was encouraged (for some reason) by the knowledge that he had not returned to Germany for some years. There was certainly nothing tying him to Paris (come to think of it, I never had the remotest idea how he spent the bulk of his time; I rather suspect he did nothing at all). At first he seemed distrustful about my reasons for inviting him, and he laughed out loud at my not-too-happy suggestion that it might be "good for him" to see Germany again. But the next day he smilingly said that the thought of returning had not brought him *"um den Schlaf,"* and he had decided to accept.

The lectures were a great success, and I renewed my acquaintance with Barbara Speer. She was as delightful as I had remembered her to be, though the shock of Paul's death still plainly showed. She looked tired, but had grown slimmer and more beautiful. With her black coarse hair gathered behind her head, she bore a striking resemblance to Falconetti as Jeanne d'Arc. After her husband's death she had decided to resume her studies, which she had interrupted in 1948, and, leaving her child in the care of her father, had returned to the university.

To make a long story short, I returned to Paris alone. I do not know exactly when Stefan made up his mind to stay on in Germany, but he didn't inform me of his decision until the eve of our departure. I was packing my things when he came into the room, handed me the notebook and said, "You'd better take this with you. It's as complete as it ever will be." When, after a moment, it sank in that he was saying good-bye, I lost my bearings and my temper as well, and I feel a surge of shame even now in recalling my parting words. I accused him of ingratitude, deception, dishonesty, insensitivity and whatever else popped into my head. He stood looking at me during my tirade with an absolutely blank expression that only incensed me all the more. When I finally wound down he said flatly, "I'm sorry, Immanuel," and walked out. A minute later I went to his room, but he was already gone, and I have not seen him since.

From Paris I wrote him a brief letter apologizing for my outburst, but received no answer. When Edith and I married, in February, I wrote again, not sure the letter would find him, and received the following reply:

> Heidelberg
> February 25, 1956

Dear Immanuel,

You will probably never understand why I stayed on here, and I don't expect you to. In any case it wasn't for Germany itself (neither the new nor the old), nor even, in the end, for Barbara, as you might have supposed. No, I just had to. It's all in the notebook.

This has been a period of great external movement—the kind of meaningless, exhausting, surface activity and involvement beneath which an immense sense of anticipation, almost dread takes shape. But I have learned to be patient, to *attend*. I know that something will happen soon: all the clocks are striking twelve.

Be satisfied with what you have of me: wasn't the notebook what you wanted? Obviously not. In any case, I wish you and Edith all possible happiness—truly, from the heart. Not many people live in the same time with each other—and you resemble each other like synchronized watches. . . .

These words, which are also the last communication I have had from him, contained a great truth: Edith and I were synchronized—by our attraction to him. In this sense his poems and the notebook were the "synchronizers," but they were also, ironically enough, the instruments that slowed down the separate, obstinate scales of our two characters at different speeds.

We could never take bearings on each other, only on him, and he was nowhere to be found but in his literary legacies.

Once upon a time (in the Thirties) when I was young and fresh from the university, I determined to collect the experiences and spiritual equipment necessary for an exhaustive understanding of the world and then (a new Descartes!) turn away from it all to reflect on ultimate things. I welcomed the war with open arms: it would be my school of life. But regrettably it was more than I could absorb, and it deferred my ambitions an hour or two too long. As I have remarked elsewhere, I found myself to be "horribly and irrevocably burdened," not so much by the war itself as by the sense of delay and impotence with which it left me. Even the few significant and liberating insights which it afforded gradually dimmed and could not be retained or regained. So I abandoned the dream of a purely reflective life. Oh, I wrote my share of commentaries: mediocre poems and essays, watched my mundane reputation grow by leaps and bounds—and became invisible to myself. I trained my eye on the great shapeless heap of bones and affairs and social furniture known as "France" and began a novel; I should have realized, by the time it entered its fourth volume, that my mind was a mammoth warehouse for *souvenirs perdus* and my book not much more than an expanding, unalphabetized catalogue of them.

An overbearing confidence in my own didactic value led me to Stefan and through him to Edith and then right on over the brink. Now that I am so ready to admit that I do not know how old I am, that such unresolved obsessions as "the war" and "France" no longer make much difference to me, I suddenly understand what he meant by "the only gift." Without it I am the last victim of the notebook, the last scapegoat. I attempted to impose my egotistical, selfish desires on the "freedom of a child," and the loss was mine. He has condemned me to go on fixing freedom in contemplations, elevating its name to an institution. Now only the name remains, and an infallible, empty memory.

But I and my interminable "introduction" are irrelevant twins. My only hope is that in laying these strange pages in the hands of others, I shall perhaps (and only perhaps) have begun to reopen some long-closed windows in myself.

Paris, March 24, 1962

GEORG LOH

Berlin/Dahlem
March 22, 1955

Very respected Frau Speer!

As managing director of the publishing house Loh and Deckeler I am taking the liberty of addressing myself to you with respect to a project we have been contemplating for some time, a project involving the eventual publication of a volume whose contents would be selected from the posthumous works of your husband. Naturally, for the realization of this work your consent and assistance must be regarded as indispensable. Before going into details, I should inform you that I had the great honor of meeting your late husband on numerous occasions, both here and elsewhere, and before his untimely and tragic death (for which you, bearing most intimately the burden of his loss, receive my deepest and most heartfelt sympathies) I had already suggested a collaboration along lines similar to those which I am about to propose, and had met with his enthusiastic approval. Now, regrettably, we can no longer realize exactly the same project, but in another form the undertaking is still feasible, and I am sure that with your most generous co-operation we can redeem even now the larger outlines of the original plan.

What we have in mind is this: to compile a comprehensive group of selections not only from his published works, but from his copious correspondence, critical writings, reviews and radio works as well, to compose a volume which, in its structure and in the fitness of its parts, would render a vital impression of the artist as the living man he was. In other words, if the metaphor is acceptable, a reconstruction in his own words of the intellectual, spiritual and emotional body of Paul Speer. In one of our conversations, I remember, he suggested that, aside from the already extant material, he might provide a number of pieces specifically composed for the volume, writings which would fill out the ultimate impression of himself "in motion" as he put it. But he reacted strongly against the suggestion that the work should contain selections from his poetry, claiming that they would conflict with the image of his person which the book was intended to project. I was slow to concur in this, feeling that the inclusion of certain poems would be essential to the evocation of the *man*. But he remained adamant, maintaining that any single poem is in itself an act presupposing another more indefinable totality, and that, if we were successful, the book itself would emerge as a kind of life poem, in which the inclusion of separate, self-sufficient poems would seem jarring and even redundant. Be this as it may, our discussions were interrupted at this point by his death, and now we must rely on you.

You may feel that this letter represents the purest audacity and presumption on my part; if so, I beg you now to forgive me. But, in my strong belief in the enduring quality of your husband's work and in his unique significance for the present generation, I am willing to take the chance that you will not. Therefore, I am asking you to consider our proposition most carefully—not only as the person closest to Paul Speer during his lifetime, but as the only person who could conceivably help us to bring our plan to fruition. Although the special passages will never be written, I am sure the wealth of material is great enough for valid substitutes to be pieced together, and that you yourself will find yourself bridging the few unfillable gaps with memoirs of your own. It goes without saying that in the assembling of scattered material (especially letters and newspaper articles) we are ready to provide you with all necessary assistance and funds.

This is, I think, already more than enough for a first letter. If you are tempted, as I hope you will be, to respond, please take your own good time and then write us, stating your suggestions and eventual obections; and I shall reply immediately in detail. In the meantime you may be certain that we stand behind you unfalteringly, and that we remain,

With high esteem,
[*signed*] GEORG LOH
Loh and Deckeler

Berlin/Dahlem
February 28, 1956

My dearest Frau Speer!

My partner and I, after having read the first draft of *Zerstückelung,* wish to express our unqualified enthusiasm over your success in having, literally, resuscitated the literary *corpus* of Paul Speer. The unfailing insight and taste which you have shown in your selection and organization are astounding; the work surpasses our every expectation.

As you have given us to know, only one small portion is still missing from the book as it stands—a kind of heading to the principal divisions of the volume. If we have understood correctly, this appendage is to be drawn from your husband's private correspondence in large part, and will be handled by you in such a manner as to penetrate the most intimate recesses of your marriage. We do not doubt that such a device will be capable of generating a deep understanding of your husband's development. What excites us even more, however, is the thought that, in your introduction of the part under consideration, you may have come upon a potent means of describing the creative process itself. Such an act of editorial manipulation, a coupling of your feminine sensibility with the straightforward masculine drive of the artist, as it were, will we feel be altogether unique in a publication of this sort, and we are eagerly awaiting its culmination, now that the bulk of the manuscript is in our hands.

Our representative in Frankfurt, Herr Feigeblatt, has been instructed to make all arrangements for your journey to Berlin by air, and to await your call for reservations. We have honored your request for double accommodation, and are looking forward to seeing both you and your assistant before the end of March, with the outstanding section in hand. Again, our heartiest congratulations! As ever, we remain,

> With all best wishes, your
> [*signed*] GEORG LOH
> Loh and Deckeler

PAUL SPEER

Because of the rapid editing and the underexposure of many shots, the theater is filled with a succession of short bursts of light. Paul Speer's face, in close-up, begins to take on continuity in this bombardment and to become a kind of borrowed montage itself. He is like a slow-motion portrait of a blond trench soldier, or a distant witness to a fire-raid, his fictitious expression abstracted in flashes from the surface of an underlying process of response.

Whose memory of war is this, for whom a reminder? Who experienced it this way—what soldier, what prisoner, what enemy, what refugee, what observer, what child? Perhaps it isn't possible, not possible at all, to comprehend even the slightest aspect, the smallest facet of the war. But we try.

Are we attracted by its horrible beauty? Do we preserve it for its mutilations, loving the recollection of pain?

Certainly, if this is how we choose to recall it, if this is what we think it was, if this is able to excite us, to move us to pity,

or turn our stomachs in instants of optical delight, demanding
acquiescence to the thrill; if this is the only way we can recall:
Then we haven't understood a thing.
We have felt nothing.
We have suffered nothing.
We have shared nothing.
And the dead are twice dead—absurd statistical sacrifices of
an unfathomable catastrophe, and victims of our obsessive con-
science and unpitiable forgetfulness.
Who will make the dead articulate, who can make himself
an organ for their voices?

> —*Zerstückelung: The Posthumous Papers
> of Paul Speer*, edited by Barbara Speer
> (Berlin: Loh and Deckeler, 1956), p. 225.

From a letter to E——— C———, dated June 9, 1954:

. . . Some single images in such a documentary film have far
more meaning for me than the entire film, contain much more
of the *essence* of war than the crazy panoply of an invasion or
the magnificent theatrical display of a battle at sea. It is as if
the incomprehensible breadth of the war as a whole, as a phenomenon—all the diffused light, all the fragments of obscenity
and stupidity and cruelty, and thoughtlessness, and irrationality
—had been concentrated for an instant in one tiny action: in
the movement of a hand, the twitch of a foot, the marvelous
uselessness of a corpse, the absurd, incongruous remnants of
family life strewn in the rubble, sprouting like weeds, too easily
recognized. The doll, the piano opened like a can, the toilet
without walls, the crude orchestration of plumbing—any one of
these or a million other flashes of *truth* has the mysterious
power to imprint itself upon us indelibly. But these epic sermons
built of them for our *pleasure*, literate though they may well be,
still tell the lies of art. . . .
Every image is a symbol of the whole, *for* the whole: a kind

of window to the abyss which is in us as well as outside of us; its surface detail, its opacity, are devoid of deeper meaning. And yet we seem to enjoy cataloguing such externals. Their ineffable fingers tease our eyes, but seldom seem to leave a lasting impression or call forth a strong response. Perhaps no single picture is potent enough, immediate or pregnant enough, so openly *transcendent*, that it can strike us blind with its light, and deliver once and for all an ineradicable message not to the eyes but to the heart, or the ear, or the body that endures. . . .

Finally we stand dumbly before our little pictures, as before the altars of minor deities. And these idols that come to signify only themselves are worshiped eventually as tokens of truth itself. We carry snapshots of the dead, amulets of fidelity, lockets with hair in them, and think them to be proofs of immortality, credentials for our memory, magical expiations of a guilt exiled to time. (The eye does not partake of time!)

We know that we are lying, though; that's the awful thing about it. And we go on lying, by mutual consent. It is not because we are constructed in such a way that we cannot admit that we are lying, either. We simply tolerate our weaknesses—because we *want to*. We employ our eyes as props for self-deception which need be no deception at all, as stilts for comfortable cowardice. We use them shamelessly to convince ourselves that we are earnest seekers after truth, when what we really want to do is make our lies legitimate, perpetuate them. So we line our pictures end to end, string images and trinkets together, concocting apologies, wording hypocritical pleas for innocence. On the other side of the epic, we think, on the other side of history, *Schicksal* and Faustian will—*there* we will be blessed, *there* the truth will comfort us, *there* we will be made strong and there time will have an end and we will be all eyes: in the final fabrication of Art, in the ultimate rationalization of Murder. And we will all *forgive ourselves* at once . . .

—*Ibid.*, pp. 228–29.

Scribbled on his desk calendar, June 10, 1954, three weeks before his suicide:

Ah me, if I took things so seriously, my heart would stop.

ALBERT OESTLER

The door opens and Professor Albert Oestler strides in; the auditorium explodes with the pounding of knuckles on desks. He slaps his papers down on the lectern, dips in his pocket for his glasses, slips them on with one hand while spreading his papers with the other, peers over the lenses at his audience, clears his throat in a sudden silence, hears it echoed by a vagrant cough, and begins to speak in a vertical, improbably deep, soft voice to the first three rows or so. After a moment someone in the back shouts, "Louder!" Oestler glances up nervously, then looks back down and continues in an only slightly more projected voice:

"Yet, as soon as a genius, or rather the awareness of his presence, has taken root in the subsoil of the German mind, the singularity of his thought begins to be domesticated and hybridized. The potted plant that results [*laughter*] continues to bear the name of its exotic parent, its cultivation is proprietary and its handling reverent, but biologically speaking, the mutation can only be described as atavistic [*laughter*]. What we want to dote upon, we first demean. Such hybrids, despite their occasional sentimental utility, are not so much the products of a native curiosity or imagination as of our inescapable desire for order and tractability. [*Another "Louder!"*] In fact, our fondness for such conservative *varieties* of genius, and our pride in their prolification under our care, enable us to attribute to them a peculiar indigenous character. In other words, our rare flowerings, after being converted into marketable varieties on our own

acreage, somehow inspire us to take the credit for the individua-
tion of the original blossom as well. . . ."

*He is a small man with white hair and a deeply lined face. He has
a clean flat overlip that opens and shuts like a flatiron on a
heavy lower one. He is impatient for the hour to go by; he is
(already) in dire need of a cigarette (Overstolz filter); he is
eager for the semester to pass; he is behind schedule on the
proofs of his new book (The Twelve-Year Millennium) and has
been appointed an examiner in this session as well. The truth
is, he would like the whole academic year to be over; he has a
sabbatical leave of six months coming up (a concession wrung
with blood from the university upon his return to Germany in
1952 after seventeen years abroad) and he is full of projects
that simply have to wait.*

". . . Nietzsche, for all his anti-German outbursts, was nevertheless one of *our* geniuses [*titters*]. He was also, unwillingly, the
prodigal prophet of our recent national behavior. But insofar
as he himself proposed the ideational means by which he *would*
be misconstrued, and understood perfectly well the likelihood
if not the virtual certainty of our abuse, he must regrettably
bear a large degree of responsibility, through his own *practical
irresponsibility*, for what occurred, in spite of his philosophical
efforts to anticipate and deflect misinterpretations. He could
never excuse himself for having been born a German—but he
was, and it was useless and perhaps unbecomingly naïve of him
to expect his countrymen to accept his critiques and insights on
his terms. He too had to be (and was) grafted onto the trunk
of the very *ethos* he found so distasteful, before he could be
appreciated by them . . ."

*Last month he and his wife allowed their American citizenship
to lapse. They are planning to build a lodge near Lake Como
and settle there after his retirement in five years. He will be
sixty in May (he is already dreading the inevitable homage of*

*a torchlight procession to his doorstep). He lost a lung in 1917,
studied under both Hermann Cohen and Max Weber, married
Helga von Herzog in 1923 and has no children. To date he has
published seven books (six in German and one in English) and
something like thirty monographs. He is a regular contributor
to the* Neue Deutsche Rundschau.

". . . perhaps the most subtle and delicate of all. But . . . he
[Hölderlin] was damned from the outset by the absence of the
rarified habitat he needed in order to flourish. This incredible
orchid withered almost instantly in our damp atmosphere,
lately known as bourgeois; his present namesake is a livid pine
whose wood is fit only for the building of coffins and the carv-
ing of Bavarian crucifixes.

"Both Hölderlin and Nietzsche, unlike as they were, suffered
the same recent fate at our hands: their great exfoliating visions
were slowly, painstakingly reduced to the seeds of national con-
formity and ground into the meal of propaganda. Fertilized by
epidemic death and unrest, by resentment and unaccepted guilt,
by the wild vacillations of an uprooted conscience, by the over-
simple distillations of manifest national destiny and racial voca-
tion from the arrogant, shoreless optimism of the Germanizers
of the nineteenth century, and by the malodorous specifics of
fanatical medicine men and preachers of disaster—fed by these,
the monstrous derivative spores sprouted wildly, invading the
cracks in the liberal intellect, infesting the popular mind, gradually darkening every window, tangling every access to the outside—until, from the wasted mind of 1921, the dark wood of
1929 sprang up, and the impassable jungle of 1933 . . ."

*He spent the middle Thirties in Switzerland, lecturing and com-
piling the material for his comprehensive study of Nietzsche
and Burckhardt. In 1938 he was offered the post of European
Rector at a famous Japanese university. He and his wife remained there for three years, without attempting to learn a*

single Zen art, without eating a single piece of raw fish. They
reached New York on a freighter in the late summer of 1941.
He is a disappointed poet and passionate amateur gardener; the
happiest days of his life were spent gentleman-farming a small
piece of land near Hartford, Connecticut, during the war.

". . . These 'mountain men,' these peasant ascetics and pseudo-
mystical revolutionaries plied the roots of our deepest instincts,
stimulated our most primitive emotions and inhibited our
rational compass so surely, so intuitively, so imperceptibly, that
they succeeded in metamorphosing the very body of Germany
without that body's becoming aware that it was undergoing a
complete intestinal permutation.

"Let us not be so misguided or dishonest as to repeat the
self-excusing lie that these men were *not really* German, either;
National Socialism was a *generic* tendency, a subnational dis-
position, long before it became a political fact—*here*. Its mate-
rializers confirmed their calling on the Western Front, under-
went their apprenticeship in Munich under the tutelage of
such occult 'scientists' as Horbiger and Haushofer, and were
initiated into the mysteries of hermetic biology and religious
agronomy in the Tibetan hothouse of Berlin [*murmurs*]. Europe
ceased to exist for them, if it ever had. From the moment of
their supposed enlightenment, they *assumed* the body of Germany; when they looked out of it, all they could see was a
virginal *Urboden* which Germany, by divine right of auto-
catharsis, was destined to populate and farm according to a
ritual plan that ultimately would lead to deification. The tele-
ological die of Germany, so to speak, was cast not by the . . ."

The bell rings: he hesitates until it stops and then finishes his
sentence hurriedly. The thunder of desk-knocking resumes. He
scoops up his papers with one hand and removes his glasses with
the other. He moves rapidly to the door and opens it; two hun-
dred students rise almost simultaneously, two hundred wooden

seats clatter upright. He steps out and to one side, and the students begin to pour out. He gropes for a cigarette, thrusts it in his mouth with a jerky, nervous motion and lights up with relief.

He seems to be waiting for someone.

RIGHT PANEL

WINTER SOLSTICE

This is Baermann's anniversary. He is wearing a black hat with a narrow brim and has just attached his new gold watch chain. He is fifty-two years old and looks sixty-five. *Grüss Gott!* said Baermann's landlady (now dead) on Christmas Eve 1935, after having shown the Gestapo to his room ten minutes before. *Grüss Gott!* replied Baermann, unsuspecting, thirty-two years old that day. Why does he wander abroad tonight? He is celebrating.

In a few moments now a middle-aged, innocent burgher is going to say *Grüss Gott!* to Professor Ignatz Baermann of the Theological Seminary, and the good professor, a little tipsy, is going to knock him down. He will spend the night in jail, but he doesn't mind. Something of the sort has happened every year for the last ten, and always on his birthday. You might say that Baermann is a glutton for punishment. Don't.

HESPERIDES

Stefan's Christmas tree shoots arrows out of hearts and closes initials with new bark. These three golden apples are fancy candles: you light the stems, they spit with flame, unraveling in threads of citric smoke.

BAGGAGE / FIRST DREAM

Stefan and someone else (Immanuel?) carry the empty suitcases back to the shop. Orange suitcases. They tell the man they don't like them. (They seem full all of a sudden.) Make us others. They *both* think: We can pay, and they turn to each other and nod. The man looks at Stefan, who blushes, and tells them how pleased he is that they can pay. Stefan realizes that the man is holding a huge pink hog on a string. Its flesh is alive and hairless, *almost* human. From this animal he will make their new bags, he doesn't have to say so. But is the hog large enough? Instantly it seems larger—and somehow *innocent*. Its skin ceases to be its own, but has not yet accrued to the bags; it quivers faintly. An affective shudder: tender, separable flesh. The man leads the animal to a large washtub brim-full of water, and opens a tap above it. A tinny-looking rod of water appears and moves slowly down to the surface of the water in the tub, entering it without agitation. The hog stretches its (no, *his*) snout to drink from the metallic stream. Stefan notices only at this moment how long and pointed the nose is. The throat, the jowls, pull taut; they seem incredibly smooth, not like skin at all. With some sort of small instrument the man begins to tap the pig's neck in several places, as if testing it. All this is soundless. He finds the "right" spot and begins to beat a delicate rhythm on it with the tool. The slaughter of the animal is imminent; Stefan knows and feels a sensation of sexual contraction, of involuntary regret. The man resembles a glass cutter rapping the underside of a pane; the pig begins to bleed, but goes on drinking. Stefan is *aware* all of a sudden that the animal is dead, even though the image contradicts him; no sound, the snout still thrust into the fine stream of tinny water, drops of blood like beads falling *tick-tick-tick* into the tub. He asks himself, Is this how dying looks? and feels that something is terribly wrong. But the method seems indisputable. He wakes up.

SNOW IN POMPEII

One briquet still sits unused; Stefan hesitates to put it on the fire, though it is all but out and the room has grown horribly cold. The water in the pitcher on the bureau is tempted with ice: a skin of cellophane. He sits and chews his tongue. A year ago it was the tinkle of fleurs-de-lis, belled Catholics. Now it is the heavy soles of Lutherans. The streets have emptied in a white epidemic, snow falls upon the ruins of the three-weeks' apocalypse: dead dolls, mangers, knives, thorns, needles, mistletoe and holly, glass balls, black hunks of stalled traffic. Sighs of organs, the town still trembling with churches. He climbs out of bed and shivering throws on his clothes to go out. Barbara will be back from Hanau this time tomorrow.

CHRIST'S CIRCUMCISION

Look: Immanuel's feet are trapped on a snow escalator. It carries him up, up until his footprints disappear. Smoothly, irreversibly. The steel teeth accept him: his flesh caresses gears. Cogs of snow are diving . . . Immanuel skiing . . . a soft descent of hair. ("My God!" said Barbara Speer at the pre-Christmas ball in the *Schloss*. "He pretends to be a poet and he dances like an elephant! Poets are supposed to have rhythm!")

DON JUAN GOES DOWN TO THE DINING ROOM

It is almost ten, the meal was heavy, their brains are marinating. Little popcorn bursts of conversation, the flak of laughter. Wilma Frobenius's smile has palsied, her eyes seem even closer together than usual: the first eighth of wine dizzied her, the second intoxicated her completely. Now she is exercising caution. Richard Frobenius has a dead pipe in his mouth, is wearing the vaguely superior, bemused look that goes with it, and nods frequently or chuckles; a thin red scar on his forehead wriggles like a worm among the furrows. Barbara is gay, not quite convincingly so: her eyes are too bright. Stefan has been studying her all evening, but even though he has recognized the effort expended in her air of lightness, he is unable to move behind the hard façade of her sociability: there is something in her volubility that has an edge to it.

The door opens. Stefan, who is sitting with his back to it, sees Barbara look up, across the table. She smiles brightly and waves. "D–J!" Everyone looks to see.

A Negro, obviously American, has just come in. He is about thirty-five, slight in build, rather handsome (à la John Gilbert). He has a tiny mustache and is wearing a Harris tweed overcoat and a pork-pie hat. He shuffles toward their table with a grin like a headlight.

"*Guten Abend,*" he says.

"Stefan," says Barbara, "this is Daniel Jeremiah Wanamaker. D-J, I'd like you to meet Stefan Brückmann."

"How d'you do," says D-J. "Yeah."

Stefan, half-rising, offers his hand. "Hello," he says.

"You know Richard Frobenius," says Barbara. They exchange nods. "But I don't believe you've ever met his wife Wilma." Wilma extends her hand: "*Es freut mich.*"

"Likewise," says D-J Wanamaker, looking her over and giving her up simultaneously.

"You don't look German to me, man," says D-J to Stefan, sitting down next to him.

"I am, though," replies Stefan. "Himmler nationalized me and Bonn upheld it."

By some act of magic a lighted cigar appears in D-J's mouth. He offers one to Stefan, who shakes his head politely ("Smoked too much already"), and one to Frobenius ("Havana": "Ach, Havana!"), who lays aside his pipe, accepts the cigar, smells it appreciatively, bites off the tip and lights it.

"Any luck?" asks Barbara, in English and in a teasing tone.

D-J laughs. "One hundred per cent," he declares. "Orin and Rudy still don't believe it, but they'll see, come spring. Those jealous jerks don't believe a thing I tell 'em."

D-J turns to Stefan. "You staying for long?"

"Could be."

"You're a German but you don't live in Germany."

"Not lately," replies Stefan. "Where are you from in the States?"

"Me? I'm from all over. I was born in Mobile, Alabammy, but I grew up in Chicago. You been there? Chicago, I mean."

Stefan nods. "Once. I passed through Mobile, too. Just in time for the tail-end of a big Gypsy wedding."

D-J regards him with a curious skepticism. "Yeah? Well I got other memories of that place."

"D-J's come here to study," says Barbara, in a faintly sardonic tone of voice.

D-J looks sharply at her and shows his teeth for an instant before he laughs. "You bet; the female sex."

Richard Frobenius rises to his feet and prods Wilma, who jumps. "It's getting a little late for us," he says. "Can we drive anybody home?"

No. They shake hands all round, and leave.

Nobody speaks for a moment. Then: "There's no reason for us to keep sitting here," says Barbara. "Why don't we move on to my place for some coffee? It's not that late."

"I'll be shoving off, then," says D-J, getting up.

"No, you come too," says Barbara quickly, almost commandingly. Stefan glances at her.

D-J shifts his feet and smiles with closed mouth. "All right. I got a little while, I guess."

Barbara seems relieved; she throws a sideward look at Stefan (who pretends he hasn't been watching her) and stands. "Whew!" she says, and titters nervously. "I didn't realize I'd drunk so much."

PRINTED MATTER

Barbara lives in a long, narrow, high-ceilinged room on the ground floor of a late-nineteenth-century house in the Bunsenstrasse. A single tall window at the back opens on to a nondescript courtyard with one neglected nut tree; she keeps it shuttered all day and opens it only on those rather mysterious evenings when the organ-grinder comes. The room is made even narrower by the bookshelves (bricks and boards) along one side; they are crammed with most of what is left of Paul Speer's library (out of fifteen hundred volumes, fewer than three hundred remain): a few relatively new art books with Swiss plates; an unassorted pile of reviews and periodicals and pamphlets, chipped and yellowing; a hand-bound volume of collages and miniatures that was a gift from Max Ernst; the complete series of *Die Brücke*; the 1920 edition of Pinthus's *Menschheitsdämmerung*; a first edition of Ariosto; an illustrated limited edition of *Ubu Roi* (Barbara wears the tiny spiral pin of the Pataphysicians); autographed copies of works by Artaud, Eluard, Breton, René Char, Pound, Gottfried Benn, Ernst Robert Curtius; a few copies of the three issues of *Bruchstücke* which she and Paul published in 1950 and 1951; various first publications of Paul's German contemporaries, all with virtually the same dedication: "To Paul Speer, without whose help and encouragement . . ."; four copies of the issue of *Die Tat* which contains Curtius's full-page appreciation of the new publication; six packets of letters to Paul, and four loose-leaf binders containing originals and photocopies of his own letters to various persons, lent by their possessors to Barbara for her use in compiling the posthumous volume for Loh and Deckeler; books that she herself has accumulated in the past year or so: odd issues of the *N.N.R.F.*, the *Neue Deutsche Rundschau, Preuves, Black Mountain Review, Perspectives, Partisan Review*, a folio of silk-screen poem prints recently sent her by Kenneth Patchen, *The Pisan Cantos, Four Quartets, Ulysses, Tropic of Capricorn, Le Mur, Women in Love, Les Bonnes, Journal du Voleur, En attendant Godot, Die Kirschen der Freiheit, Fragebogen*, and an East German edition of *Caspar Hauser* . . .

BLACK TOBACCO

Stefan and D-J are lodged like two pashas in mounds of pastel-colored pillows on Barbara's bed (which is otherwise hard as a slab: shortly after Paul's suicide she slipped and fell, suffering a slight injury to her back). Barbara is seated in one of the two folding chairs near the radiator. She has put on her dark-green pullover (wary of drafts: the back persists); her face is pale and sagging a little, but she does not want to sleep. The room is thick with the smoke of cigars and Gitanes; outside it has begun to rain; heavy drops of slush on the lids of garbage pails. It is well after midnight.

Stefan explodes with laughter.

"That's disgusting!" cries Barbara. "Useless cruelty! Why do you brag about it?"

"How it was, though," says D-J. "And that's nothing. Did I ever tell you about the time we—"

"No, and I don't want to hear about it, either," says Barbara emphatically.

"Oh come on," says Stefan. "He doesn't expect us to believe him."

"It's the gospel truth!" D-J retorts, his eyes bulging with sincerity.

"So much the worse for you, then!" cries Barbara. "There are lots of other things we could talk about than the war, especially your version of it."

D-J folds his arms and shrugs; Stefan suddenly bursts out laughing; Barbara frowns. "What's so funny?" she asks. He stops laughing and looks at her. They all sit; a gutter spills over outside. "It's not that grisly story about the tramp on a bicycle, is it?" Barbara asks, beginning to waver.

"No," says D-J. "It's not. It's a true story about the end of the war . . ."

THE BURGOMEISTER'S DAUGHTER AT
THE END OF THE WAR

"I guess it must of been along about March or April and we were taking ten villages or so without resistance, most days. Once in a while some crazy fool'd take a potshot at us, but everybody was inclined to be real apologetic when that happened. All you had to do was drive in in your tank and sit there in the middle of the *Hopped-plots* and look mean, till the infantry caught up a couple a hours later. That was the textbook way of capturing a town, or got to be. But this p'ticular town was different, they told me I wasn't just supposed to take it, I was supposed to *occupy* it too, for a while, until they could shift some troops from some other sector to come in and do the job. Now it shouldna been my job in the first place, but I was 'way off ahead and on my own more or less, and that All-American ass-hole Withington got jealous and decided that was as good a way as any to tie me down. Anyway, this town was just a little dump not too far from *By-wrought*, which as a matter of fact I captured too (yes, but no music) one week later. The Germans had pulled out lock stock 'n barrel to regroup a few miles back; this town had been a supply place, but the soldiers there was all S.S., according to our intelligence. There wasn't much of a chance of them coming back, but it wouldn't of been no trouble for one of 'em to sneak back with a bazooka or for any local people who got it into their heads to do something foolish to give us some trouble if they knew one tank was all there was likely to be for a few days, and I was damned if I was going to have myself or my crew suffocate in that tin can like a sitting duck waiting for them doughboys to show their face, no sir. But orders is orders, and so I figured we had just better make some kind of strong impression on those people and put a little bit of organization into our occupation, I mean make good 'n sure they knew they were occupied and we hadn't just dropped in for the scenery or for them to have a chance to play he-ro.

"Well when we drove in they already knew we were coming, so they had a welcoming committee all picked out and waiting lined up in the *Hopped-plots* in their Sunday clothes. Theyda been carrying flowers if they thought they could get away with it. *Naturally* there wasn't a swastika anywhere to be seen, you coulda looked till kingdom come for one. Same thing with pictures of Hitler—*who's he? Oh, we got a picture of Bismarck in the schoolhouse, sir, and that ole man there, he's got a autographed picture of the Kaiser in his bureau draw, but Hitler? Who dat? Not us, oh no, not us.*

"Well, I told my boys to keep a close eye on their ole daddy and to point the turret gun at the church tower and then I climbed down with a submachine gun slung across my arm and sauntered up to that welcoming committee. All right, I said, who's the burgomeister here? and the fattest one stepped out of the line in leather short pants and said I am, and started to rattle off something in German a mile a minute until I put on my best Chicago smile and said, That will do, you speak English? A little, he said. Soldiers? I asked, and he looked real surprised, like he'd never even heard the word before this very minute. So I repeated myself, saying I didn't like to have to, and he made a motion with his hands like somebody running, which was supposed to mean they were far, far away by this time. Okay, I said, where's your house? At first he pretended he didn't understand, he put on a big smile and woulda come up closer if he dared, but instead he just stood there rocking back and forth and smiling, until I moved in and screamed in his face: I asked you where's your house? Well, he and his cronies went into a quick huddle and then he came back and said in pretty good English, We have quarters already prepared for you in the schoolhouse, sir.

"Now I'm no fool. I gave him a poke in the belly with my gun barrel and I said very sweetly, That's all very nice of you, I'm sure you got my interests at heart, but I think maybe it hasn't entered your mind, *mein Hair*, that as of right now *I* am the burgomeister of this crummy town, and as such I naturally expect to live in my own house. I let them buzz that over till it'd sunk in and then said, And I wouldn't like to think there was anybody who objected. Well, a thin man with blond hair and a long scar on his face stepped out of line and said But—so I knocked him down with my fist, and that was my first act as burgomeister. In no time flat I was on my way to my house with the welcoming committee leading the way, my Sherman right behind me, and everybody in town lined up and quiet as a mouse on both sides of the street.

"When we got there there was a good-looking girl about twenty-five standing on the front steps, all quivery and puckered up to get hysterical if she got half a chance. She latched on to the fat man, who turned out to be her father, and he must of told her he was now the ex-burgomeister, because when we got inside she ran up to me and started squawking like a chicken. There wasn't much I goddam well could do but give her a little slap to shut her up. I didn't like to, but anything else'd've been a waste of time. Her ole man got red enough to burn up, like he was about to have a stroke, he was an old guy and full of beer. If he'd of had a gun, he'd of killed me, that's for sure, he just couldn't stand the idea that he had to do his little part in losing the war. So I kept that gun very carefully between me and him and started looking around. What's this door here? I asked. It's my study, he said. Well you don't touch a thing in it, I said, 'cause I may just want to do some studying myself. How many bedrooms you got? Two, he said and I knew he was all set to lie about everything, so I stopped asking questions. We all trooped upstairs and I made him point out four bedrooms. Open the door to this one, I said, and he kind of hesitated and said, There's someone in there, so I kicked it open. There was a young fellow about the same age as the girl lying on the bed in his underwear. He didn't have legs from the knees on down. He was scared shitless, he started babbling in German, which the ex-burgomeister answered. I asked what'd he say, and he said, he asked who you are and what do you want. Well I hope you told him I'm the new burgomeister and this is my bedroom, I said.

"Listen here, said the ex-burgomeister, and about that time I blew my stack. God damn it all to hell, I said, I'm just about out of patience with you people. *You* listen to *me*: I'd be packing if I was you, because you got exackly *five minutes* to clear out of this house, and if you're not out when those five minutes are up, I'm gonna start reducing the population of this village.

"All this time the young fellow on the bed was putting on his artificial legs. As soon as he had 'em on he walked up to me and said in very good English: What are we permitted to take with us? I was so het up I guess I expected trouble from him too, but here he was talking like he had some sense, which would've made him the only one so far. But just at this moment who should come tearing in but the girl. She let out another one of those godawful shrieks of hers and threw herself around the young guy's neck. He said something to her and she calmed down a little and stared at me with blood in her eye. Meanwhile, the ex-burgomeister had got started off on another tack, telling me a mile a minute this was his son-in-law and he'd lost his legs in Russia and this girl was his daughter, which I already had figured out for myself and this was their room and he didn't care so much about himself but as a soldier myself I would understand what it was like to lose your legs and surely I wouldn't put a disabled veteran out on the street. I let him run on like that just long enough for me to get good and pissed off all over again—I could see my little occupation going down the drain—and then I said, I'm very touched but you got just one minute left, so if you got clothes or personal effects you want to take with you, you'd damn well better be collecting 'em.

"Just then one a my boys called up from the street: Cap'n are you all right up there? and I started over to the window to say yes, when that crazy girl made a dash at me. If she hadn't been so eager to dig my eyes out, she coulda grabbed the gun out of my hands, I was pretty careless. As it was she had just enough time to lay open my face with her fingernails (I still got a scar here, see?) before I clouted her one with the gunstock and laid her out cold. Everybody gasped and took a step toward me, but stopped when they saw that gun leveled on them. For about half a second I was going to kill 'em all, I'd been killing people for a year without letup just about, and it woulda been easy. But that passed, and when they all saw how close they'd come to getting killed, couple of 'em almost passed out. The young guy had gone down on the floor next to his wife, she was all right, already beginning to come around. Anyway, suddenly he looked up at me and said in German, but I understood: *You African swine*, in a real empty voice. Now here's the funny thing: I can't tell you what that mighta provoked me to do before that, I'd a cut that man to pieces. But all of a sudden it got to be just too much in the opposite way: it made me want to laugh out loud. So I walked over to him and said, Say it again, *Superman*. And you know what? he *blushed*, I swear he blushed, and his lips kind of quivered, and he shook his head. The thought passed through my mind to make him take off his artificial legs and crawl out of the house, but it was only a thought, and I'm glad I didn't, now, though then I could just as well've done it as not.

"That's all. They left, and I didn't have no trouble at all for the five days it took the doughboys to get there. And that's how I occupied that town."

THE PRINCESS AND THE PEA

Stefan and Barbara are lying side by side, naked. Stefan is smoking and staring at the ceiling. Barbara props herself up on her elbow beside him. "You're not the first since Paul," she says.

He laughs. "Why tell me?"

"I wanted you to know, that's all. I don't want you to think I'm someone I'm not. It hasn't been easy."

"No," he says. "I don't suppose it has."

"You're the only one I've told."

"Why?"

"I don't know—I don't like confessions."

He glances at her.

"I mean, I don't like to have to explain things when there's nothing to explain."

"Can I just ask you something?" he asks with an odd smile.

"Yes . . ."

"You're not afraid of falling in love with me, are you?"

She reddens and frowns and drops her head down on to his chest, to hide.

He makes her look at him again. "We'll have to watch out for that, won't we?" he says.

DOWN BY THE LEVEE

Stefan finally has a proper room—in a private house near the old bridge, overlooking the river. He got it through D-J, who popped into Oleo's Eisdiele this afternoon sporting stovepipe boots, jodhpurs, tweed jacket with leather elbows and a riding crop. He has joined the Ziegelhausen Riding Club. He was about to go for coffee at his landlady's and asked Stefan to come along.

The house is an old one, and set so close to the river that the ground floor is flooded once every couple of years when the river overflows its banks. As a result, the downstairs rooms can be safely rented only during the winter season—and come the deluge, even the people upstairs are obliged to take to row-boats to get in and out of the house. No one seems to mind; this calculated risk lends the place a romantic air which it certainly would not possess otherwise, and Frau Isenfels (Brigitte to some) never has much trouble keeping it rented.

Brigitte's own apartment commands a view of the stairs lead-ing up to the first floor, where D-J and Stefan have rooms on either side of the kitchen (with "cooking privileges"). There are three other students in the house: two on the second floor and one in the garret. The second-floor occupants shared the coffee invitation; the young man is a *stud. phil.* named Thorwald von Berg; *das Fräulein heisst* Liselotte Wolfenbüttel and is immersed in Romance languages. The fellow in the attic, described with some disdain by his *Kommilitonen* as a "perennial student," is named Reinhardt Gerstenmaier, and was not on hand for coffee (though he would have been if his rent had been paid).

Brigitte herself is about fifty, and twice a widow (first husband Otto Flügel fell under a locomotive in 1932; number two, Karl-Heinz Isenfels, met the same fate under a tank at Tobruk ten years later). Beneath a certain surface weepiness, Frau (*Witwe*) Isenfels is an emotional ox. She has eyes for D-J, and only D-J; he primes her like a pump and she weeps and laughs joyously while he pulls her leg. Their conversation (if you can call it that) is in an unknown dialect of German: a kind of guttural snowball fight. But look: she sits and inhales loudly the odor of his manhood (Thorwald embarrassed, Liselotte languishing); anyone else would wake up one day and discover he had bitten off more than he could chew. Not D-J. He has perfume to spare and a cast-iron stomach.

PAUL / ONE

"The first time I ever set eyes on him was in the autumn of 1947. It was my first semester here, and his fourth, and one day he happened to sit down directly in front of me in *Hörsaal* 10. I fell in love with the back of his head. Don't laugh, I really did, I couldn't stop staring at it, I didn't hear a word of the lecture. His head was perfect, it was *separate* from the nape, and long from back to front, and beautifully balanced, *posed* so delicately on his neck. (I can't stand people whose heads grow straight out of the back of their necks!) About halfway through the lecture he must have felt my eyes on him; he began to squirm. Suddenly he turned round and looked at me, half irritated; I blushed and averted my eyes. But when he turned back to the front I went right back to boring holes in his beautiful head until I had got him to turn round again, blushing this time himself and compressing his lips in a deprecating smile.

"He was waiting for me when I came out; I would've died if he hadn't been. He smiled the same tight-lipped smile as before and asked me, Well, what's the verdict, Fräulein? Do I need a haircut?—and laughed, and I laughed too.

"Pretty soon we were spending every hour out of class together (he was studying philology, I was in the Anglistics department); we took long walks, no matter what the weather, or sat for hours holding hands across the oak-topped tables of a dozen *Stuben*, telling our lives, sharing secrets. He was innocent and enthusiastic and nervous; he told me he had never met a girl he could spend more than five minutes with before. He was a virgin. I wasn't, I'd had a little—adventure I guess you'd say—during my labor service in the summer of 1944, when I was not quite seventeen. It was weeks before the idea ever crossed his mind that he was in love. As for me, I wanted him from the first moment I set eyes on him; it got so bad I couldn't sleep. And I could feel him tremble when I touched him, too; and when he kissed he shook all over, like a young boy. . . ."

TRISTAN

Reinhardt Gerstenmaier, attic inhabitant, is encountered for the first time as Stefan is carrying his suitcases up to his room.

On the stairs they hesitate and nod to each other, but do not speak.

Gerstenmaier has a fine head, Schilleresque, just made to be buried in some white and heaving, heavenly bosom. A long thin face with quivering nostrils and a deep groove on his upper lip and thick converging eyebrows that lean on each other like the sides of a fur tent. (The flaps turn back to permit a quick glance into the docile gray obscurity of the interior, where a tiny flickering fire of twigs smolders but throws no shadows.)

THE PARTRIDGE

For the first time in almost a year Freddie Bühler swings into Oleo's Eisdiele. A storm of voices greets him; a broad smile lights up his face. His right leg is missing below the knee (bomb, Hamburg, 1943: he was fifteen then), the trouser leg is neatly doubled and pinned to his side pocket, he uses hand crutches. He is wearing a short duffel coat, unbuttoned, and a soggy felt hat that makes him look at least thirty-five.

His eyes light on Barbara; he waves to her to be patient (a lordly gesture, since she is anything but impatient to see him), makes a triumphal tour of the other tables and returns to where she is sitting with Stefan. They stop talking and look up at him. He takes off his hat and coat (underneath, a short-sleeved shirt and sleeveless pullover, muscular forearms) and sits down, looking much younger. He has ash-blond hair and a reddish face with conflicting blue eyes. He shakes Stefan's hand and turns to Barbara, who smiles politely; she seems a little wary of him. Without being asked, he immediately launches into a full description of his travels in the last six months: an odyssey from London to Trieste in the role of tourist guide to an American couple. As he rattles on he keeps twisting about and waving to people, or glancing uneasily at the door, and lighting a chain of cigarettes (Camels), each of which he only half smokes before lighting the next. Barbara is growing restive: Freddie is relating something about a night in Pigalle with the husband, a crisis, a fight with the wife (Amsterdam?), she is slipping into his bed on every possible occasion (Stefan purses his lips and looks a little pained), and the husband is pretending, but only pretending, not to care (Lausanne? Milan?), but actually biding his time, looking for an opportunity to do him (Freddie) dirty (Barbara motions to Frau Riegel) and in Trieste (at last!) accusations, police, the wife runs away, money is owed to Freddie, the man has a gun in the glove compartment (Frau Riegel comes; Stefan has change ready), the wife is suddenly back, loves them both (hates them both) and more police (Freddie lets out a whoop as a tall blonde comes through the door) and the money question remains unsolved (Barbara and Stefan rise as one) and . . . (Good night) here is Freddie, broke and back in town!

PAUL / TWO

"I made it happen: I seduced him; he didn't know what was happening. Afterward I spent the night with him, in his room . . . he was like a baby, docile and nervous . . . so nervous! . . . yet he hurt me, as if it were the first time.

"The next morning we could hear his landlady puttering about in the hall. We made love again—twice—our hearts pounding away at the slightest sound from outside. At about eleven the landlady (I can't remember her name) knocked on the door and said she had fresh sheets for the bed. We held our breath and pretended there was no one there. Finally we heard her sigh and go plodding off down the hall. Paul whispered in my ear that she had brought fresh sheets only yesterday. I couldn't help it, I started to laugh and he got furious with me, he was that jittery. Finally we heard her go out, and we got dressed and crept down the stairs like two criminals. When we got outside we took off running and ran smack into her coming out of the Kaiser Kaffee-Geschäft on the corner. All three of us stopped dead and just stared at each other for an instant, then she said, Tch! tch! Herr Speer, I never expected such a thing from you, and shook her head and went home. But you know what? She ended up giving us her blessing (I wish I could remember her name!). Once we'd started we weren't going to stop, and my room was out of the question: to get to it you had to pass through every other room in the house, like train cars, something out of Dostoevsky or Kafka. (Oh, now I remember: it was *Feucht*, that was it!) Frau Feucht was only about forty I guess, and a widow, her husband had been a postman. It seemed to give her some kind of vicarious pleasure to aid and abet the romantic sin being perpetrated under her roof. She came to be very friendly and confidential with me, told me all her troubles and her life story, confessed that her husband hadn't been much of a man (I was convinced she wore him out) and finally admitted that she had had her eye on Paul herself, but that she was happy he'd found such a pretty girl, *that* was all right, and she didn't mind. It got so she was bringing us breakfast in bed in the morning and extra lumps of coal for the stove, and even sitting on the edge of the bed with us in it just to talk. It sounds peculiar, I suppose—but it wasn't; it was an easy, relaxing kind of natural intimacy.

"Still, for a long time, Paul had to be reassured of a thousand and one things before he felt it was *right* for us to make love. Weeks passed before I ever saw him completely naked (and that's an accomplishment in a small room!) and it used to upset him terribly if he caught more than a glimpse of me. I found it pretty ridiculous, but it was no good trying to shame him. His sexual ignorance was abysmal, he couldn't bear to have the act be an object of a conscious attention. Only gradually did he begin to take a kind of deliberate pleasure in his body and mine. Perhaps it was a good thing—sex never lost for him the quality of a sober ritual. . . ."

SAMSARA

Fräulein Gerber is forty-three (according to D-J, who should know), short-legged, long-waisted, sweet-faced and creamy-complexioned. Every evening, after her lectures on Faust and phonetics at the Translators' Institute, she comes into Oleo's with a small, limp, varying entourage of French, Swedish, Italian, English and American girls (all supposedly learning German).

She is a born Buddhist, a dimpled dreamer; she has a fried-potato *karma*. She belonged to the party: it was her one and only marriage. Now nothing is real to her any more; she wears a faintly murderous gentility like widow's weeds. If she doesn't want to believe something, it isn't true, and what she believes she believes apologetically; but her humility is of the sort that makes her ashamed to ask the waitress for sugar when she has forgotten to bring it. Whatever inconveniences she suffered during the occupation she attributed to the inexorable nature of Years-After-a-Lost-War; with the eagerness of a Girl Scout she joined the ranks of the denazified. It was "as it had to be" and "what was expected of one." Fräulein Gerber treads water in *Schicksal*.

But she is an old maid, and D-J (ubiquitous) rubs on her "condition" (as he calls it), implying an invisible sensitivity, inventing a nonexistent intellect; he has her so flattered and titillated she can't sit still any more. Only once in a while she suddenly "finds herself" angry at him and disappears with acidy eyes and a high chin. When she appears again, D-J allows her to forgive him without too much ado, and Fräulein Gerber cannot disguise her gratitude for this complaisance.

In the hall outside *Hörsaal* 11 stands Professor Albert Oestler, his head averted from the stream of students pouring out but watching them from the corner of his eye. He bites the filter of his Overstolz, hungrily swallowing smoke. A smile lights his face, he says, "Brückmann!" and Stefan turns to him. Together they head for his consultation room.

Grüning the assistant stops them just outside the door. "Excuse me, Herr Professor, someone is waiting for you inside: a woman."

"Ah yes, thank you," says Oestler. He ushers Stefan in, saying in a whisper, "This will only take a moment."

As they enter, a middle-aged, heavily made-up woman with dyed hair, feather hat and dangling triple string of imitation pearls springs from the professor's swivel chair and bounds toward them. Oestler has his hand outstretched and has just opened his mouth for formalities when she emits a horrendous bosom-and-pearl-heaving shriek, slaps the cigarette from his left hand and grinds it into the floor. "Arrgh!" she cries, and thrusts her face into his, sparks flying from her eyes. Oestler's mouth opens and shuts like a fish's. He swallows and backs away.

"Unspeakable!" she booms. "*Ich bin Frau Birnenhof!*"

"*Ach, so, ja,*" says Oestler.

"*Ja!*" she says, leaving no doubt about it.

Oestler glances about frantically, hoping to find something to distract her. "Frau Birnenhof, may I present Herr Brückmann?" he asks weakly.

She leans back, squints, musters this morsel critically, then spreads her lips, baring an unbelievable array of gigantic teeth in a man-eating smile, and offers her hand like a piston. Stefan grasps it gingerly and says, "*Es freut mich.*"

"Say it again!" she cries.

"*Es freut mich—*"

"Aha!" she shouts. "I thought so!" She leaps back, points her finger in his face and announces triumphantly: "Hungarian-American!" She tweaks his chin, bug-eyed, convinced. "Right?"

Stefan stands paralyzed. "Right!" she shouts.

Oestler is moving round to occupy his chair before she can reclaim it. His hand is caressing his cigarettes covertly. He sits down; already she is leaning over his desk on the other side, lionlike. "Now!" she roars. "Let us get down to business. I have another appointment in exactly"—she hoists a fleshy arm; her wristwatch is ingrown, like a gold tourniquet—"seven minutes."

"Please, do sit down," says the professor, weakly. She glances round warily, assures herself that there *is* a chair, and deigns to crouch upon it.

"Enunciation!" she hisses, pursing her lips like the opening of a tobacco pouch. "Repeat after me: *Ah-nungs-lo-sig-keit.*"

"*Ahnungslosigkeit,*" says Oestler, too indifferently for his own good.

She springs to her feet and pounds her fist on the desk. "*Nein! Nein! Nein!*" Oestler goes white. "Louder!" she bellows. "*AH-NUNGS-LO-SIG-KEIT!*"

He slaps his hands down just in time to prevent all his papers from being blown off the desk. At the same instant Stefan, who has backed into a corner at a safe distance, sneezes. Frau Birnenhof whirls about and throws him a menacing glance. "*Gesundheit!*" she commands. (God said, Let there be Gesundheit, and there was Gesundheit.)

Back to Oestler she turns, balefully. "Well?"

The word was trembling on his lips; for an instant he drops it, but redeems it just in time and tosses it to her hastily: "*Ahnungslosigkeit.*"

She rolls her eyes and groans, showing her gums. "*Amerika* has ruined you!" she says. "Never in my life have I heard such a miserable '*Ahnungslosigkeit.*' Never! Say 'Ah.'"

"A?"

"*Nein! Ah!*"

"*Anhh—*"

"*Ah! Ah! A-a-a-a-ah!*" (Berlin Zoo, 1932, thinks Oestler.)

"*A-a.*" He shrugs apologetically.

She slaps her brow and flops disgustedly into her chair. Planting an elbow on the desk top, she fixes him with a red-clawed finger. "All right!" she says ominously. "We are left with no alternative—exercise!"

"Exercise?"

"*Ex*-ercise!"

"What kind of exercise?"

"Glottal, dental, palatal, laryngeal and pulmonary exercise. The requisites for speech are *all* missing." Frau Birnenhof heaves with conviction.

"Oh," says Oestler.

She tosses her mane. "I shall return tomorrow at this time with a complete list of training routines, and we shall go over them together, *care*fully, and discuss *pro-ce-dure.* You have a long hard journey ahead of you, but be not discouraged; it is the journey to speech! the way to your own personality! And it is never too late—not even in a case such as yours. In the meantime I adjure you, in the name of sanity and our mutual endeavor, to abandon that unspeakable *habit!*"

She rises and stretches. Oestler finds himself incapable of getting up. Stefan stands by at the door. She stalks across the room and stops directly in front of him, unlips her teeth in an even more carnivorous smile and swipes him playfully across the face. "Hungarian-American!"

Oestler has finally managed to lift himself out of his chair, but is moving only reluctantly toward the door, afraid that his proximity could detain her. She wheels about with outstretched arm. "*Auf Wiedersehen, lieber Herr Professor!* Until tomorrow then!"

The windows rattle; the professor smiles wanly and mumbles something inaudible.

"One last word!" she roars, as the door is already closing behind her. "*Gargle!*"

WHO CAN READ WHITEHEAD?

Oestler falls into his chair; for an instant it looks as if he is going to burst into tears. He is too upset even to remember his cigarettes. Stefan sits down in the chair which Frau Birnenhof has just evacuated and offers him a Gitane with a smile. Oestler glances at the package and laughs. "Oh! No, thanks, I'll have one of my own."

They light up and sit for a moment, convalescing.

"Who on earth was that?" asks Stefan finally.

Oestler blushes apologetically. "She's supposed to be a voice teacher. I've been getting so many complaints about my inaudibility lately I thought I'd better do something about it. Vollmer promises we'll have an amplifying system some time before the turn of the century, but in the meantime I thought it would be a good idea for me to find somebody who could help me strengthen my voice. I lost a lung in the First War, you know."

"Oh . . ."

"Anyway, I found this woman in the directory; she wasn't in when I called her last evening, but I left a message and she called me at home at seven this *morning*—scared my wife half out of her wits." He waves a finger at the Gitanes. "Do you really like those things?"

"I didn't start smoking at all until about a year ago, in Paris. Immanuel was always offering me cigarettes, and finally I started accepting them—out of inertia mostly, I think. I can't say I really like them, only sometimes. When things change, I'll stop. And don't ask me what I mean by that."

Oestler regards him quizzically. "How did you come to know him—de Bris I mean?"

"That's a long story," says Stefan. "You shouldn't ask if you really want to know." He laughs. "Nice exchange—he took me up, I took up his cigarettes."

"I met him last autumn for the first time, at a conference in Normandy. All the arguments were drawn up long beforehand and nobody had come to discuss anything, I thought, but de Bris made what I thought was a pretty intelligent non-Marxist speech, naïve and a bit too humanist for my taste, but honest, and so I had dinner with him. It was a surprise to see him here. . . . How did you happen to come to Germany with him? Or is that another question I shouldn't ask?"

Stefan shrugs. "I'm not clear why I've done anything I've ever done. Things just happen, and I let them happen. The trouble is, I overestimate my strength, I take it too much for granted that the people who come my way must have come for some reason—silly metaphysical flair. I treat them all the same way, from my point of view; I expend all my energy on them, until things build up inside me and suddenly I can't any more, and then I just run away. As for why I came to Germany with Immanuel, the real reason, if there is one, had very little to do with him—though why I stayed did. In one way or another, as soon as I asked myself, I knew I might as well come back, perhaps even *had* to, as if the time I spent in Paris had been only a kind of stopover and I was really on my way back all the time, without knowing it." He lifts his shoulders in embarrassment.

Oestler is still staring at him, strangely. He chuckles. "I have to confess I asked de Bris a lot of questions about you. But he didn't enlighten me very much. He said you weren't very helpful when it came to yourself. I'm beginning to see what he meant." He smiles, not kindly: provocatively. Stefan frowns. Oestler goes on. "He thinks very highly of you, though. I was often tempted to accuse him of exaggeration, in fact."

Stefan says nothing; Oestler reads the look as modesty.

"Well then," says Oestler after a moment, "we have time." Stefan glances up at him; Oestler is still watching him steadily. "What I wanted to ask you is if you would come over to my house on Saturday evening for dinner with me and my wife. I've invited a few people, mostly students, to drop in afterward for coffee, and we'll just sit around and talk. This sort of thing's gotten to be a regular Saturday ritual—hangover from America. My colleagues here tend to look at me with a jaundiced eye because of it; familiarity between student and professor shouldn't be encouraged, they say. But I'm all in favor of it. Will you come?—not that you're exactly a student."

"I hope I'm not—but yes, I'd be happy to; thank you."

"Good," says Oestler, rising and coming round the desk. Stefan stands, Oestler takes his arm and they walk to the door. "You know," he says laughingly, "I told Vollmer that Whitehead once said he wouldn't have felt alive as a teacher if he couldn't have had students *around* him as well as before him, and do you know what he replied? 'Yes, but who can read Whitehead?' "

PAUL / THREE

"Often he read aloud to me: he had a light, sweet voice, not dramatic at all—it was as if he were speaking the words to an unheard music. He read Stefan George and Hölderlin and Georg Heym and Rilke, in a soft, liquid German, with just a trace of Bavarian dialect. Mostly for effect—he'd spent the first ten years of his life in Vienna, both his parents had been Austrian but had gone on to Munich not long before the war. The whole family was musical: when Paul was a child Anton Webern was a frequent house guest; his father played the violin and his mother the clavichord . . .

"He was sure of his calling as a poet, but he was reluctant to show much of what he'd written up to then to anybody, me included. He'd changed his mind about a great many things since his mother died, he said; for one thing, he'd stopped imagining he was going to be a German Rimbaud. Hitler was his would-be Verlaine, he said, and the war an Abyssinia he never got to—so he'd destroyed most of his earlier poems. . . ."

SHADES OF A *WANDERVOGEL*

Adolf Weichart is a *Studienrat* (sixty-four years old last New Year's Day) attached to the Translators' Institute; he also gives private German lessons at DM 2.50 an hour. He and Fräulein Gerber are *"per du"* (onetime romance?), but they nevertheless address each other respectfully as "colleague." He is quite tall and walks with a stoop, bowing his huge, maney head as if searching for lost pennies, licking his lips incessantly. He can walk for days without eating, without sleeping, without thinking, burning slowly, internally, invisibly. His nose, which is swollen from years of booze and hay fever, is fuzzed with fine white hairs that make it resemble nothing so much as a small, worn, pink tennis ball. But though his appearance is that of a pathetic and affable deliberate buffoon, there is a look in his eyes (a blur not of hurt or pain but of lurking violence or secret vice) that stifles any urge to mock him. He was broad and muscular in his youth (no classic), but grew immense in the late Twenties and Thirties (away, unwinding his youth in Venice and Alexandria and Algeria; away, buying back his youth in mirrors). The war caught him somewhere there in North Africa and burned the fat away, leaving his skin (which has the disreputable color of boiled chicken) to hang like a postwar *robe-de-chambre* from his repatriated frame.

PAUL / FOUR

"He was slender, delicate in build, but finely proportioned and a little above average height. His horn-rimmed glasses made him look terribly serious and at least ten years older than he was; when he smiled he looked ridiculous in them. But without them he was an eternal adolescent who never turned twenty. . . .

"He talked with passion, always, and this passion seemed to come from some invisible reservoir behind his nervous system, not in it; on the surface his energy never belonged to *him* at all. When it came through, it left him exhausted and a little irritated—and those around him too, often as not. But when he focused on a subject and began to talk about it, you could be sure he wouldn't let up until he had demolished it. You can't imagine how attractive these obsessions of energy were—nothing was more characteristic of him as a *man*. I'm not just talking about the power to sway people, either, or the force of logic. Maybe obsessions was the wrong word, it would be better to say *possessions*, because I really do believe that the source of these fits of work and talk that came over him lay outside him; I could only look on and admire, or just *listen*. That's why I say I don't mean logic or conviction—their level was one that was familiar to me, I could touch it, sympathize with it. Whereas his *mind*, his *thinking*, appealed to me as *feminine* (if I can say such a thing), his drive, his energy belonged to another order of things to which I had no access. Oh, I'm getting things all muddled up; it's so hard for a woman to try to define these things she *feels* about men...."

SPELEOLOGY

Freddie's place: a tiny room on the fourth floor of an old office building owned by an uncle of his. Originally furnished with nothing but a sink, intended as a storeroom or workroom. Freddie has filled it now, however, with several disastrous pieces of cast-off furniture—a sagging bed, an ancient table, a sofa which when you sit on it disgorges (still) half a dozen mice and wheezes great clouds of dust (pre–First World War), a few dewickered wicker-bottom chairs, a supine two-legged magazine rack, etc., etc. As this furniture menagerie arrived piece by ignoble piece, Freddie sat ready with a saw and promptly cut the legs off the bed, the table and the chairs; now only a Japanese dwarf could distinguish them from anomalies in the floor. There is no cupboard—clothing which is not simply dumped on the floor is thrown at nails in the wall (most of which by now support huge canvases in stretchers); sometimes a shirt or jacket catches, thereby disguising a "painting" if not improving the general appearance of the room. One small window looks out (infrequently) on a dreary stone wall; it is usually curtained with a filthy bedspread that looks as if a chicken had bled to death in it (though Freddie swears it is household enamel). A radiator next to the sink radiates enough heat for a barn (Freddie does not seem to perspire) and provides sufficient boiling water for one cup of Nescafé in the morning.

THE STRANGER FROM THE TROPICS

Reinhardt Gerstenmaier (no stranger at all) in a frayed white linen suit with a threadbare lapel (the temperature outside is fifteen degrees below zero Celsius), pants sagging almost to the thighs, two top flybuttons unlatched (brown bone monsters), the legs piled up like concertinas around his ankles.

He turns: the seat seam stands agape.

He is letting his beard grow: it is three days old now.

His soul is being eaten by invisible moths (or mouths?).

BATEAU IVRE

Weichart's solid belching laugh fills the intermissions of a Friday night in the Cave. His party never changes: future lawyers bald at twenty, dueling scars, hay-haired philosophers with rimless glasses and conditioned manners, a few tight black-haired girls: a White Russian cabal plotting counterrevolution under the very noses (under the counter) of the bearded jazz bolsheviks. Except for the *maître*, who is loyal to Steinhager, all are drinking Libella fruit punch.

He sits with arms around them all, a lurching rowboat; his passengers hold fast. He starts to wheeze and springs a leak, the bottom of his voice falls out, masts capsize, he roars; his face inflates like a lifebelt. The order to abandon ship is given: a hundred vessels attend his S.O.S.

But somehow, somehow, he hauls in his oars and leans slowly forward, bailing his lungs out; then falls back high and dry and water-eyed. The sea is oiled with saxophones.

THE CANNIBAL WHO NEVER SWALLOWS

Don't think I didn't know what was going on between you and Immanuel—I did.

What do you mean by that?

You know what I mean. I don't care, but I'm not blind.

No, you're not blind—you're just crazy, that's all.

PAUL / FIVE

"Whatever plans we made to spend that first vacation together came to naught—they were pipe dreams anyway. I went up to Hanau to my father, and Paul went home to Munich and started to work. Though his father (who'd been maimed in a building cave-in in 1945) could afford to pay for his tuition and room rent, Paul had to provide his own food and pocket money. His stepmother, Elisabeth Raabe-Speer (I'll tell you about *her* another time), was rather well off in her own right, but when Paul had refused to study law, which was what *she* wanted him to do, she'd sworn he wouldn't have a penny from her toward his studies. I guess his father was too indifferent or resigned or something to try very hard to make her change her mind. It wasn't a matter of pride, that's all I know. Anyway, Paul had been working every vacation in a small publishing house for the glorious salary of thirty-seven marks a week.

"We wrote to each other almost every day, but there was one thing I didn't tell him. By the time we returned to the university in May, I was a little over three months pregnant. I was afraid to tell him in a letter, I was sure I'd never see him again, it was my fault it had happened, not his. Oh, I started to tell him, a hundred times, then tore the letters up. But that was how my father found out—I left a letter lying on my writing table one day and he saw it. He told me right away and quite openly that he knew, and I'll always be grateful to him for leaving the decision as to what to do to me. When I said I wanted to marry Paul, but that I had to *see* him and talk to him, and let him make up his own mind, he let me go back to the university.

"So I went back and worked up the courage to tell Paul. Actually it had nothing to do with courage; I just blurted it out. Paul turned very white for a moment and then asked, 'What can we do? 'I'm going to keep it,' I said defensively, 'whatever we do.' 'Of course we'll *keep* it,' he said scowling, 'I didn't mean that.'

"We got married in July, just before the summer holidays, in a civil ceremony at Hanau. My father gave me away; he'd met Paul for the first time about three weeks before and liked him from the first moment. I had a brother who was killed in the early days of the war—and though Paul couldn't have been less like my brother, my father was overjoyed to have a son again.

"Paul's parents got no wind of the marriage until we went and told them; he hadn't been afraid of his father or what *he* would say—it was his stepmother he was worried about—and I can assure you, he had every reason to be worried . . ."

ACROTIC LIFE / SECOND DREAM

Suddenly, upon the painless discovery of a blue line running up his left arm on the inner side, he becomes aware that he has blood poisoning. He is afraid in an abstract way, it is dangerously advanced, and yet he is not really *inclined* to take it seriously. He starts to make his way to a doctor's office, but there are numerous, half-humorous delays. The entire dream is actually contained in the one instant when he sees the doctor standing across the river from him, with his back turned, and it occurs to him that he might die, is going to die. His denial of the knowledge jars him rudely awake.

PAUL / SIX

"Raabe-Speer must be almost fifty now, but she doesn't look it. She's a cold, tall, perfect icicle with raven hair; there's not a line in her face or a crease on her throat; she's like an embalmed queen, upright, incorruptible.

"In her youth she was on the stage, in Hamburg I think; her first marriage was with some matinée idol of the Thirties; during the war, while he was at the front, she met Egon Speer (not long after Paul's mother had died); he was in uniform, an engineer and a dashing forty. When her husband died in Italy later in the same year, she and Paul's father got married almost immediately.

"Once an actress always an actress—she can play every role to the hilt, from loving mother and adoring wife to social butterfly and lofty innocent martyr and, when the chips are down, whore and fishmonger too. Most women seem to *recognize* her somehow, perhaps because they see parts of themselves, or out of jealousy, I don't know; but *men*—they fall for every trick in her repertoire. Whether it's her beauty or whatever it is that blinds them, it hypnotizes them so thoroughly they don't feel any pain at all while they're being devoured. And I'm not just talking about Paul and his father, either.

"But I was prepared for a quite different person, too, from the one that confronted us when we arrived in Munich to announce our marriage. Paul had painted me a picture of a stern woman, all right, but a just one, a kind of female Jehovah. But the minute we faced each other I had a terrible premonition of danger. And I wasn't wrong, either: no matter how often I let myself be talked into believing there could be something good, something honest or selfless in that woman, it always turned out to be exactly the opposite. There's no way to describe her so she'll appear as monstrous as she is, without seeming ridiculous. I have no doubt that she's insane; it's just that there's no name for the pathology. I have to give her credit, though: no matter how mad she is, she's diabolically consequent; she lives in another world of I-don't-know-whose making, a world where nothing is ever forgiven or forgotten, where imagined slights, imagined transgressions, provoke convulsions of hatred and revenge that real ones never could. The horrible thing is, a real reason of some kind, absolutely consistent with her view of things, her own *interest*, lies at the heart of everything she does. She's always doing the right thing, in her own eyes, and her victims seem to be only too happy to give her almost a written permission to do her worst; they just lie down and die. . . .

"Paul's relationship with her was a strange one. (From her perverted standpoint she was in love with him; I was a *rival* from the moment I set foot in her house, and I was supposed to behave like one; the fact that I was the one who was *married* to Paul didn't give me any special privileges, as far as she was concerned—and I can't tell you how many times I was tricked into taking a defensive position, and I always ended up in the back seat.) Paul was around seventeen when his father remarried; you'd think that a boy that old would never have entered so wholeheartedly into the artificial family scheme established by the remarriage. But Paul had loved his mother excessively—it was an expression of *his* need, not hers; she loved him, but it always seemed to me, from the way he spoke of her and from things he let fall, that his mother had been quite conscious of his too-great dependence on her and was rather disturbed by it. He never portrayed her as having been too possessive, and yet that is what she would have to have been to have justified the tremendous reliance he developed. There's no way to know now, of course. What I think is that, to some degree at least, he sensed that she recognized and feared his peculiar dependency, and—whether consciously or instinctively—he himself had made her fears seem exaggerated to her, or tried to, just to protect his need. In any case, her death came as a terrible shock to him (his father was in Germany but away from home during most of the war years); but the possible emotional consequences of it hadn't even begun to make themselves felt when Raabe-Speer arrived on the scene. And so Paul immediately embarked on an elaborate rationalization through which he replaced his mother with her, not as love-object (he didn't have to *love* his stepmother, as long as he *stood by* her and satisfied certain other requirements she made), but as a mother-substitute onto which he could rebind all the broken strings of his dependency. The situation must have looked quite different to *her*; as I say, she had no qualms about falling in love with him, he was easy prey, and the accident which Paul's father suffered within two years of the time they married, and which left him almost completely disabled, left her (for a time at least) with no other emotional preoccupation than Paul. She didn't waste any time: with a sure instinct she grasped Paul's make-up, his particular needs, and began to play on them to her own ends, until she'd managed to seduce his loyalty and had rubbed it into a kind of passionate servility that she could manipulate with ease.

"Her first reaction on learning that Paul and I were married was to accuse me of having robbed her of her son—*her* son!— and of having become pregnant on purpose so he would marry me. Then she became more tragic in tone; she began to bewail

the inevitable loss of a talent that would never be allowed to
unfold now, with the responsibilities of wife and family—a
talent which only *she* had ever appreciated. Paul protested
(not too strongly) that she had only made it more difficult for
him to study what he'd wanted to, and she faced him down.
For your own good! she screamed. Did he want a divorce?
She had lawyers, they could crush the marriage, annul it, she
would send him back to the university, anywhere he wanted, oh
he must get a divorce (with killing glances in my direction),
this could only end catastrophically. . . .

"But by the next morning she had switched to another line;
she was miles ahead of either of us. She fell on us at breakfast
with a glistening, magnanimous smile that would've melted an
iceberg, and said, 'My children, the first shock of hearing that
two people as young as you both are had got married caused me
to behave in a way I realize was deeply *unfair* (she used the
English word); I beg you to forgive me, and to accept my
blessings on your marriage.' She was just as sweet and understanding as a dish of whipped cream; my mouth fell open. She
went on: she had accepted the fact of our marriage, for better
or worse. There was the child to think of, and Paul's career
(she must have used that word 'career' fifty times). Did he
want to go back to the university? If he did, and agreed to
transfer to Munich, she would lend him the necessary support.
He could pay her back when he became famous, that was how
much she believed in him. Without even waiting for a reaction,
she turned to me, and with soulful face began a long speech on
my duties and responsibilities, now that I had married an artist.
She praised Paul's great gifts to the sky, quoted Goethe, and
informed me that it was both an honor and a challenge to
have married one of the 'select of God' (I swear!), and she
hoped I would live up to the task—if I could, and did, then perhaps everything would turn out for the best after all, and would
I stay on in her home as her guest, and so on and so forth . . .

"Well, we took the bait. From one point of view we had no
alternative. And Paul was so ready to jump at the chance, so
relieved at her change of heart, I just didn't have the courage or

foresight or whatever to stick to my misgivings. In the face of that woman's incredible dissimulation, her *effrontery* that looked like anything else but, I wilted. I even began to think perhaps *I* was the one who had been hysterical when we arrived, that I had willfully misinterpreted, willfully provoked her first re-actions—perhaps it had been nothing more than the quickly regretted, quite natural outburst of a highstrung, adoring mother (or stepmother—I never had one), in which case I would really be jeopardizing Paul's future (and mine, and the baby's) if I deprived him and us of her help; where could we have gone, what could we have done?

"I've rather neglected Paul's father in all this. But by the time I met him he was only the shell of a man, he was forty-five and looked sixty; his accident, which had occurred when he was only forty-one years old and still in the prime of life, had paralyzed his entire right side. And his hair had turned com-pletely white almost overnight. The news of our marriage made little outward impression on him; he smiled wanly and said, 'Oh? Well then, good.' I liked him, he was always vaguely sym-pathetic to me, but he was so withdrawn, always tired and listless and without much interest in anything. I managed to spend a little time with him each day—either reading out loud or talking with him until I saw he was growing fatigued.

"One day he said to me quite unexpectedly (this was after we'd been there a few months, just after Max was born), 'If you should ever wonder why I bother to go on living, it's because of two things, my dear: because I know it takes less courage for me, the way I am, to live as I have been left to live than it would take to die—and because I love *her*. The second reason may be the harder for you to accept or understand, but it is by far the more important to me.' I'll admit, it was hard for me to understand. If Raabe-Speer was sticking around for anybody in particular, it was for Paul. His father had a day nurse, and his stepmother lived at the other end of the house, in a room adjoining ours. When his father was wheeled out in the morning, she appeared and planted a dutiful kiss on his brow, and the same thing happened at night before he went off to bed; but I doubt that she ever spent more than ten minutes a day with him during the whole time I was in that house. That wasn't what mattered to him, though. He had been an exceedingly handsome and virile man, and he had played the field. He had never loved Paul's mother, or worshiped her the way he did Raabe-Speer; he had relied on her—she was an unassuming, forbearing, shy familial anchor, a genteel, domesticated woman and not a man's woman. Raabe-Speer had been a conquest, and now I don't think he dared ask himself why she stayed on with him, after his incapacitation—or perhaps he knew, remotely. In any case he was endlessly, unquestioningly grateful that she had, and his desire to go on living was rooted in his gratitude for her presence.

"That was the environment in which our child was born and in which we spent the first year of our married life. Life in the tomb, or something like it. Until I escaped, and I mean *escaped*, I never even felt that my child was my own. Raabe-Speer appropriated him *spiritually*, and appointed me nanny and diaper-changer. She didn't want physical contact with him, although she had to reassure herself fifty times a day that he was still there. She didn't want to be reminded that this little creature was a physical being at all—when it became obvious that he would have my hair and eyes, she would have sent him back for another model if she could; her hot and cold pride in him was exactly like the one-sided satisfaction that the owner of a well-oiled and polished precision tool has in his acquisition before he has learned to use it. . . ."

CAMERA OBSCURA

They are sitting on the rug by the bookcase. Books and pamphlets are spread all over the floor around them.

"Here they are," says Barbara, finding a yellow envelope behind *Menschheitsdämmerung* and *A History of the Great War*.

She opens it and removes a bundle of photographs, slips off the rubber bands and begins turning them over like odd-sized playing-cards. When she reaches the fifth or sixth she hands it to Stefan. It is a bad snapshot of two fuzzy people standing near a fuzzy tent.

"In France," she says. "Summer of 'fifty-two."

"Is that *you*?"

"I was a bit chubby, wasn't I?"

"I'll say. Doesn't even look like you."

She hands him another. It shows Paul in profile, holding a laughing baby close to his face.

"Frankfurt," she says, "after we ran away from Munich. It's one I took; the light makes his hair look awfully dark." She goes on shuffling without really paying much attention.

"Wait," says Stefan, catching a glimpse of something. "Can I see that one? . . . No, the one before."

She hands it to him, a rather large informal portrait of Paul wearing glasses. He looks forty. The print is poor, but its dullness lends the picture a certain soft, appealing quality. "I never liked that one," she says. "It's a good enough likeness, but he has his hair combed back, and that always made his brow too high."

Stefan looks hard at the photographs and then shivers involuntarily, as though he'd been struck by a draft. "When was it taken?" he asks.

She thinks back. "I'm not sure exactly—during the time we were bringing out *Bruchstücke*, I think . . ." She takes it from him and turns through the pile until she comes to another postcard-sized photo: it shows Paul seated in a garden chair, in a white suit, without his glasses. "This is my favorite," she says, handing it to him. "It's the way he looked when we met. Everything is right: his hair brushed over to one side—and you can almost tell his eyes are green, can't you!—the deep lines down from his nostrils to the corners of his mouth, and that beautiful smile, hardly a smile at all . . ."

The photograph trembles slightly in Stefan's hand:

Hannes.

"So Paul went back to the university; he studied hard and shut poetry out of his mind for the time being and became very thin and irritable. He didn't show any consistent interest in the baby; for weeks at a time he could completely forget it. I was always there when he got home, bored, but just as much in love with him as ever. We seldom went anywhere, never did anything together. Oh, twice I managed to get up to Hanau to see my father, once a short visit with Paul and the baby, once alone. Raabe-Speer was in and out, I'm sure she had a lover, although she was circumspect enough about it. She ignored me almost completely; I kept out of her way generally, anyway. Paul's father sat like a mummy, too listless even to read. Paul had to have a separate room to study in, often as not he fell asleep there; we were sleeping together less and less frequently. Often right at bedtime Raabe-Speer would trump up some reason for wanting to talk with him, and then keep him up until two or three in the morning, until she was sure I had fallen asleep. Or she would edge us on until we'd had a fight over some silly trifle, then play the arbitrator, carefully leaving one small spot unresolved so she could be certain one of us would land on it later on and start the fight all over again. It happened too often for it not to have been calculated. . . .

"I don't know how I stuck it out as long as I did. It could have gone on that way for another year at least, until Paul had his degree, maybe even longer; I'd have gone out of my mind in the meanwhile, that's all. But one day—not long before Christmas in 1949—Max knocked over the tree, Raabe-Speer threw an hysterical fit, Paul took her part more or less, and I just couldn't take another minute of it. I didn't discuss it, I went up and packed, I had to get out of that house; I was afraid they could (*she* could) still talk me into feeling I was in the wrong, or being selfish, or stupid, and I *wasn't*. The first moment that Raabe-Speer left the house for a second and Paul wasn't looking, I took off and went to Hanau.

"I waited for three weeks, the three most miserable weeks of my life. My father pretended I wasn't there, turned away all callers, refused to answer the phone. Finally Paul came; he had fought the most terrible struggle of his life, inner and outer: he'd broken off his studies and walked out of that house too. For whatever it cost him, and however unwillingly or unprepared he might have been to do it, he had, *finally*, spoken for himself, for his own life and mine and the baby's. . . ."

WHAT DOES A HERO WEIGH IN POUNDS?

Barbara is off at a seminar (Chaucer); Stefan, who has begun to help her with the organization of material for *Zerstückelung*, is in her room sorting a huge pile of correspondence, trying to put the letters (including a great many undated ones) into some sort of chronological order. He comes across this one, printed in India ink, and stops to read it:

Darmstadt, 13.VI.1955

Dearest Barbara,

How wonderful to hear from you after all this time! Käthe and I read your letter with tears of joy and admiration. What courage you have shown in your decision to return to the university! how wonderfully you have weathered the trials of this past year!

I was moved more than I can tell by what you said of Paul's regard for me. You may rest assured that the feeling was deeply reciprocated, and that I shall always bear the terrible wound of his death on my heart. There is no way, except in my work, that I can ever begin to repay the great debt that I, among so many other young poets, owe to him

—for his personal friendship and for his just criticism and unfailing encouragement.

That this is so makes it all the more difficult for me to say what I must now, in answer to your request for copies of Paul's letters to me, however. I understand full well how intense your desire must be to compose the work for which you have been commissioned, as a tribute to Paul, the husband and the artist. But I, for one (and how regretfully you cannot know!), must refuse. If it were only because of the intimate content of many of the letters, I could still make a selection of passages of a more objective nature, copy them and send them on to you. But there is a more serious reason for my refusal, and I have searched my conscience thoroughly and painfully before deciding to give utterance to it, for I fear you will misread—and I do not want to hurt you. But here it is:

Paul was a great artist, very likely a genius, who at the time of his death had produced a small body of poems and poetic essays which will eventually, I believe, establish his reputation as one of the great poets of our time, not only in Germany. That this may be said of the work of one who died so young does not lessen our sense of personal loss, but it is a source of healing certainty: his life was not altogether wasted. This knowledge is what lends me courage to say what I must.

There have of course been many correspondences which must be regarded as integral parts of their authors' creative work. But Paul's letters, it seems to me, are not of this order. Not that they are inferior; no, but they sprang from another intention, had their origin in another area of his being. No matter how intense they may be in feeling, no matter how urgent, the ideas and reactions expressed by Paul in his correspondence (with me, at any rate) are not to be confused with his art. They are *directed* in a way that his poems are not; they are expressions of the man, the friend. They are not exalted, they are *personal*—not merely in the privative sense of the word (for who am I alone?) but also in their nakedness, their tone of apology (so often!), their reliance upon sympathy and understanding, their willingness (nay, eagerness) to err and be corrected. How can I give them away? I cannot, Barbara—either to curiosity or for the derivation of analytical "clues" to his character. Paul is dead now, my *friend* Paul; and I see no reason why I should help deliver him to the eyes and brains of those who would not understand, who *need* not understand—to those who do not possess the warrant of love that would entitle them to gaze upon the man himself.

Please do not misunderstand me, my dearest Barbara. I am not refusing *you* these letters—I am refusing the *use* of them to the world. I am of the belief that every great artist bears within himself the seeds of a great *man*. But (perhaps only in our epoch) these seeds may flourish only in his art, only there may such a man transform, immortalize his human suffering and transcend it. Paul's greatness is there, present, accessible to all. What business does anyone have in wanting to piece together the details of his daily, mundane life, or the fragments of his past? Of what genuine value or interest can it be to anyone outside? Case histories are always like skins on the verge of being discarded. Paul's art is of a piece, self-sufficient; it will make its way (*his* way); it is the only true statement we may expect from a man who was crucified on the cross of art-and-life. All the rest is the unreadable debris of his struggle to live as a man in a world for which the artist was not meant—to adjust to an inferior life which he knew was not his own, not the one envisioned but unreachable perfection and completion.

Paul's last letter to me contained the following lines; it is like a tiny but significant footnote to all his letters and perhaps to his life as well:

Herbst und wieder herbst und immer herbst—
    warum kein segen?
Hart war der weg und nun nicht mehr—
    wohin der regen?

Do come to see us soon, dear Barbara, and bring little Max, and stay, and let us talk (we are not so far away, after all, here in Darmstadt!). Käthe joins me in wishing you every blessing and joy in life.

In warm remembrance and affection,

KARL-HEINZ HARDENFELD

POSTPRANDIAL PRATTLE

PROFESSOR IGNATZ BAERMANN: Who knows? Perhaps the consonant provides the link, by way of pictures, between the phenomena of the natural world and their linguistic notations.

CHRISTIAN BROEDESACKE, *stud. phil.*: Nonetheless, the expressive content of the noumenon is best evoked by the vowel.

PROFESSOR ALBERT OESTLER: Then the vowel would lie at the root of the dualistic error, which is not the case.

JOSEPH LIEBLICH, PH.D., UNIVERSITY OF JERUSALEM: Especially not when it preceded the consonant as an attempt at speech.

STEFAN BRÜCKMANN: But what makes you so sure it did? Perhaps language itself, *our* language, has imposed this priority conception on us. I can't see how hissing or gritting one's teeth is a less legitimate articulation than saying *Ooh* or *Aah*. Or why it should come later. . . .

AND SO ON

"I was simply unable to read Goethe until I was forty—"

". . . about the same age I *stopped* reading Rilke—"

". . . more *Streusselkuchen*, Herr Professor—"

". . . No, my dear fellow, there is no way in which the doctrine of the eternal return may be rationalized so that it will conform with the Christian eschatological bias, which is fundamentally Persian and Semitic in origin. You must understand, in the Greek conception of the *kosmos*—"

". . . all the elements, in some mysterious fashion, are also present in another concatenation that re-evokes, instantaneously, the full affective presence of a past perception which may no longer be remembered *per se*, but only through—"

". . . heading for a door, I open it, pull it shut behind me, and at precisely that instant I am awakened by a real door slamming. How do you explain that? Is it possible to dream backward, compressing time so that—"

". . . We must start speaking English; our young friend Mr. Kallergis is not able to follow, I'm afraid—"

". . . No, please, I understand; I just don't have anything to say—

". . . *exactly!* In the second book, with its intentionally looser form and its anticipated moral, we are given a kind of—"

". . . I know, dear. I just wish Frau Birnenhof could see you, she'd—"

". . . have caused a sensation, no doubt about it. It's certainly the first time that a young Jew has been so outspoken about his impressions of the 'new Germany'; but I feel that, no matter how honest your outrage may be, there is simply no acoustical backboard, as yet at least, for what you have to say. We are still too easily put on the defensive. Even the most purely objective statement appears polemic in the highest degree to the average German reader, who is no longer accustomed—"

". . . if he ever was—"

". . . notorious for reading portions of an unfinished work aloud to just anyone—"

". . . and a friend is apt to be the worst judge of everything but the extent of his own jealousy, especially when he is also a writer—"

". . . laughing behind his back at Brod—"

". . . and the oversights! Soon someone will come along and inform us with documentation from the shorter pieces and *The*

Trial and *Amerika* in particular that Kafka was secretly converted to Roman Catholicism; mark my word—"

". . . the typical Marxist error. And what examples! Imagine: a small smiling girl on a sunny street, holding an ice-cream cone, against all the cathedrals and festivals of—"

KAMAKURA

". . . what I have never been able to understand: how this man, so engrossed in Zen, and after having spent five years in the mastering of one art, after having submitted to such a discipline, could have returned to become a rabid Nazi—"

". . . in the *Buch-Gemeinschaft* a couple of years before the war, and Suzuki or—"

". . . Besant. But Steiner, on the other hand, had—"

". . . Count Keyserling—"

". . . after *Sein und Zeit,* pounding the lectern in a Storm Trooper's uniform—"

". . . if it is true that Haushofer did accompany him through China and Tibet—"

". . . the concave world, the stars, light bulbs—"

". . . exhibited in Edo Park. Great flowering chancres, viscous wounds, mutations as landscapes, animal and vegetable and mineral interchangeable, indistinguishable, the visible psyche, the sexual organs as dehiscent fruit or rotting stones, ashes and vivisections, and everywhere, in a thousand metamorphoses, the great white cloud—"

". . . that first lecture he gave, on *Moby Dick,* which I had never even heard of. But my! how he hated the Japanese! . . . and Yamaguchi just bowed and smiled, and went back to Tokyo almost every day for another six weeks. Can you imagine: No, thank you, we won't go on any bloody Japanese steamer! Why, they'd have slit his throat with the greatest of pleasure. How he did it I don't know, but Yamaguchi booked passages for them on an American ship, finally, and the day they left the whole faculty turned out and went down to the station to wave them off, and all the professors' wives brought flowers, and wept, they actually wept! But he was adamant to the last in his hatred. . . . I had the overwhelming sensation that I was walking directly into the spiritual landscape described by Lawrence in *Kangaroo*, which I'd read just a couple of years before, except that this was America and not . . . in a terrible state, bottles and trash everywhere, the bed unmade and black with dirt. It came as a shock to me to see him reduced to such circumstances, and of course there was no question of his being able to repay me the money at the time, and he never did. But you mean to say he is now well known? . . . the rats. I believe the estimate for all of the United States is now three or four per person. We had ten thousand or more, some seasons . . . incapable, in its rigid superficialities, of delineating the subtle distinctions so necessary to—"

THE DANCE OVER FIRE AND WATER

JOHN KALLERGIS, *exchange student*: No, I don't know what it's like, and as I'm always being told, I was too young at the time to remember the last one. After all, I was only ten when it began and fifteen when it was over with. Besides, being an American, I am automatically excluded by nationality from any discussion about what it was really *like*—even if I'd been a soldier it wouldn't make any difference; the mere fact of my birth marks me for some reason as a person who couldn't and shouldn't care less—as far as you Europeans are concerned, anyway. I guess you've cornered the market on war. Everybody agrees you're more *sensitive* than we are, and suffer more, and all that. *Why* is another question. We're just expected to sit up and listen like good little boys and girls when our elder cousins talk, and we're supposed to pretend that we all grew up in the same great big house with you, too—but we didn't. That's our loss, you say then; but I'm not so sure. I'm not sure about a great many things, not even about how much *you* should have to say about the war, either. There's such a thing as being too close, too involved, I think; and people who've lived under the weight of things much greater than they could bear or comprehend have either been crushed by them eventually, or else they've done the best they could to forget, and the quicker the better. Obsessions are atavisms, it seems to me. Anyway, I get sick and tired of being told by you how I should look at things. Your age and your experience are your worry, not mine; I never heard so many explanations and self-justifications in my life as I have since I came over here—I didn't ask for them, and I don't need them, either. They leave me cold; they aren't *my* business—not in the way you want them to be, anyway. You can't teach me and yourselves all in the same breath. If you want to justify things, or simplify them so you can forget them, or lock them safely away—convince yourselves first. I can't be of any help—remember? I didn't go through it, I wasn't torn to pieces, I saw nothing firsthand, and I don't have to spend the rest of my life trying to glue pieces together or trying to forget.

But I'll tell you something: I *do* have something to say about the war, or I *will*. It has to do with *conscience*, and I'll find the way to "delineate those subtle distinctions." It is people like me, of my age, brought up the way I was and in the place I was, people for whom the war was very far away and yet unimaginably close, sentimentally, affectively close, ubiquitous. It prodded us continually, as a condition, inescapable, whispering to us in a milion ways about its existence *out there*, as an *It*. Already, when we still couldn't grasp it at all, we felt the coloring of it in everything around us, more intensely every day as we grew—and now it is people like me who are its only accumulative children, the only people, or almost the only ones now, who are still concerned with that big It, who have to be, who still have the war unresolved inside them, and know it has to be resolved if we are to go on to anything at all. We are the only people with no hard feelings, with no science but what we feel, mistaken as that may or may not be, and no teacher but memory and a conscience willing to be blemished, if that is the way to a resolution of ourselves and of that war. . . .

PAUL / EIGHT

"With my father's help we finally found a tiny flat in Hanau for next to nothing, and Paul got a morning job in a copy bureau. It didn't pay much, but we got along. And Paul came slowly back to his writing. The first thing he undertook was a series of translations—all from American poets—as an experiment; at first he had no particular thought of trying to publish them. Most of the ones he chose were from the older generation: Pound, Williams, Marianne Moore, Wallace Stevens. But he worked with some of the younger Black Mountain poets as well, and began to correspond with them.

"What he tried to do was not so much *translate* the poems as recast them. The first thing he did was break them down into a peculiar root-German all his own. I made the interlinears; his English wasn't perfect by any means, and we discussed single words for hours sometimes. He had an incredible ear, a sense of weight and balance, and he sensed the richness, the *Rohstoff* as he said, of English. And so he sat, and painstakingly broke down the fixed structures of his own tongue in analogy to the American poems, until he had provided himself with the raw material for new patterns, new syntheses in German. He tested rhythms, the weights of words, like an assayer, consciously trying to strike new tones, revive exhausted resonances, straining the flexibility of his German to what often seemed to be a breaking point. But never quite. I read aloud, and for hours he just sat tapping the point of his pen on the sheet of paper before him—the margins of his work sheets were always covered with thousands of tiny dots, as if they'd been sprayed; he heard, and tapped, and his rhythms took shape. The results were little less than miracles: they were genuine transplantations, faithful to the originals but completely German in the reading.

"And yet the process itself interested him more than the results; what he was striving for was the creation of new lines of movement for his own poetry—and for that of others who could read and *hear*. I remember one day—he'd been reading Pound's *ABC of Reading*—he came and showed me the passage that says German verse hasn't done anything new for about seven centuries. He was furious. 'But if he weren't right, I wouldn't care,' he said. That little book really fired him up; he decided it was directed at him personally, and he set out to shake a hidebound traditional poetic diction into new life; he wanted to perform a kind of deliberate poetic alchemy: from gold to lead and back to gold again, as a first step, with the poet himself being tempered in the heat he generated . . .

"I have the translations, I'll show them to you one of these days. In many ways I prize them even more highly than his own published work, not only because I was so closely involved in their creation, but because they are living attestations to his birth as a poet. Under that self-imposed discipline, his ear for the intrinsic *musicality* of his own language became incredibly refined—more precise and natural than that of any German poet within memory, perhaps . . .

"I encouraged him to submit them to publishers, thinking perhaps he might receive a commission to do an entire series. And he did. But we were terribly naïve. Although we were in touch with the authors concerned, almost all of them, we hadn't thought to secure rights on a legal basis, and the German publishers we sent them to simply took up options and wrote back to us saying how much they admired Paul's work, but other arrangements had been made, *regrettably*. What they'd done of course was use us as tipsters. Later, when the first German translations did appear in print, there wasn't a doubt in the world that many of them had been lifted almost bodily from Paul's. And there was nothing we could do about it. In the end none of them were ever published in book form, not one. We printed a few in *Bruchstücke*, but since then almost every one of the poets he chose to experiment with—and pointed out—has appeared, with great success, in far inferior translation...."

THE PLEASURE DOME

Picture a dozen (more or less) intense poetry-lovers (some youthful, some not) crouched or sprawled on coats and cushions around a table top at one end of which Freddie Bühler presides like a Buddha perched on an isosceles triangle of two forelegs and one lower, book in hand—a table top on which two cracked teapots stand, as well as a dozen tumblers and a dozen ceramic cups (from the Feuerbacherstrasse ovens of Honoré Lambert, late of Vallauris by communal consent), one lidless jar of honey and a jagged tin of Four-Fruit marmalade, a number of knives and teaspoons and unmatched plates, two cellophane packages of *lachs*, a pound or so of "Rama" margarine, a half pound of Tilsiter, a wedge of Brie, a roll of handcheese with caraway, four or five varieties of cold cuts and sausage, a Swiss loaf, several packages of whole-corn bread, pumpernickel and cracked wheat, *Quark* with chopped onions, and three bottles of cheap muscatel (labeled Spanish) from Jakob Seltzer and Sons, Wine Merchants, Schlierbach/Neckar. Picture the progression of events: full-mouthed and dumb the coterie attends Freddie's thin-voiced reading of African primitive poetry; just as darkness falls the tea runs out; Thorwald von Berg, kneeling and brandishing his arms, has just begun his recitation of the prologue to *Faust*. But picture further the ritual of wine, the deep-blue haze of *Gemütlichkeit* and Reval smoke that has settled by nine P.M., when finally *The Waste*

Land (*Macht's schnell! Polizeistunde!*) has faded into religious silence and the table is a sticky shambles and the crowd is about to move on to the Cave, and resume in another key.

THE MINIMALIST

Stefan runs into Baermann at the little post office just across from the old university, and learning that they are both heading in the direction of the Bismarckplatz, leaves with him.

"Is Lieblich still here?" he asks.

"No," says Baermann. "He's gone back to Berlin. That's where he lives."

"I thought he said he was from Tel Aviv."

"That's where he grew up. He was born in Berlin. He and his mother went to Palestine in 1936."

"Oh."

"That's what I say. He is a very confused young man, that Lieblich. And bitter. Like his mother. I knew his parents, once. His father was a very clever man, a strong man. One of the last real Jews of my acquaintance."

Stefan says nothing.

"You too are a peculiar fellow," says Baermann. "But I don't think you're confused."

Stefan laughs. "Thanks."

"No, I mean it. Down in the depths you have a sound sense of humor, a kind of Yiddish skepticism. . . . You're *not* by any chance a Jew, are you?

"No, not yet, I'm afraid."

Baermann shakes his head and chuckles. "Now there's an answer for you!—I should ask, *hein?*" He lets out a sigh. "Well, who is any more? Only by birth, never by predilection. Look at me: I was born a Jew, raised a Jew, educated by Jewish professors, imprisoned and persecuted as a Jew; I watched Germans kill Jews, and here I am, teaching watered-down Old

Testament theology to the *goyim-Studenten*—by preference. Also just a little by force of habit, I suppose, but that's a recent development. . . . I love Germany, you see."

Stefan looks at him; Baermann smiles.

"You don't know what I'm saying—that's all right."

"No, I understand; I just wanted to see your face."

Baermann says nothing for a moment and then goes on. "*Ja!* What the Germans did to us they did not knowing that the very minute they began there could no longer be such a thing as a German Jew. By surviving, and by coming back, I became a German. Now I'm helping my countrymen to heal their self-mutilations, or trying to—and not without self-interest. I want to heal myself, and I couldn't do it if I were still a Jew. . . ."

"And Oestler?"

Baermann seems surprised. "Oestler? What about him?"

"Where does he fit?"

"*Fit?* He doesn't fit at all. Oh, he is a good man; yes, Albert is a good man, liberal, a coward of a lovable variety, jealous of artists, awed by scientists, afraid of men of action and distrustful of theologians. I have known him most of my life"— he glances at Stefan—"*except for seventeen years.* And exactly *those* seventeen years are why he does not fit: he was *needed.* Now he is neither Jew *nor* German, and though he pretends to be one or the other and sometimes both, he is not. His prognosis of national illness and his foresighted desertion of the ailing body were the first symptoms of his own disease; now, when that ravaged body seems well on the way to physical recovery, he returns to it, to search obsessively in the history of its pathology for clues to his own irreversible decline. Innocence is expensive. . . . Still, the university is fortunate to have him—as a reminder of bygone days, when such ambivalent men still had a place, in a secular and more-or-less organic society. Others can gauge the extent of their loss, their depletion, on him; they can listen and watch, and they will see that he is right intellectually and wrong morally, necessary as an analyst but useless as a guide. You see, most Germans are latent schizophrenics these days: they cannot oscillate without obvious choices, and there are none. As an ex-Jew I feel a great regret for this state of affairs; once upon a time the Jew represented a kind of opposite pole to the German, and Germany itself was the resulting creative tension. Now that the Jew has been alienated, like Lieblich, or absorbed, like me, or eliminated, like *most*, only the second-rate *déracinés* like Oestler find an echo. Genius wounds, deeply, but now the best are dead, and mediocrity can kill. . . .

"As for you, my young friend: don't try to be a Jew—even a perfect imitation is still an imitation. Be a German, if you can; without a few real ones, we will never again be Jews, and without Jews no Germany. . . ."

PAUL / NINE

"There was another side to that first year in Frankfurt, though. Paul went through awful sieges of depression. He wouldn't be able to work for weeks on end, and the very sight of the baby infuriated him. He lost his temper with me over nothing, and for the first time began to talk about killing himself. A few times he worked himself up into an insane fury—really hysterical outbursts—you can't imagine what it was like. One day I couldn't stand another minute of it and burst into tears and began to scream back at him; I don't know what I said, but he slammed out of the house, shouting that I could consider myself lucky if I ever saw him again.

"But he came back, after a couple of days. Though I saw him dead a thousand times, he came back, and when he did, he was another person. He clung to me like a child, followed me around the house all day, never mentioning the blowup or his absence, and obviously begging me silently not to, either. He went to work like a man possessed; but for a long time he had to have me in the room with him. Not talking, just *there*. Every once in a while he would turn round, wait until I realized he was looking at me, then smile and squeeze both eyes together for a second and turn back to his work. And when he made love to me, then, it was as if a great spring had broken through inside him, and he couldn't contain it, and he seemed to be trying to dissolve deep inside me. . . .

"That summer the idea of bringing out a little magazine of our own began to take shape. Everybody we mentioned it to told us we were out of our minds; we had next to no money at all, barely enough to stay afloat, but when Paul sold a series of essays (four in all, entitled 'For a Postwar Surrealism') to the *Allgemeine Zeitung*, and was paid the unheard-of sum of 360 marks, we decided to invest our little windfall in the plan. We knew that it would be only a drop in the bucket, but the bug had bitten us, and so we sat down and drew up glorious outlines for a literary review that would set the world (or at least Germany) on its head.

"It was a time when the few purely literary magazines in Germany were devoted almost entirely to translated material, and were having a pretty rough time of it; even the larger, well-established critical periodicals supported by publishing houses weren't doing too well. We didn't care; we were going to go about things differently, and on a smaller scale. The whole 360 marks, just about, went for postage on letters to everyone we knew and didn't know, describing our intended publication and begging for money, subscriptions, and contributions. Paul was even ready to approach his stepmother for help, but I vetoed that. We set up an elaborate subscription plan, printed brochures and mailed them all over Germany, Switzerland and Austria. Paul had been doing odd newspaper jobs—book reviews, *feuilleton*, that sort of thing—and we were relying on the contacts he had made for a critical reception that would bring us a swarm of subscribers. Paul talked a small printer into doing the first issue for us on credit; we borrowed on our faces, on sheer gall. By the time the first issue came

off the presses in September, we had the grand total of sixty-
three official subscribers and a debt of something over three
thousand marks. But we were both ecstatic. The entire issue,
from the first page to the last, had been written by Paul himself,
in the peculiar fever of contrition that had come after the outburst, and as a one-man effort the magazine was phenomenal.
It opened with an essay, a kind of manifesto called 'The Poet
at Mid-Century' and was followed by three of Paul's translations from Pound and two from Wallace Stevens, a study of
Gottfried Benn's later work, and four original poems, plus
reviews of two young German poets whom everyone else had
absolutely ignored.

"Well, we mailed it out and carried it out by hand and placed
it in any bookshop that would have it, and then sat back to wait.
For three weeks that's all we did: *wait*, getting more and more
discouraged as the days dragged by without a peep of response.
Paul was about to explode again, I could feel it. But then it
began to happen: letters came on the same day from each of
the two poets whose work Paul had reviewed, thanking him
and asking if they might contribute to the next issue. And then
other letters, from the most unexpected quarters—a beautiful
one from Benn himself, saying that the magazine had given
him the same sensation he might have had 'if a friend reported
dead on the front suddenly turned up alive'; and a warm
request for three subscriptions from a retired professor of German literature at the Sorbonne. But I will never forget the
morning (or the look on Paul's face) when the postman arrived
with a copy of *Die Tat* and we discovered that the entire front
page had been devoted to an article by Ernst Robert Curtius,
in which he called *Bruchstücke* 'the most promising and unexpected publication on the German literary horizon since the
Twenties.'

"Even though our subscription list never rose above 150,
our spirits soared, and we brought out a second and third issue,
and they were every bit as good as the first. Now the whole
burden was no longer on Paul; we were swamped with con-

tributions; the third issue was devoted entirely to poems by young German poets, with the exception of two American poems translated by Paul, and the lead essay. It was the first time that most of them had appeared in print. After that we came to our senses; the magazine had received unheard-of acclaim but not one bit of financial support—it was clear that if we tried to keep it going we were headed straight for bankruptcy. But *Bruchstücke* had made its mark: it had enabled Paul to clarify his own objectives, it had granted a dozen young artists of talent the opportunity to appear in print, and it had shown, as one correspondent said, 'that German is a modern language after all.' It was a fabulous *succès d'estime*, an affirmation of belief in the German language and the postwar rejuvenation of German literature. . . .

"Suddenly Paul was corresponding with dozens of people, he had more offers from other periodicals that he could possibly handle; he began to write for *Südwest Rundfunk*. He compiled a volume of his first poems, the new ones—it was published in the summer of 'fifty-two, while we were in France. We were able to pay at least the interest on our debts, even though we couldn't reduce them by much (Raabe-Speer obviously thought we had become millionaires; she began to hound Paul for the money she had spent on his studies in Munich—we paid that in a hurry, I can tell you).

"And Paul began, for the first time, to show some real affection for Max, who had just turned three. He was happy, he said, to see that he was going to look like me and not like him. He grew quieter inwardly; I could feel it in everything—in his work, in the greater span of his patience, even in his lovemaking. If I had to put it in a word, I'd say he was gradually becoming my *husband*, that he wasn't any longer just a sensitive boy playing at being a man. He saw it happening too, and I think it came as somewhat of a surprise to him; he had feared more than anything that he would lose his—I don't know what to call it—not depth, *geniality* perhaps, if he ever shifted his erratic balance even partly onto the back of another human being. Up until then I don't believe he had ever really regarded me as his *wife*—I'd just been an unnamed feminine someone he needed without wanting to admit his dependence. In a sense it had taken almost four years of marriage for us to *be* married."

THROUGH THE FLOWERS

"When we first came here," says Oestler, pointing to a snow-bank, "I tried putting roses in over there—"

"Mm," Stefan says, after twenty minutes of touring the professor's buried flower beds.

"—but it didn't work. There used to be"—he lays a hand on Stefan's shoulder and points up at the eaves toothed with icicles—"a drainpipe that emptied from up there, a big one, and it must have left some sort of poisonous residue in the soil. The first year the blossoms were beautiful, but the second they looked like shrunken heads." He laughs at his own simile, and changing the position of his hand presses Stefan across the sluggish driveway round to the back of the house. "Nothing much back here; just the odds and ends of last year's bulbs, and a few flags I've managed to keep going from the specimens I brought with me from Connecticut." He glances at Stefan, who nods with politely feigned interest. "My wife takes up most of the ground with her herbs—both cooking and medicinal. She *uses* them all, too; the house smells like a pharmacy half the time,"—he smiles and Stefan smiles back—"forty-four varieties at last count, of which about forty move into the house with us for the winter, either in pots or to dry."

He kneels and brushes away some snow near the back steps; a thick clump of parsley appears, black-green against the white. He plucks two sprigs and stands up. "One of the outsiders," he says, sticking a piece in his mouth and offering the other to Stefan, who shakes his head.

"It's good for you," Oestler urges him.

"No thanks," says Stefan. "Never touch the stuff." He shivers.

"You're cold. Let's have some coffee. It's not exactly the best time of year for strolling in the garden."

Stefan laughs. "Well, I didn't want to be the one to say it."

MUSICA ANTIQUA

Frau Frobenius (of sweet smile and narrow eyes) has served them baked beans with bacon and garlic. "*Unerhört!*" exclaims Stefan, stuffing himself.

"We had to eat so many during the occupation," whines Barbara, imitating a *Hausfrau*.

"Not what *we* ate," says Richard Frobenius.

Frau Frobenius smiles (sweetly).

Harpsichord, recorder.

"Coffee everyone?" asks Frau Frobenius as they leave the table.

Richard Frobenius opens a bottle of Dujardin and turns the record over.

"No one eats now the Jews are gone."

"No chicken fat, no big fat garlicky dills—"

"Not even rice very often."

"Black pepper, what about black pepper?"

"Real *lachs*, smoked—"

"The bread's still good."

"Once in a while a nice Thüringer—"

"Ugh!" snorts Wilma.

"The liverwurst is pure *Schmalz* most of the time."

Coffee. Richard Frobenius breaks open a box of Dutch cigars.

"My uncle received a shipment of Brazilian tobacco in 1939," says Barbara. "Kept it hidden all through the war and made a fortune afterward. But he never smoked himself."

"Remember *mukafuk*. Can you still buy that stuff?"

"Don't anybody knock *mukafuk*," says Stefan. "I have fond memories."

"Better than weeds boiled in a helmet," declares Richard Frobenius.

"My uncle's cigars were the best in Germany until 1947," says Barbara.

"How wonderful!" Wilma exclaims.

"Yes, those were the good old days," Richard Frobenius says. "To the good old days of 1946 and '7!" He hoists his cigar in a toast and pops it in his mouth.

"Are you by any chance related to Leo Frobenius?" asks Stefan.

"No—but my father was," replies Richard Frobenius. "I'm not related to anybody now except my wife." He points to the scar on his forehead. "My good-bye to everything else."

"Oh! tell them the fraternity story," suggests Wilma.

"Yes," he says, "by all means the fraternity story. A moral tale. One night I was in The Owl, in the back room, having an early dinner, and a young brother came in in full regalia—blue, pink and yellow. He had a scar from eye to chin, with visible stitching (which, by the way, reminds me of another story, about a shipowner's idiot son who got his long-sought-after gash, a real beaut, and trotted off to the doctor to get it sewn up. Blood all over the place. 'I want a real scar,' he announces: 'not too bright and not too light, not too thick and not too thin—what can you do for me, doc?' 'How about a zipper?' says the doctor)—anyway, this gaudy *igitur* comes in, sits down opposite me and begins to stare at me. Just stare. Well, after a while it made me nervous and so I asked him, 'Would you mind telling me what's so interesting?' He blushed and stammered, 'Your scar, sir, it's beautiful; it's the most beautiful scar I've ever seen. *Wenn ich fragen darf*, what fraternity did you get it in?' Now I was never one to squelch a compliment, so I replied very seriously: *Germania-Russia*, in impeccable Latin. My young admirer wrinkled his brow, thought for a moment and then declared, really confused and concerned, 'I'm afraid I never heard of that fraternity; was it by any chance before the war?' "

DAS MARIONETTENTHEATER

The women depart for the kitchen; Frobenius lays on Scarlatti and pours Stefan another cognac.

"I've been wanting a chance to talk with you," he says. "Do you mind?"

"No," says Stefan.

"Maybe it's none of my business, but I'd like to ask you a simple question."

"Go ahead."

"It's just this: Do you love Barbara? I don't mean do you want to marry her, just do you love her?"

"Yes," Stefan replies.

Frobenius leans back. "Good," he says. "That's all I really wanted to know. And I believe you. I don't want to see her hurt. She doesn't just need a lover."

"I know that," says Stefan.

"Yes, I think you do," says Frobenius, and after a second, "Has she spoken to you at all about . . . this past year here? Intimately, that is?"

"A bit, pretty guardedly. She wants me to know certain things, but I'm not supposed to speculate on them. Of course I do, anyway, and she knows I do; that's healthy enough—what I'm not so sure of is whether *she* knows she doesn't just need a lover."

"Do you think that's all she sees in you? I can assure you it's not."

"No, but it's not that simple—she isn't free to admit her feelings to herself. Paul is like a telescope she holds up to her eye backward to make me seem farther away than she knows I am. Perhaps I shoudn't say it out loud, but I can feel us coming to an impasse one of these days—Paul will be there like a wall that neither of us can climb over, and she won't even want to try—there's already a latent resentment in her that anticipates that moment, and which helps her to prepare herself for the end of our relationship. I don't want that, but I don't know exactly what to do. If our relationship were purely erotic, then the aftermath wouldn't be destructive in the way I'm afraid it will be if things go on this way without changing. But it isn't just erotic, and because I do love her and see how close she comes sometimes to loving me, to slipping out from under the burden of Paul, I feel an awful frustration. She needs a shock of some kind, something to smash that telescope, that wall that's looming up, but I can't manufacture it—even if I could, I don't know if I'd have the right, things are too precariously balanced, I'd only make her hate me afterward. . . ."

Frobenius is regarding him thoughtfully. "Well, what *do* you think could bring about this . . . shock?"

"If I knew that, I wouldn't be sitting here talking so remotely about the whole affair, as though the outcome were a foregone conclusion. It's strange you know: she talks to me about Paul for hours, and I'm sure what she says is honest—*accurate* would be a better word. But somehow I know it's all incomplete, one-sided—not as though she were deliberately leaving things out, but as though there were some things she didn't know how to tell me in terms of *him alone*, and not by way of herself. She talks about herself realistically enough, but the only time Paul takes on substance in my mind is when she speaks of his 'work.' The rest of it is all 'the marriage,' and it's a marriage I can't really believe in, except from *her* side. Paul is a kind of marionette—no, not even that, a *doll* she animates *now* for my benefit. I have the ugly feeling she is quite unconsciously trying to lead me around into a concurrence with the guilt she feels—"

"But what guilt?"

Stefan shrugs. "I'm not a very good analyst. I listen and I know what I hear; but when I draw conclusions I always end up exaggerating, I'm afraid. She *is* asking for a vindication of some kind, though. . . ."

"For the suicide?"

"Not exactly, no—Oh, it set the wheels in motion, but the guilt sense was already there. It's as a fact of their *marriage* that she can't accept the suicide, I think; and now she's trying desperately to convince herself that it happened *outside* the marital framework. Only her memory won't let her—"

"Talk talk talk," cries Wilma, emerging from the kitchen. "Here we come, ready or not," says Barbara.

THE IMPENETRABLE OUTLINE OF HUMAN BODIES IS HORRIBLE

The reading of the protocol has already begun in Oestler's Russian seminar (which Oestler for some reason has asked Stefan to attend) when the door opens and a stranger steps quietly in. Oestler looks up and smiles understandingly, and motions the fellow to come sit down beside him at the end of the long table. Stefan regards the newcomer closely as he creeps along behind the students on the opposite side; he is frighteningly, almost convulsively thin—and pale, pale. His hair is long, dark hair shot through with veins of pure white. Thirty years old? Forty? Slender, knotty arms that do not swing.

With lowered eyes he sits down at the corner of the table; Oestler leans over and whispers something to him (the protocol drones on) and after a moment he glances over at Stefan, who is still watching him, frowns faintly and drops his gaze again instantly. Stefan suddenly finds himself trembling, inexplicably; he looks at his hands—they are twitching uncontrollably. His eyes go back to the stranger and his skin begins to tingle. The room is warm. No; a strange feeling has come over him—akin to that of imminent loss, but in reverse, if that can be, like watching himself fade away in a mirror. Affectively, he feels threatened, but by what? He tries to fix the sensation. He lights a cigarette, his fingers still quivering (all around him students are opening books and shuffling papers; Oestler is speaking. Something.)—my body . . . what is it doing? saying? Do I know this man?

Throughout the remaining hour a verging nausea, under the voices a ring of precipitous danger. Purely internal; no clues; his eyes bounce from that blank face, those bony shoulders. The stranger does not look at him again; a tiny artery clings to his temple like a fishhook, his face is immobile, white and yellow-ish alternately. His knuckles are white pebbles on his fists. Stefan: what do I really see? When did this exchange (for it *is* an exchange) begin? drop for drop, the teeth of caves, growing in darkness. Siren of warning, unfamiliar reaction . . .

THE LOST YEARS

After the seminar they meet; it is Oestler's idea. The stranger's name is Peter Faber. He shakes hands with Stefan, but his eyes are elsewhere, anywhere—flying in seen but unpredictable pat-terns, like flies in the invisible dimensions of an enormous room.

They sit down in Oestler's study; gradually the sounds from the hall and stairway become fewer, until they are left in com-plete silence. Soberly, ceremoniously, Oestler begins to interro-gate Peter Faber. Faber replies to each question directly and with a surprising lucidity, throwing occasional glances in Stefan's direction: no, there is no one now . . . yes, he was twelve years a prisoner . . . mostly in the Urals . . . eighteen when he was captured . . .

Oestler is all sympathy, exaggeratedly patient (or so it seems to Stefan; he wonders that Faber does not notice, or, if he does, does not care). The rosy light from the single lamp near Oestler's desk is kinder to the young man's face—that is, it makes it possible to see that he *is*, after all, a young man.

Stefan's throat is still tight, though he has relaxed somewhat; he does not want to know Faber, he has never *wanted* to know him. A thousand repressed faces forcibly recall themselves in his; there is something macabre, insistently repellent about his entire physiognomy: he has the rigorous look of a dead man. Twelve years! Even martyrs die after a few hours; what he must have been through!

But what is Oestler doing? What does this mutually agreeable inquisition mean? Stefan grows increasingly uncomfortable. Is it for me? Is he using Faber as a lever to pry me open? Why should I have to witness this debasing spectacle? The years have names, and I know them—

A chair scrapes, and Stefan realizes that he has not been listening for some minutes. Oestler and Faber are getting up. Stefan rises just in time to accept Faber's stiff bow-and-handshake (easier to break a man than recondition him!).

"Good night," says Faber. "Forgive me, I am still not well. I've only been back a few weeks. I hope that we shall have the opportunity to meet again some time soon."

Stefan lets the door close, then turns to Oestler, who is wearing a peculiar smile. "I'll be saying good night, too, Herr Professor."

"You have a moment, don't you?" says Oestler, softly.

Stefan shrugs. "Yes, I suppose so," he says reluctantly, and sits down. Oestler comes round and sits opposite him.

"Poor fellow," he says, "depressing."

"Yes," says Stefan.

"He came to me early last week, to ask if he might be allowed to sit in on my seminar. He won't be able to commence regular studies until the autumn. One can't fail to see that there's something wrong, out of the ordinary about him, but I didn't know exactly how to find out what it was. I thought perhaps he had been in some sort of sanitorium; it never occurred to me that he might have been . . . where he was. As it turned out, it wasn't necessary for me to ask: he simply came out and told me— strange how people react to just a little sympathy—he seemed almost eager to talk about it. Terribly moving. Of course I said I'd be delighted to have him in the seminar. . . ."

Stefan waits. Oestler sits with eyes lowered, kneading his hands; he glances up to find Stefan watching him. "I . . . am not quite sure how I should put this," he says, weighing his hesitancy as much as his words, "but I was wondering all evening, for the past several days in fact, if perhaps you wouldn't, well . . . be willing to cultivate this young man's friendship." He lifts his glasses and massages his eyes. "What I mean is, more precisely: would it be possible for you to spend a little time with him, just an hour or two on occasion, until he's become . . . acclimatized, let's say, to life in—here in Heidelberg? It must be an almost overwhelming experience for him, to say the least. I'll do what I can to help, of course, have him over to the house and so on, but I feel he needs—and would be most grateful for—the company of someone who is . . . you know, more—"

"More what?" Stefan interjects.

The blank question is unexpected. "More . . . his age," says Oestler, querying Stefan's question with his answer. "He has no friends here; he must feel as though he had landed on some strange planet, another world than the one—"

"Why me?" asks Stefan, with the same bluntness.

Oestler flushes this time. "I am only trying to be of help to a young man who is very much in need of it," he says. "That should be self-evident. I have turned to you in the belief that you are a person, perhaps *the* person who could, *ja—understand* Peter Faber, his sensations and his problems. Naturally, no one is forcing you to undertake anything you don't want to, and most certainly not if you would find it disagreeable—"

"Which I would," says Stefan.

Oestler crosses his legs. "I don't understand you, Brückmann. To be perfectly frank, I find myself rather disappointed by this reaction of yours. But perhaps I am not being just; I admit I had allowed myself to picture your response to my request quite otherwise, and may therefore be guilty of having misled myself." An audible note of annoyance has crept into these last words.

"No, you have every right to be disappointed in me," says

Stefan. "The very sight of Peter Faber threw me into a nervous turmoil; for me to have anything to do with him is out of the question. Don't ask me why. His appearance, or just *him*—everything started to come in on me at once, and I felt caught, and all my alarm bells began to ring. No doubt that's my fault, as much as or maybe more than his, but there is nothing I can do about it—at least nothing I am going to *try* to do about it. I'm sorry."

Oestler seems thoughtful, but then he shakes his head, and smiling tightly raises his eyes to Stefan. "Don't you think you might be exaggerating your . . . nervous sensitivity just a little?"

"No, I *know* I'm not. I practically had to force myself to come in here with you after the seminar; it would have been better for me to say sorry, I have to run, and do just that—because I *knew* something like this was coming . . . sooner or later it had to."

Something like *what?*" Oestler asks.

"Like this," says Stefan. "Tell me, quite honestly: Do you really think I could be of help to him? Did you ask me to, purely for *his* benefit?"

"Most definitely not for *mine*," says Oestler, growing irritated.

"Then why did you have him repeat all those things?"

"*Things?*"

"You know what I mean—that whole story you say he'd already told you; question by question, answer by answer you let him tell it again, you let him go *through* with it. For whose benefit was that, his or mine? You could have introduced us, waited until he'd gone and then told me yourself. What was the point of the *performance?*"

Oestler stands. "Now see here!"

Stefan rises as well. "No, I'll finish, now I've started. Why did the poor bastard have to recite for you? Who was that for? Did you *enjoy* it?"

Oestler takes a step toward him. "Herr Brückmann, I forbid this tone!" he says hoarsely. "You do not know me so well that you are entitled to . . . question my motivations or my honest intentions. Have I made such a mistake in investing confidence in you? in taking you into my home as a friend and equal? It would seem so!" His voice begins to rise. "It is impossible to attribute your gross breach of . . . taste, of respect, to your age; there is no excuse for it, you are not a child! And I can assure you that next time I shall be less generous, less gullible when presented with the singular phenomenon of a young man who has suffered much but shows few outward signs of it—I shall be forced to infer that he is innately insensitive and congenitally immune to civilized breeding and the feelings of others, and that any attempt to befriend or assist him would be a wasted and perhaps dangerous effort! Now kindly take your leave!"

Once outside, Stefan begins to feel a certain remorse—not so much for having precipitated a crisis in his relationship with Oestler (once he remained it was almost unavoidable) as for having provoked the older man (and for this he takes the blame) to such a naked, unsettling, and ultimately useless outburst against him.

But there is no undoing it now.

THE WIND IN THE WILLOWS

Weichart's voice is gone, but he cannot dispense with laughter. He chain-smokes and gropes for approval on the knees of his companions. A shredded whisper, then a heaving burst of hilarity; you can hear the throat tearing out. Unshaven for days now. (He coughs into a stiffened knot of red bandanna.)

THE TOKEN

"Yes," says Richard Frobenius, "I'd had a couple of semesters here back in 'thirty-nine and 'forty, before being called to the 'defense of the fatherland.' I didn't get back to the university until 'forty-seven; I had plenty of silver in my head but not much in my pocket. One of the first people I met was Barbara. She was a peculiar sort of girl, plump, bright-eyed, serious. We went out together once or twice, and just talked; she showed a real understanding for things not many girls of her age did, even in those days. I fell in love with her, or thought I did; I felt good when I was with her, in any case, and that was rare for me. But every time I felt tempted to get romantic, she steered me in the opposite direction—she knew what she wanted, and it wasn't me. She didn't give me a chance to get all worked up; she wasn't a teaser.

"Anyway, she met Paul before long and that was that. When they got married a few months later and left, we lost touch for a few years. I went on and took my doctorate and became acquainted with Wilma Schlegel; she was looking for a husband and I decided it might as well be me.

"The re-encounter with Barbara was by far-fetched chance, if such things ever are. In the summer of 'fifty-two Wilma and I took a long camping trip through southern France and one evening pulled into a tenting ground not far from Uzes, on a river, and lo and behold, who should be there but Barbara and Paul. Barbara had put on still more weight but hadn't changed much otherwise. She and Wilma struck it off right away (Wilma's one of the few women Barbara's ever been able to get on with, as a matter of fact), and the four of us joined forces for the next few weeks. I hadn't really known Paul before, except by sight. Oh, I'd seen *Bruchstücke* and was running across his name more and more frequently in the newspapers, but I couldn't make the mental connection between the name and the bespectacled adolescent of 1948. Well, he was brilliant, no doubt about it; he knew everything, there was literally nothing he hadn't read, and he had the rare gift of a mind that was both retentive and synthetic. But you know, I never really warmed up to him. He was cruel, I felt, just below the skin. His imagination ran away with him, it was obsessive, it led him to play with people, all the time, and I didn't like it. I didn't see any reason for it.

"Now, if I tell you some things that I've never mentioned to anyone else, it's not only because they may in some strange way be useful to you, but also simply because there's never been anyone else with whom I've talked about Barbara the way I have with you. I have confidence in you, I think you understand her. I must only ask you to keep what I'm about to tell you to yourself, for your own—edification, let's say. But somebody has got to help Barbara, and I can't; I'm not much good as anything but a leaning-post, friend-in-need sort of thing. I don't know if there's anything you can do either, but I'll tell you my little story for what it's worth, even if only to fill in a few blanks on the other side of your picture of Paul. . . .

"A few days after Wilma and I arrived, a small trailer pulled up not far from where we'd pitched our tents, and in the week that followed we got to know its occupants pretty well—they were two very chic Lesbians from Paris. Now I don't know why it is, men never seem to have much trouble spotting them, but women themselves are almost completely oblivious, and even when they *know*, they go on resisting the knowledge as if their lives depended on it. Anyhow, Wilma and Barbara were both blind as bats, whereas it didn't take those girls in the trailer more than two seconds to fix their sights on them with what seemed to me were pretty unmistakable intentions. (The masculine partner, by the way, went for Barbara, not Wilma.) Soon our wives were spending the better part of the day over at the trailer. Paul didn't notice, or if he did, he didn't seem to care, but after a couple of days I sat Wilma down and had a little talk with her. The only effect was to make her furious; she said I had a filthy imagination and she'd talk and associate with anyone she damn well pleased.

"I began to realize, and this is getting to the point, that Paul was taking great secret delight in Barbara's attraction to the other girl, and was even subtly encouraging it. I don't want to make this sound more serious than it was—on the surface it would have seemed quite amusing to an outsider, I'm sure—

but when I saw that Paul was not just playing a harmless game, but was deliberately goading Barbara on, beyond her quite innocent enthusiasm for the girl in question (who, it seemed, was really very bright and cultivated)—well, it disturbed me greatly. I couldn't imagine what was motivating him, but whatever it was, it was downright perverse.

"The situation came to a head when the trailer girls suggested a dinner '*seulement pour nous femmes*' in the trailer. I put my foot down and told Wilma I'd hogtie her if necessary but this was one soirée she was going to miss. I tried speaking to Paul about it, but he just laughed and said, 'Let them go if they want to so much; they're not schoolgirls. They'll let us know *what happens*.' That did it. Then and there I marched over to the trailer and told that pair I knew what they were up to, and they'd better lay off. I got called a Nazi and a few other things for my troubles, but the seduction party never took place, and the next day, after a tearful farewell, during which the two Lesbians and our errant wives exchanged little gifts and what I thought was an inordinate number of kisses, the trailer pulled away. I don't recall what Wilma's friend gave her—a bottle of cologne or something like that—but I do remember what Barbara's suitor gave *her*, because I saw it again, under rather peculiar circumstances—circumstances without which I wouldn't be telling you this as a prelude. It was a tiny amulet of hand-wrought silver filigree, on a chain, quite a fine little antique piece, actually. We all admired it, but I didn't give it any more thought—*then*.

"A little over a year later I happened to find myself in Paris at the same time as Paul and Barbara (we'd been corresponding) and we made a date to meet one afternoon at the Cluny. It was raining, I remember, but I came on foot from the Louvre. All sorts of people were milling about in the entrance when I entered the café. Barbara had said on the phone that they'd be waiting upstairs.

"Barbara was slimmer than I'd ever known her; she looked like a different woman. She had cut her hair much the way it is now, and she was really beautiful. But there was another, subtler change in her as well, I discovered, after I sat down. Usually I'm not so astute, but somehow I recognized, or sensed, right away that a certain odd aggressiveness had crept into her manner. It manifested itself as a kind of protectiveness toward herself and toward Paul, proprietary, as if she didn't quite trust him to speak for himself and didn't trust herself not to. I've seen the same thing in other 'artists' wives,' but then it was usually the very quality for which their husbands had married them, not an acquired characteristic, as this most certainly was.

"Paul was playing a game of a kind, and he went right on playing, off and on, when I sat down, to Barbara's growing irritation. Once in a while he'd stop for a minute or two and listen in on our conversation, without adding to it—and then he'd start up again. Finally we stopped talking and just watched him. What he was doing was this: From where he was sitting he could observe the people coming up the stairs, and whenever anyone coming up caught his fancy he began to spin a fictional biography for whoever it was, and went on inventing until the person had found a table or someone more interesting came along. For example—and with no attempt at an imitation; just so you get the idea—a dowdy middle-aged woman in a soggy hat got a treatment that ran something like this: Madame Geneviève de la Tour, age fifty-four, born in Reims and sin in the shadow of the Cross, wed at thirteen to an unfrocked acrobat, thrice rewed, six legitimate children, two ill, one cat more than that, hysterectomy, ex-contralto, last climbed La Scala on St. Nicholas Day 1922, *vorübergehend* concierge in a mortuary in Menilmontant . . . and so forth, much more than that. It was funny, some of it, but there was also a hysterical ring to it all. I laughed in spite of myself, and kept glancing at Barbara. She was tight-lipped and white. Something was going on, but I had no idea what.

"It stopped raining outside, and the lobby began to clear. Paul fell silent. Suddenly he leaned over to me, confidentially, and said, 'How's Wilma? Still safe and sound?' 'Yes,' I replied, 'she's fine.' He smiled. 'Good,' he said, 'that's what I like to hear.' 'Oh, *Paul*,' said Barbara.

"At just that moment Paul started up again: 'Gaston du Gard, trop tard, bâtard, canard, en garde . . .' Barbara gave a start; I turned to see a young man coming up the stairs. He came straight to our table, nodded, looked questioningly at me and sat down. He was pale, clean-shaven and well-dressed, and very young, not more than twenty. Paul mumbled introductions (the name was really Gaston, it seemed, but I wasn't sure about the 'du Gard') and then the two of them began a whispered conversation. Barbara started to squirm; I couldn't get her to look at me. Finally she burst out angrily with: 'For God's sake, stop it!'—and they both looked up, startled, Gaston a little shamefaced. Paul slapped his hands on the table and said, 'O pardon, pardon. Gaston, say pardon.' 'Pardon,' said Gaston obediently, without a shade of irony. He was trembling, I noticed. Barbara got up. 'I'm leaving,' she said; 'I'm sorry, Richard.' Paul reached out and grabbed her arm and yanked her violently back down into her chair. 'No, you're not going anywhere,' he said sharply, 'and if any apologies are made, I'll make them, not you.' She sat quietly for a moment; I thought she was going to cry. But suddenly she bent forward and shouted at Gaston: 'Why don't you go, then? Why don't you get out of our lives?'

"I still didn't have the vaguest idea who or what Gaston was. For some reason I felt a little sorry for him. 'I'll go if *he* tells me to,' he said, in a ghostly voice; 'I didn't make any of this happen, *you know that*.' Barbara looked at Paul, pleadingly; I held my breath. Paul released her arm, which he had still been squeezing, and turned to Gaston, and nodded. 'Yes, Gaston, go on,' he said. The blood drained from Gaston's face, he stood up shakily, opened his mouth and then closed it again. He reached in his pocket, removed something and stretched out his hand to Barbara. 'It really wasn't my fault,' he said; 'Take it back, please.' Barbara made no move; Gaston opened his hand, and the little amulet from the year before fell on the table. Without another word then, he turned and left and ran down the stairs. I glanced at Paul: he was watching him go, and I saw that his eyes were full of tears. I couldn't make head or tail of the whole affair. 'Gaston du Gard, trop tard, pardon . . . ,' said Paul.

"Not another word was spoken until we were out on the street, where we parted. I never saw Paul again, or Barbara either (although we exchanged one or two letters) until she came back here last year. I've never gotten up the nerve to ask her what it all meant—and she's never once referred to it of her own accord. Perhaps, eventually, you can make something of it; God knows I've tried, but I'm afraid it's too irrational for me. . . ."

THE EYE CAUGHT BLOOD, CAUGHT FIRE

Gerstenmaier hungry, Gerstenmaier thin; only a spark somewhere deep in the mesentery keeps him alive. He is moved by forces of which he knows nothing; when a specific intention ascends to the level of consciousness, when it looks as if he might be obliged to act and *know* it, he begins to shake with unstoppable cold and paranoiac ague. He has, in other words, the makings of a perfect *German* revolutionary: that is, a revolutionary for whom an act so overt as picking his nose in public has far more earth-shaking abstract connotations than loading a real pistol in the privacy of his room, to go and kill the Kaiser.

When, for example, he was in love with Bernadette (or was it Nathalie?), he burned like a cactus inside, intense and black, and by telepathy worked his way through her skin like a tiny worm, making her itch (he thought) with irritation, pity, curiosity. Ah, those few weeks: the silent pain, the stirrings of his death, the inviting smell of schizophrenia; he tracked her in his eyes from cloud to cloud, and his tongue filled his mouth when she landed. He could stare at her for hours then, his eyes would blur with steam while he smiled a smile inferring an immortal *we* in a tragic conspiracy.

Of course, she never noted his existence.

"Paul's father died very suddenly in early April of 1952. Raabe-Speer looked ten years younger in black, so she wore it for about a month, then rented the house in Munich, sold a few things and moved to Frankfurt, 'to be near the only person I have left in the world.' I avoided her as much as possible, but Paul was halfway excited to see her, and what could I say? I was sure she was up to no good, but I had no idea what she might come up with. I found out soon enough: one day Paul presented me with a *fait accompli*—she had talked him into letting her underwrite our debts on *Bruchstücke*. I went wild when he came out with that little piece of news; he hadn't even consulted me before signing the papers. It was all to our advantage, he said, it would save us money in the long run and give us more time to pay the debt off. I was speechless at his gullibility, but there was nothing much I could do but swallow it and hope for the best. Hah!

"With a business sense like his I could see he was capable of signing our souls away if she told him it would be 'to our advantage,' so I managed to drag him off to France that summer. We left Max with an aunt of mine (couldn't ask my father to keep him that long), put our things in storage and simply took off for three months. And it was wonderful; neither of us had felt so free in years. We met people and more people (Immanuel de Bris, for one); we even ran into Richard Frobenius, whom I hadn't seen since Heidelberg. He looked much older and had got married since I had last seen him. He was really funny, up to his neck in the process of being domesticated, all jealous and jittery and wrapped up in Wilma. Paul was wicked: he teased the pants off poor Richard from morning till night...

"Well, when we returned, Raabe-Speer had another little surprise waiting: we'd sent her a check while we were gone—

to pay the storage on our things—and she'd applied it as a payment on our debt. As a result, half a dozen cartons of our most valuable books had been auctioned off. When we got back it was too late; I just sat down and cried. She wasn't moved in the least by what she'd done. 'First things first,' she said. I must admit, that shook even Paul up quite a bit; there were some really valuable books among those lost—a complete collection of *Die Insel*, for example, and a number of books his mother had given him in childhood.

"Other than that, there's not much to tell about the next year or so. Paul was doing more and more work for the radio and began getting some good television commissions too. It was the sort of work he could do in his sleep, practically, without sapping the energy he needed for his *own* work. The second volume of his poetry came out and actually *sold*; we made another, shorter trip to France—to Paris this time—to arrange the terms for the publication of a 'selected poems' in French. All the editors who'd rejected his earlier translations and then turned round and legally stole them, all of them were at the doorstep day and night, literally begging him to come to them, on any terms—suddenly they wanted his name. And the nice thing was, he could afford to say no. . . ."

CROATIAN LUNCH

According to the blackboard in Moritz's hashhouse (across the street from the Cave), today's menu (one mark twenty) is fried pig's liver with fried onions, purée of potatoes, peas and carrots and green salad (two rusty leaves with frail cider vinegar). "Rice à la Freddie" is also available, at seventy pfennigs. Beer, milk, coffee, sprudel to drink (the Coca-Cola man has stopped delivering until a hundred and twenty-nine missing bottles have been paid for). If you want plain water you have to beg for it at the back entrance to the kitchen.

Vera Eichhorn (redhead) is working the counter, handing out numbered priority slips, calling out orders when they come up, admonishing customers to bring back their dishes when through, and railing at everyone stupid enough not to have the exact change. Behind the counter, in the minute kitchen-cubicle, Moritz himself is busily forking slivers of liver in and out of the pitch-black grease in a pitch-black frying pan. Beside him, wearing an old straw hat as a shield from flying oil, perches Freddie, peeling raw potatoes into one huge pot and beating boiled ones to a pulp in another. On first glance it appears that his missing leg is buried up to the knee in mashed potatoes.

In a corner near the stained-glass window, under a poster still announcing last year's visit of Sidney Bechet, Peter Faber is sitting alone, waiting for his order of rice. One by one the extra stools have been filched from his table, clearing a space around it, so that now, as he sits with his hands folded on his books before him and his legs drawn up tightly beneath his chair, looking out over the room unblinkingly, he seems to be presiding over festivities of some kind.

Vera Eichhorn calls out his number. He does not respond. She shouts it a second time, impatiently. The other aspirants for food glance at their tabs; then their voices pick up the number and turn it into a chant: forty-four! forty-four! forty-four! The number enters Peter Faber's thoughts like a distant signal; he cocks his head and then looks down at his folded hands. He spreads them absently and glances at the moist scrap of paper clinging to one palm—forty-four. With a start he jumps up and heads for the counter.

"Are you deaf or something?" demands Vera Eichhorn.

He shakes his head. "I'm sorry," he says.

"Other people are waiting, you know," she says.

"I'm sorry," he says again.

She snorts and reaches for his tray, swings it around and slams it down in front of him. "Liver," she says. "That's one mark twenty. You want anything to drink?"

He doesn't seem to hear; his eyes are glued on the tray.

"Come on, I haven't got all day!"

He begins to shake his head, slowly, and opens his mouth to get his breath; more and more strongly he twists his head from side to side, and a thin whine of protest emerges from his throat. He seems to be gagging. Vera Eichhorn grows frightened.

"What's wrong?" she asks, staring into his face.

For answer he flails out with his hand and swipes the tray to the floor. Vera Eichhorn howls; people jump up.

"No-o-o," cries Peter Faber, and tears from the place like a drunken man, his head lolling. Outside, in the narrow street, he stops behind a beer truck and lets spasm after spasm rack him until he brings up blood.

DEAD SEA SCROLLS

An article entitled "Chancellor and Church," which appeared in the January issue of *These und Synthese*, has been causing quite a stir in academic circles. For the first time since halcyon days, Professor Erich Vollmer has essayed to pronounce on political morality, but his piece, regrettably, betrays no greater acuity than his onetime contributions to the *Frankfurter Zeitung*. In fact, no one seems to be in agreement with anyone else as to what epoch he is referring to. A reviewer in the *Tageblatt* holds that he is speaking of the late Roman Empire, but this is obviously the mistaken result of a too-hasty perusal of the essay, which mentions Adenauer in every other line. A more careful (but anonymous) reader, in a letter addressed to the editor of *T.u.S.*, ventures the opinion that "Adenauer" is a metaphorical way of saying "Kaiser Wilhelm," and supports his view by reference to a little-known work called *Kaiser and Church*, by Waldemar Wentz, published in Graz in 1920. In the same issue, a Lutheran clergyman persuasively insinuates that "Kanzler" might well be replaced in every occurrence by "pope," in which case Adenauer (for whom, to be sure, no seat of government is given) would not have to be translated. Oestler is reputed to have remarked, with obvious sarcasm and in private, that *Weltschmerz* means ulcers and *Seinsgrund* hemorrhoids if a single word in Vollmer's article means anything at all. But the only man who has hit the nail squarely on Vollmer's head is Dr. Ignatz Baermann, who this morning, within the hearing of at least fifty students, shouted from one side of the Hauptstrasse to the other, "So what are you trying to do, Vollmer—write your own Dead Sea Scrolls?"

PAUL / PARENTHETICAL

". . . I feel like a prisoner condemned for life to a cell whose tiny window looks out on the backyard of his own past . . . his memory for binoculars . . . he watches every move that's made there . . . but none of the relatives or loved ones whose actions he observes realize they're being watched . . . they all think he's dead. And maybe he is . . . or *I* am . . . *Some*body is . . .

"Paul and I lived unreal lives . . . those years . . . when his father died . . . Raabe-Speer like a vulture . . . France . . . all unreal . . . We played at being whole, brilliant, free, important, young, innocent, European . . . twenty or a hundred years too late or too early . . . It was a hoax we pulled on ourselves . . . we pulled . . . all the stops . . . used up energies, moral energies we didn't have, not ours, our generation's . . . We concluded pacts . . . absurd . . . we were mad, both of us, insane . . . two years . . . back and forth . . . all invitations accepted . . . a thousand people in and out of our lives . . . a two-year moratorium on everything . . . Seven or eight thousand marks of debts—who cares? Max—he'll grow . . .

"*Die neger und die bärte / haben immer recht / Wer sind wir?* Paul said . . . greater and great extremes . . . what we wanted . . . how does one go about converting literature into life? Make it literature first . . . not worth the price, I'll tell you . . .

"Was it our incapacity? Were we fundamentally dishonest? All our advisors said so . . . they all had beards . . . but it looked like we'd come through . . . *Now I cannot abide the thought of what I loved and no longer love, nor the memory of what I still love and have lost* . . . Who said that? I did. Paul had his back to the wall . . . oh the walls came tumbling down, and there I was, his enemy from behind . . . I wasn't enough . . . I wasn't . . . Oh, I'm drunk and maudlin . . . why did you get me drunk this way?"

SELF-INFLICTED SEBASTIAN / THIRD DREAM

Someone he knows but cannot quite identify runs up to him in a dreadful condition—beaten, clothing torn to shreds, face a mass of bruises. Who did it? Stefan asks. Paul Speer, the other says, resigned. But why? Stefan asks. The other shrugs helplessly. What will you do about it? asks Stefan. What *can* I do about it? replies the other dejectedly; it's no use, who would believe me?

Stefan awakens with the realization that the face, the affective impression of the beaten figure in the dream were those of Paul Speer himself.

MID-FEBRUARY

"What are you doing?" Stefan asks as he comes in.

"I'm painting my nails," she replies, spreading her fingers and admiring them.

"*Green?*"

"What's wrong with green? We're going to a carnival dance, aren't we?"

He shrugs and smiles. "I thought I was going color-blind. Can I use your razor?"

"Look," she says proudly, "I've already done the toes."

"Oh, marvelous," he says. She glances at him suspiciously, but he has gone to the washbasin, and she cannot see his face. He removes his shirt and begins to lather his face. He moves over slightly to watch her in the mirror: she is wearing a look of tremendous absorption and painting her right thumbnail, touching the little finger of her left hand to the index finger of the right, to hold the brush steady.

"There's a fresh blade on the shelf," she says, without looking up.

He changes blades and starts to shave; she begins her left hand. He can hear her humming under her breath: *O Tannenbaum.* He smiles.

"It's Paul's birthday tomorrow," she announces suddenly. He looks at her in the mirror, but says nothing. She does not take her eyes off her hand. "His twenty-ninth," she says after a moment.

A long silence.

"I never thought before," she says. "You're both Aquarius. You're not at all alike."

He laughs.

"Should we be?" he asks, turning to face her, half-shaven. She blows on her nails to dry them. "Um hmm."

He laughs again. "Well, that poses a problem. Should I be more like him, or he like me, or should we strike an average?"

"Don't be facetious. I'm serious."

"Does the astrology go with the green fingernails?"

"Very funny."

He goes back to shaving. She paints her left thumbnail. When she has finished she starts to screw the brush back into the tiny bottle; her hand jerks unexpectedly and tips it over on to the rug. "Oh damn it!" she cries. "Oh damn it all to hell!"

She drops to her knees beside the stain and stares at it. Stefan, his chin dripping, lays aside the razor and crouches beside her. He lifts her face up; she is furious.

"I hope you're happy!" she cries, and charging to the dresser takes out a bottle of polish-remover and a cloth, with which she begins to scrub the green polish from her nails, viciously.

THE JOYLESS STREET

Weichart is dead. On her way back from the funeral, her face at half-mast, Fräulein Gerber runs into D-J and lets herself be coaxed into a nearby *Lokal,* where she dabs at her eyes with a paper napkin and pours out her heart.

It seems the old man had left his room (in the Bunsenstrasse) a week ago, carrying a small suitcase, destination unknown. Two days ago he returned (late at night) and rang the house bell until his landlady (Frau Hilde Laub) awoke (with fragile heart) and let him in. At first she didn't even recognize him, he was in such a terrible state—"as if his insides had been sucked out," his hair "like Struwwelpeter's," pale and grizzly, his clothes in tatters, and trembling violently. Frau Laub began to cry when she saw him. He apologized profusely for rousing her from bed (his teeth chattering, a mere thread of a voice, tears streaming down his cheeks too), but he had lost his keys, his wallet, everything, somewhere, he didn't know where any more. Once inside, he went straight to his room (refusing bouillon, refusing tea, refusing schnapps) and locked himself in, leaving Frau Laub in palpitating distress just outside. She kept calling out his name until he answered her: "*Ja, ja,* still here—go on to bed now." And finally, hearing the sound of his ragged breathing on the other side of the door, she went on back to bed. It must have been after seven that he went out again, because it was not until then that she fell asleep. He had taken his briefcase, with notes and papers inside, and a few personal effects, as if he were planning to be away overnight, and had shaved himself and changed his clothes. At eight o'clock he was crossing the courtyard of the Old University, when he suddenly stopped and toppled like a hollow tree, leaning and collapsing at the same time, not far from the fountain. Some people saw him fall, but he was already dead when they reached him. His ninety-three-year-old mother, who lives in the East Zone, was not permitted to attend the funeral on such "short notice."

PAUL / ELEVEN

"Just before Christmas of 1953, Raabe-Speer telephoned from Berlin to announce her engagement to an architect named Eller. It was the first we'd heard about the romance; we didn't even know she'd gone to Berlin. But she also informed us, in a tone that sounded as if we were supposed to be heartbroken, that she wouldn't be back in Frankfurt for some time. Hurrah!

"The transfer of our mortgages to her still rankled me, but by February we had reduced our total debt to a little less than five thousand marks. And at the same time we'd put enough aside to make a down payment on an apartment in a new housing development. Max had started to go to kindergarten—at a school about halfway between the place we were living in and the new apartment, so that when we moved in he wouldn't have to be shifted. And with him away mornings, I worked too, at an American elementary school, putting every penny I made into the new apartment. I can't tell you how excited we were . . . we were delighted and eager as children with a new toy . . ."

THE BLUE RIDER

It is a bitterly cold, damp evening, not yet midnight. They are in the *Anlage*, walking home from the Cave. The pavements are glazed; Barbara has slipped and scraped her hand; now Stefan is holding her tightly by the arm. As they pass the Bunsen Monument, Freddie skids alongside them and asks if he can walk with them. They are rather surprised by his appearance: he was still holding court in the Cave when they left, and they have not stopped anywhere along the way. He is wearing a light gabardine, altogether inadequate, and appears to have lost his gloves. Stefan offers him his but he refuses with an odd smile. They move along slowly, without talking; every once in a while Freddie stops, and wavering on one leg hands his crutches to Stefan and blows into his hands, which are literally blue with cold. Each time, Stefan again offers him his gloves, and each time Freddie refuses them, always with the same pinched smile.

When they get to Barbara's place she asks him to come in for a coffee and to warm up a little before going on. Hmm, he says, and follows them in. Once inside the room he lets himself down on the bed, drops his crutches on the floor and stuffs his hands in his pockets. His teeth begin to rattle violently. Barbara urges him to take his coat off; no response; she glances at Stefan, who sits down cross-legged on the floor. After a moment Freddie shudders and looks around as if suddenly realizing where he is; he pulls his coat off slowly, works it out from under himself and hands it to Barbara to hang up. Barbara puts some water on to boil, sits down and lights a cigarette; she rubs her eyes. A nervous silence. Stefan has taken a folio of color reproductions of expressionist paintings from the bookshelves and sits turning them one at a time into his lap. Freddie wears a blank smile; he cranes his head to examine the lithographs on the wall behind him. Barbara gets up and opens the window a crack; a little snow sifts in from the sill. She makes the coffee; Freddie regards her, grinning. They sit holding their cups in both hands. Franz Marc's brilliant horses play at Stefan's knee. Freddie clears his throat; the others glance at him instantly.

"Shall I tell you a story?" he asks.

SWEET ENOUGH TO EAT

"A traveler to a distant land has been invited by some wealthy landowners to their country estate. They have spread a fabulous feast to welcome him—huge roasts, game birds, venison and suckling pig, baked fish, all sorts of vegetables, and salads and melons, cheeses, rare wines and so on. The table, which is placed in the center of a spacious salon with windows on three sides, is set for twelve people. Just as he is sitting down, the traveler happens to glance up. He sees that from an opening in the ceiling almost directly over his head a small child, bound hand and foot and quite naked, is slowly being lowered on a rope. He watches openmouthed. The lowering stops, leaving the child suspended at a point about three feet above his head, only lightly swaying. The traveler sees that it has been smeared with honey; its eyes are open and impassive, and it hardly seems to be breathing at all. The traveler looks about him; no one else at the table is paying the slightest attention. So he turns to his hostess and asks, 'If you will permit me, may I be so bold as to inquire of your ladyship the purpose of the child above my head?'

"Her ladyship smiles cordially and replies, 'First of all, you should know that it is the custom here to open all the windows once a day at exactly two o'clock, and to allow them to remain open for exactly one hour.'

"The traveler consults his pocket watch; it is two minutes to two.

" 'When this takes place,' the hostess continues, 'the flies are of course free to enter, but because the hour of their entry coincides with that of our midday meal, we are obliged to make some provision for keeping them occupied, else they would descend upon the table and consume our food. It is for this reason that a child is procured and dipped in honey. There is no more effective lure: the flies cannot resist it.'

"The traveler is aware that the room has been getting darker all the time his hostess was speaking, and now, when he hears a sound like the cutting of wood with a power saw, he looks to the windows opposite him and on either side and sees that they are black with flies. He turns to his hostess. 'But why is the child so acquiescent?'

"Her ladyship blushes. 'You must really forgive us,' she says. 'It isn't always easy to obtain a fresh child every day. This one has had to serve a week already, I'm sorry to say, and it is almost dead.' She lifts her hand cautioningly. 'But don't be concerned; even if it should die during the course of the meal, it will serve its purpose. The flies will not detect the difference.'

"And so the windows are opened and the meal begins . . ."

MUTUAL LACERATIONS

A long pause. Freddie is terribly pleased with himself for some reason. Stefan is simply staring at him. Barbara stands up, and in the same instant Freddie asks, "Do you have a pair of scissors?"

"Yes," says Barbara, "What do you want them for?"

"Let me have them, please," says Freddie.

She fetches them and hands them to him, warily.

"And my coat, please," says Freddie.

Barbara takes the gabardine off the hook and lays it in his lap, frowning. Freddie grins. "Thanks." He takes a deep breath, hoists the coat high with one hand, stabs the scissors into the right shoulder, readjusts them and quickly severs the arm. In the same way he amputates the other arm as well, hacks through the heavy seam just below the collar, makes a little gash at the point where the backstitching begins, lays down the scissors and tears the coat completely in two. Stefan and Barbara are hardly breathing. Freddie seems to have forgotten all about them. Methodically he dismembers the two halves of the coat, until nothing is left but a heap of rags on the floor by his foot. He lifts the scissors up to his face and regards them intensely for a moment. Then he sighs, his eyes dart to Stefan and then to Barbara, briefly; unexpectedly he smiles, lays the scissors down on the bed with exaggerated care, leans over and picks up his crutches. He pulls himself erect. "Good night," he says, debonairly, and swings past them both to the door. They hear him clumping out and hear the front door close.

THE MODEST EPHEBE

A foggy morning. Reinhardt Gerstenmaier keeps popping in and out of Oleo's, pestering Stefan to "spare a few minutes," until finally he gives in. As it turns out, the thing most on Gerstenmaier's mind is Mallarmé. And so they walk round and round the block by the breakwater lock in the Neckar (river barges lined up for passage, the winter river high and fast and dense gray-green), with Gerstenmaier chuckling madly, triumphantly waving his arms, expostulating wildly, loudly, striking sudden poses of abysmal earnestness in which he freezes until Stefan takes his arm (feels him quiver) and gently urges him on.

As a result of this little stroll, Gerstenmaier lies awake most of the night, wondering if he dare suggest the exchange of the second person singular with Stefan. Stefan, on the other hand, has caught a cold.

PAUL / TWELVE

"In late April, just before moving into the new apartment, we left Max with my father and went down to Baden-Baden on a visit to an old friend, Frau Olvig Grumbeck, the widow of a famous psychotherapist of the Twenties. August Grumbeck, who died in 1934, had been German, but the old lady was Swedish—from Uppsala, I think. Paul used to tease her about her woodchopper's accent, saying that after sixty years in Germany she hadn't even got through one tree with it. 'My *dear* young man,' she always replied, 'I have never found it worthwhile to learn German as a language, when it is so much easier for me to go on speaking Swedish with German words.' She had the most delicious schnapps I've ever tasted—like a rare *marc*—and she always offered us tiny cigars from a lacquer case, then took one herself and nursed it all afternoon . . .

"She was slowly going blind, but she still kept up a tremendous correspondence, lately, as her husband's friends all passed away, with young people she was interested in, or had read about. I don't know how she knew so much about what was going on—she had to read things practically letter by letter with a huge magnifying glass. Paul and I got to know her through *Bruchstücke*—one day in 'fifty-one a letter had come from her, saying she had read Curtius's review in *Die Tat*, and she would be happy to become a subscriber; Paul wrote back and they began to correspond. Her letters were quite amazing— what an insight she had into Paul, even before she'd met him personally! I remember once she wrote, 'You're a Werther with a Jewish soul; you'll never be able to worship your own idols. *Vorsicht!*'

"Some of her husband's early monographs had influenced Freud greatly, but Dr. Grumbeck never joined the 'movement' in any official way . . . he preferred to settle down in Baden-Baden, which he called 'the heart of German landscape'; he founded a small sanatorium, chose his patients from an army of postwar incurables and then cured them—or let them die doing things they wanted to do but which had been forbidden them because of the advanced stages of their diseases. He was a fine linguist, knew at least half a dozen languages well enough to read and converse in them—he was convinced that through word associations it was possible to trace through to the roots of a patient's ailment, even when the source, or 'direct cause' as he said, was an accident and not a physical malfunction. Accidents differ from diseases only in that their effects are more rapid, he said, and he held that psychic disturbances derive from physical as well as earlier psychic causes, whereas physical ailments could always be traced to psychic roots. He was somewhat of a Paracelsian: he liked to think of himself as a soul-diviner (psychician, he called it, half-jokingly, in his book *Ego Over, Ego Under*) rather than a physician. He didn't treat his patients, he tried to help them take possession of their own bodies.

"He scoffed at the idea of a 'national' medicine, much in vogue at the time. Yet he could never escape a certain dualism in theory and practice, one which Paul called 'German *id*-ealism': a concept of ethnic conditioning below the conscious surface of the mind that was both mystical and biological. He obtained fantastic practical results with his patients, but his 'methods' were not teachable. He spent his life attacking cancer as a psychic disorder, arrested a hundred hopeless cases, and then died of it himself when he was barely sixty years old. Paul said the body had reasserted its priority over the mind, but Frau Grumbeck wouldn't hear of it. No man who devotes his life to the re-establishment of harmony in others, of psycho-somatic *balance*, she said, no such man can escape the deliberate unbalancing of himself; he must place his own body on the scales. So that even though the ultimate object of all his efforts be his own wholeness, as healer he is always last to be healed. Eventually his body does assert itself, or reassert itself, it has to—the total spiritualization of the body is a terrible concept—but the fact that the body then insists on more than its own rights, and often in the most drastic way, is still no proof of its *priority* over the spirit. The goal is still a balance which only the spirit can impose. . . .

"During that same trip to Baden-Baden Paul and I went to see a documentary film, a French one, one of the first full-length war documentaries to be shown here. The theater was packed with French soldiers and their wives—we were almost the only

Germans there—and all through it we had to listen to their comments. At least I did; Paul sat like a wax figure throughout; he never once turned to me, and when we came out he refused categorically to talk about it. That same evening in our pension he wrote the little piece which asks, Who will make the dead articulate? but it was only recently, in going through all his correspondence, that I realized how profoundly the film, or no, not exactly the film, but something about what it implied, had affected him—and to what an extent that had coincided with his own frame of mind at that moment.

"We visited Frau Grumbeck again the next morning, for the last time. She saw right away that Paul was preoccupied, and she asked him what it was, but he just shrugged it off. But when we left she took me aside for an instant and whispered exactly these words in my ear: 'Something he has seen or heard has burdened him with an extraordinary sense of guilt, an inordinate sense. Watch him; he needs you as a woman, as he has never needed you before.'"

RESONANCES

Barbara in the Cave, wearing slacks and a navvy blouse, her legs crossed standing, nails painted silver-pink, cigarette, laughing unconvincingly, expecting someone, anyone, to come down the stairs, pinching the straw of an interminable Coca-Cola . . . unhappy, bored, hypnotized by the earliness of the hour and the unimaginable time still to be spent here. By choice. Gerstenmaier hovering about Stefan, Freddie's leg blocking traffic, his watery voice cutting smoke. Black and green lines on the crude walls, a clarinet, the sudden crystal xylophone. The girls have all been dipped in water, none of the boys have pants that fit. A table tips over and bottles break, Herr Doktor Jura Herbert Braun runs in, Venetian blinds come down, the music stops. Stefan hardly recognizes her: Where are you, Barbara?

TWO CLOCKS OUT OF TURN

Something of his dream remains and continues to unfold, just out of reach, even after he has awakened. He hardly speaks throughout the day, and often the dream comes close to breaking through to the surface of his mind. But it was present most clearly in the exact instant of waking, as always, just before his wits tied up and he quickly began to hate himself again. In that instant he felt he was a tiny particle of truth, that he wore a transparent body. Now he realizes with pain that the self he relinquished then has gone on dreaming, but his waking attempts to regain the dream are useless. He and the child of his dream (the child of simple truth) share the same disappointments, but they will never look each other in the eyes.

THE YOUNG WORTHY

The floor of the garret where Gerstenmaier lives is tremendous in area, but the slope of the roof on both sides is so sharp that no real walls have been left at all (except at the ends), and there is only a narrow channel down the middle where one can stand upright; it is more than a little like the peak of a pyramid. At one end is a small window through which a puny finger of light tickles the darkness.

Gerstenmaier switches on the light: a single hundred-watt bulb suspended like a hypnotist's device low over the bed (which for some reason is planted in the exact center of the room). Stefan hesitates in the doorway; for a moment in the glare he has the ugly sensation that he is entering an abortionist's operating room. Gerstenmaier moves on over to the window, knocks it open and then switches on the gramophone (the needle has been left on an unfinished record, and as the turntable drags into motion, a low groan is heard). Gerstenmaier turns to face him; the light hangs between them; Stefan cannot see his face. (The gramophone begins to sound like one; the record turns out to be *Parsifal*.)

"*Bitte*," says Gerstenmaier.

Stefan enters, still unused to the light; all he can see is the bed. It is rumpled and filthy. Gerstenmaier steps toward it from the opposite side; Stefan sees his face, white and embarrassed, as he stoops and hastily pulls a rusty-looking quilt over the bedclothes. "Please, sit down," says Gerstenmaier. Stefan glances around. "There," says Gerstenmaier, pointing. "Just push the books on the floor. Will You have a coffee? I'm sorry I can't offer You anything else."

"Thanks, don't bother," says Stefan, placing the books carefully on the floor.

"No bother at all," says Gerstenmaier, and plugs in a coil heater.

"I can't stay very long," says Stefan. "You said You had something You wanted to see me about."

Gerstenmaier rummages about among cracked coffee cups and moldy pots and pans. "Yes," he says.

Stefan waits for him to go on, but hears only an Ah! of discovery. He looks around, tired of trying to penetrate the light barrier; the place is a shambles, a firetrap of books and periodicals and old newspapers, broken records, odds and ends of apparel.

"What was it, then?"

"Wait for the coffee, please," replies invisible Gerstenmaier. "It is something very important."

Stefan picks up a book lying near him and glances at the cover: it is volume one of *The Foundations of the Nineteenth Century*. He leafs through it, comes upon a line drawing of Dante Alighieri, alias Aigler, and puts it back down. Gerstenmaier comes round the bed carrying two cups, hands one of them to Stefan and then sits down opposite him on the edge of the bed. "So!" he says.

Stefan smiles helpfully.

Gerstenmaier smiles back at him, then jumps up again, rushes over to the gramophone, and lays on *Des Knaben Wunderhorn*. When he returns he has a book in his hand. He holds it out to Stefan. "Take it, I beg You!" he says huskily. "As a gift."

Stefan accepts the book from his hand; it is an old paper-bound copy of *Ich und Du*.

"Look inside, please," urges Gerstenmaier.

Stefan opens the book; it is a first edition. There is an inscription in a strong vertical hand: "*Georg Flemmig, im Gedächtnis der gemeinsamen Stunden und zu einem Zeichen der gemeinsamen Ewigkeit. Weihnachten 1922. Martin Buber.*" Stefan looks up at Gerstenmaier, waiting with moist eyes. "Really, I couldn't accept this," says Stefan. "It must have a personal value for You."

"Oh, please, You must, I beg You, You must. It is what I wanted to talk to You about," says Gerstenmaier, tears welling up in his eyes.

"But . . . I don't understand. I've never read it, if that's . . ."

"Not about the book . . . I wanted to talk, no," stammers Gerstenmaier. "Ach, don't You see? You would be making me a gift as well. . . . The *title*."

Stefan's stomach contracts slightly; he really does not understand.

Gerstenmaier gulps the rest of his coffee like a double shot of schnapps, and then leans forward toward Stefan. "I . . . want so much . . . to be Your friend," he says. "Please take the book . . . to signify that I may be permitted to address You as . . . *thou*."

Stefan nearly laughs out loud; he takes a quick swallow of coffee and says in a very serious tone: "But You can call me *thou*, it isn't necessary to give me the book. It must be something You want to keep . . ."

Gerstenmaier reaches forward and takes Stefan's right hand in both of his and presses it warmly. The tears are streaming down his cheeks. "Oh, I thank . . . *thee*," he cries, overjoyed. "I hadn't dared to . . ." He chokes and can't go on.

Stefan stands; he feels the cruel reflex of his laughter rising in him again, and he is not sure he will be able to contain it this time. "I must run," he says, and adds, "my friend" in helpless cowardice.

"I understand, I understand," gushes Gerstenmaier, rising to escort him to the door. Stefan is praying that his new "friend" will not be inspired to kiss him; he can already hear the *Sturm und Drang* of Gerstenmaier's brain ransacking itself for literary parallels replete with embraces.

At the door Stefan turns with his hand already out; Gerstenmaier glances at it and then squeezes it in both his own again. "Goodbye, my friend, for now. I thank thee."

"*Ach, nichts zu danken,*" says Stefan, and pulls out of Gerstenmaier's kneading grip, leaving him to stare after him tearfully as he starts down the stairs.

He has already reached the ground floor when he hears a frantic voice from the eaves shouting his name; he stops and waits as Gerstenmaier charges wildly down the stairs to him, waving something in his hand.

"Thy book," he cries. "Thou hast forgotten thy book!"

PAUL / THIRTEEN

"Six weeks we had been in the new apartment, six weeks— nothing was wrong, had gone wrong. Oh, in the first week they discovered that the plumbing hadn't been installed properly, and for a week or so we didn't know when the water would be running and when it wouldn't. Max was in seventh heaven, he had a room all his own, Paul had started to work the first day we moved in and hadn't let up for a minute—the only thing he complained about was all the letters he had to write and couldn't find time for. He was happier, *evener* than I'd ever seen him, with a healthy distance from all the petty things that always upset him so much. Nobody could have said that he'd suddenly become an extrovert, but for him the mood was almost euphoric; we were both a little drunk with the sudden relaxation we felt . . .

"We'd even had a visitor, a young American poet, a Negro from California named Robert Ashburn with whom Paul had been exchanging occasional letters ever since publishing one of his poems in the third *Bruchstücke*—one that had appeared in an obscure little magazine called *Solvent*, in San Francisco. We'd just missed him the last time we were in Paris, but now, he told us, he was on a Fulbright in Marburg. When we asked him why he hadn't got in touch with us before, he replied very seriously that he'd been ashamed to until he'd learned some more German. And he had—you'd have thought he'd been speaking it for years; it made a great impression on Paul. For the three days he stayed with us, the two of them hardly slept, they talked so much. I never saw Paul take so strongly to anyone as he did to 'Bop,' as he called him. I liked him, but I found him strange, too intense—I guess he frightened me a little; he was so tall and fine-featured and yet so very black. . . .

"He said he planned to go to India when his year in Germany was up (end of July that would have been)—and as far as I know he did. He sent me a handwritten poem shortly after Paul's death, with no letter . . . but I've heard nothing of him since. Would you like to see it?"

MAHAYANA (to Paul Speer)

. . . under the rose-apple tree, premonitions of his future . . .

The buck become an eagle
folds his talons and flies
without past—
Our ivory's companion's gone!

His airless shell retains
a teardrop: *The body's only consolation
is revulsion toward itself!*

Now should we rush to declare
the cruel reprisal, refusal of love?
or *attend like the birds in the rain
the letup of pain?*

No earth between the legs of mud
and *heads that dawn in clouds . . .*
from here it seems the mountains
are wasted in parentheses,
and I am left clutching
a world without words
to make room for some small sorrow.

—ROBERT ASHBURN

PAUL / THIRTEEN (continued)

"But that day. It hadn't rained for a week, the sky was clear
and there was no rain coming. We awoke to a breeze—*I* awoke;
Paul was already up and in the bathroom, singing. I had never
once heard him sing before by himself, only with others, and
then reluctantly. The sun was pouring in, it was cool, an unlikely summer day, so unlike what we were used to that something was wrong with it already. How can I put my finger on
it? Sometimes things open up and become unnaturally clean,
sterile, and it disturbs you without your knowing why, makes
you restless. You open all the windows, you wander round undressed; things seem too simple, lazy, there's no hurry and yet
you feel impatient all the same. You find you've got up an hour
before you normally would, and everything's off. That's the
way that day was. . . .

"Paul went out and came back with a dozen fresh rolls, saying I could throw last night's away. While we were drinking our coffee, Max toddled in with nothing on, carrying his toothbrush. Without a word, Paul spread butter on it and we both lost our breath laughing at the look on Max's face. We split our sides over everything in the newspaper: it was full of the most hilarious news in the history of the world. It was still early. I made a second pot of coffee, we ate all the rolls, a good half dozen each. The sun kept pouring in. Max sat in Paul's lap. I suggested we go out to spend the day with my father, take a boat on the river, just walk around. Max could afford to miss a day of school. But Paul said, 'Oh, let him go, he'll be out at one. There'll still be plenty of time to go somewhere. I have some work to do, wait for the afternoon.' And so we did.

"Yes, we waited for the afternoon. I took Max to his kindergarten, and Paul disappeared into his study. I came back with cigarettes for him and washed the dishes and tidied up. The morning crawled by, the radio played to itself, and the longer that day lasted the more it was as if it hadn't really begun.

"I left the noon meal ready in the kitchen and went into the study to tell Paul I'd only be a few minutes, I'd pick Max up at school and then we'd eat; and he said, 'All right, I'll be waiting.'

"*And that was all he said:* 'All right, I'll be waiting,' and a smile, and back to work, and I went out.

"It was when I got to the school and was standing out front under a tree—I know now exactly how it felt, what kind of tree it was, what I was wearing—it was then that I had just the most fleeting sensation, like a prickly heat, that . . . that what? Nothing really; it passed, but something, somewhere, was wrong, things were too regular, and yet not regular at all—cars going by, the glare, a house I'd never noticed before across the street. My stomach felt light, a double feeling, desirable and hateful all at once. That passed too, Max came running out, it would be *his* day, at least. I took his hand and we skipped along down the shady side of the street, with him tugging at my hand, exuberant. I remember that walk under the trees as a tunnel echoing with Max's laughter, a tunnel through the dense sunlight; you could smell the melting tar, dust; the grass was glistening, the leaves were yellow.

"We came to the corner where we had to cross the road to our house. All of a sudden Max pointed at something behind us, I don't know what; I turned to look, I was carrying my purse under my arm, I dropped it—why did I drop it?—and bent down automatically to pick it up, and in that instant he let go of my hand and darted out into the street. I spun back around, almost losing my balance. He was halfway across and a man on a motor bike was coming. I cried out, Max twisted around, laughing, startled; the man put on his brakes and leaned sharply to one side to avoid him, but brushed him anyway as he went by. Max fell down, half under his own impetus, I screamed and dashed out after him. I snatched him up; he was too frightened to cry. The man dumped his bike on the traffic island and came back to us, white-faced. I was trembling terribly, and I don't remember a word he said, only that he was furious. I slapped Max, hard, the only time in my life that I have really hit him—and it wasn't to punish him, either. It seems to me now that I wanted to stop something by striking him, hold something back, change the direction of that day. Then there was a policeman there asking questions, and I said it was my fault, and I had to listen to a lecture from both him and the driver; I thought they would never finish. I kept looking at our house and it kept staring back at me out of the light. Finally the policeman went away and the man drove off and I wrenched Max off his feet and ran with him under my arm like a parcel across the street and into the house and up the stairs, shaking more and more uncontrollably, biting my lips until they bled . . .

"And the door to our flat was locked. I hadn't taken a key. I didn't bother to knock, I began to pound on that door, I tried to kick it in. I'd *known* it would be locked. Max began to scream, people came out of other doors, they pulled me away and held me, I was hysterical, I couldn't make sense, I couldn't catch my breath. Someone called the police. I was weeping insanely, I didn't have to wait: *I knew.*

"Finally the police or the fire department or somebody came and broke the door in, and the gas came pouring out. It was exactly what that day itself had smelled like from the very moment I woke up in it. . . ."

THE SOUL IN HANDCUFFS

The following week-old letter is awaiting Stefan at the American Express this morning:

Le Parc de l'Air
16.II, 1956

My dear Stefan,

It may be this letter will never find you, but I rather fear that, like my last, it will reach you and then lie unanswered. I sincerely hope that this will not be the case. Granted, you have made your decision and we must *both* abide by it: I may no longer make demands of you (that *is* what it means to you in large part, is it not?). But oh, my young friend, you will learn all too soon that to be free (or to free oneself) of a discipline (even as gentle as mine) is less to escape from onerous duty than from responsibility, and without the acceptance of responsibility there can be no life incentive. None of us lives in that Rabelaisian monastery where one may do as one pleases (and whether this is to be lamented or not is an abstract matter). But my purpose in writing again is not to arouse old resentments or to repeat the admonitions of my last letter. Let me say merely that I still expect as much of you as I ever did, and pray you will not lose yourself in meaningless pursuits or unworthy environments. There is so much to be done, and you have so much to *give*.

Le Parc de l'Air (you will have noted that this letter is
not from Paris) is a small *domaine* not far from Arles, and
it is where Edith and I have come for our honeymoon. Yes,
we are married—for almost a week now—and both of us
are happier than ever before in our lives. I hope this announcement will not come as too great a shock to you, but
that you, upon reading it, will even share in our happiness.

Do reply! A few words will suffice to reassure us that we
have not lost all traces of your regard. Your continued silence
(unless, of course, this letter should return) must signify
only one thing: total indifference. And that I should regret
more than I can say—not for my sake, but for yours.

We expect to return on the 23rd to Paris, where, not without trepidation, we shall await your reply.

If you are still in Heidelberg, please convey my best wishes
to Frau Speer and remember me to Professor Oestler, who,
as I am sure you have come to appreciate, is a man of great
sensibility and personal charm.

Your

DE BRIS

For a long moment Stefan stares off into space, looking as if
he were trying to make up his mind whether to laugh or cry.
Finally he stuffs the letter into his pocket (rather viciously) and
goes out.

At noon he meets Barbara in the swarming canteen of the
New University; he has not seen her for over two days—she is
going through the ordeal of composing the memoir that is to
accompany her compilation of Paul's "posthumous papers."
She is distracted, listless, her eyes are black with fatigue, she has
an enlarged pimple on her neck at the collar line, almost a boil.
Now, sitting there in all that uproar, drinking milk soured by
interminable cigarettes, listening to her disconnected complaints, fretted by her run-down appearance, he begins to feel
an empty disillusion, a weary indifference taking the place of

his sympathy, and he is greatly relieved when she dashes off to class.

He spends all the afternoon in an out-of-the-way café, writing and rewriting his reply to Immanuel's letter, until he is satisfied that his words neither intentionally lie nor deliberately speak the truth.

But when he has already dropped his letter in the box and it is quite beyond recall, he suddenly has a clear vision of Edith, reading it, only Edith, and wishes for an instant, for her sake, that it might have contained other words: some cryptic phrase of sympathy that only she would understand.

SCENE FROM A *BILDUNGSROMAN*

They have been to the late showing of *Le Jour se léve* (*Originalfassung*) at the Kino Camellia. When they come out it has just stopped snowing and the air is dry-cold; an edgy wind is picking up; specks of powdery snow are flying. He cautiously lays his hand on her shoulder, sure that she does not want to be made conscious of his touch. They reach the bridge without having spoken a word. She glances up at him suddenly; tiny snowflakes are clinging to her face without melting. Then she looks back down.

"Say it."

He feels her shrug under his arm. She gives a little self-deprecating laugh; they walk on; she wipes away a strand of hair that blows into her eye.

"The last time Paul and I were in Paris . . . we saw an American version of the same film—with Henry Fonda I think it was. Paul loathed it; he said he didn't understand how Americans could be so vicious and sentimental at the same time . . . But I liked it, I hadn't seen the version we saw tonight, didn't even know it was originally a French film until he told me. I said, pretty lamely I suppose, that the people in the American version had been believable enough. Paul just laughed and said, 'Since when is it necessary for people to be believable; who is believable?' "

They reach the other side of the bridge; the wind blows them across the street. They start down toward the Bismarckplatz.

"I still like the other one better," she says, "but I couldn't really say why I liked it, then . . ."

"How does it end?" he asks suddenly. "The same way?"

She looks at him sharply. "Have you seen it?" she asks.

He shakes his head.

She stops abruptly. He turns back to face her and finds her angry. "What's wrong?" he asks.

"He doesn't die!" she says vehemently. "That's how it ends, that's how I liked it. Why should he die? Is there any reason— except to make people think they've seen something or understood something they haven't? The American one didn't have a happy ending, it was just more believable, that's all; nothing to do with logic, or acting, or art . . . Gabin was marvelous, but he didn't have to die . . . that isn't the way it is!"

He takes her arm; she jerks it away.

"I was only asking; I don't disagree," he says.

"I'm not asking you to agree," she cries irritably. "Paul told me, I remember he told me the French one ended with his death, and do you know what he said? he said that was *regrettably* the only possible outcome . . . And I said no; life may not be logical, but art *can* be, there's no call to play around with things until they seem more irrational than they already are. Why make that kind of distinction between life and art? he asked. His death is logical enough, either way. You haven't even seen the other version, wait until you do and then get upset, if you want to . . . Well, I've seen it, and I was right; *he* wasn't . . ."

Her lips begin to quiver; she is ready to cry.

"Come on," he says gently. "It's too cold to stand here this way . . ."

They start walking again.

"I'm sorry," she says.

"There's nothing to be sorry about," he replies.

"*Do* you agree with me?" she asks.

PAUL / FOURTEEN

"In the evening of the same day that Paul's death was announced in the papers I received a telegram from Frau Grumbeck expressing the shock and grief she had felt on reading the news. A letter would follow, she said, and on the morning after the funeral it came. It was too soon for me to hear what she said in it—without beating about the bush she spoke what was on her mind. It cut me to the quick, that letter, and though I know now that it did help to diminish, or at least inhibit, the formation of guilt feelings in me, *then* the letter irritated me, it seemed so objective, so pompous, so indifferent to the effect of Paul's death on me . . . and, in many ways, I still haven't got over it.

"She said this: she reminded me of her last words a few weeks (it seemed years) before, about his needing me as he had never needed me before, and said I might think, in recalling them now, that I had left certain things undone, that in some way I had failed him as a wife, or as a woman. Her reason for writing was to forestall any such thoughts—have them later, she said, when you can grapple with them, but not now or for a long time—we all fail, she said, and we all run the danger, in recognizing our failure retrospectively, of wanting to take all the responsibility for it on ourselves, especially when memory is so ready with verbal props to help us accuse ourselves. 'I am retracting my last words,' she said, 'for a later time when you will be better able to fit them in the larger perspective of your memory of Paul himself, not of your *marriage*. Mourn *him*, and not the loss of anything else.'

"I felt immediate resentment—I had the right to mourn in

my own way for as long as I liked, hadn't I? But the letter said, 'Read on, dear Barbara, don't stop now,' and I did, getting more and more outraged at her presumption. She had made a mistake of judgment, she said: she had had a great regard for Paul always—but she had developed a too-readily forgiving *weakness* for him. By this she felt she had slighted me and cheated herself; she had been forgiving herself for her own errors as a wife by watching their repetition in me. She had overlooked, or ignored, Paul's natural selfishness as an artist; she had been tolerant of it at my expense. She begged my forgiveness—can you imagine?—for not ever having incriminated him, for not having had the courage and for being too selfish to express an insight into his character that had been manifest to her from the beginning. . . .

" 'It is no comfort to say it now, but the ultimate vital *fault* was in Paul,' she said (with my poor dead Paul!). 'We women are only human, especially as wives, and more especially as wives of artists; no matter how often we feel we can touch on the nerve center of our husbands' art, on their masculine power, we still remain rooted in life at a much more primitive, invariable, more *logical* level (these words are hers), and we are never capable of a total sacrifice of ourselves to their ends, no matter how much we love them or they love us. We must go along, *but we must not leave the ground.*'

"Paul knew this, she said, he knew it with an intuition we would normally describe as feminine; he resisted not merely the downpull of his own individual self, as a *particular* man, but the burden of marriage, the responsibility of fatherhood, every isolating checkweight on the mundane human level as well. He despised his own complexity and yet wanted to extend it to embrace the multitudes, *in his mind*, all human experience, *in his mind*. It drove him to try to become completely artist, completely actor, demiurge and destroyer, at a distance; to become totally self-sufficient and independent and infallible. He came to take every death but his own seriously.

"Ultimately we women do not care for art, she said, we mean something else each time we use the word; we don't believe that things are so complicated, so *wrong* even as the artist would have us believe, or at least so *incorrigible*. And we are not altogether mistaken, not in human terms, and not from our own limited standpoint, our own more immediate perspectives. The weight we exert, the pull, is not meant to be total; but from it must come the tension out of which the new human form emerges, the form which is neither god nor dust. There is no other way. It may never be demanded of us that we alone create this tension, just as there must be a willingness, a recognition on the part of the man, that he cannot go the whole way alone—no matter how powerful, how self-sufficient, how potently alone he may feel—he must still make the one overture to life and accept the one responsibility of a single alliance that will precede his art. And this is what he promises, whether he knows it or not, or is ready or not, in the moment he marries. You didn't fall down; Paul's death is a burden his own memory must bear, she said. For you to try to take it on yourself would be equivalent to letting him absorb you, take you off to nowhere. Do not let yourself be destroyed by what your memory of him, and your love for him, must now relegate to *his* incompleteness....

"I read that letter I don't know how many times that morning, weeping tears of pure rage and frustration—and self-pity. I've read it a thousand times since then, and even though I accept now that what she said came from her heart, and that she felt she had to say it then and not later, I still have not forgiven her....

"She begged me to come down to see her, but I never did— for one ostensible reason or another. The real reason was that I couldn't bear to face her; beneath everything, I knew I would try to defend Paul, and I wasn't sure I could . . . . She was right, after all, in a way that no one has a right to be. And now she is dead, too....

"I'd just laid the letter aside when Raabe-Speer came in. Eller, who'd turned out to be a sympathetic sort of fellow, waited out in the car; they were on their way back to Berlin. She didn't waste time or words. She just looked me in the eye

and said with a straight face, 'Well, are you satisfied now?' At
that moment I knew what kind of people had run the concentration camps; if I'd had a gun I'd have shot her without a
twinge. She wanted to make some things clear; she would pay
the remainder of the debts, but in exchange she wanted the
rights to all of Paul's published works, in perpetuity. I stammered no, I would pay the debts off, I wanted to, they were
mine now, the debts, the poems, all that was left of him. 'The
only thing you have left is a filthy conscience,' she said, 'and I
won't take that from you. As for the rest, we'll see what the
courts have to say....'

"I saw, all right. Within a few months she had closed down
on everything, including the apartment. The one *thing* she
didn't take from me was Max—though she went as far as to try
to have me declared mentally incompetent. It's a good thing
she didn't keep it up just a little longer, I'd have been worse
off than just incompetent....

"When she finally left that day, I was on the verge of total
collapse. My father tried to get me to lie down, but I was
beyond listening. I couldn't see, I couldn't hear, I couldn't
think. I wanted to explode, to fill up all the space I felt around
me; the feeling reached to the tips of my fingers. I ran out of
the house, got exactly as far as the top step on the porch, tripped
and fell down the stairs and landed on my back. I was knocked
out cold. When I awoke the doctor was there; I was face down
on the pavement on a blanket and he was prodding my back.
I was still drowsy enough to feel perfectly blissful until the next
morning; I'd done very nicely, I thought...."

"OPEN THE DOOR," SAID GOLDEN

Stefan has just passed the entrance to the public baths in the
Bergheimerstrasse when he hears a voice cry "Hallo!" He turns
instinctively ("Open the door," said Golden; "one time it will

be your angel.") and Peter Faber, all smiles, grotesque, his long hair flopping waterlogged, jogs up to him swinging a dilapidated satchel.

"*Guten Tag!*" he says heartily.

"*Morgen,*" replies Stefan, taken aback. "Been swimming, I see."

"*Ja,*" nods Faber, vigorously, still beaming, "I go every day. For my system," he adds.

"Oh," says Stefan. "You'd better be careful, you'll catch cold."

"*Ach, nein,*" Faber protests. "Not me."

Stefan shrugs and speeds up; Faber trips along beside him, wielding his satchel like a schoolboy.

"Are you going to the lecture?" asks Faber hopefully.

"Oestler's? No, not today. You?"

"Oh, *nat*urally," replies Faber. "It's the last one of the semester."

Silence. Then, as they come to the Bismarckplatz, "Are you going up the Hauptstrasse?"

Stefan almost lies, but then says "Yes" and unconsciously slows down. He has never seen Faber so animated before; he suspects that the performance is for his benefit, and he cannot imagine why. But the thought leads him to ask himself pointedly, forming the words in his mind, why he has always found him so repulsive; uneasily he glances over at him. At the same moment Faber skips a step or two ahead of him, turns around forcing him to stop, and as it he had been reading his mind, blurts out:

"Why do you persist in disliking me so?"

Stefan's mouth falls open; he shakes his head. "But I—"

Faber wags a finger in his face. "No," he says reprimandingly. "Don't say you don't when you know you do."

"Really," Stefan says, irritated at being trapped this way.

"If I sense it so strongly, it's better that I let you know I do, and ask you why," Faber insists. They are blocking the narrow pavement; people push by them muttering. Faber draws Stefan into a doorway. "I don't mind if you think I am a fool," he says evenly, almost confidentially, "because I *am* a fool, it was my fate to be *made* one . . . but I am only my *own* buffoon."

Stefan makes it plain that he is not even listening.

"I don't mind if you don't want to be seen with me, or don't want to talk with me; you have the right to avoid me—or perhaps the *need*; how can I know that? But you have *no* right to despise me—in yourself I mean—not even now at this moment when I'm forcing myself on you. . . ."

He hesitates a second, and Stefan takes the opportunity to step back into the street. But Faber yanks him back; his eyes grow alarmingly wide. "Look at me!" he says harshly, still not raising his voice. "Do you know how old I am? My birth certificate says I was born in 1926, and that would make me thirty. But do you know how old I *really* am? No, and who does? who *could*? I am a curiosity, a specimen, a useless pitiful anachronism—I look it, I feel it, I *am* it. Yes! It is purely incidental that I am also a weakling, I am that too, it is even a joke of a kind, because by all rights, being weak I should have died. Now I need all the pity I can find, from all those who have pity to spare and are only too pleased to bestow it, and from those who have none but whose laughter will do—their pity enables me to hate myself, and not them, for having been too weak to die. You see, I know how to use it, their pity, therefore I deserve it. I'm not insensitive; the more hypocritical the pity, the more clearly it defines the distance between me and their world, *this* world I have come back to, gives me to know the confines of my weakness, and tells me what I have to hear: that I am no more *essentially* dead than those who pity me.

"But you, *you* have no pity to show me; no, you even despise me. Congratulations! You are different from all the rest, you are stronger; and that is what I do not understand. You are the one person who should be able to look at me and *comprehend* me, how I could become what I have become. It should be the easiest thing for you to do, the most *natural* even. You just don't *want* to! What are you afraid of seeing—your*self*? or do you think you have already? In *any* case, it's no solution when you pretend I don't exist. Not much may be left, but for you there is something—separate from you, contemporary with you, and not at all despicable. Your recognition of it, your acceptance, is *necessary*—for me to *take* pity, and for you to *refuse* it. . . .

"Reject me if you like, but as a *person*, not the generalization, the abstract of what you fear. Only *see me*, make room for me, for an instant, *once*. Otherwise, one day even the pity of Christ himself won't be enough to justify my life. That is not a threat, it is the *truth*."

Suddenly Stefan's chest tightens in a sharp cramp; involuntarily his hand goes out and touches Faber's sleeve, staying him. The most concise pain he has ever felt shoots through him, piercing the armor of years to the sensible heart of memories behind it. For an instant he neither breathes nor sees. Then slowly, in a cautious exhalation, the pain relents. Peter Faber reappears—anxious, distinct.

Neither can bring himself to break the silence, not for a long time. It is a real silence: the street is a mute procession on a screen. Then finally Stefan takes Faber's arm and says, "Come on, you'll be late for Oestler's last lecture."

"*Ja*," says Faber. He wipes his mouth with the back of his hand, and smiles.

BREAKING CAMP

Reinhardt Gerstenmaier, of spurious mention, constipated and frayed by unrequited love, boards the *Strassenbahn* that flies by Königsstuhl, and reconnoitering on numbered trees, departs for Denmark to learn Danish and read Kierkegaard in the original. He leaves behind a tragedy of unpaid bills, of trash and worn-out records (Mahler, Schumann, Wagner), unmixed feelings and unbroken hearts. Adieu! *Tschüss!*

"Please don't touch me."

"I'm not touching you. You must get some sleep."

"No . . . I want to lie this way awake, and have you talk to me. Come just a little closer. There, yes there. Don't touch me, though. Oh, it's so warm. Things keep swimming by . . . and the flies!"

"There aren't any flies."

"I close my eyes and listen to you breathe, I open them and I can't hear you any more or see you. Tell me you're here . . ."

"I'm here, but sleep, go to sleep."

"If I could only be sure, really sure . . ."

"Poor Barbara . . ."

"Paul . . ."

"Yes . . . but sleep."

"Tomorrow . . . the day after tomorrow . . . at last . . ."

AMOR FATI / FOURTH DREAM

Stefan is being pursued by a car. He can run just fast enough to stay a few feet ahead of it. Perhaps even faster, but he knows that he would tire after a while and the car would run him down. If he turns to either side the car turns too, and he realizes that though he is in a certain sense its captive, he is nevertheless determining the direction in which the vehicle moves.

He manages to twist about and run backward for a few seconds without change of speed, so that he can look into the car. Without surprise he sees that he is himself the driver; at least there is a strong resemblance, although the driver seems a little older and wears a look of fierce resolution, of iron will.

For a moment or two Stefan stares straight into his eyes, but he gives no sign of recognition. With a skip (flighty, light-hearted) Stefan turns away and resumes his forward movement, and gives no more thought to the driver.

He is confident that he has the stamina to keep on going as he is for a long time, perhaps indefinitely—but for some reason the small distance separating him from the car begins to become irritating. There is something so absolute about the gap, as if it were an invisible, fixed bond. But who has tied it?

The sameness becomes intolerable, and so he begins to formulate a plan: he will slow down by infinitely tiny degrees (sure somehow that the speed of the car will remain constant), cutting the distance imperceptibly until he touches the vehicle. *First.* It is important that he make the contact; he feels an influx of extreme confidence, all the excitement of a great discovery. And so gradually he alters his pace—or rather, as a sensation, his pace slows down of itself. Easy: he feels the growing nearness of the car in the hollow of his back. He is almost gliding now, his movement is so smooth; each careful stride brings him closer and closer. *Now:* let himself be touched, nudged, borne, lifted by that force behind him. As it enters his body, his eyes are already choosing a new route. . . .

For a split second, as active, external dreamer, he sees his own face, up close; it seems a little older and is wearing a look of fierce resolution, of iron will . . .

He leaves the ground . . .

ISIS IN LOVE

He awakens suddenly, just before dawn. Barbara is turned on her side, with her back to him, toward the outside of the bed. He uncovers himself carefully, not to disturb her; her back lies bared for a moment from the shoulders down to the triangle at the base of the spine. Nothing has any real color yet; her flesh is a rotogravure. Just above the coccyx one vertebra stands out a little more than the others, out of line, accentuated by a touch more light. It has something watchful about it, he thinks.

She shivers; he pulls the covers back down around her; she rolls onto her belly, her face still hidden from him. He steps over her, out of the bed, brushing her accidentally with his leg; she stirs faintly.

His lower belly is swollen, stretched tight and a bit painful; he is erected. His skin refuses to react to the chill; he does not want to wake her entirely. Quietly he opens the door and steps across the hall to the bathroom.

When he comes back in he is still half-tumescent, and his flesh has contracted with the cold. His teeth are on edge and he is awake. The light has changed: the room is gray-blue; in it two or three yellow objects stand out: a blouse, a bookjacket, a lampshade.

She is lying on her back now, he sees, with her arms folded on top of the blankets, and as he approaches the bed, she turns her head to him. Her eyes are open and fixed on the level of his waist. He stops beside the bed and smiles down at her; she glances up into his eyes for an instant. An uncertain smile jerks at the corners of her mouth like a tic; she drops her eyes again. Suddenly she draws a deep breath, tremulously, like a child after long weeping. He regards her face from above; in the half-light it *is* the face of a child, large-eyed. The sight of it warms him; at the same moment he feels an involuntary sexual thrill that both excites and embarrasses him. He leans over to kiss her, to sit down and cover his nakedness—but she looks up quickly with startled eyes and says huskily, "No, just stand like that, for a minute. Please."

He straightens up; a strong apprehensive urge passes through him. She is breathing heavily. She raises her hand: it will be to caress him.

When she touches him he quivers involuntarily. Her hand is killing the desire he felt; he struggles not to lose it, inwardly, but outwardly he remains passive. She begins to win a ritual of her own from the contact with his sex. He is left outside it, growing weaker, helplessly cut off from her private act of adoration. His legs tremble; he is up to his waist in cold water; he shrinks until he cannot stand it any longer, and then steps back, out of her reach, without being conscious of having meant to.

She looks into his face, questioningly, then twists away and buries her face in her pillow.

ALL THESE DREAMS OF INADEQUATE ANGER

"It's you, not just your body, that lies down with me, and it isn't only my body either, but me, and the time is right now, not last year or five years ago, and if we make love we're making it right now. I'm in love with you here, not you there, and I wanted to think there was just the faintest, wildest chance that you might be in love with me, or that you could be. I didn't care if you could accept it now or not, or how much time it would take to rid yourself of the compulsion to keep on looking for him, whether in me or in anybody else or in all other men for that matter. But you can't understand that he's dead, or you won't, and no matter how many lovers you have now, how many substitute phalluses you find, you won't change that and you won't have him back, and you can't go on loving him this way, by proxy. He's dead, all but the words. Listen: Paul the artist and Paul the husband, they weren't the same man even, they never were, never would have been; you couldn't put them together then, and you haven't done it now. You've finished the book, like a personal solution to a puzzle, but it's only a testament, if it's that: an effigy; but his body is still dead. Whom do you think you are holding when I'm in your arms in the dark? who is there when you close your eyes? Do you watch yourself do what you do, say what you say? think you expiate a guilt you want to feel and can't, by wasting your body in a useless magic, this insane erotic ceremonial you think will recreate him?"

PERIHELION

A dark young man is afoot in Berlin, for the first time in many years, walking aimlessly, carelessly, around the peripheries of his memory.

A certain house in Moabit is no longer standing.

No one is alive in the Brunnenstrasse, or over the line.

He drifts along in a benign insanity, with tears stinging his cheeks. The pavements seem new, untrodden; even the cobbles in the streets have been turned. Lost voices, exiled songs, off in the elms, within the unsprung buds.

He sits for a while on a bench (Leonce paws the ground, gnawing fistfuls of grass); over there somewhere, well guarded, shades of tenement dwellers fly their shrouds from the backbones of courtyards, tiny brown boxcars lie idle for miles, the smoky stench of cabbage and coal fire lingers in preliminary spring.

(But only one stone swan stands upright still, one Jewish Pavlova in a wide white sea of rubble.)

EVERY MORNING BEFORE BREAKFAST

On the terrace of the Hotel am Botanischen Garten Barbara Speer is sitting with Georg Loh's representatives Rudolf Munin and Eugen Hugin. It is ten-thirty in the morning; Stefan has been up and out since dawn. Loh (it was announced when they arrived last evening) is "regrettably" out of town; Deckeler is dead (died suddenly!); and until Loh returns, Hugin and Munin are in charge. Make the best of it, Barbara!

At this particular moment she and Munin are making plans for the day (he is a pudgy man with slick black hair and yellowish fingers). Hugin seems to be listening (raptly and agreeably) but he is not. Beneath the table his tapered hand (immaculately cured) rests laxly on the ribs of a stray female Dalmatian; slowly it moves, without changing attitude, down the dog's side toward the haunches; the dog's breath quickens.

(Barbara laughs.)

Hugin's fingers tuck in slightly at the first knuckle, exerting a slight pressure; a blue racination of veins becomes visible, and three white ligaments.

(Munin titters.)

His hand moves down, down, almost imperceptibly. The bitch cocks her head, twists it down and sideward, attentively: her tongue rolls out redly.

"He will be back tomorrow, though, won't he?" asks Barbara.

Hugin's free hand takes up his coffee. He holds the cup poised before his mouth, but does not drink.

"*Always*," says Munin.

Barbara turns to Hugin. His eyes are on her, unblinking. The cup is still at his mouth.

"Have you read the manuscript?" she asks.

"Hmm?" he murmurs.

She turns back to Munin. "Have *you* read it?"

(Hugin drains his cup.)

"Yes, I've read it," says Munin. "Have *I* ever *read* it!"

Hugin suddenly squeals; the dog yelps and springs away.

"We've *all* read it," he says. "Do you know the Heine Routine?"

"The Heine Routine?" asks Barbara. "No, I'm afraid I don't."

Hugin and Munin join hands and recite, sing-song:

"I am a German poet,
Well known throughout the land;
When famous names are mentioned,
My name is first on hand."

"I know *that*," declares Barbara.

"Wait, you haven't heard the rest:

"But what I lack, my baby,
Is lacked throughout this land;
When grievous pains are counted,
Mine's right here in my hand!"

"Aouu!" cries Munin.

Hugin giggles. "I guess I know one when I see one."

Munin gasps. "Yup! Yup!"

"What do you mean?" asks Barbara, quite confused.

Hugin puts on a serious face. "That we just can't *wait* to get our hands on the rest," he says.

Munin topples from his chair, convulsed.

THE HÖLDERLIN ROUTINE

After an exhausting afternoon of zoo and war memorials, they find Stefan back at the hotel, have dinner there and then repair to Barbara's room with several bottles of Doppelgänger Rotkopf '47.

Now the bottles are all empty, Stefan has passed out on the bed, Munin has developed a cramp in his left thigh, and Hugin is massaging it. Barbara seems resigned, too tired to move.

MUNIN: Harder! . . . *Ach, ja, so.* . . .

HUGIN (*to Barbara*): You mean you've never heard of the Hölderlin Routine, either? Tut, tut, and you a poet's widow!

BARBARA (*unwillingly*): No, I haven't, and I'm not so sure I want to, either.

HUGIN: Come, come! You haven't *lived* until you've heard this one. Your ignorance must be rectified at once!

MUNIN: Get with it and rectify this, you second-rate Gründgens!

HUGIN (*striking a poetic pose*): "The gods are not the property of men." (*To Munin*) Better?

MUNIN: Keep kneading.

HUGIN: "They belong to the world. And when they smile upon us, we belong to them . . ."

(*Munin bats his eyelashes and simpers.*)

HUGIN: "Just feast your eyes on this Aglaia! See how she smiles at me and makes me her prisoner."

(*Munin curls his lips in a revolting smile and claps his hands on Hugin's shoulders.*)

HUGIN (*aside*): "That smile doesn't only belong to whoever owns her, either."

MUNIN (*pouting*): I'm not an Aglaia, I'm a Pomona. (*He groans.*) A little higher . . . *ummp! ja*, there.

HUGIN: "You're an Aglaia if *I* ever saw one. But by Gad, the *water* here . . ."

MUNIN (*alarmed*): What water?

HUGIN: Stop spoiling the routine! ". . . the water here should be more limpid . . ."

(*Munin snickers.*)

HUGIN: ". . . Like the water of Cephissus or the Erechthean Spring."

MUNIN: The *what* spring?

HUGIN: The Erechthean!

MUNIN: Oh, thorry.

HUGIN: I'll bet. "A goddess deserves something better than this muddy hole."

MUNIN: Well!

HUGIN: "But then . . . (*quaveringly*) we're not in Greece."

MUNIN: Ooh, are you a *Greek*, sir?

HUGIN (*dejectedly*): "No, I'm afraid not. Alas and alack, it's my sorry lot to be a . . . *German*."

(*Munin faints dead away.*)

BARBARA: Is that all? I don't see the point.

HUGIN: All? *All?* [*He lifts his eyebrows, lowers his eyelids and devises a soulful expression.*] The *point* is immortality.

BARBARA: Immortality?

HUGIN (*emphatically*): *Im*-mortality!

(*Munin, recovering miraculously, starts playing an imaginary violin.*)

HUGIN: "All that is good in thought and deed, every beautiful thing, is immortal, a Genius that never forsakes us. Invisibly it accompanies us throughout our lives, right to the [*sotto voce*] grave. But then! then from the grave it takes flight, and goes forth to join the great armies of other Geniuses throughout the entire world . . ."

MUNIN (*clutching at his throat*): Urgh, agh, I can't breathe for all the *Geniuses* in here!

HUGIN: Will you kindly shut up and let me finish! ". . . throughout the entire world, working incessantly toward its completion and transformation and perfection."

(*Munin, feeling neglected, limps over to the bed. He looks Stefan over, jiggles the bed to make sure he is asleep, then sits down and begins to stroke his hair. Hugin is watching from the corner of his eye.*)

BARBARA: Go on.

HUGIN: Ah! You like this part better, *hein?* Where was I?

BARBARA: Perfection.

HUGIN: Oh yes, so I was. Well: "These Geniuses, *gnädige Frau*, are births; or, if you will, segments of our soul. And only in these parts is the soul immortal."

BARBARA (*moved*): How beautiful!

HUGIN: Wait! There's just a little more. "So it is that the great artists of all ages have left us representations of their Geniuses in their works . . . but not the Geniuses themselves. No, their works are but reflections on the steamy surface of our earth, like the image of the sun upon the sea—or better: upon the dense fog that surrounds us." That, my dear, is the Hölderlin Routine.

BARBARA (*suddenly anxious*): But Paul, what about *Paul?*

HUGIN (*seemingly pained*): Paul? Paul? Ah, no, dear heart, not Paul. Perhaps once, a long time ago, perhaps then *that* Paul had an immortal soul. But now, now . . . I fear that soul has fled. . . .

MUNIN (*leaping from the bed*): Oh, where is my immortal Paul, immortal soul, immortal Paul? Where *has* his Genius gone?

(*Barbara begins to cry, softly.*)

STEFAN (*starting wildly out of sleep*): What's going on?

HUGIN: She's been laughing so hard she cried.

MUNIN: She's been crying so hard she laughed.

STEFAN (*furiously*): Why don't the two of you get the hell out of here!

BARBARA (*reprimandingly*): Stefan! You're their *guest!*

PALIMPSEST

Georg Loh rises from behind his desk (hardly taller standing than sitting). He strides forward with outstretched hands to greet his guests.

"Ahh, *at last,* dear Frau Speer!"

Stefan stands slightly behind her and watches him come; it is a good ten yards from desk to door.

"He usually doesn't get up at all," whispers Munin. "This is a special occasion."

But here he comes, across a polished hardwood landscape on the fourteenth floor of a concrete mountain. Behold:

A strange mixture of primitive and refined characteristics: an oversized peasant's head perched on a slender neck, and a narrow chest branching off into short arms with incongruously tiny hands . . .

He releases Barbara from his embrace and turns to Stefan. "And this is Herr . . . ?"

"Brückmann," Hugin says.

"Herr *Brückmann.* So!"

He is almost three inches shorter than Stefan (which makes him five foot six or so). He has one tiny eye (the other is patched), a low forehead, long rusty-gray hair and bad teeth. He is not quite sixty and resembles an old woman.

And Stefan recognizes him, in spite of *everything*.

TOM THUMB

Hugin and Munin are flanking Loh; Barbara (who has been with him all day) sits opposite; Stefan (whoever that is!) has the place beside her. The restaurant (Grotto in the Woods) smells of scorched flesh. Everyone has drunk too much Rinpils.

LOH: Herr Brückmann, you're not eating! This is a celebration.

STEFAN (*shaking his head*): I'm sorry, I never eat much.

LOH (*belches and loosens his necktie*): *Dis-moi ce que tu manges, je te dirai ce que tu es.* [*He swivels his one eye toward Barbara.*] Well, my dear, enjoying yourself?

BARBARA: Oh, yes. It's hard to believe I—we've only been here two days.

HUGIN: We took her places, we amused her.

MUNIN (*nodding*): Least we could do.

(*Stefan makes an impolite noise; Barbara glares at him.*)

BARBARA: (*to Loh*): They were really terribly kind.

LOH (*throwing his arms about them both*): My two right eyes, my lexica, my world-at-large, my boys!

STEFAN (*challenging him*): How did you lose your eye?

LOH (*lowering the shutter on it*): My eye? [*He applies himself to Hugin and Munin; they shrug.*] Oh, the war, the war . . . one pays, but one grows wiser.

STEFAN (*unsatisfied*): When did you lose it? What year?

HUGIN: 'Forty-three.

MUNIN (*simultaneously*): 'Forty-four.

STEFAN (*quickly, insistently*): Well, *when?*

LOH: 'Forty-five, if you want to know. Why are you so interested in my eye?

STEFAN (*dissimulating*): It makes you look like a pirate.

LOH (*starts, sags, and then roars with laughter*): Ah, ah, ah! By God, you're a delicious child! (*To Barbara.*) You were so right, my dear! Paul would be proud of you.

BARBARA (*uncertainly*): Do you really think so?

HUGIN (*resentfully*): Hunh!

MUNIN: That's what I say.

LOH (*still chuckling*): Take that to heart, my boy; I can see their point. When you're not very tall you have to eat.

(*Hugin and Munin, mollified, laugh raucously.*)

FAUST, PART THREE

A tear rolls out from under Loh's patch.

"There, there, Herr Loh," says Barbara comfortingly.

"Please call me Georg."

"*Georg.*"

He smiles bravely, runs a hand through his yellowish hair and then lays it like a confidential crab on hers.

"Heinrich Deckeler's death was a terrible shock. He was the only true friend . . . the only . . . soul-partner of my life."

He shudders.

"His heart?" Barbara asks.

"His heart? Mm, *ja*, his heart . . . *my heart*. You must understand: we were like . . . the two sides of a single coin—no, that's banal. We were a predestined attunement . . . he was the stationary pole, I the erratic . . . he was the sun and I his planet . . . he the axle, I the wheel . . . he the pylon, I the ox upon the threshing floor of history . . ."

(A dozen more such metaphors; Barbara sits and nods like a woman in deep mourning.)

He draws a dreary breath. "I ran away in 1915 when my father died. My heart gravitated to Germany, I went to Munich, cities are a fire for youthful anger, I met Heinrich, we went in the army together, to the artillery. Even then, when he was hardly more than a child, he was a saint, whose rare depth, whose love of country, whose truly serious mind and whose conscience transfixed me . . . his being became an anchor for my no-less-

German spirit, however unformed it was then, however far
apart our lives may have taken us. He was always there . . . *I
knew.* And still (this is crucial to your understanding!) I could
not be other than I had to be—*then.* I was the templar, he the
guardian, I the outer, he the inner, I the undisciplined, he the
serene, I the vagrant, he the rooted, I profane and he somehow
the worshiper. . . . None of the others, none of those whose
ways crossed or coincided with mine ever recognized in me
what he did. They threw themselves away; I was the seeming
instrument of their decline. In reality, however, I lived already
on another plane where I was answerable only to him, even
when I myself did not know it . . . Caesar was the first to go,
and Blum: I could not help them, circumcised by Birth, de-
capped by Law! Then Däumler, in Berlin, during the second
period of my life spent with Heinrich (that wasted too! I was
still young, still blind and hungry!) . . . caught in the mesh
between us both he was, not altogether his fault . . . but then
his son, he too, the spit and image of a second chance, and
doomed by chromosomes! [He laughs.] Do not ask. There is a
wonderful irony involved in thinking aloud, my dear . . . Rad-
shinski too, poor fool, I tried to help him—ha!—three years . . .
fate set us down on common ground . . . Enough!"

His face relaxes; he leans closer. "At long last, out of my
wanderings, home from the long war, the one long war, the
spent energies, the dissipating excess of freedom . . . home from
the crusades, the driving urge to conflagrate, destroy, consume,
externalize, reform, transform . . . home from the alchemistic
world I came—and Heinrich was waiting, and took me into his
arms. He showed me the very nature of my soul, a soul unraveled in a labyrinthine trek to nowhere—each turn, each
dead end, each climax that had seemed a station on the road to
infinity, was in the end no point in a road at all, but a pile of
meaningless stones: my runes, his timbus. I devoured his life;
he was my character unrealized, my Demian; I had betrayed
him from my very youth."

He sobs and clutches Barbara's hands in his.

"One hope . . . *Paul* was his legacy to me . . ."

Barbara gasps.

"Yes, Paul. Dearest Frau Speer, you must return! Your Paul, our Paul will vindicate us both. We have no other part to play but that of restitutors now . . . how else to exorcise our ghosts, our failures, but by giving them bodies again! Tell me you *will* return—for Heinrich's sake, for our sake, but more than all [huskily] for Germany's sake. This work we have undertaken must be realized: at stake, in microcosmos [whispered], *is the world's rejuvenation.*"

"Oh, yes!" cries Barbara, transported. "Yes, Georg!"

He chokes with emotion. "Ach, how can I thank you, dear Frau Speer . . ."

THE PROOF OF THE BIER IS IN THE TEST

"But why did you do it?" Stefan asks. "That's all I want to know."

"Didn't," says Loh.

"I couldn't have *invented* you!" he cries.

"Why not? You've lied before, haven't you? Anyway, lies are only enhanced by occasional truths; it's not consistency that matters, but reiteration."

"No. Lies are like Alice's looking glass: once you're through it, it doesn't matter which direction you take; you can advance or retreat or go around in circles, but you always come back to the point where you entered. And there those 'occasional truths' are inescapable and valid. Which is to admit I've lied, but not about you. You're an entering-point."

"Mm," says Loh, unimpressed. "You have an answer for everything, haven't you?"

"Answers merely take the shape of their questions," replies Stefan (with admirable aplomb).

"Every man his own artist, *hein?*" scoffs Loh. "All right then, answer this!"

He removes his patch and blinks a perfectly healthy eye. His hair has been hennaed and clipped.

"Heinrich, old friend!" cries Paul Speer from the door, and rushes into his arms.

"See?" shouts Loh triumphantly. "Where is your Hannes now?"

"*Where is my Hannes now?* That isn't Hannes, it's Paul. And Heinrich isn't *your* name either!"

"You *are* a nuisance," declares Loh. "You can't have *everything* you want."

"I don't *want* you *or* him—I only want to know why you killed Hannes."

Loh plants his hands on his hips. "My dear fellow, I'm getting just a wee bit annoyed. Would you mind telling me what there is about me in particular that makes every jackass with a skeleton in his closet want to saddle *me* with it? Every day there's another one of you—*angels of the dead* on my doorstep. I've been wished to death, pinned to death, stoned to death, chopped to death, spelled to death, spiked to death, and I don't know what-all. It's pretty damned tiresome, I can tell you. Now here *you* come with your little bag of bones to pick. Go away, boy! And take my patch off this instant!"

Stefan yanks it off in astonishment and hands it back.

"How'd I get it in the first place?" he cries, peeved.

Loh offers it ostentatiously to Paul. "Want to try it?"

"Oh, thanks, Heinrich," says Paul, and slips it on with pride.

Stefan gives him a disgusted look; Paul smiles back blithely. "Where's Barbara?" he asks naïvely. "Shouldn't she be here?"

"Most likely she's out looking for *you*," says Stefan.

"*Still?*" exclaims Paul, disbelievingly.

"Oh, don't mind him," says Loh to Paul; "little Negro is disgruntled."

Stefan is about to say something, but just at that moment Barbara bursts in, perspiring and out of breath. She goes straight to Paul and kisses him dutifully. As she does so, she catches sight of Stefan and straightens up surprised.

"Well, I see you two have already met," she says.

Paul nods, rather indifferently.

"Ha!" cries Barbara at Stefan. "I told you so!"

"You needn't be vindictive," says Stefan, hanging his head.

"That's right," Paul says, pulling her round to face him. "It took you long enough to make up your mind. Where've you been all this time?"

"Good boy!" says Loh. "Spoken like a true ingrate. I think she's done pretty well all round, considering everything."

"I'm sorry," says Paul.

"Shut up! Shut up!" Stefan screams suddenly. "Leave him alone!"

Loh seems greatly astonished. "My! My!" he exclaims; "what on earth provoked that little outburst? Leave *whom* alone? Why don't you just sit down somewhere and hold your tongue, and if we want your opinion we'll ask for it."

"No!" he shouts, beside himself. "I won't stand by this time and let you go through with it."

Loh spreads his hands innocently. "With *what*, demented child?"

In desperation Stefan turns to Paul. "Don't let him, I beg you. I don't care about anything else . . . *please*."

Paul shrugs, helpless, resigned; his eyes are mild as lambs' eyes.

"Barbara?" Stefan asks, hoping against hope.

She throws her arms about Paul and glares at him defiantly.

"Well," says Loh, "there's your answer, and don't say you didn't ask for it."

NIGHT THOUGHTS

He dreams he cries out—but comes to in a silence of dead weights and darkness. Barbara is leaning heavily against him; her flesh is warm and damp. His right leg is carbonated, the sensation is unbearable. A sharp light keeps exploding in his eyes, illuminating nothing, heralding nothing. He cannot sleep then; his wakefulness, he knows, is a state he will have to endure, somehow.

Baermann said: Be a German, if you can.

And Oestler said: You feel nothing.

And Immanuel: You and your filthy innocence! Take sides! Between the myth of lost or coming community, your ridiculous dream of universality, and the unavoidable consciousness of pain, you can't erect a legend.

And Moon: I died a day too soon, Stevie-boy. One more day, and I'd've handed you the world on a platter, *my* world. One word of submission. But no, you're a cheat, I hate to say it, you never loved a soul in your life, and you never take the rap for your selfishness either. But I forgive you. Come on back. Here, look, here are my hands . . .

And Paul. He can feel it: even Paul is beginning to take part in these recriminations. Through Barbara, whose reproaches he allows, can't help but allow for the time being. But she is more and more Paul's advocate; soon she will say: Paul is your pattern, if you want me.

There is no way she can avoid it, he thinks. I will have to hear him, abide by him, take his place, if I want her. I could do it, too, but would she want me then? Right now she needs me still, but Paul is gaining ground. Do I love her enough (would it be love?) to make myself the object of her guilt? Must I mourn Paul as well?

Oh, damn the dead! demanding, unrepentant. Turn back! look down! touch our faces! embrace us! swear you won't forsake us!—not our memory, *us*, ourselves, intransient substance, incorruptible . . . body! Helpless, cowardly, impotent! Hateful voices, locked in space and speaking: *Time.*

(Only Golden . . .)

But oh! God, I don't know now how strong I am. I do love her. I want, I wanted to see it out. I hoped, I thought . . . I never expected this. What? What have I *come back to?* Has my own motion restored this moment? Did I will this insane confrontation? What apparition is Loh? . . . another, *the* other . . . where? Were the time and place of my declared history never

mine at all? Is there no fundamental distinction between them?
—between Hannes and Paul, between Lokowandt and Loh? In
pursuing the one face of Hannes, where have I come? Is there
another version of myself, and this a purely spurious innocence?
How can I know?

MORITAT

On a rather mysterious evening this time of year, the Widow
Barbara strides into a courtyard somewhere behind the Alexanderplatz. She is high-heeled and smoking, well-painted and
loudly dressed; before her she pushes a battered barrel organ
mounted on doll-carriage wheels. Just behind her, gorged with
smiles, comes Loh the *Bänkelsänger*, in burglar cap and red
bandanna. He is followed in turn by Paul and Hannes, two
underfed look-alike urchins who carry his gear. Last but definitely least, dragging his feet at the end of a long leash that ties
him to Barbara's rig, is the mangy bellboy monkey known as
Stefan.

In the center of the courtyard the procession comes to a halt,
and Loh's assistants hurriedly assemble a metal rack. Faceless
tenants of the houses hang themselves like bedding from the
sills. From the lopsided crossbar of the rack, Hannes (or is it
Paul?) unfurls a folio of oilcloth sheets on whose cover is
painted, in crude Gothic letters, the legend: A WINTER TRAGEDY.

Loh produces a long wooden pointer. He raps sharply on the
organ (Widow Barbara starts to crank), jabs the Stefan-monkey
fiercely (he begins to dance) and snaps his fingers at his two
stooges. They unveil the first tableau: The interior of an old
barn, hay and starving horses. Loh begins to sing, throatily:

"In this barn, midst hay and horses,
Two tired boys have found a nest;
Day for day without resources
They've been fleeing to the West. . . ."

Widow Barbara waves and grimaces at the anonymous gallery. Loh signals for his lackeys to uncover the second tableau: Two ragged waifs are lying in the hay; from a beam over their heads hangs a sprig of mistletoe. Loh points and sings:

"Of the two this one's the older
Though the younger leads the way.
One grows weak, the other bolder
With the passing of each day . . ."

He stings the Stefan-monkey to jig-time and winks at his helpers, who avert their eyes as they display the third tableau: with fiendish glee the younger of the two boys is bringing an axe down on the head of the other.

"Witness now with shame and sorrow
What this picture doth betray;
Let your eyes recoil with horror
From this scene no words portray . . ."

A chorus of groans from the watching façades. The Stefan-monkey begins to screech and protest; he tries to bite Loh's leg. Widow Barbara decelerates her grinding to a moan-and-thump tempo, to which Loh beats the beast to death. The pointer breaks; Loh casts the bloody thing away and claps his hands, the music speeds up and the next tableau is shown: The murderous child, blue-black in color, grins with axe in hand. Breathing heavily, Loh sings:

"There was ne'er an act more gruesome
Any time or any place—
Nor a more unlikely twosome:
Mark ye well his cruel face!"

An outcry of hate from the windows; the two apprentices are sobbing loudly; Widow Barbara peaks her eyes dolorously and grinds more slowly. Loh himself reveals the last tableau; majestically the sun comes up over a tiny barn almost lost in a vast landscape of snow. He plants his feet on the monkey's corpse, spreads his arms to his audience, and sings with great pathos:

> "Aye, from that scene most foul and gory
> Let us all now homeward wend;
> Take this moral from my story
> (For without one there's no end):
> Love yourself and don't be sorry;
> You can always lose a friend."

The tenements shake with applause. A downpour of Weimarer billion-mark banknotes and twopenny pieces buries the lifeless monkey.

THE BEGGAR OF MY SORT WHO COMES TO SUCH A PEOPLE

Now, in a moment, the door will open, and Paul of flesh and blood will enter, a pale and assertive bridegroom. I'll be the tell-tale smoke of cigarettes, I'll have to fly away.

She is untouchable now. But I love her.

Love her? It was hopeless, more hopeless than I ever imagined.

Three hours still. I dare not sleep. Loh has weapons, I can't hold out against him.

This is no mirror; its surface is truth.

O vast stagnating spring of Germany, where are your real cities, your real excursions?

VERNAL EQUINOX

I know how I hung
on the windcold tree
   swung there for nine long nights,
wore a spearwound
was offered to Wotan
   offered up self to myself,
on the powerful tree
that hides from Man
   the root from which it sprang.

—The Edda

Stefan is suspended over a void, his feet lie miles below him, he is cold, colder than he has ever been before. He is staring upward at a white sun, and no matter how he tries he cannot take his eyes off it. Below him myriad voices are shouting in a cacophony of unknown languages. If he could only see where they are coming from they would cease to cry out—this he knows—but he cannot bend his head down. What are his feet groping for? Nothing. He can flex his hands, but there seems to be something wrong with his shoulders: he makes an effort to raise his arms and feels them begin to swing like huge pendulums. He goes over the roster of his invisible body in his mind, reading off part after part; each member responds as a voice to its name, but there is still no unity. Each one, as soon as he has identified it, starts to expand and fill the void beneath him, assuming an exclusivity that terrifies him. If only he could see!

Now only his face remains, but he is afraid to name it. He has called upon his eyes; he closes them now as they too begin to swell; the white sun is still up there, above him; he opens his mouth and adds his voice to the uncounted voices beneath him. But it is immediately drowned in them, and is inaudible even to him . . .

He has become all eye now, and this eye is fixed on a somehow familiar crucifixion. The white sun is in him, too, insistent as a cold and screaming tooth. He begins to circumnavigate his dangling body, exploring its contours, reading its lines in the sharp light he projects, counting its pores, its socket-caves, the fine hairs that float upon it like angel seaweed, the moles that lie like oilspots. The navel is a shallow crater; beside it a spring sends forth a thin blue stream that glides unbroken down to the shoals on which his useless sex hangs shipwrecked. He moves away, on to an unknown geography, where the eye is divested of all senses but its own, and is deaf to the voices, and glides along a ridge of islands in a narrow sea, lax in the down-scent of his death.

Behind his head he hesitates—and then invades it, to repossess the world of his body . . .

Stefan, in mammoth proportions, is being sucked through a narrow transom, and as his head comes through, last of all, he cries out with the pain and at last hears his own voice. All at once there are other voices, this time known and distinct, but he is too exhausted to listen and identify them. He lies very still and feels the nearness of certain forms, floats with his eyes closed, growing gradually warmer, letting the successive waves of an incoming tide wash over him, gratified by his permissiveness and the soft, sure restoration of himself.

LOT'S WIFE

"Stefan

He tries to open his eyes, but they are tightly sealed.

"*Stefan.*"

He opens his mouth and for an instant forgets how to make a sound come out.

"It's me—Barbara."

He concentrates on her voice.

"You cried out. Are you all right?"

He licks his lips; his eyes refuse to open. "Yes," he says. "All right."

"Do you want a doctor?"

"No, it's passed now."

"What happened?"

He tries to smile. "It's nothing new. I'll be all right now."

"You didn't show up; I got worried."

"Have you been here long?"

"Only a few minutes. I ran into D-J on the way up; he didn't even know you were—we were—back. But what is it?"

"I can't open my eyes yet, that's all."

"You must be famished. Can I get you something?"

He rolls his head back and forth on the pillow. "No, I'm just worn out; it's all over. . . . Is it night?"

"No. It's Tuesday morning."

"Three days?" he asks, unbelievingly. He shuttles his head and laughs.

"Why do you laugh?" she asks.

"I guess because I knew it couldn't be night."

She says nothing for a moment. Then, "I have to go up to Hanau."

"When?"

"In a little while. . . . Max is sick; my father called."

"Oh?"

"It's only a cold, but he has weak lungs. Anyway, I haven't seen him since Christmas, and I miss him," she says, vaguely defensive.

"I've never seen him at all," he says. No response. "When will you be back?" he asks.

"In a couple of days, not more; I still have a lot of things to clear up here," she replies. "Why don't you come up tomorrow, if you want to?"

"Where?"

"To Hanau—there's an extra room."

Wrinkles appear in his brow; he titters nervously. "You know, I really can't get my eyes to open—or don't want to. It's silly."

She touches them lightly with her fingers. "They're all mattery. . . . Will you come?"

"Perhaps," he lies, and gropes for her hand. She lays it in his; he squeezes it.

"Will you be here when I get back?" she asks, in a strange voice.

He purses his lips but does not answer.

"You won't, will you." Not a question. He frowns; she lays her hand on his forehead.

"Please don't," he says, as if he were in pain.

She pulls her hand away. "I'd better be going. The train

leaves at two and I still have to pack my bag. Do you need anything?"

"No, I only want to sleep; I'm too exhausted to think straight . . ."

"I'll tell Frau Isenfels to look in."

"Never mind; it's really nothing now."

"Are you sure?"

"Yes."

Finally she withdraws her hand from his and stands up.

"Well," she says.

"Barbara . . ."

"Yes?"

"I . . . just wanted to say . . . I do love you."

No answer; her mouth makes some kind of strange, moist sound, and he hears it.

"Will you kiss me?" he asks.

She leans over, her hands propped on the edge of the bed, and touches her lips to his. His arms come up and around her and pull her down on to him. She loses her balance, wrenches away and stands up.

"*Auf Wiedersehen!*" she says, as if scoldingly. "*Auf Wiedersehen*, Stefan," in a different tone, a little farther away. Stefan hears her open the door, chewing on his lips; then, in a muted voice he says, "*Leb'wohl*, Barbara . . ."

He has no way of knowing whether she has heard him or not, but there is a long silence before the door closes. Almost instantly he falls into a deep and dreamless sleep.

ANONYMOUS LIFE

Stefan scratches his eyes until he gets them open. It is dark. He sits up; the blood falls to his feet like a gush of lead, hardens and rebounds inside him; he buries his face in his hands, low, to keep from passing out. After a long while he stands up cautiously, walks to the window and looks out. The full moon is over the church; the clock in the tower says 7:30.

In the mirror he verifies his yellow eyes, his sallow face, his three-day beard. He shakes his head, runs a hand through his hair and begins to dress, tittering nervously at his dizziness. He tugs on his overcoat, losing his pullover sleeves somewhere around the elbows.

THE POET INCUBUS IS SHED

Barbara steps down from the second car of the yellow motor coach, sneezes twice without warning and leaps the ditch, slipping as she lands on the other side. Her traveling case pops open, spilling its contents in the grass. She drops to her knees exasperatedly and begins to rake things back into the bag. She weeps softly as she does, unaware of her tears. Under the light of the street lamp she seems to be praying. *Paul is dead.* She snaps the bag shut and catches sight of the backs of her hands; for no reason at all she lifts them close to her face, tilting them so the light will fall across the veins obliquely, and then leans slightly forward, inspecting them. *Paul is dead.* Her jumper slides up, baring a tiny portion of her back: the flesh draws tight and the vertebrae protrude. She is choking with tears and she still does not know it. *Paul is dead.* She rocks back on her heels into a squatting position and stands upright. An amulet on a tiny chain is left lying in the grass, like a silver scribble. *Paul is dead.* She jogs down the Martin-Lutherstrasse, swinging the bag, her hair jagged as a boy's hair. There is a light burning on the porch. The upright roof-supports slide by it. She hops up the steps, half conscious of an ache in her left breast as she raps on the door. Steps: her father. The bare padding feet of a child: Max! She crouches in anticipation. *Paul is dead! Leb'-wohl*, Barbara!

MAN IS A WONDERFUL, WOUNDABLE ANIMAL

Oleo's is hopping. Fat Carlo is sweating away behind the bar, dipping and dripping in the ice-cream bins. He looks up for an instant as Stefan comes in, grins, and then reapplies himself. The Moped Gestapo, installed on the left, is demanding *Der Stürmer* from Emile, spastic fifty-year-old alumnus of Theresienstadt. But all he has left is *Die Abendpost*. A delegation of straw-hatted Bavarian tourists from a pullman bus has occupied the Polish corridor, and just beyond them a group of Italian and Swedish girls from the Translators' Institute are eating spaghetti and lining up sleeping accommodations with three boys from the English College, a prince with a Porsche and an American soldier named Tannenbaum. Fräulein Gerber just left for the evening performance of *The Concert at Sans-Souci* (her all-time favorite film) at the Studio-Lux.

Stefan hangs up his coat and sits down in a far corner, with his back to the mirror. Frau Riegel hustles by; he orders a hot chocolate, then pulls out his cigarettes, lights one and plants both elbows on the table. He has no idea why he came in—force of habit, most likely. He recognizes almost no one. "Eine Kleine Nachtmusik" comes on in the jukebox. The Bavarians are laughing uproariously and shouting for more beer. Emile is screaming at the Gestapo in a high-pitched voice: the large American archaeologist with glasses at the next table is getting nervous. Stefan shuts out the noise and sets himself the mental exercise of determining how many times he has come to this place with Barbara. But all times except the last melt into one: wax effigies in all the chairs at once. For the first time since his return to Germany he has the sensation that *Germany* is where he really is. Medieval carnival, peaked roofs and tilting walls; snapshots of castles; polyphony; wallpapered plaster; *Konditoreien*. Somehow the walls of the town have not crumbled; suddenly the connection between the affective body of his memory and the ordinary haphazard figures of this place, this moment, is real. He touches his forehead: still a slight fever. Even Berlin (so distant already) and Loh (he speaks the name aloud, softly, exaggerating his lips, and shivers when his heart fails to react), yes, *especially* Loh, belong to that interim world to which Immanuel brought him, and not to his remembered Germany, not to him. Now who belongs?—there is only movement, clatter, there are only these voices, this particular evening. The figures are real enough, solid enough in any case. Hypothetically. But he realizes that he is not taking them seriously, and for the first time reads his relaxed indifference as a warning; he is ready to *forgive* them, but for what? for being what they always have been? Were the absence and dissociation only *his*? If so, he has imagined his history; he thinks: No way to tell, not by examining myself. Rational refutation: if what happened did not happen to you, to whom did it happen and what *else* happened to you? He smiles at his own sophistry; he is still sick. Yes, he smiles at himself. Not at *them*.

His cocoa comes; he says "*Danke schön*" and Frau Riegel moves on. Automatically he fishes in his pocket for change, lays sixty pfennigs on the table, sucks the blob of whipped cream from the top of the chocolate, wipes his mouth with the back of his hand and lets the rest lie.

Suddenly a gust of wind inflates the heavy drapes on the door. Two small hands appear in the rift and part them. Two children enter: first the very dark girl of about twelve to whom the hands belong, and then a boy of ten or so. They are immediately recognizable as Gypsies. Both are wearing outsized overcoats that reach to their ankles and are smiling an identical put-on smile. Frau Riegel heads for them with wild peasant eye, her hands fluttering with the anticipated pleasure of shooing them out. But Fat Carlo leans over the counter and bars her way with an ice-cream scoop. She folds her arms and bides her time.

The two children stand very quietly just inside the door until every eye in the place is on them. Then the girl steps forward and declares in a clear, ringing voice:

"We . . . are . . . acrobats!"

A few laughs. One or two people clap. Without a movement of her head, with her chin high, hesitating on the next, already-formulated words of her spiel, the girl glances sharply about the room, appraising. The crowd falls silent. Only the jukebox persists: Glenn Miller's "Chattanooga Choo-Choo." The girl hoists her arm dramatically (the sleeve is huge); her hand is bent back stiffly. She licks her lips. Her hand flips down as if on a spring and points at one of the Bavarians.

"If the gentleman . . . with the *beau*tiful hat [laughter] . . . will be so kind . . . as to assist us in our preparations . . . the performance will begin."

The gentleman with the *beau*tiful hat, more than a little drunk, is prodded to his feet by his friends, and stands meekly awaiting orders, numbed by all the eyes upon him. The girl takes a single step closer; he glances around nervously, stands hulking and weaving, then stares down at her. She waves her arm (all sleeve).

"These tables—back! One table must be cleared and put—*here!*"

The Bavarian jumps as if stung. The occupants of the deported tables are already evacuating. He lifts a table; a spoon slides to the floor. Carlo nudges Frau Riegel, who rushes over and starts gathering up empty bottles and dirty dishes. The girl dances back to where the boy is still standing, and the two of them remove their coats at once, revealing harlequin tights, brightly colored but filthy and much-patched. They toss the coats over a chair at the Gestapo table (Emile has escaped) and advance to the center of the room, where by now the required space has been cleared and the empty table set. The choo-choo has run down; more "Nachtmusik." The girl curtsies mechanically, the boy crosses his feet, spreads his arms and bows almost to the floor. The girl cocks her head, tilting her chin upward as she does. She bares her teeth in a ridiculous professional smile, and announces:

"Ladies and Gentlemen! Pay good attention! Tonight and tonight only . . . you have the exceptional good fortune . . . to be able to witness . . . a sing-ular performance . . . of acrobatic skills! My brother" (she extends a flat indicative palm; he shows his teeth) "and I" (she drops her head down and snaps it back up smartly) "will now execute for your enjoyment . . . some of the most daring . . . the most breathtaking . . . the most incomparable . . . feats known to man!"

Applause. She bows. Her brother bows. She snaps her fingers; the boy, deadly serious, takes a step, lays his hands on the edge of the table, throws his legs into the air, hesitates in a handstand, lets one foot at a time down on to the table, and then flips himself upright. Applause. The girl stretches out her hands, backs up a step or two, then trips toward the table, abruptly leaves the floor, turns a full flip in the air, and lands in a crouch beside her brother. She springs upright. More applause. They bow and hop down.

Since the two children entered, Stefan has not taken his eyes off the girl. His immediate reaction was one of embarrassment, and he turned away, only to find himself facing her in the mirror, which he had forgotten was behind him. And so he turned back toward her to watch. As it became clear that she was fully in command of the situation, that she was *going to stay*, he began to feel a strange sensation of correspondence, of identity, by which he is both intrigued and disturbed. Now, behind the smooth façade of her performance, behind the mean and underfed dead earnest of her body, behind the dictatorial manner and the practiced confrontation, the manner that *works* because it is incapable of doubt—behind these he searches for something: a phantom, a warrant for his feeling, signs of a forgotten self. All he *sees* is a body, one that responds perfectly to a discipline that is not imposed by anything outside itself, by any onlooker, nor even by the requisites of the feat it is performing, but rather by some unidentifiable regard of itself (as well as he can make out) as *instrument*. This instrument extends itself unfailingly to include its environment; the more difficult the feat, the greater the ease with which it seems to perform—as if by the implicit consent of the spectators, though they themselves have unwittingly and willingly become the functions of its executions. Yet they are not being used; no, for a few minutes now (whose minutes?) they have experienced a genuine release from the burden of regarding, of determining. They have simply *responded*. And Stefan too has submitted to this flexible instrument, letting the thought of a personal meaning behind its mechanics dissolve within the pleasure of its presence.

There is no longer any applause; the bodies of the girl and boy join and disengage like the two sections of a Chinese puzzle. Everyone is suspended in a huge breath, deep and successful, that has risen and caught and now awaits the signal for its release. The small boy is trembling with application, his tights are drenched with perspiration, his teeth are clenched, blind to eyes. The girl does not seem to have tired at all. Her dark skin is dry. Only the whites of her eyes glisten, and her smile wears on, impersonal, artificial, impertinent; through it a steady hiss of commands, half-words, holds her brother on a line. He attends as she drops to a split on the table, twists her back leg around and comes to a sitting position on the edge, leans back, lifts her legs, plants her feet beneath her and worms her body slightly back. She extends her hands to the boy and snarls; he bristles and then hops forward, plants his hands on her knees, crabs together, and springs to a full handstand on them. Then, reversing the placement of his hands suddenly, he lets his feet fall one at a time into her uplifted hands. Her legs begin to rise; she wears the same fixed grin, the boy scowls with exertion. Her elbows come down on the table close to her sides, drawing his feet close together; simultaneously she heaves her legs into an upright stance; the boy releases her ankles and stands on her palms with outstretched arms. He bends his knees, she thrusts upwards and he flips off the table; instantly the girl slaps her hands down on the table, wrenches herself in one motion into a handstand, separates her legs until she is doing an exaggerated standing split, rocks slightly forward and then back, tilting in a kind of cartwheel to the floor beside her brother. The boy wipes his nose on his sleeve; he is bobbing with exhaustion. The girl bows, releasing him, releasing everyone: the performance is over.

Stefan sits quietly, still watching the girl, half hypnotized by her. She has spoken again; he did not hear what she said. Her brother has slipped his overcoat back on, and now, holding his pockets out (so that he resembles an absurdly tiny pregnant bear), he is taking a collection from the tables nearest the door. The girl has produced a tambourine from somewhere and is making her way to the back, nudging and encouraging, wearing the same rigid smile, counting each take with quick eyes, saying *Danke!* again and again with the same toneless voice, the same automatic tick of the tongue.

Stefan, seeing her close in on him, has a sudden urge to run. But he knows he cannot. Is there more to her than her manner? he wonders. Why did he feel the way he did when she first came in? Why should he have felt anything at all? There is probably nothing behind the surface of perfect discipline except a buried child, already atrophied, unreachable by any will, by any insight or response—a child (like himself?) so self-contained that if she should be touched would be entirely unreceptive, or who, even if affected, would have no use for the contact, a child far too wise and too hard to care. Stefan sits now, unable to move, heaping hypothetical scorn on her, doubt after doubt, inurement after inurement, humiliated by this crass projection of himself.

But when she comes to him, last of all, and his far corner is suddenly the only remaining pocket of silence and resistance, and everyone around him has paid and is already forgetting, reducing the moment of his release to a safe and meaningless residue of memory or anecdote—now, when she comes to him, last of all, thrusting her tambourine into his face, confident, appraising him with (it seems) the same bruised, implacable apathy, the same past-knowing armor, the same brash, impossible *motif* of smile and feral, unrelenting eyes—when she comes to him now, rattling her tambourine in his face imperiously, he suddenly knows what he must do, and takes courage and lifts his eyes to hers. She hesitates an instant, utterly impassive, then shakes the thing again impatiently, challenging, but ready to faze him out.

But he is committed now, too; his hands relax, he feels a sweet wave of assurance rise in him, and he breaks into a broad grin. She stares back at him, not acknowledging him, until a light veil of strain wets her eyes. She resists blinking; the two red dots at the corners of her eyes begin to swell; slowly she lowers the tambourine. Her lips twitch once, twice, and then— oh! he gets her to smile, a real, thawing smile, an unbearable smile which he holds until it grows to a warmth that melts her face, and make her only, and *still*, a girl of twelve. He reaches forth instinctively and takes her hands in his; the tambourine tinkles; her hands go limp, give in. He stands and leans over and kisses her on the forehead, she murmurs—pain? joy?—he releases her, frightened; he is losing control of the rising emotion inside him, nameless, he will burst—he knows it: he will burst—he wants to cry out, he snatches his coat and runs blindly from the place, dizzy, quaking with the knowledge of impending life.

ISHMAEL ON THE OTHER SHORE

Foolishly, blankly, he wanders with unbuttoned overcoat across the old bridge and then along the bank of the river toward Neuenheim, never losing the moon, struck with it, a little feverish still. Headlights slide above his head, the high black water of the Neckar sucks at the grass by his feet. He tries to penetrate the moon; he doesn't even know what day it is. He decides it must be after the twentieth, around the equinox; but his assumption is not so much a conclusion as a wishful explanation.

GOD'S VEHICLES

A clock strikes ten as he is crossing the Three-Bow Bridge: he has been walking for an hour. Up ahead of him lie the fairgrounds, but there are few lights. He walks on and comes to a narrow dirt road that runs alongside an open field. He turns down it: a train of wagons is lined up close by—detached wooden trailers propped up on jacks or blocks of wood, and a couple of black automobiles. He reaches the end of the row; behind the last wagon a fire is burning, and around it are sitting half a dozen Gypsies, talking in muted voices. Stefan draws near; they catch sight of him and fall silent.

"What do you want?" asks an old man, impatiently.

"Nothing, I . . ."

"Why are you standing there then?"

"Some children, *kako* . . ." The word slips from him unconsciously.

"Ah? *Halt tu ninna yo mello rom?* (Are you also one of us?) Come close and let me have a look at you."

Stefan takes a step toward them. "The children . . ." he says, foolishly.

"What children?" the old man asks, scrutinizing him. "Are you one of us or aren't you? Speak up!"

"Yes," shrugging.

"Sit down then."

A boy of about sixteen pipes up: "I think he's a *busnó*."

"Be quiet," says the old man. "Who cares what you think? I invited him to sit with us." He turns to Stefan and asks, somewhat more kindly, "What is your name?"

"Stefan Brückmann."

"Hah!" cries the boy.

"And the other?" asks the old man.

"Murshkar," Stefan replies, in a low voice, glad of the fire as he blushes.

The boy laughs rudely.

"I said be quiet!" commands the old man. "These children," he says softly to Stefan, "did they send you here? We weren't expecting you."

"No. I just thought I might find them . . . it doesn't matter."

"Where are you from?" asks a man from across the fire.

"I'll ask the questions," says the old man. "How are your mother and father, your sisters and brothers?" he asks formally.

"They are dead, *kako*."

The old man nods understandingly, as if he had suspected as much. "May your life be all their unlived years—a long time?"

"Yes, a long time."

"Do you have a cigarette?" asks the old man.

Stefan extends the packet; the old man takes it and passes it around, and hands it back to him empty.

"How much longer will you be here?" Stefan asks.

"We're leaving in the morning," says the old man, lighting up with a stick from the fire.

"Where will you go?"

"Oh, to the north for a while, then west, and then south," he says vaguely.

"We're going to Saintes-Maries for the festival!" the boy volunteers.

"Yes, we'll get there sooner or later," says the old man. "Have you been?"

Stefan shakes his head.

"Nor have they," says the old man, indicating the others. "I was there many times, but long ago, when we *rom* still had no automobiles, in my parents' wagon, then with my own when I married. Now my wife is long dead and my children too, all but this one (he points at the boy). His name is Farthi. He's a good enough boy, but the dead ones seem better. The further back

I think, the better things seem to have been—for us, I mean—
but perhaps I am wrong, I'm a *phuro rom*, after all. . . ." He
lapses into a long silence, and then asks, suddenly: "Can you
write? Have you learned to write?"

"Yes," Stefan admits reluctantly.

"You see!" shouts Farthi. "He's a *lavengro!* He's come to
write about us, to spy on us!"

"Ho!" snorts the old man. "What would *you* have to tell him?"

"I knew a *lavengro* once," claims the man across the fire. "He
was a gentleman, a real *baro rai*. He paid well, too."

"I didn't come for that," Stefan protests.

"Shh," says the old man. "Don't mind them. We have our
life, you have yours. I only asked; I like you, I'll tell you a story
for nothing, and I know all the *paramishe* there are—even one
with a hero named Murshkar."

"I'll bet!" cries Farthi. "There's no such story. Why haven't
we heard it before?"

"Because it isn't for you and you're only going to hear it
now, that's why," says the old man, moving closer to the fire
and spreading his hands. . . .

THE STORY OF MURSHKAR

Brothers! Friends of my soul! Come close to hear. My health's
just fine, may yours be too! If it isn't, have some of mine! Now
listen and believe.

All this happened in a time when some things had been and
some still hadn't, but this was told to me by a man who saw it
with his eyes. In those days the age had passed when all men
were kings—but there was still a true king of Gypsies, alive and
recognized by all the tribes. He ruled the *Puszta* and the
Délibàb above it, and held court in a city that straddles a river.

His wagon was the finest ever seen between the Tisza and
the Rhône. Its ribs were blacker than the darkest brow, its nails

were of brass that gleamed like a bride's eyes. The canopy, which was of lambs' wool strengthened with pure gold wire, was trimmed with yellow tassels like shreds of thin-skinned lemons. Beneath the chassis (in a hidden place) was fixed a box filled with the fortune of fortunes—more gold and silver than you or I have ever seen or ever will. This treasure had been his father's and his father's father's, but neither the king nor any other *rom* might touch that gold until the day we all come home again (lest the *mulos* enter in at night—right now!—and grind us all between their teeth).

One day came and then another, and on one of them the king was old. So he called his only son to him, the prince called Murshkar, and said, "My son, the time has come when you must marry. My head is bending beneath the weight of too many days, and will not support many more. Go out and find you a wife, a princess, and my *vardo* and all I have will be yours. You will have a surname and the honor of guarding a fortune that no one may spend until the day we all come home again. And one day the women lamenting my death will heed your voice and fall silent, and strew the hair they have torn from their heads in your path, to soften your way." He showed Murshkar a fine sturdy horse and made it his, and gave him a wallet containing many gold coins. Then his uncles struck him hard upon the head and shoulders (as is the custom still) and he stood fast, like a man. So his father blessed him, while his mother wept and wailed in a corner and hid her face.

Oh, away he rode, toward the west, wearing a red and yellow suit (his royal colors) with silver buttons for show, his purse in his pocket and a fiddle for luggage. A prince he was, a fine young man! And he sang with his father's blessing, for with it any mountain may be climbed, or so I've heard.

But he had not gone far when he met a gaunt and ragged man who greeted him and cried, "Stop for a while, Brother Stork, Young Prince, and play me a tune on your fiddle. I'll play you a tune in return if you do."

"I've a long way to go and no time to squander," replied

Murshkar, slowing down but a little. "For I'm off to find me a wife, a princess."

"Oh, but give me a mile of your time," said the vagabond, "and I'll hide for you." And with this he sprang high into the air, turned head over heels, or heels over head, flip! flop! and landed on his feet. Then Murshkar knew that the man was really a minstrel magician such as they have in those parts, called *rejtösik*, and so he decided it might be a good thing if he came down from his horse with his fiddle.

"Well, all right then, what shall I play for you?" he asked.

"You can play me a winter song or a summer song, a flower song or even a tune that maidens dance to," said the man. "But don't stop till I hide."

So Murshkar began to play, very slowly at first and then faster and faster, until so many notes burst from that *boshomengo* of his that the trees sprouted new leaves and new birds appeared to sing in them. The *rejtösik* scurried over to a bush, grabbed up some things he had left hidden in it, and hurried back—all with a very strange step, as if his feet didn't quite reach to the ground. Then he sat down not far from where Murshkar was standing and began to arrange his hiding gear. First he took a pig's bladder and stretched it over an old shard from the third day of Creation, then he took a thin reed, or piece of cane, I'm not sure, and stuck it into a little hole in the bladder and pushed it down until it touched the inside of the shard.

Well, Murshkar played and the birds sang their heads off, and the *rejtösik* began to sway back and forth in time with the music. Then he spit on his hands, rubbed them together, folded them tightly on top of his head, closed his eyes so they looked like the dried-out nipples of your old granny, and suddenly stopped rocking. Very straight and still he sat, with his eyes squeezed together, for a minute or so; then he took his hands down from his head, laid the left one lightly on the piece of pot to steady it, and stuck the first finger of the other in his mouth. When he had got it good and wet he brought it out and com-

menced to stroke the reed with it. Ever so gently, back and
forth, but what an odd sound it made!—like a brake on a
wagon wheel or a thousand furious bees. Murshkar couldn't
hear what he was playing himself, but he dared not stop.

Now the *rejtösik* started to sing, if you can call it that, in a
very low voice to begin with, and using words that Murshkar couldn't quite hear or make out (if they were words at all).
Oh, he got awfully worked up, that *rejtösik*, and sang louder
and louder, all aquiver from top to toe. And he sang like a dog,
sang like cats making love, he whinnied like a horse, and
mooed, and cooed, and brayed and howled and bellowed and
snorted, until the veins on his neck stood out like reins pulled
taut, and the sweat just exploded out of his face. And he sang
these words finally, and Murshkar ceased to play, because he
knew the *rejtösik* had hidden:

Brother Stork, Sister Dove,
Your feet are bleeding—
Not my eyes have cut them
But the hands of hairy children.

Come, come! Magyar children!
Go bind their feet with music!
Drums, drums! Magyar children!
Go heal their wounds with violins!

Here I hide, I hide in songs—
Ayy! Old laws I hide in!

And right there the *rejtösik* opened his eyes, but the eyeballs
had rolled back into his head and Murshkar saw nothing but
white. It scared him half to death, I'll tell you.

"Hey! Where have you gone?" he asked, and shook with fear.

"Far away from here . . . where the moon is," said the *rejtösik*,
and sure enough, his voice came from far, far away.

"Oh! And what do you see there?" cried Murshkar.

"Fire," said the *rejtösik*, after a little while. "I see bones too, and burning wheels, and a white sky. And the sun is neither far nor near but deep within."

"Do you see me a wife?" asked Murshkar, not too hopefully.

"Arrrr . . . more fire, *men* on fire! I hear screams." And just to prove it, the *rejtösik* let out a bloodcurdling scream of his own, again from far away, as though he were deep in a hole. Murshkar would have liked to run, but he couldn't move, not so much as a hair. Now the *rejtösik* resumed his singing, but in such a distant voice that Murshkar had to kneel down beside him, as close as he dared, to make out these words:

Wash your eyes with St John's Wort,
Hee! Get away, devil!
Jump a fire with the one you court,
Hee! Get away, devil!

Whitsun Rose is three times red,
Hee! Get away, devil!
Winter wed is winter dead,
Hee! Get away, devil!

Princess Snow and Princess Ice,
Hee! Get away, devil!
Snowborn son has lost you twice,
Hee! Get away, devil!

Flesh of horse or heart of man,
Hee! Get away, devil!
He will eat you if he can,
Hee! Get away, devil!

At this the *rejtösik* started to shiver and shake all over, his face turned dirty white, and he began to rub the reed in the bladder again. With his eyes clammed shut, he rocked to and fro for a few seconds, and then made more animal noises, until at last he was back and shouting at the top of his lungs. Bam! his eyes popped open and he jumped to his feet and danced all around Murshkar, doing handstands, turning cartwheels, and chanting: "Do, do, do rey-do! Off you go! Off you go!" And snatching his instruments up from the ground he ran away and disappeared—either behind a tree, or perhaps up into the sky or into the ground (for there weren't many trees there). As for me, I can't tell you which it was.

Well, old Murshkar stood wonderingly and still frightened for a while right there where he was. Then he decided he'd wasted about enough time and so he mounted up and whistled off like the devil's sneeze to overtake the sun before it sank again into its cave at world's end.

He rode and rode and hardly ate and didn't stop at towns. Every morning he resumed his race with the sun, and every night he fell asleep exhausted underneath the stars. How many days he rode I don't know, but as time passed the sun grew tired. Murshkar was up and riding for an hour or two already before it crept up on him. For a while each day it kept him company then, and told him long stories of strange places it had seen in its travels, but its voice grew older and older and finally faded out altogether. So Murshkar and the sun parted company.

He ventured to address the moon, who kept crossing his path all alone, thin and shy and cold. She didn't turn her back on him, but she hid her face behind veils, and it was only after many evenings, when he had already spoken many times to her, that she finally showed him her eyes, black and hollow, and said (in a voice strangely deep for a girl): "You ..."

"Me?" asked Murshkar.

"You," said the moon. "Where do you ride, so hard, so far?"

"I'm a prince," replied Murshkar. "I must find me a wife, and I've no time to squander."

"Ah," said the moon. "Come wander. Come marry me."

"But I hardly know you," said Murshkar. "What is your dowry?"

"White flowers and water," said the moon. "The night is my father, and I am the princess of reflections."

"And would you come away with me?" asked Murshkar.

The moon drew fog across her face and tried to blush. "These are my ways, up here, dark ways. I cannot leave them."

Murshkar sighed. "All well and good, then. Let us ride together, but I can't marry you."

"I see, I knew," replied the moon, and shivered. Her teeth began to chatter and the trees replied by dropping all their leaves. The earth shrank.

Murshkar grew cold. He buttoned his jacket up tight and rode on silently. And when he looked up again, the moon had disappeared.

Early one morning (not the next) Murshkar came to a river whose farther side he couldn't see, for all the mist that hung around. He looked for a ferry, but there was none to be seen, so he rode alongside the stream till he came to a mill with its wheel turning and smoke coming out of its chimney.

"Hallo!" he cried. "Anyone in?"

A man appeared in the door. He was short and broad-shouldered and had bushy red hair. He was wearing an apron and brushing his hands on it.

"A fine good morning to you, friend," said Murshkar.

"I suppose so," said the man, looking him up and down.

"Could you be so kind as to tell me what place this is?" said Murshkar.

"It's the boundary of the Ice Kingdom, the *only* boundary," said the man. "I take the tolls."

"I've come a long way," said Murshkar, "and I'm mightily hungry."

"Do you have money?" asked the man. "If you do, come on in."

So Murshkar hitched his horse to a stone with a cross on it and followed the man into the mill. A pot of water was boiling over the coals in the fireplace; Murshkar sat down beside it to warm himself.

"How much money do you have?" the man asked.

Well now, Murshkar didn't stop to think that this question

might be out of anything but very natural curiosity—that's how green he was!—and so he promptly took out his purse and emptied it on the table. "I don't know exactly," he said, and began to count the coins. At the sight of all that gold the man jumped as if he'd been stung by a wasp. "Yow!" he cried, and began to scurry all about the kitchen; in no time flat he had a place set for Murshkar, and one for himself too. He peeled a sack of onions and a peck of potatoes faster than you could take off a pair of gloves, and threw them in the pot that was boiling over the fire. "Just a minute or two," he said then, and went outside, while Murshkar kept right on counting. After a bit the man returned with some large chunks of meat and tossed them in the pot as well (it was a wonder how it held all that food!), then sat down next to Murshkar and put his arm around him in a friendly sort of way.

"Um hmm! but you're a fine-looking fellow!" he exclaimed. "How is it you've come this way? You're not from these parts."

"I'm a prince come to find me a wife, a princess."

"Well I'll be blistered!" cried the red-haired man, clapping Murshkar cordially on the shoulder. "You've most certainly come to the right place for that."

"Oh, goodie!" Murshkar exclaimed. "I really do hope so, for my father is old and tired and I've no time to squander."

"No mistake about it," said the man, watching Murshkar drop little stacks of coins back into his purse. "The King of the Ice Kingdom is going to be mighty happy to see you. You see, he has a daughter named Cold Sophie, and she is the most beautiful princess that you or I or anybody else ever laid eyes on. Yes sir! And she's been waiting for ages now for some handsome fellow like you (and a prince, to boot!) to come and set her free."

"Set her free?" cried Murshkar.

The red-haired man put on a very serious look (it makes the tears come to my eyes just to think of it) and shook his head mournfully. "Aye, it's a sorrow and a shame. But she's under a spell cast on her seven long years ago."

"A spell?" gasped Murshkar, horrified. "What kind of spell?"

The red-haired man rolled his eyes and said, "She was born in a time of great want, the people of the kingdom were starving and the king had no money to relieve their suffering. So when Erlik the king of the underworld came and offered all the gold the dwarfs could mine in twelve years, in exchange for the princess at the end of that time, the king her father gave in and pledged her to the dwarf. But when the twelve years was up and Erlik came to claim her, she cried out, Better my head should fall from my shoulders than marry you! Well, when the dwarf heard that he flew into a screaming rage and started jumping up and down. Have it your own way! he shouted, and kerplop! her head was in her lap."

"Ow!" groaned Murshkar.

The red-haired man raised a finger. "Ah, but she wasn't dead. Oh no. Her head just sat there blinking and gulping in her lap. And when she opened her mouth no words came out, and when she picked her head back up with her little hands and tried to stick it back on her neck, it burned like all the fires of hell—so horribly she had to put it right back down again. And it's been that way ever since."

This was almost more than Murshkar could bear. "How can the spell be broken?" he demanded, ready to set out at once.

The man slid even closer and pinched Murshkar's ear. "No one knows that but me, I'm afraid," he said confidentially. "How much gold did you say you have?"

"I didn't say," said Murshkar. "But if you want to know—I have three hundred and thirty-three pieces all told."

The red-haired man threw his arms around him and kissed him soundly on the nose, then jumped out of his seat, crying, "That'll do exactly! That'll just do!" He leaped over to the fireplace, lifted the pot off the fire and plonked it down on the table. "Let's eat now," he said, "and I'll tell you what to do."

Well from that moment on things happened so quickly that Murshkar didn't have time to think. So his purse vanished and he began to eat the stew (which was hot and filling but pretty odd-tasting, to say the least)—while the red-haired man told him this:

"First find the ferry that will take you over the river. On the other side is a road that goes only one way. Follow it until you come to a town that lies at the foot of a mountain. The mountain is a fortress, the strongest in all the world. In its depths, in the deepest chamber, Cold Sophie languishes with her head in her lap..."

(Now of course this was said much more slowly and with many more words than I've used. The red-haired man seemed to be just as hungry as Murshkar, who had difficulty in understanding much of the time, the man kept his mouth so packed. But the strangest thing was, every time the man took a bite he flipped a bit of stew from his spoon into the fire, where it snapped and sizzled with all sorts of weird noises—like the clump of hoofs on soft earth, or the squeals of a horse whose ear is being bitten.) With his mouth crammed full the red-haired man went on:

"If you were to try to get into the fortress all alone, you wouldn't get any farther than the first of nine great doors, all locked and barred and guarded by ferocious white dogs (some say black), each one ten times whiter (or blacker) than the one before."

"What do I do then?" asked Murshkar, discouraged no end.

The red-haired man popped a piece of meat the size of your head in his mouth, and spat juice into the fire, where it snorted. "Well," he said (and swallowed the meat half-chewed), "today is the first day of the twelfth month. Right? You must reach the town by the day after tomorrow at the very latest. Preparations will still be under way for the great feast of diggers three days from now. It's the one time each year that the fortress is open to everyone in the land, and the whole day is spent in merrymaking. And it's the only day on which the princess may be seen."

Murshkar's ears pricked up at that, you may be sure. The red-haired man licked his bowl. "When you enter the town you'll find signs everywhere announcing the holiday and listing jobs for cooks and entertainers. Hire yourself out as a fiddler: that way you'll be admitted to the innermost hall for the grand ball. Now there is where the princess will be sitting, at her father's side. Seven times she's sat there, with her head in her lap. And never once has she so much as smiled."

"But how can I break the spell?" asked Murshkar impatiently.

"One thing at a time," said the red-haired man, clearing the table with a swoop of his arm and leaning toward Murshkar. "When all the guests are assembled and the banquet's about to begin, Erlik will suddenly appear. Each year, on this one day, he returns to ask her hand again, prepared to lift the spell if she will only consent. (Who knows? perhaps he really loves her.) But each time, without fail, when she sees him approach she lowers her eyes, and when he speaks to her she pretends she has not even heard him. And not all the entreaties and tears of her poor father can make her change her mind. So the dwarf stalks out of the hall in a fury and the spell remains in force until the next time."

"I understand all that," said Murshkar; "but what do I do?"

"This time, when he approaches her—"

"But how will I know him?" Murshkar interrupted.

The red-haired man giggled, as if this were the funniest thing he'd ever heard in his whole life. "You'll know him, no doubt about that, my friend. When he approaches the princess and before he has a chance to say a single word, you must step quickly forward from wherever you are standing and start playing the liveliest *csárdás* you know. Play it faster and faster, and while you're playing move slowly toward the princess yourself. The dwarf will start to dance when he hears the music, he won't be able to help himself, and once he starts he won't be able to stop, either, not as long as there's music for him to dance to. He'll dance himself right out of the castle and back into his hole, and he won't stop until he's reached the center of the earth. As for you, when you're right up beside the princess, you must get down on your knees and put your head just as close as you can to hers (but don't stop playing!) and whisper these words in her ear:

> "Princess Ice, pray thaw for me
> And wash away this fairy.
> A prince's eyes saw far to thee
> And chose thee then to marry.
> Princess Ice, put on thy head:
> Today's the day that we shall wed.

"Then and there the princess will pick up her head and put it back where it belongs, and the dwarf will hightail it from the place and the spell will be broken. But take care! If you stop playing for even an instant, he'll cease to dance and turn you to stone on the spot."

Murshkar got up. "Thank you," he said. "If that's all, I'll be on my way, I have no time to squander." And so he rushed out of the door.

When he got outside he looked around for his horse. But it was nowhere to be seen. He whistled and shouted, but his voice just lost itself in the gray fog and there was no reply. His stomach began to growl and he felt sick all of a sudden. He ran back inside. The red-haired man was counting the money.

"Where's my horse gone to?" cried Murshkar, in a panic.

The red-haired man looked up at him and smiled wickedly and shrugged his shoulders. "How should I know?" he asked, innocent as innocent can be. But just then from the chimney came the sound of a pitiful whinny. Murshkar jumped, and his flesh crawled.

"What have you done with my horse?" he screamed.

The red-haired man clapped himself on the belly and belched. He stood up; he seemed shorter. He began to laugh, and his face turned as red as his hair. Murshkar didn't know what to do, so he asked again, this time pleadingly, "What have you done with my horse, please?"

The face of the red-haired man suddenly became mean and menacing; he looked like a demon of some kind, and he opened his mouth and a horse's voice came out. "What did you think you could buy for so little gold?"

Well with that, Murshkar flew into a wild rage. He looked round and grabbed up an axe lying close by the door and ran at the little man, all set to chop him clean in two. But all of a sudden the fellow sank straight through the floor, zoop! like that! and pulled the whole mill, sticks and stones and sacks and flour (if there was any) and fire in after him. In the wink of an eye Murshkar found himself standing alone near the river on a bare patch of ground. Not so much as a mite remained of the mill, and, oh did he feel bad; his stomach was upside down. He just staggered over to the place where the red-haired man had disappeared. There he found his empty purse lying on the ground, and he let it lie, for all the good it did him now. He couldn't even think; he wandered over to the upright stone with a cross on it. The reins of his poor lost horse were still tied to it. It was just too much for him. He sat down and buried his face in his hands, and wept as he had never wept before. No gold, no horse! How would he find him a wife, a princess? What would his father say? What a fool he was! He was simply sick with shame and self-pity.

Well, he couldn't sit there forever. After a while he began to think about getting across the river. He'd go on foot to the fortress if he had to. He knelt down to pick up the reins of his horse (never tell when they might come in handy), and as he did he saw something strange on the stone. Under the top, which was carved like a roof, he saw three little windows. They were covered with glass panes, and behind them were tiny paintings. That made him curious, and he sat down on the ground to examine them more closely.

Now the first picture showed three men, two of whom were wearing beards. The older one of these had a white beard and was clothed in a flowing robe; the other had a dark-colored beard and he was almost naked. The third man was very young, not much more than a boy, and he was dressed in a striped suit like a uniform. All three were seated on thrones, side by side, and in the air around them hovered children with wings.

The second picture was completely different. The young man in the striped suit was in it, lying on his back on the ground, and bent over him, with his hands on the boy's throat, was the red-haired man from the mill. This picture sent chills up and down Murshkar's spine.

But the third picture was the simplest. It showed the young man again, kneeling in prayer this time, and underneath him was written in plain letters: *Pray for my soul, who passes here.*

And so that is what Murshkar did, though he had never prayed before (and it wasn't as easy as it looked). But he thought if he hadn't been meant to obey the command, he would never have seen it.

Off he went then to find the ferry that would take him across the river. It was a long walk and he almost missed the place, which turned out to be under a bluff on a bend in the river, and out of sight from the road. But as he passed the spot he suddenly heard a voice calling out his name and went to see where the voice was coming from.

From the edge of the bluff he looked straight down. A tall man with a white beard and long hair (like the old man pictured on the stone) was standing on a little pier to which a raft was tied.

"Come on down, Murshkar," shouted the man.

"How?" shouted Murshkar back.

"However you can," the man answered impatiently. "I suppose you want me to come up and fetch you?"

"No," said Murshkar, ashamed of himself. "I'll find a way."

And so he did.

"Hurry," said the man, already pushing off.

Murshkar jumped aboard. He looked about him. The river, which from above had seemed so peaceful, splashed and heaved all around them, and a dense fog obscured the shore, though they couldn't have been more than a few feet out as yet. Murshkar couldn't even see his own feet, or the edge of the raft. He grew fearful, and turned around to see the ferryman, but found only the man's face, floating and oddly glowing.

"Don't be afraid," said the man. "Just stand still, or sit down, if you must."

"How did you know my name back there?" Murshkar asked.

"I only carry one passenger at a time," replied the man. "If it had been someone else, he would have had a different name, wouldn't he?"

"Yes, of course," said Murshkar, just a little confused, "but—"

"But it was you," said the old man. "Well, don't worry your head about it, and don't ask questions now. There'll be time enough for that later on, if you get where you're going and do what you want to do."

So Murshkar didn't say anything else, and the man must have turned his face away, for Murshkar saw nothing but fog and felt nothing beneath his feet, as though the raft were fog as well.

Then suddenly he heard the man's voice shouting "Jump!" and without thinking he jumped. When he landed (and what a long time it took!) he found himself on a road high above the river. It was snowing. He looked around in wonderment; below him the river, frozen solid, stretched like a broad metal trough into the distance, and there was no sign of either raft or ferryman. So Murshkar blew on his hands to get them warm, then thrust them into his pockets and shivering with cold tried to get his bearings. But he could not find the sun: the sky was equally dull and lightless wherever he looked.

So he began to walk, and walked on and on, and the sky was always the same color, not dark nor light, and he didn't know how much time had passed, and there was no one to ask. He grew terribly discouraged (as well he might have!) and began to doubt that he was anywhere at all, and to feel great pangs of helpless regret and reproach. What a simple fool he'd been! First his money and his horse—his poor horse!—and now this. Oh, he was sure he'd never find a wife. Why had he wandered so far? The tears began to trickle down his cheeks and drop off his chin, freezing as they fell . . .

[In the distance, a clock begins to strike the hour of midnight: the old man hearkens, then looks at Stefan.]

Perhaps another wanderer (if there was one) trod them under foot, then left his own a little farther on. Or perhaps, when spring came, they melted and gave birth to berries—to tiny bitter-white and salty-tasting berries that birds ate.

Hah! Who cares very much what becomes of tears shed in despair upon a winter road?

The last stroke of the clock wavers and fades; a breeze is picking up. The old man claps his hands on his knees. "That's all," he says. "We must be up early. If you want more, you'll have to finish it yourself; there are many endings to such a tale...."

STONES FROM THE NAVEL

Murshkar, he whispers, and his heart swells painfully.

Murshkar, he says aloud, and the night air, like a harsh rebuttal, jostles him and hustles him along.

Murshkar, he cries, into the darkness.

And suddenly a child's face, the dark glowing face of a twelve-year-old, appears before him, smiling. He feels her lips against his brow; and then their faces diffuse, into one warm reflection on the finite pool of memory.

THE GLASS MOUNTAIN

A summer country where nothing stops the eye, the ground light-green and yellow, plowed belts of black. Murshkar is walking; he is carrying a ring-shaped loaf of bread, and every step or two he leans down and plucks an herb and tastes it.

Suddenly he remarks, with a kind of surprise, that the sun is really a puncture in the sky. He glances at his hands; they are the color of flour paste. He touches the fingertips and they melt together and grow thick, like candle stubs. He lets the ring of bread slide from arm to arm.

He sits down and tries to pry his fingers apart, unsuccessfully. So he eats through one side of the bread (it tastes like paper); the rest falls and rolls away, hobbling, across the empty fields. He thinks: No birds—but just then a swarm of them pass and light not far away on a hill. Instantly the hill becomes a quarry from which black dust rises.

All at once a terrible screeching and bleating fills the air. He springs up and looks around. Directly behind him, across the road, thousands of pigs are milling and jostling and squealing: a sea of swine of every shape and description.

He walks hesitantly toward them: they shrink into an indistinguishable mass of flesh, a welter of bodies. He hears a harsh laugh and with a start recognizes the red-haired man, knee-deep in carnage, bounding about, stabbing and slashing with a long knife. A cry chokes in Murshkar's throat; his arms tingle and his legs go limp. In a wink the red-haired man stands astride a huge mound of corpses, drenched with blood as with red, liquid light. He begins to laugh again, more and more shrilly, until he is no longer laughing but whinnying like a horse. The heap bursts into flame, a gigantic bonfire. Murshkar's skin prickles; he shudders violently; he stretches out his hands: they are shriveled but separate. A thick column of flame and smoke shoots up and then collapses in rubble. A snow of ashes drifts into a black silence.

Murshkar walks into the charred remains; bones snap beneath his feet, ashes eddy up like butterflies. He spies his purse; joyfully he snatches it up and looks inside: it is filled with tiny glowing coals. He removes one and weighs it in the palm of his hand. It is cold and heavy, and blinks like a star or a glass eye. He drops it, and thinks: *There is no grail.*

Suddenly a cloud rushes by and stuffs itself into the sun-

perforation like a sponge in a drain. Murshkar begins to feel warmer. The sky in the distance lets itself down slowly like a wide blue awning, until it touches the horizon. On it is painted a glass mountain, and Murshkar is able to see all the way to its heart. There, infinitely small and far away, the princess sits and weeps with her head in her lap.

He strides confidently toward the mountain; it sails forward to meet him. . . . The road begins to slant downhill between sloping fields. On all sides peasants come running, dressed in bright garments, waving handkerchiefs and staves. He smells honey and hears flies. The mountain looms near. . . .

Then he is on horseback, on his own horse, and holding his violin aloft like a banner. It *is* a banner, red and yellow and forked. Bands are playing.

He passes through the wall of glass.

People press around him, cling to his sides, strew flowers in his path. A blue rain begins to fall. Posters peel from walls. His mother kisses his boot. He catches sight of his father in a gable window, young and nodding, with white teeth. Doves cluster. His horse's hoofs clack like pistol shots on the cobbles.

The crowd sighs: Aah! and sinks to a thousand knees. Shutters fly open, roofs sprout leaves and grow together above his head. His horse moves swiftly, gliding on delicate hoofs. House fronts blur . . . Suddenly, near as doll's doors before his eyes, huge gates swing open and he sails through them alone. He shuts his eyes an instant in his flight, and then re-opens them—on *her*. He gasps at her beauty, which is the beauty not of youth but of agelessness. His eyes burn, his hair stands on end.

He realizes that he has landed in a vast hall, with walls of woven lances and an arched ceiling tiled with shields. Portals wide enough to admit whole legions lead in from every side. Within the hall hundreds of long tables are sagging under the weight of roasted animals, the full year's harvest, great tuns of wine. Exactly in the center of the hall stands a table as large as a plateau, larger than all the other tables put together, and on it, in a pewter vessel the size of a warship, lies a gigantic fish, baked and garnished with oak leaves. Bench after bench beside the tables is groaning with guests: men and women and children of every description. Murshkar turns round and round; everywhere he looks it seems he recognizes friends, but if he lingers on any single face it blurs or fades away. He is caught in a warm giddiness of welcome, a sensation of arrival. He is reflected in a thousand mirrors, endless samovars, in golden smiles, a world of polish and glistening eyes.

Cymbals clash. Murshkar tastes the dull green skin of brass; his mouth turns dry. The floorboards part, and up comes Erlik, pick in hand and snarling. It is Loh, or Lokowandt, and now he is truly a dwarf. He stalks past Murshkar without recognizing him, and plants himself squarely in front of the princess. A great bowl slides off a table, spilling oranges across the floor. Murmurs fill the hall like a litany.

Hannes Däumler (Paul Speer?) steps forward boldly. For an instant he stands close to Murshkar, who feels his breath and his mouth like a cut lemon on his ear. A shiver of delight passes through him.

Lokowandt-Erlik stamps his foot; chandeliers quiver, light bristles. The princess turns her head face down into her lap and sticks her fingers in her ears. The king hides his face. Hannes leaps forward with a cry; the dwarf whirls about and points his pick at him; he freezes and turns to stone. All the people in the hall seem suddenly to have turned into statues as well, and Murshkar knows with certainty that it is time for him to play. He lifts his fiddle and strikes the first note; Lokowandt stares at him and drops his pick. Murshkar is all fingers, all arms. The princess turns up her face and smiles faintly. The dwarf opens his mouth and his eyes spit real fire. Hannes's statue topples and breaks among the oranges. Murshkar plays like a windmill, like spokes on a runaway wheel. Lokowandt gnashes his teeth and stamps one foot and then the other. The statues begin to clap in time. Murshkar is everywhere, watching himself, playing faster and faster and faster; the walls move closer in. Lokowandt howls and dances; his red hair leaps like flames; crude nuggets of sweat burst from his ears.

Still playing, Murshkar kneels beside the princess and whispers words of his own making in her ear: words spoken and instantly forgotten. Ah! the princess raises her head with both hands, and places it squarely on her shoulders. A smile transforms her face. Murshkar kisses her soundly on the brow. The ceiling of the hall flies away. A fragment of stone leaps from the floor and cracks the dwarf between the eyes. He yelps and bleeds and then vaults away over all their heads like a screeching cannon ball. Hannes leaps up whole and embraces Murshkar, whose violin bursts into a hundred silver sparrows. The princess rises and takes his arm. A roar of applause and water fills his ears ...

They are flying on the raft and there is no fog, and the earth is neither above nor below them. The old man with a white beard turns his face to Murshkar and asks, "Do you understand now how I knew your name?" and Murshkar answers "Yes" and sees that the old man is his father, *afer all*.

"Look!" says his father. Murshkar turns round. Behind him are standing two young men, both alike and unalike.

"Are these my brothers?" asks Murshkar, unable to remember.

The princess smiles. "They are our sons," she says, and ceases to resemble anyone but herself.

They ride a red-and-yellow wagon over swells of hair. Pods explode. Tall, dead prehistoric fish stand on their tails beside them: a fence of pines around a dark island. But a tiny fire begins to flicker in the interior, and flares up until it becomes as bright as the sun itself, and its warmth is incredible.

They pass again the barrier of glass, returning.